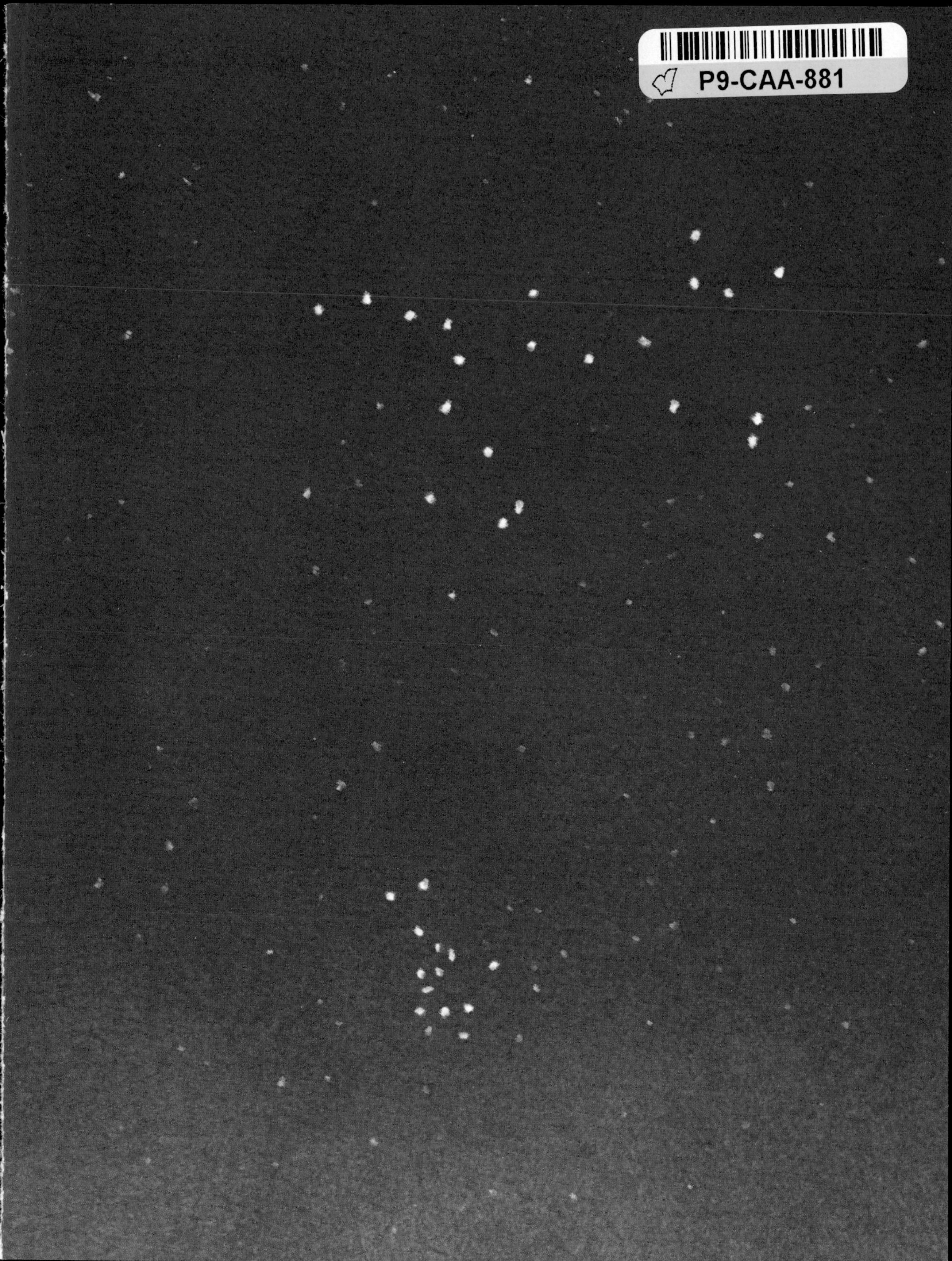

PETER & ERNESTO

a tale of TWO SLOTHS

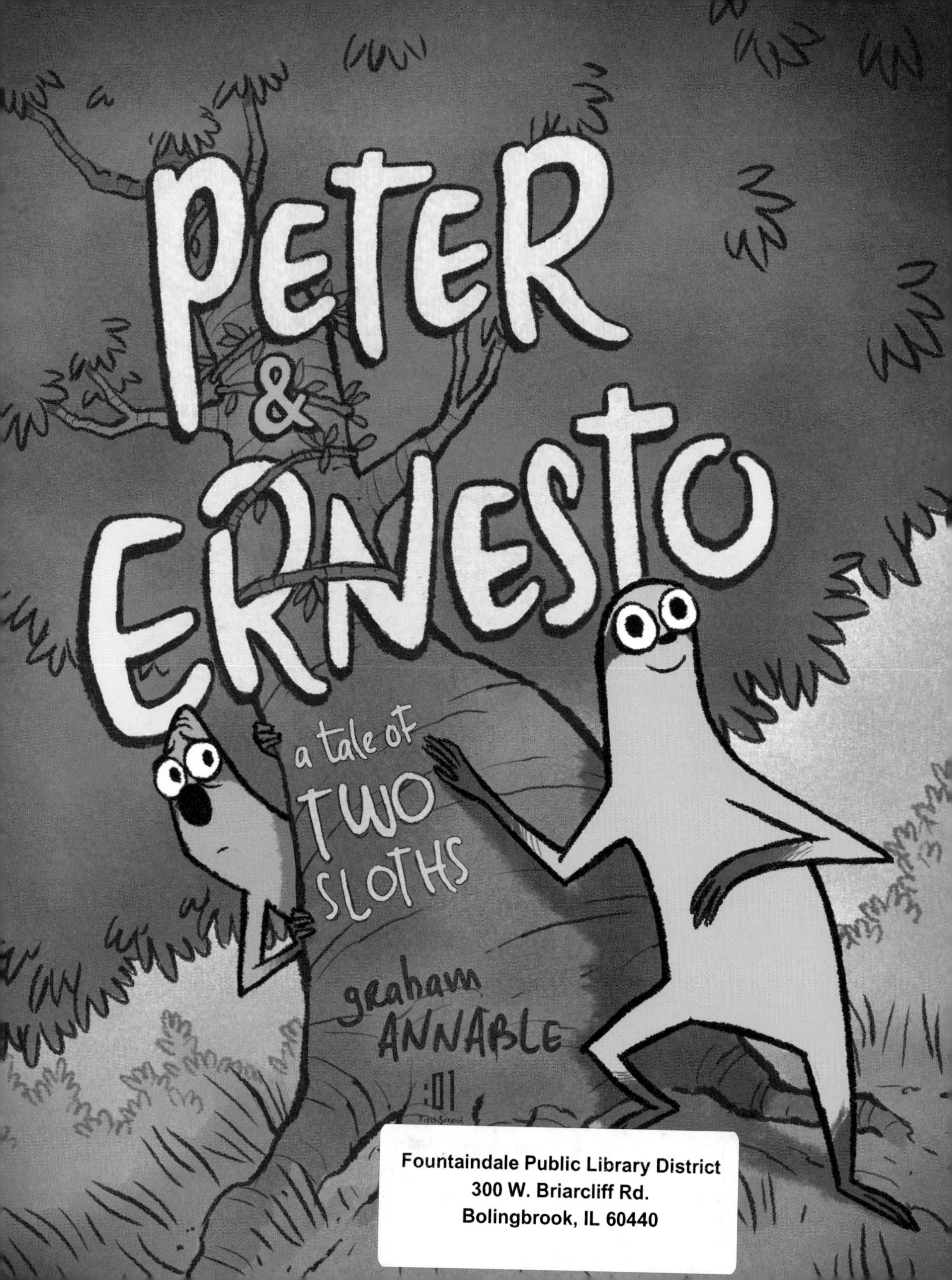
PETER
&
ERNESTO
a tale of
TWO
SLOTHS
graham
ANNABLE
:01
FirstSecond

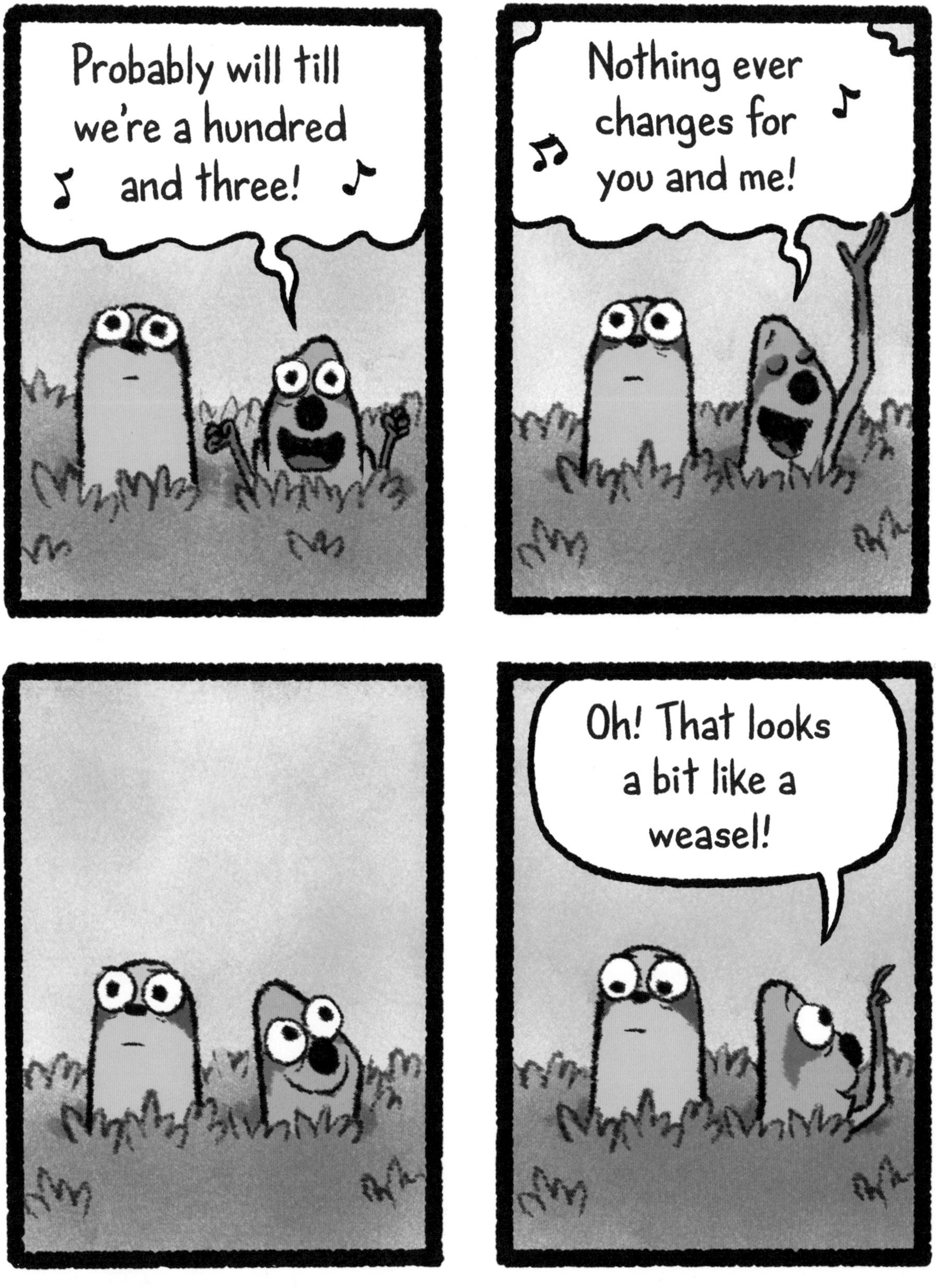
Probably will till we're a hundred and three!
Nothing ever changes for you and me!
Oh! That looks a bit like a weasel!

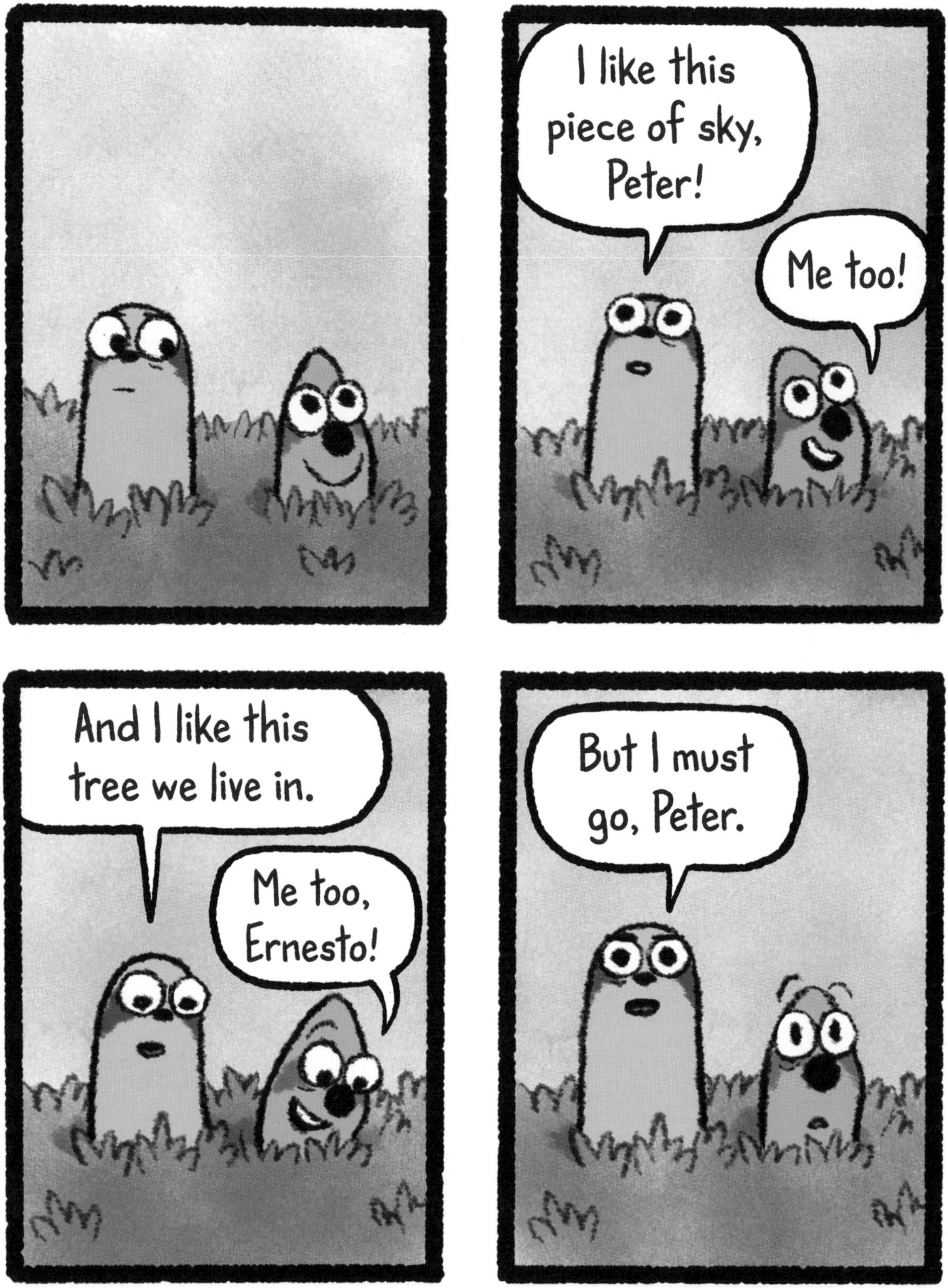
I like this piece of sky, Peter!
Me too!
And I like this tree we live in.
Me too, Ernesto!
But I must go, Peter.

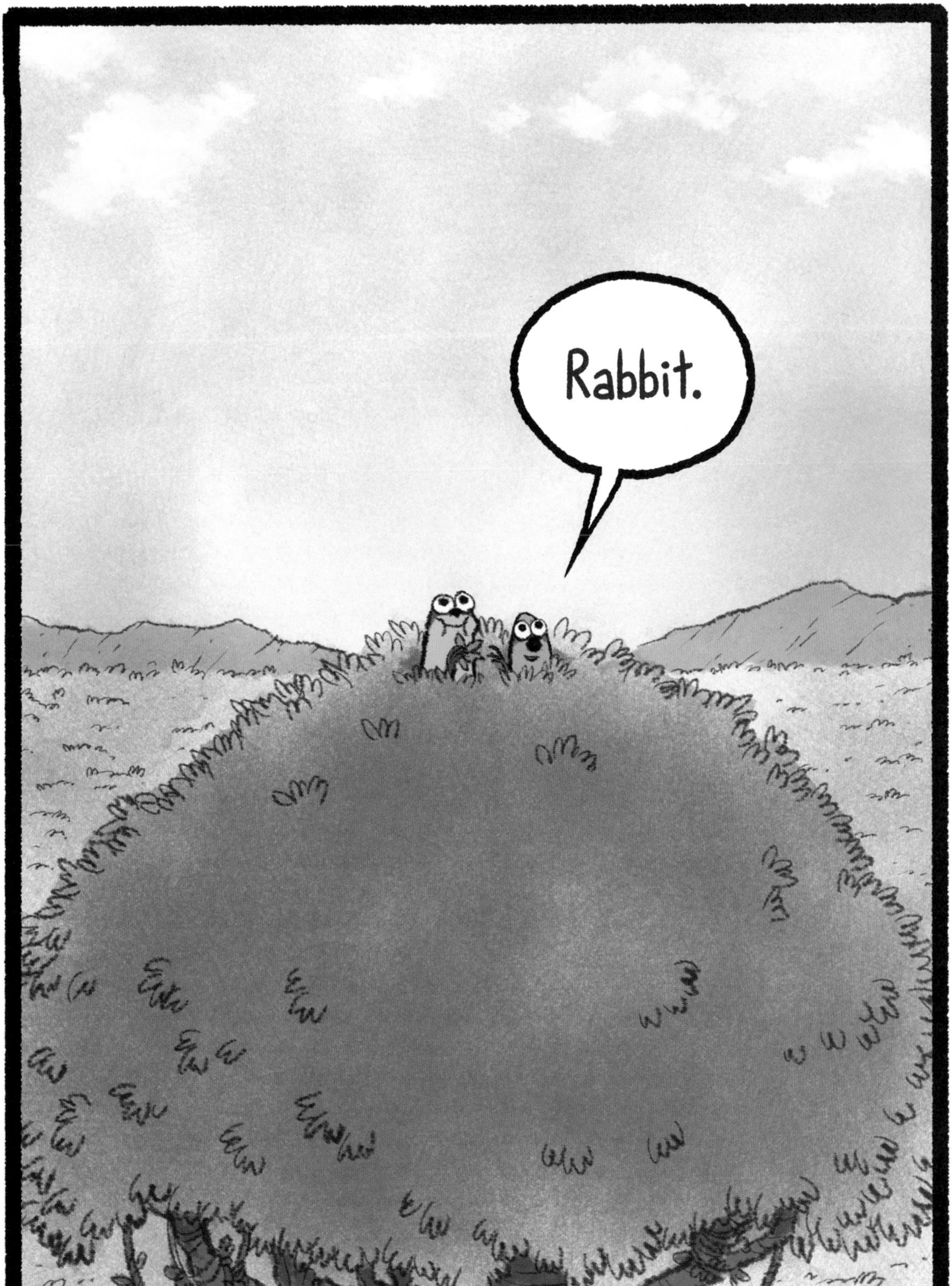
Rabbit.

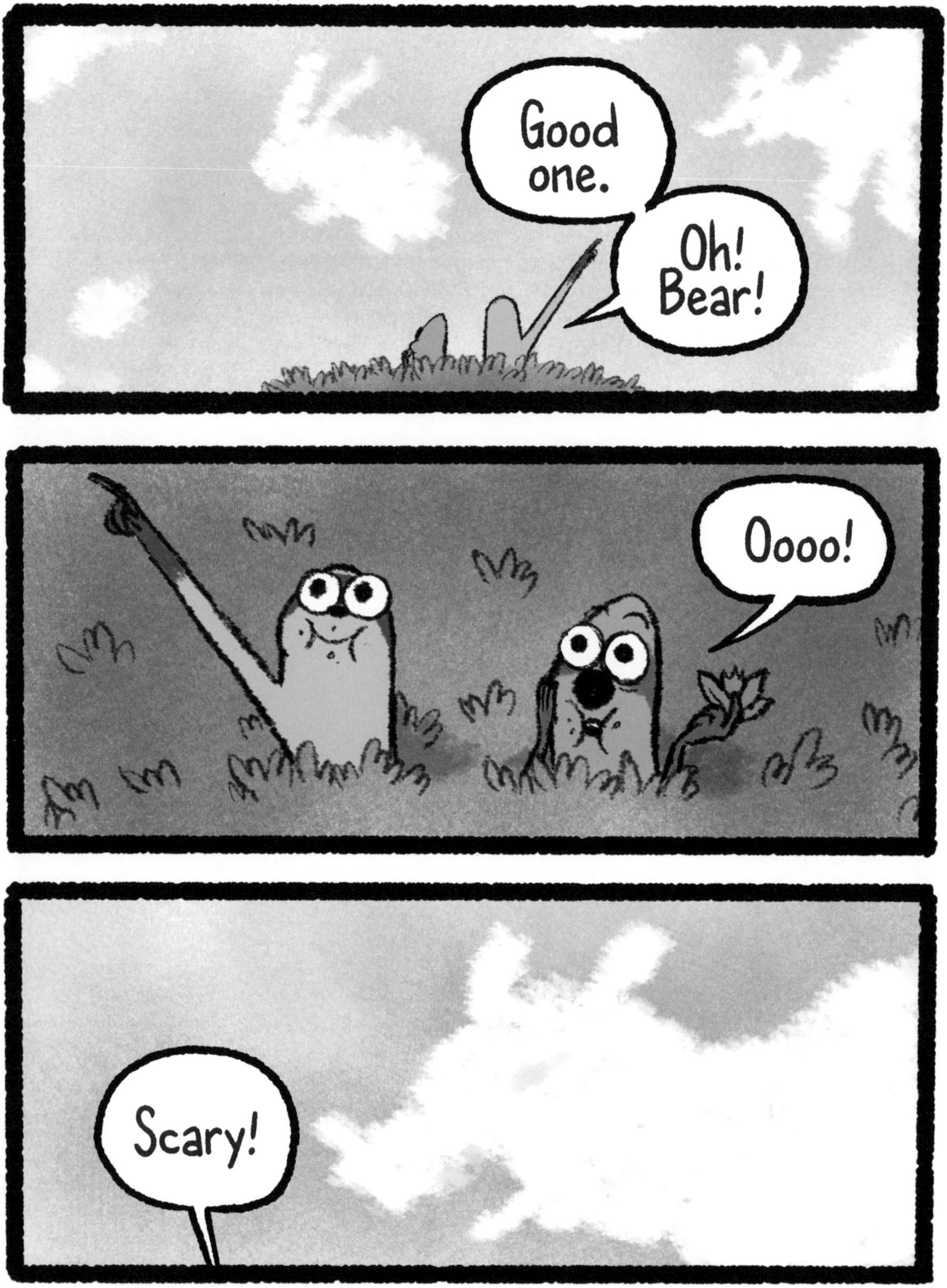
Good one.
Oh! Bear!
Oooo!
Scary!

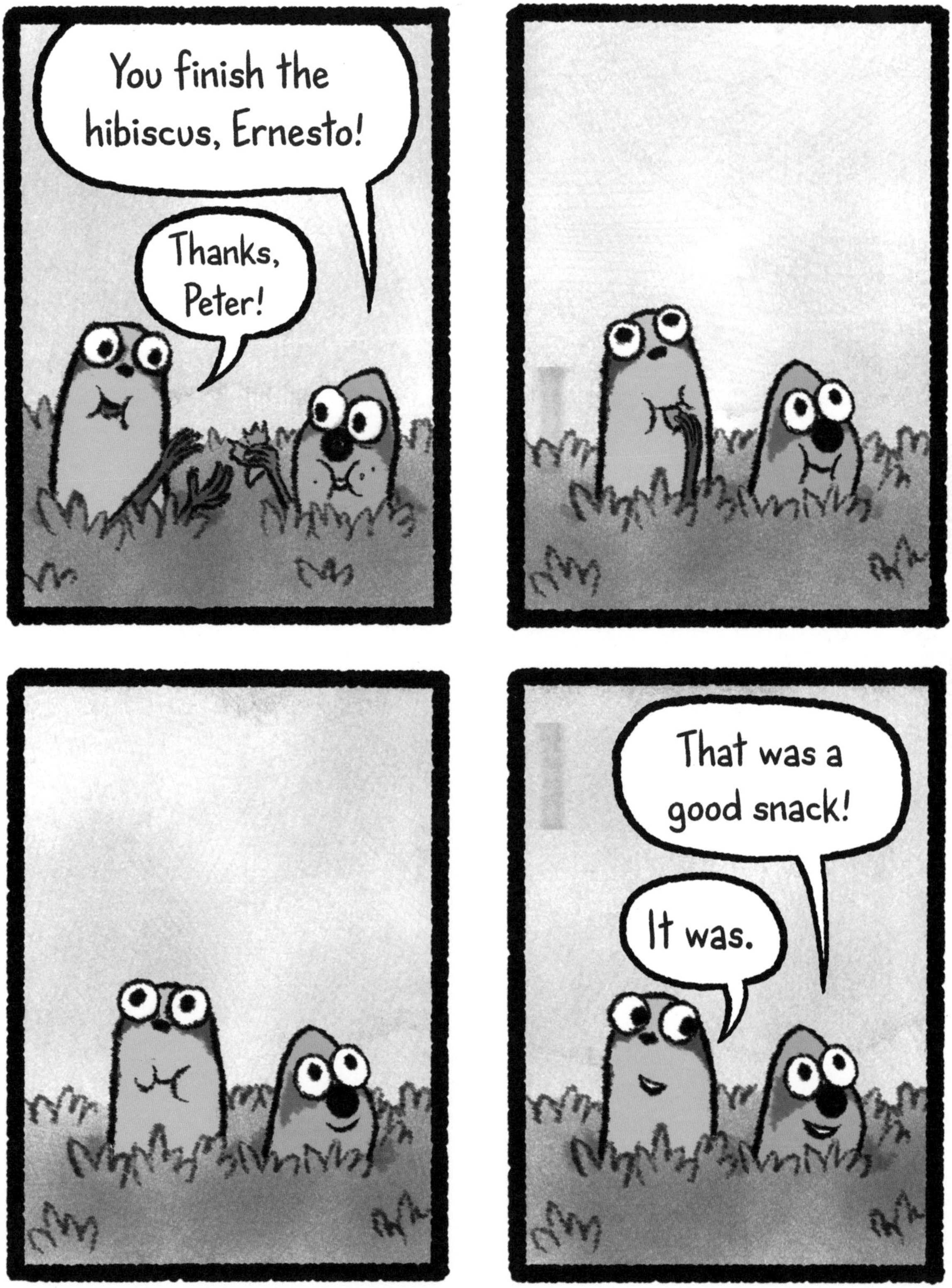
You finish the hibiscus, Ernesto!
Thanks, Peter!
That was a good snack!
It was.

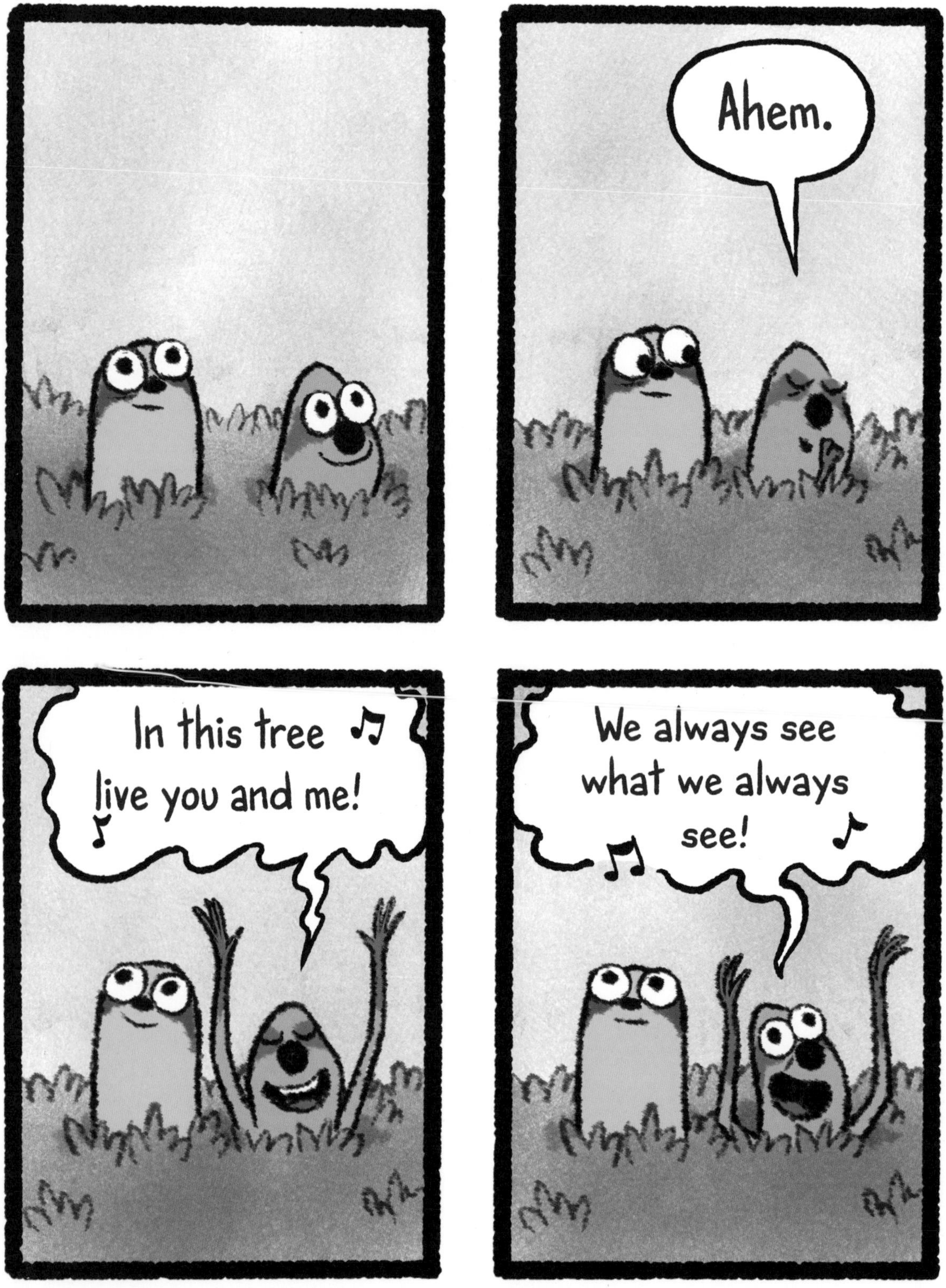
Ahem.
In this tree live you and me!
We always see what we always see!

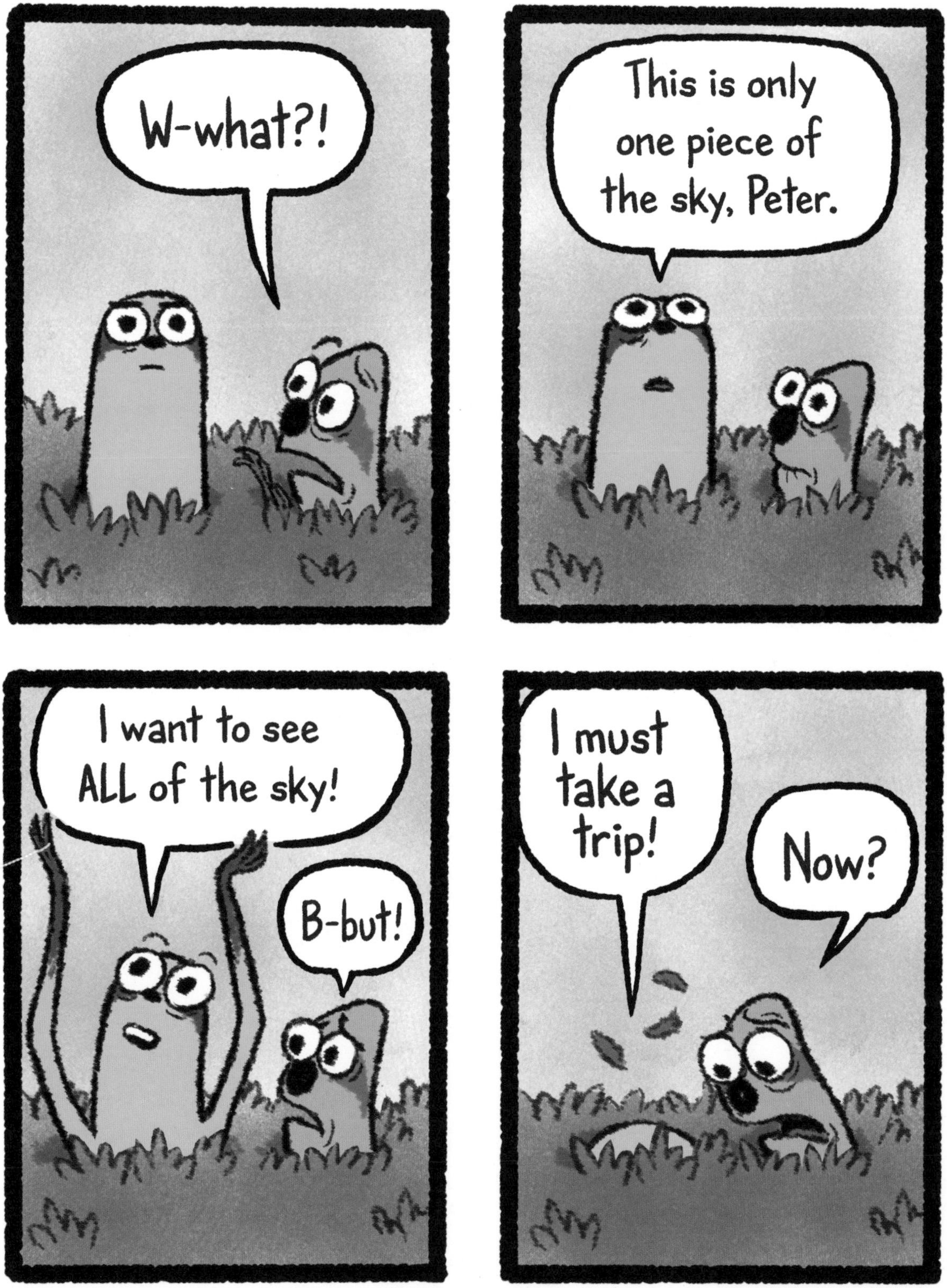
W-what?!
This is only one piece of the sky, Peter.
I want to see ALL of the sky!
B-but!
I must take a trip!
Now?

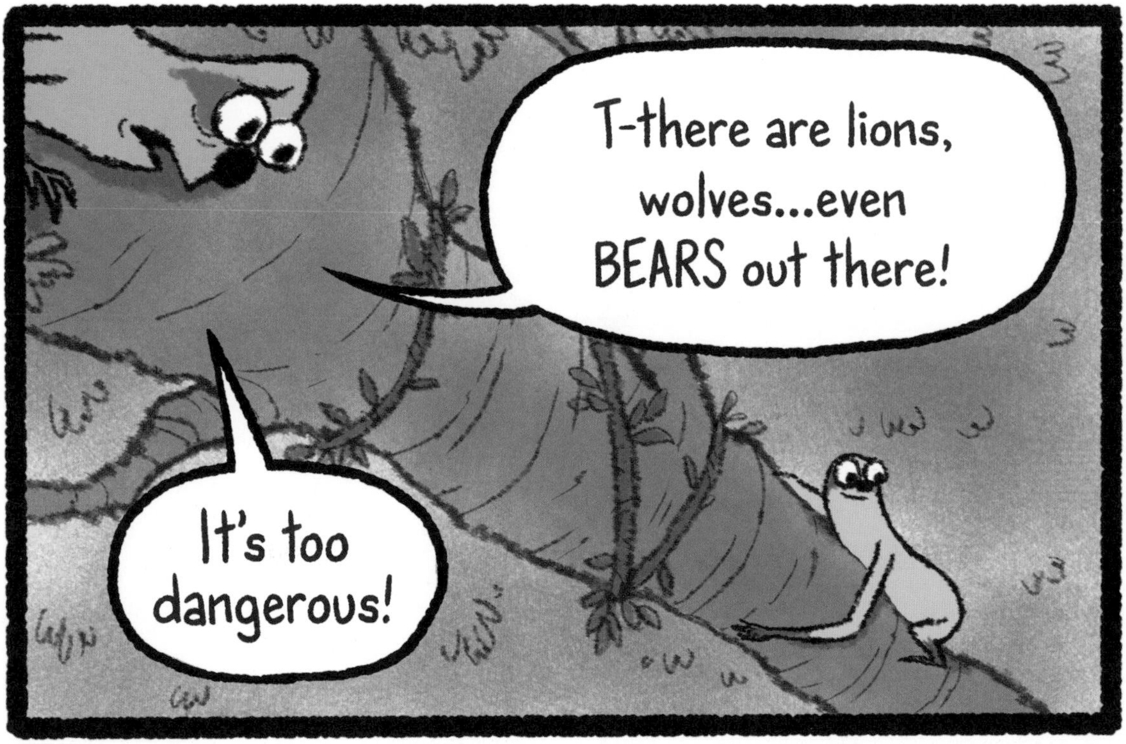
T-there are lions, wolves...even BEARS out there!
It's too dangerous!

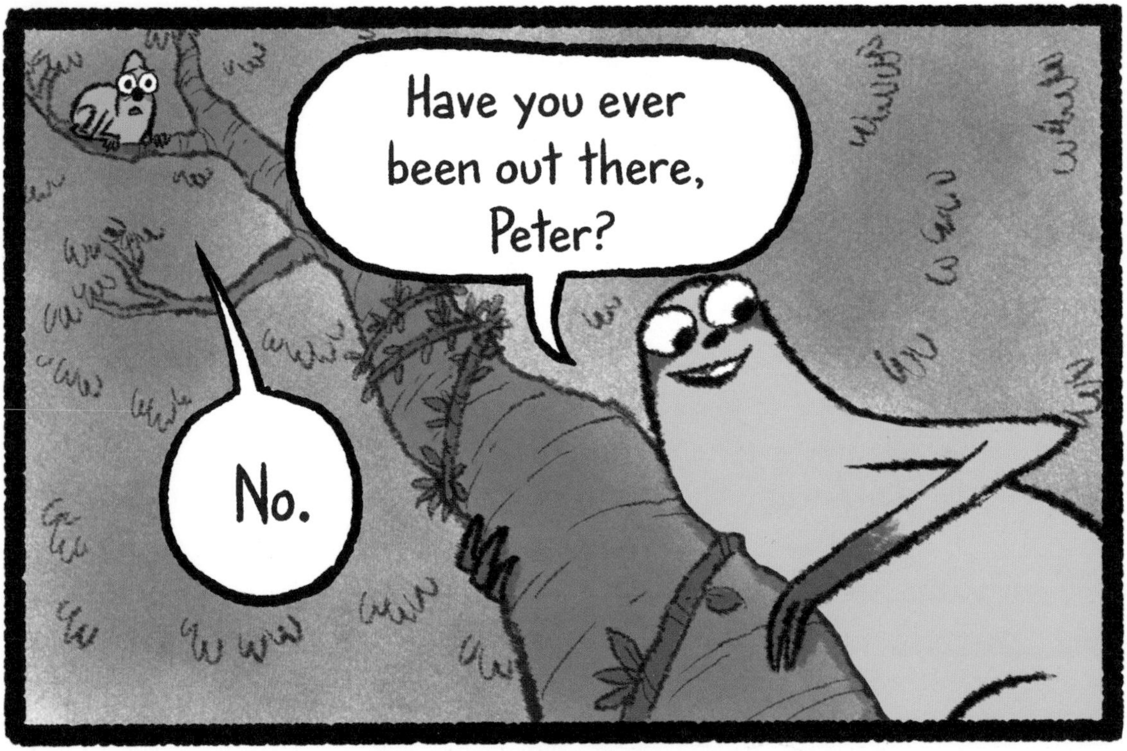
Have you ever been out there, Peter?
No.

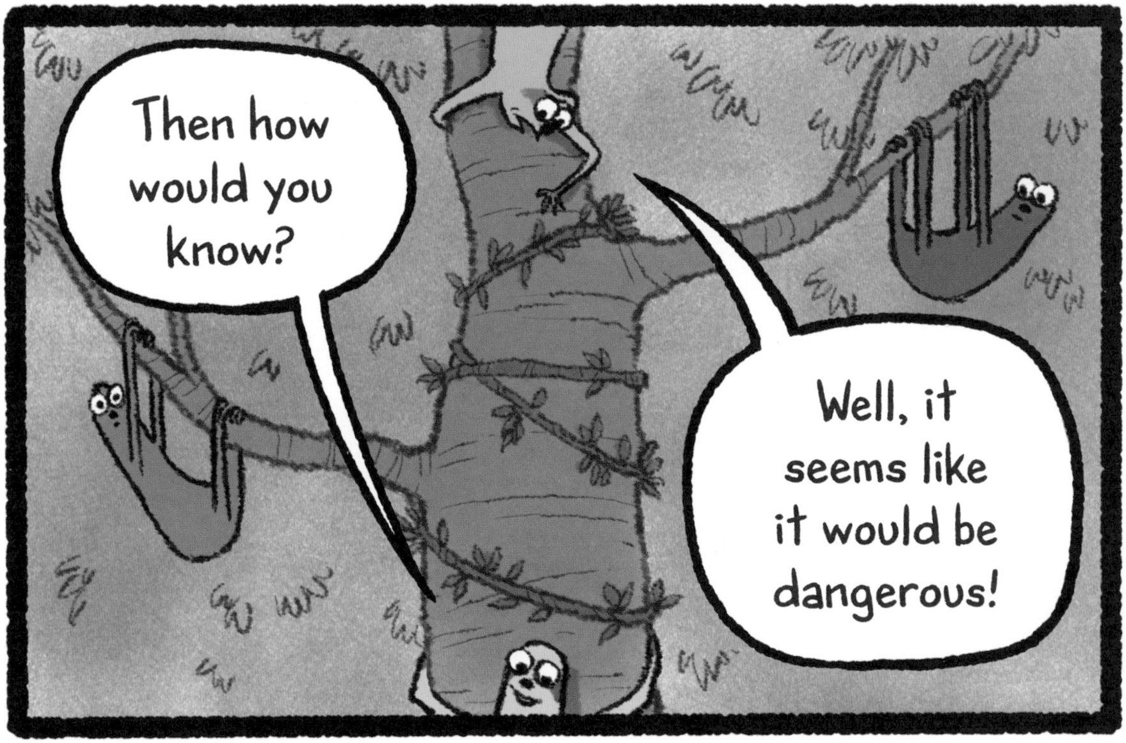
Then how would you know?
Well, it seems like it would be dangerous!

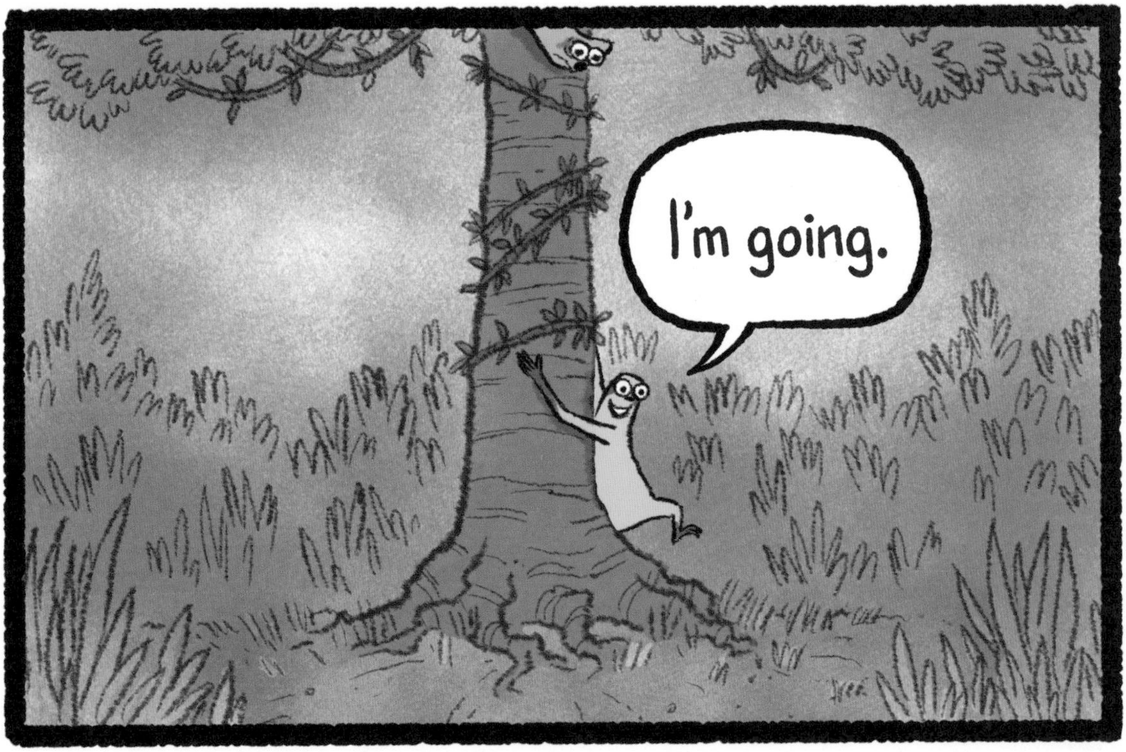
I'm going.

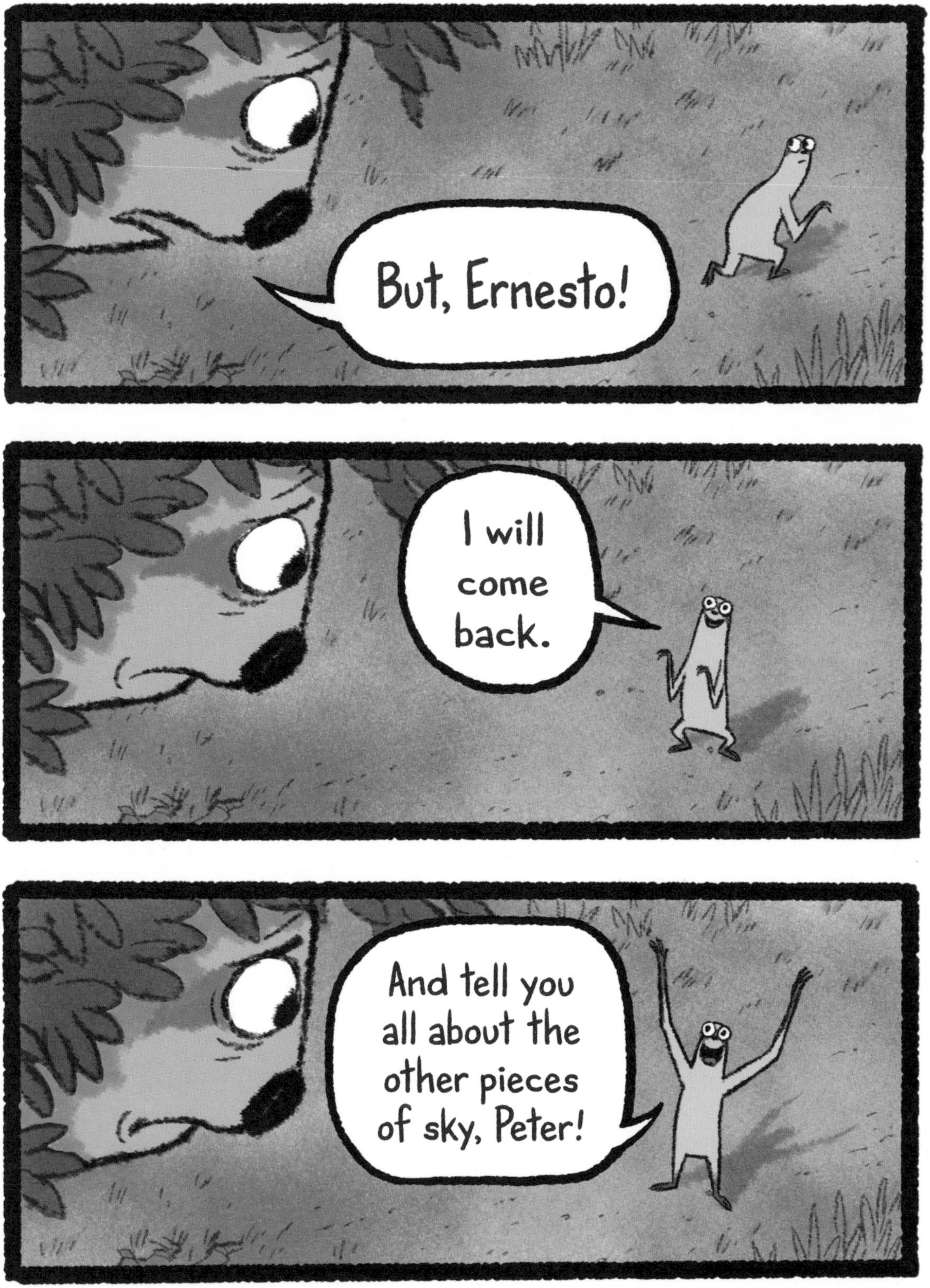
But, Ernesto!
I will come back.
And tell you all about the other pieces of sky, Peter!

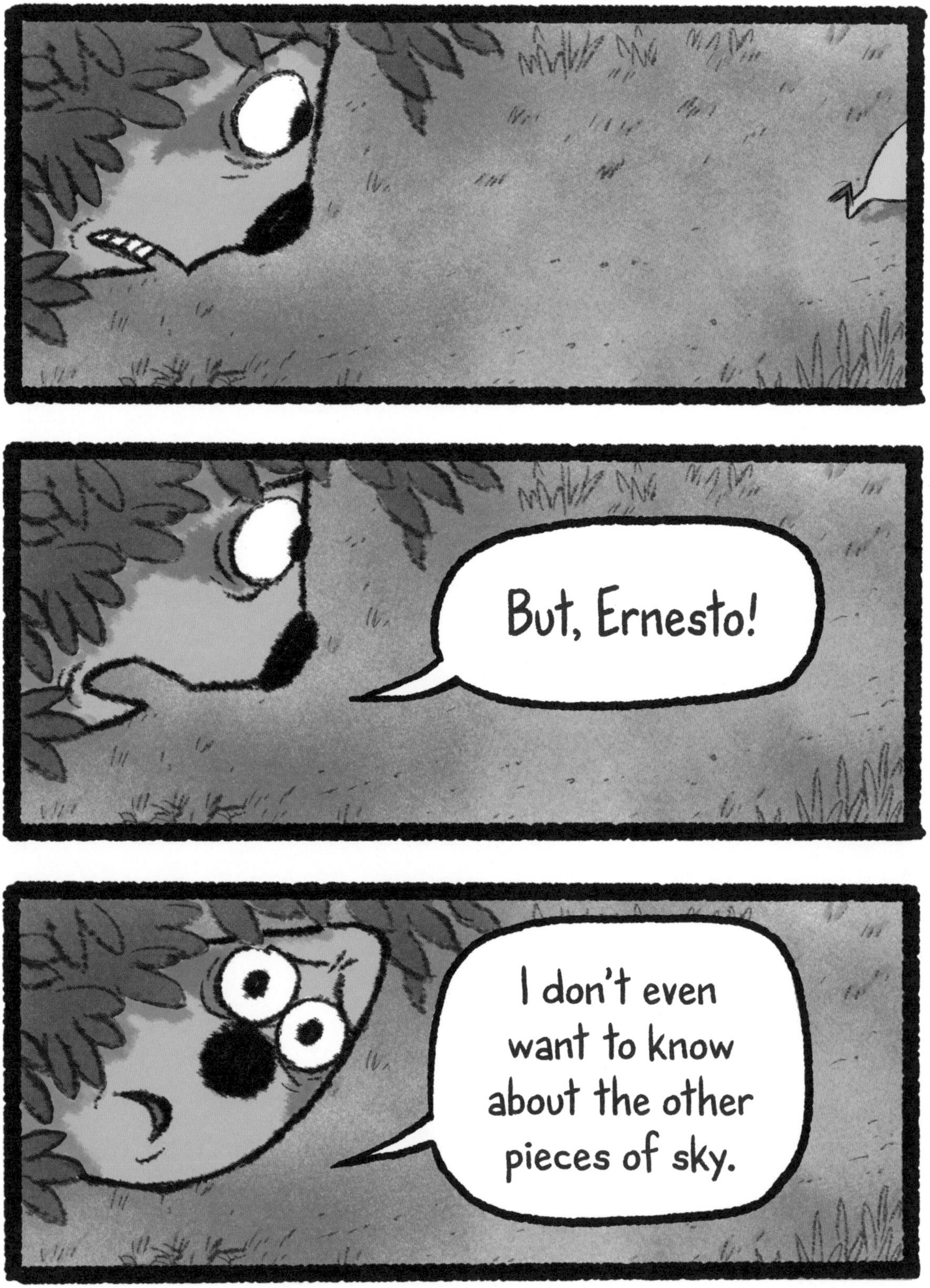

But, Ernesto!
I don't even want to know about the other pieces of sky.

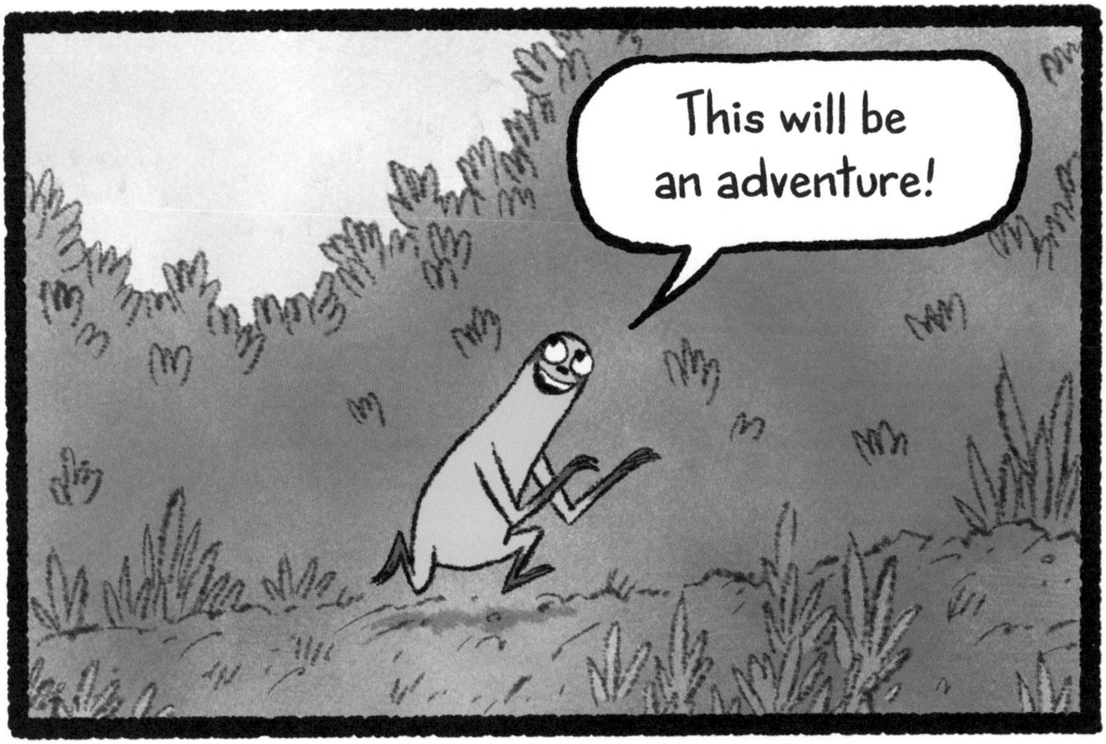
This will be an adventure!

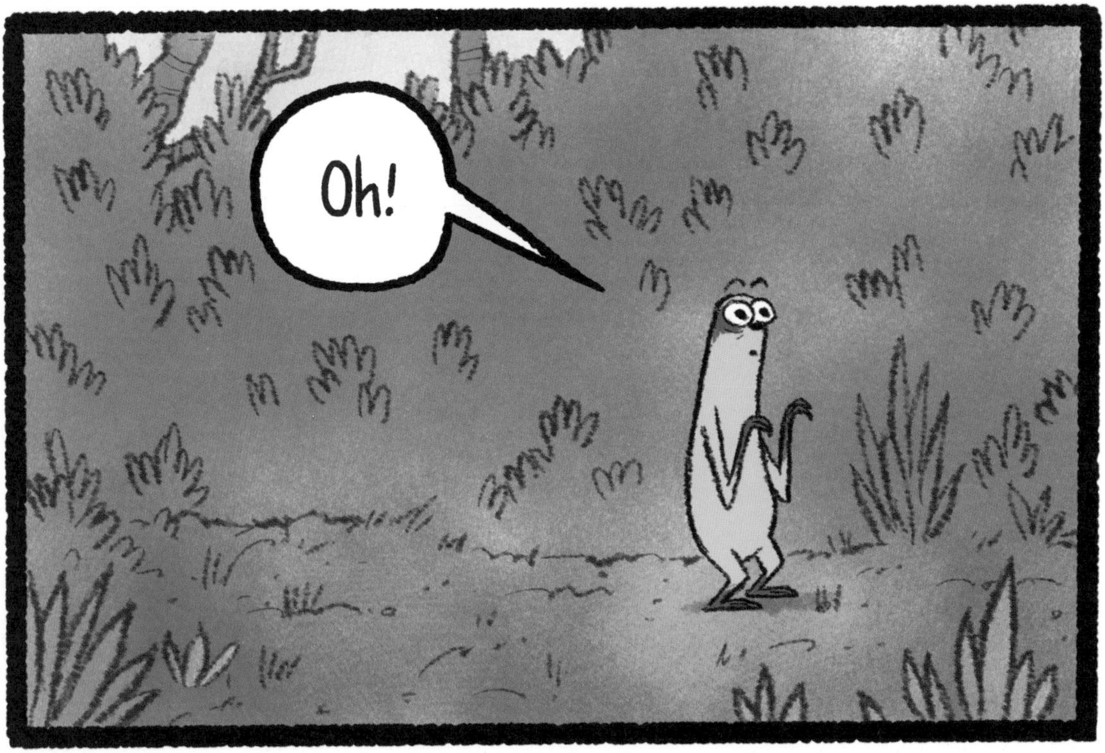
Oh!

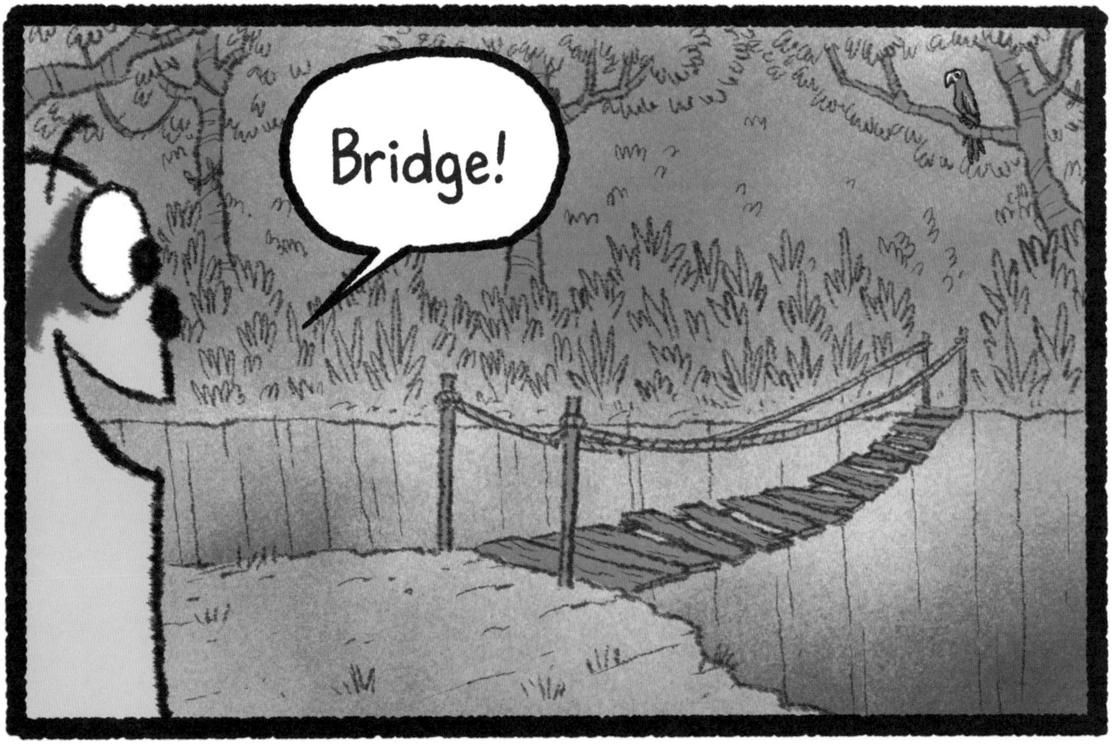
Bridge!

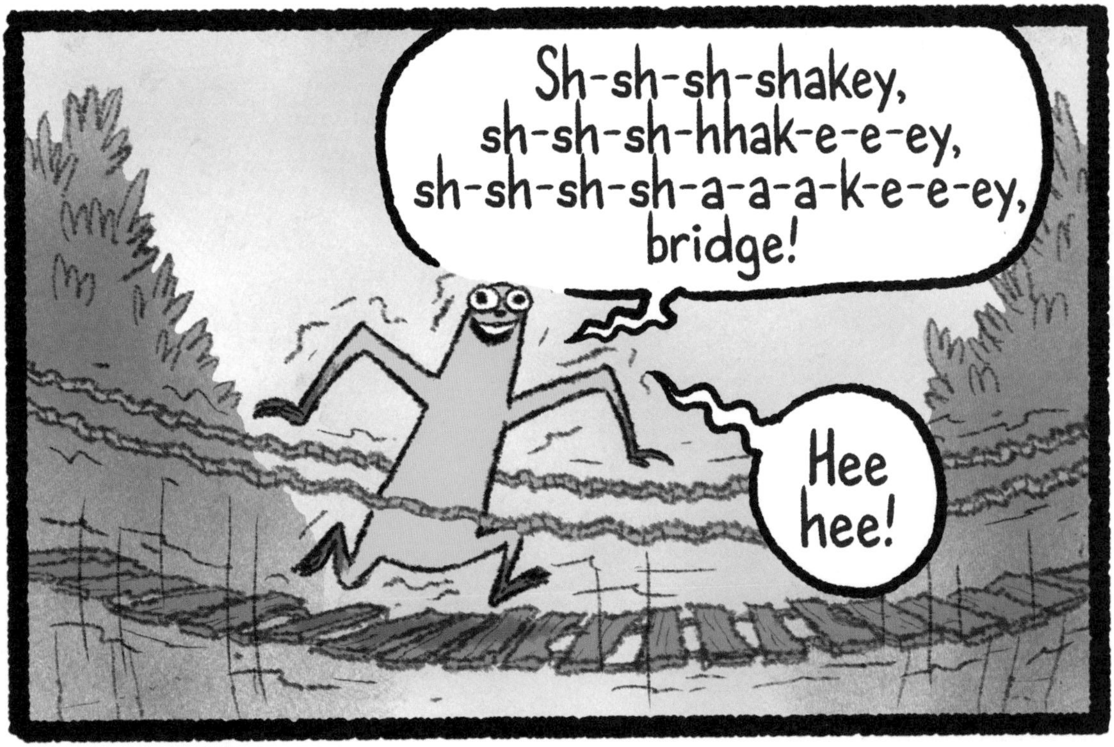
Sh-sh-sh-shakey,
sh-sh-sh-hhak-e-e-ey,
sh-sh-sh-sh-a-a-a-k-e-e-ey,
bridge!
Hee hee!

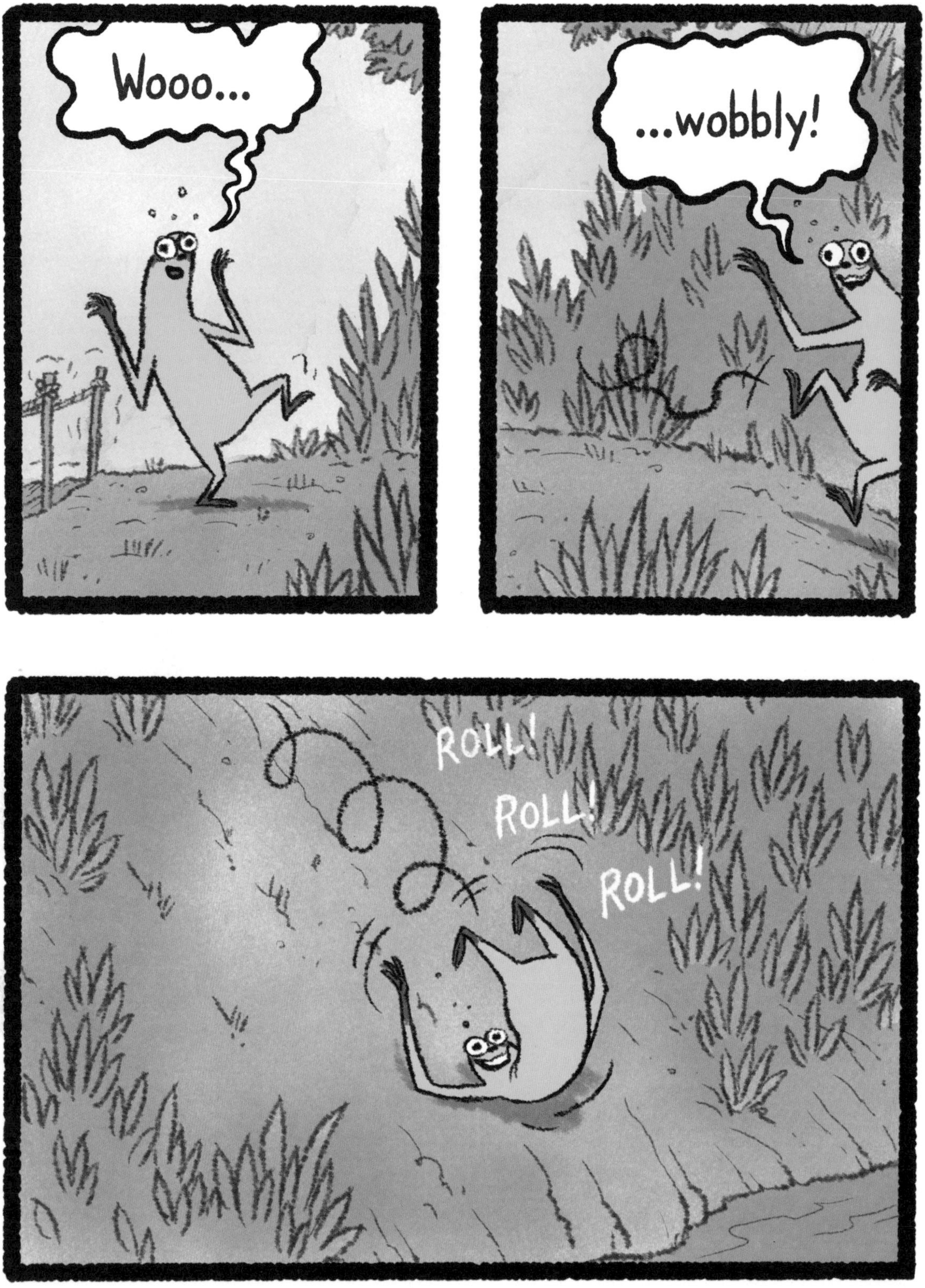
Wooo...
...wobbly!
ROLL!
ROLL!
ROLL!

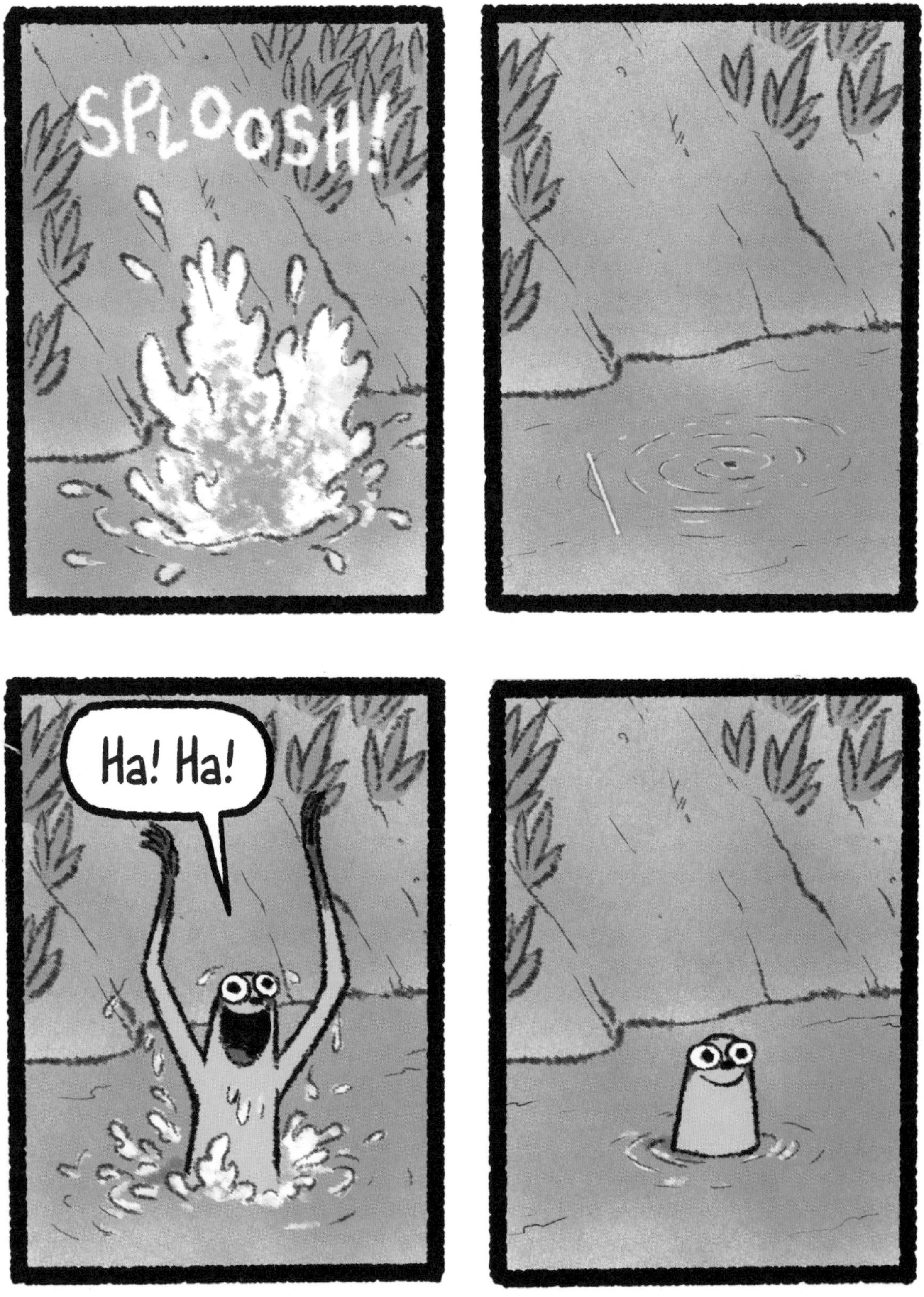
SPLOOSH!
Ha! Ha!

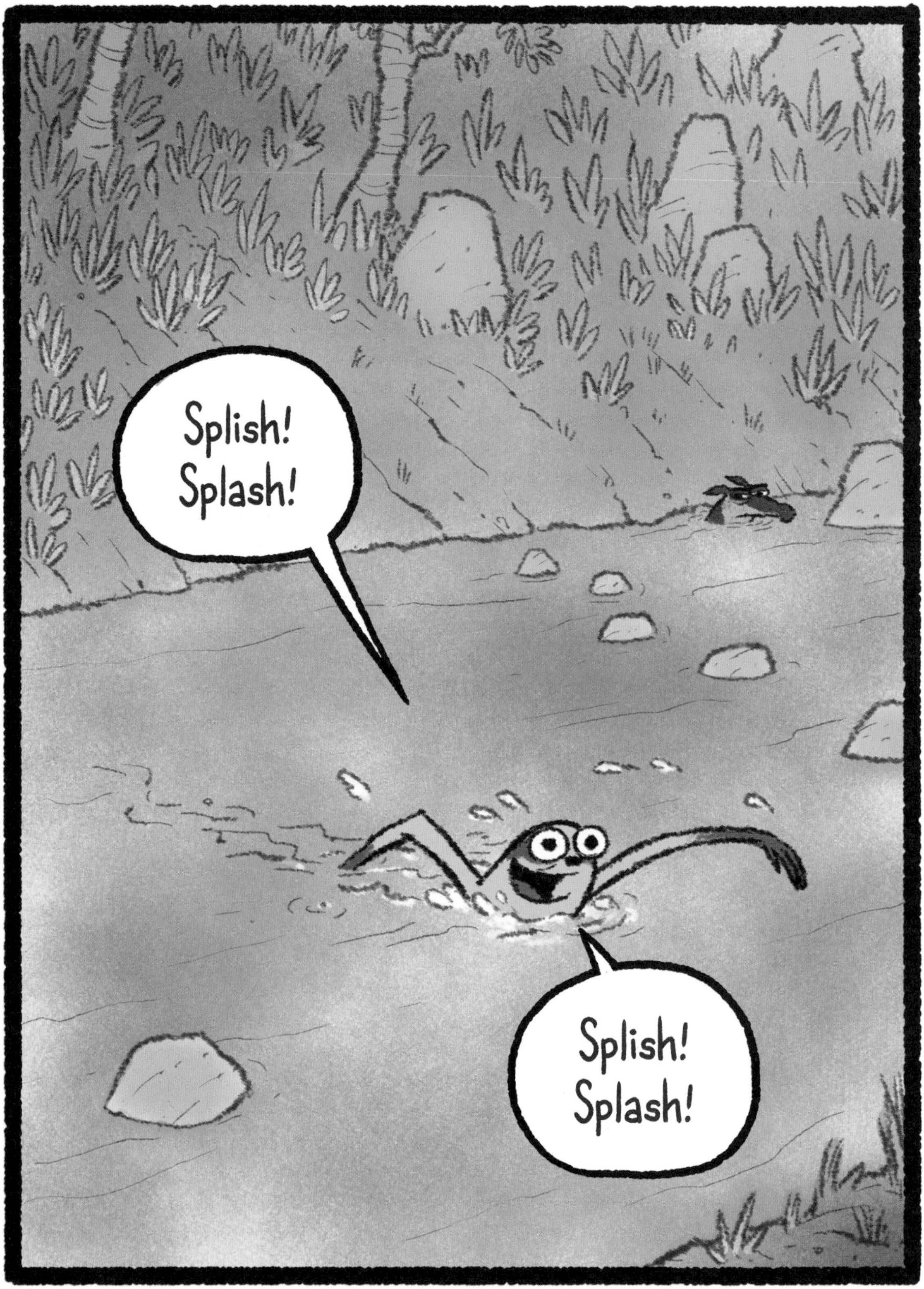
Splish! Splash!
Splish! Splash!

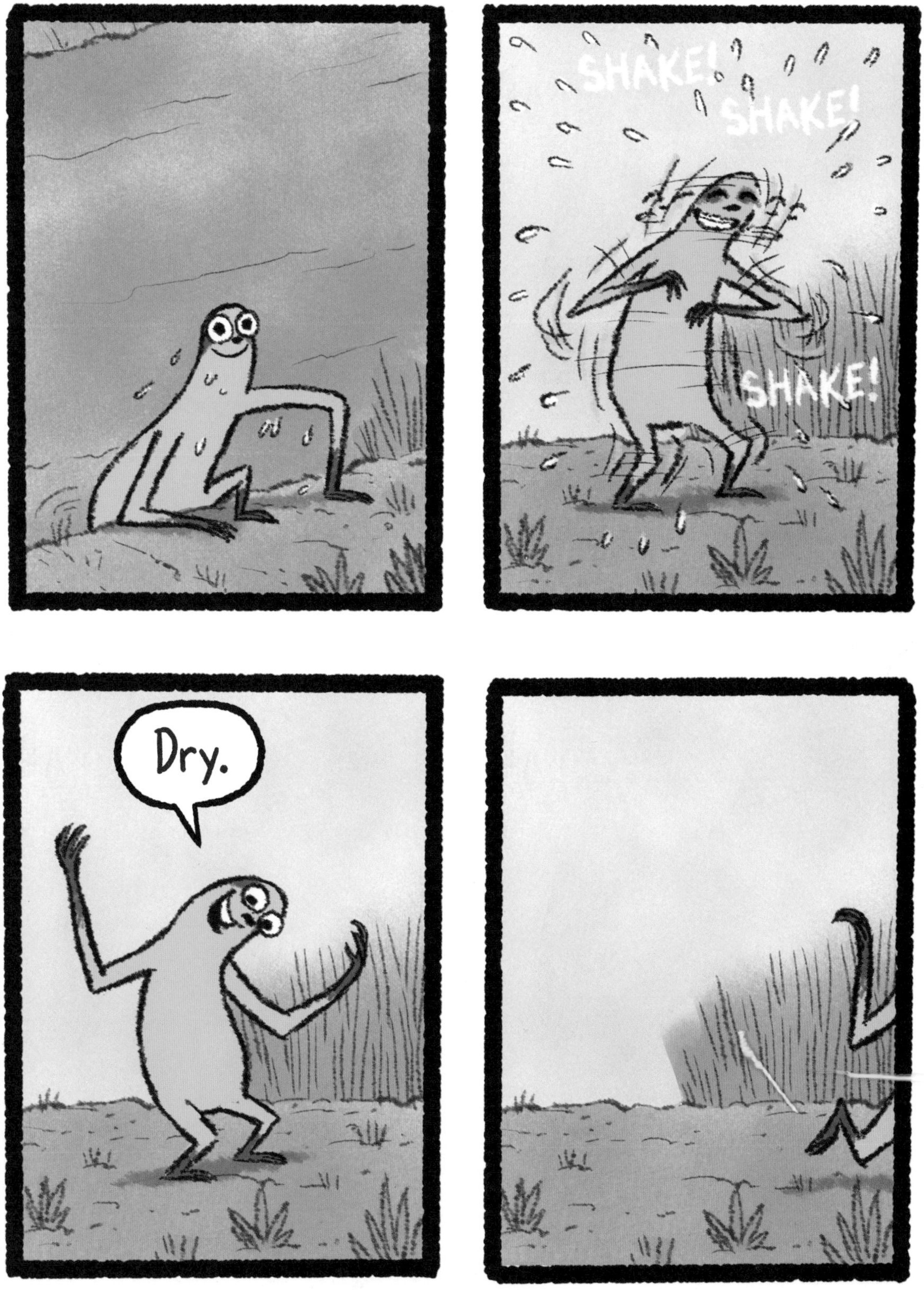
SHAKE!
SHAKE!
SHAKE!
Dry.

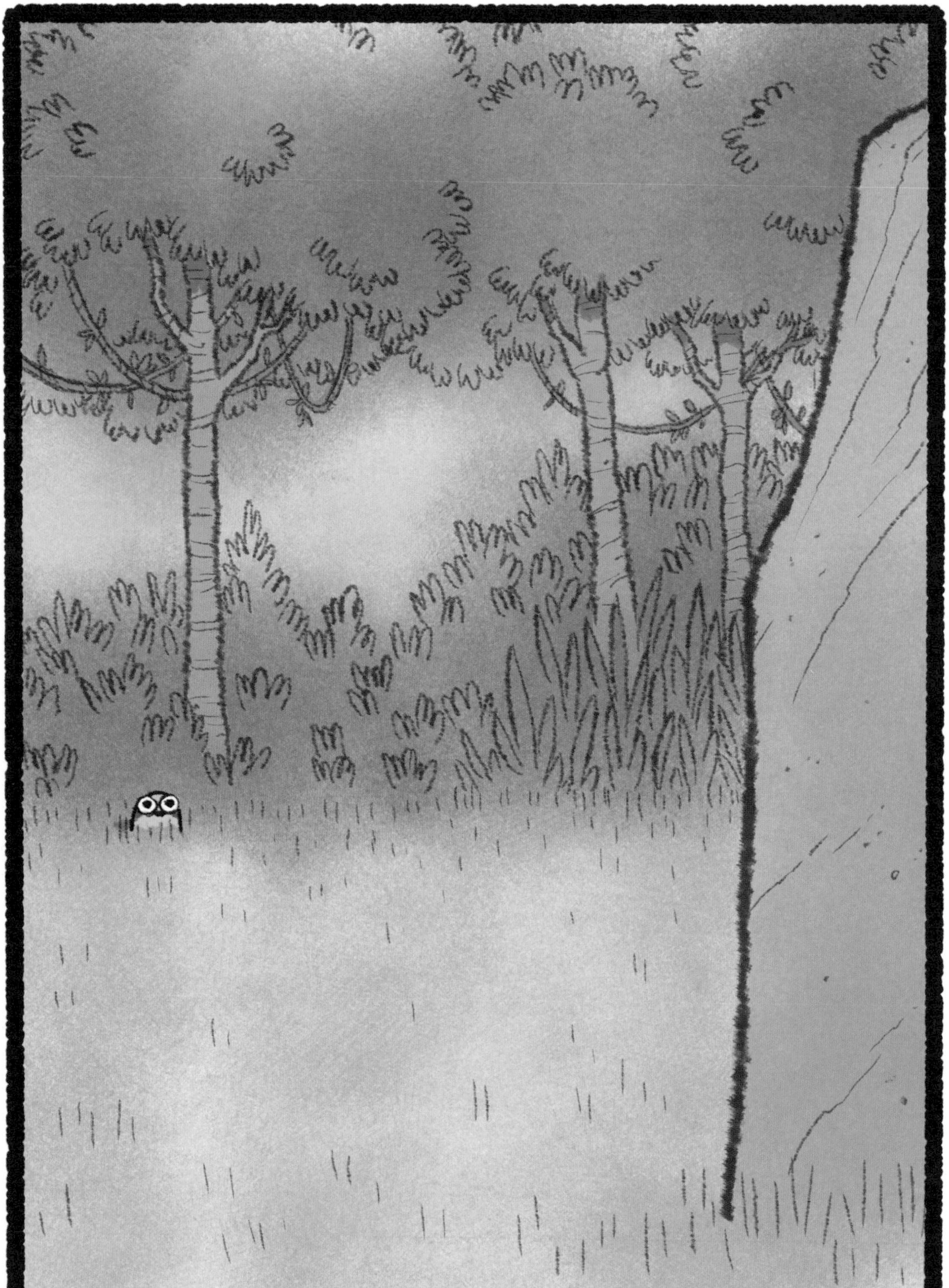

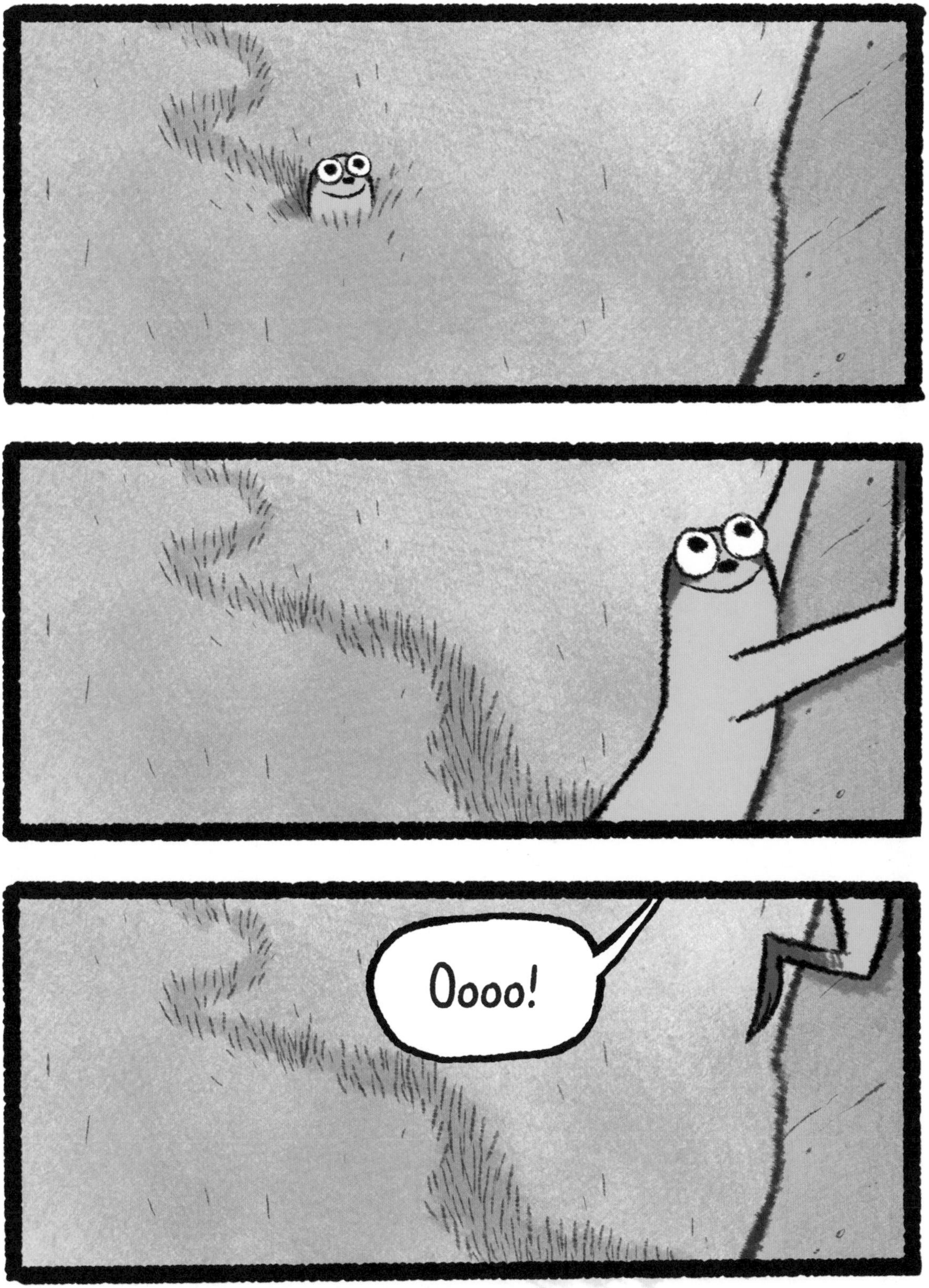
Oooo!

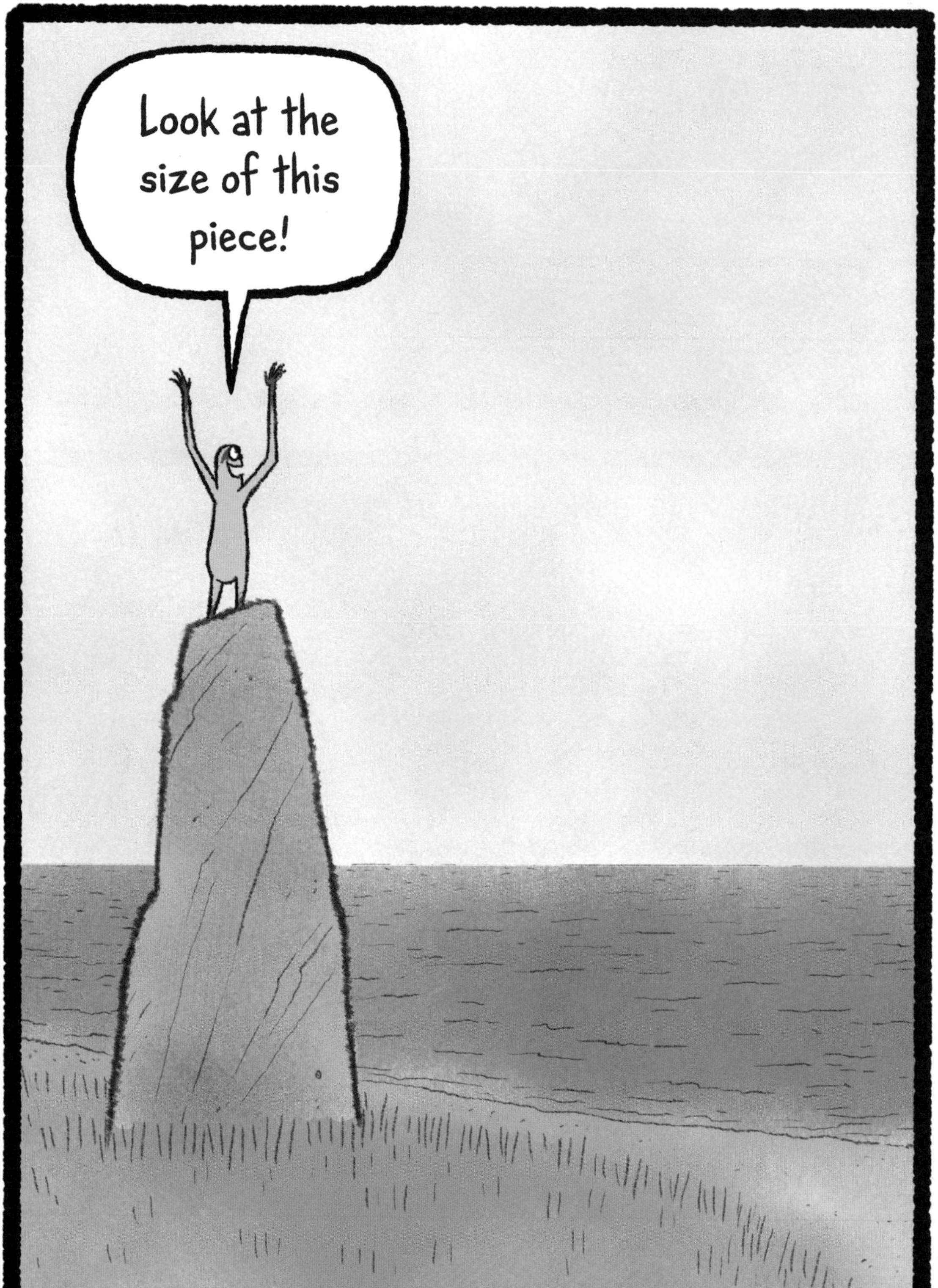
Look at the size of this piece!

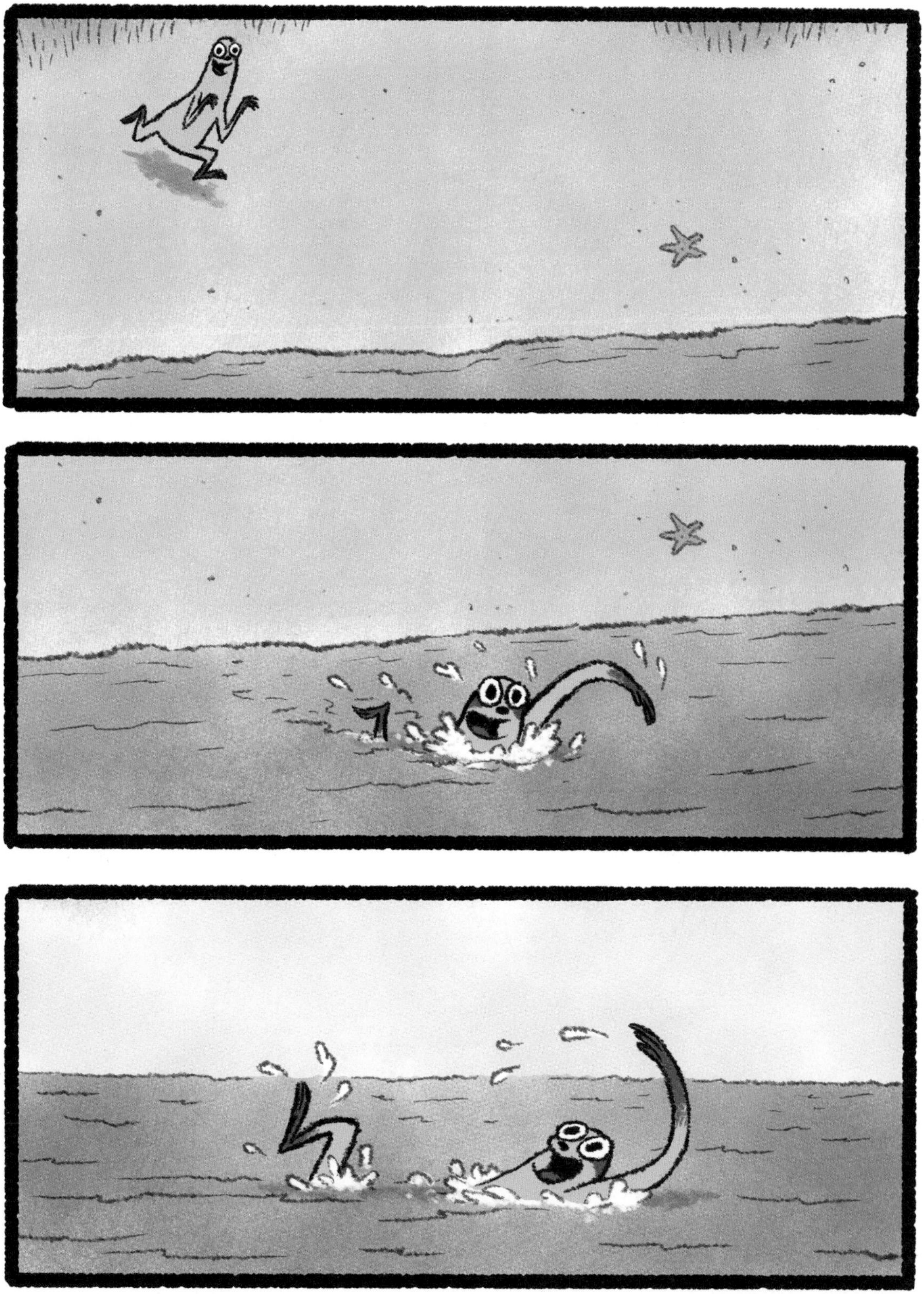

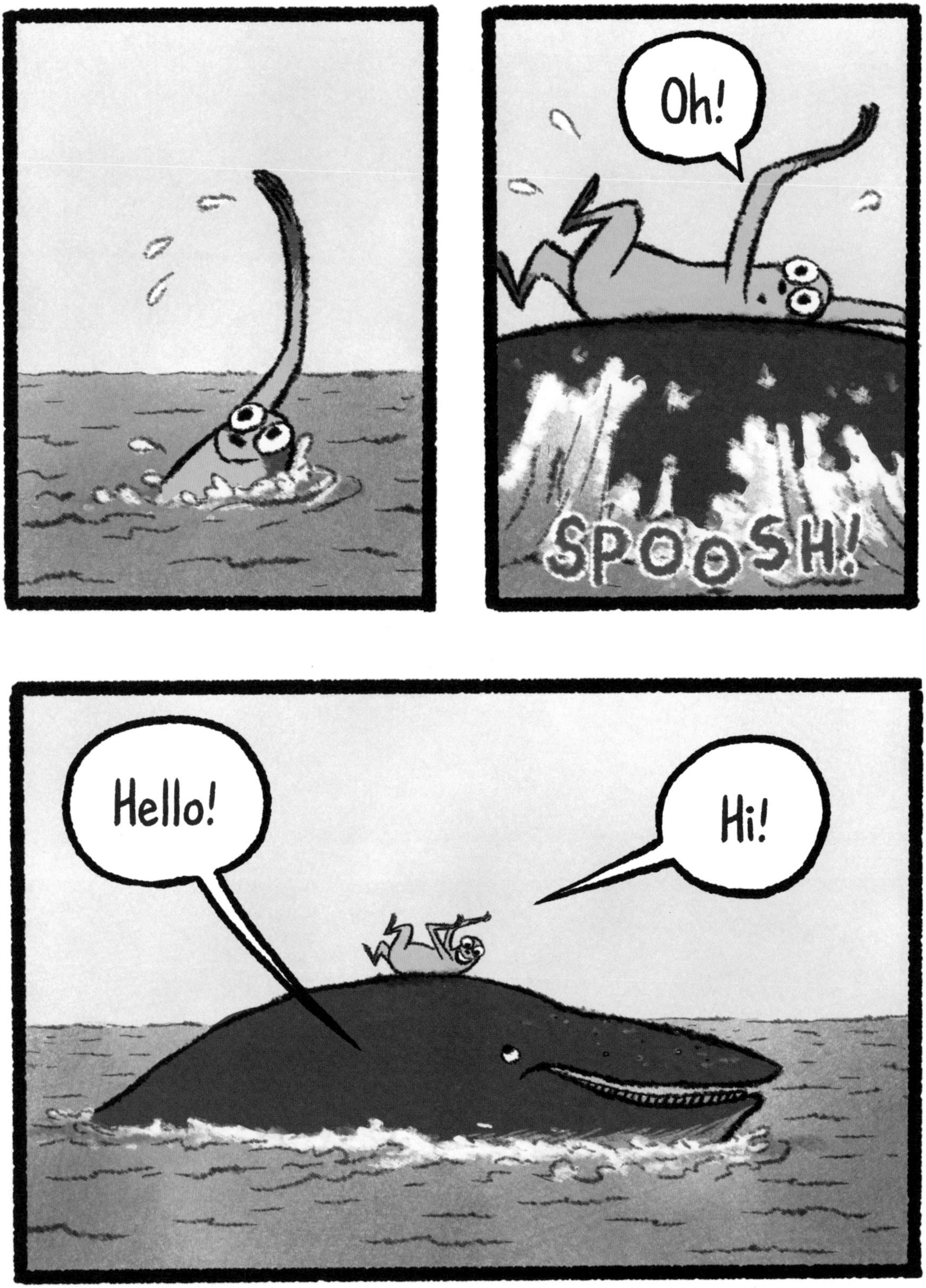
Oh!
SPOOSH!
Hello!
Hi!

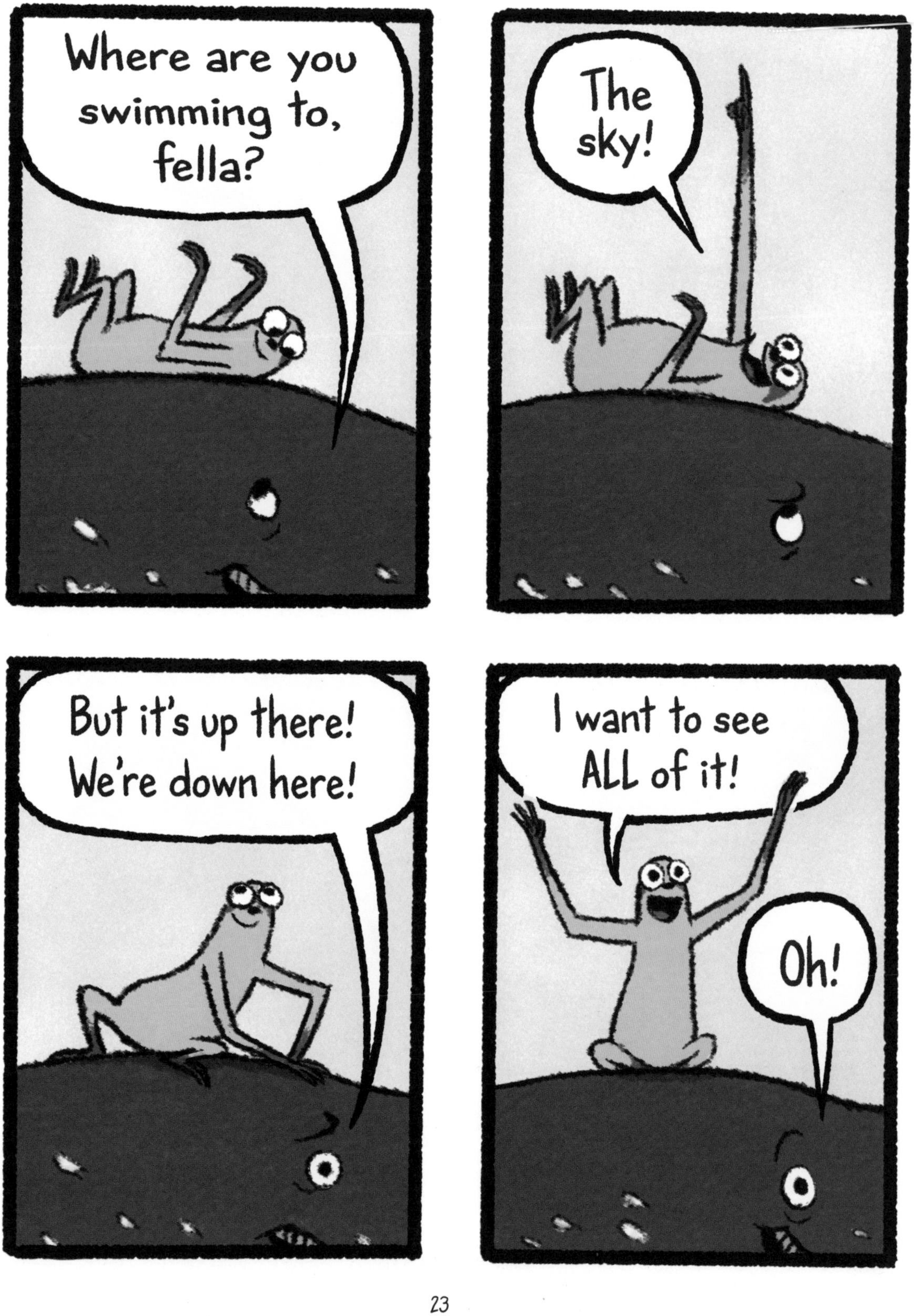
Where are you swimming to, fella?
The sky!
But it's up there! We're down here!
I want to see ALL of it!
Oh!

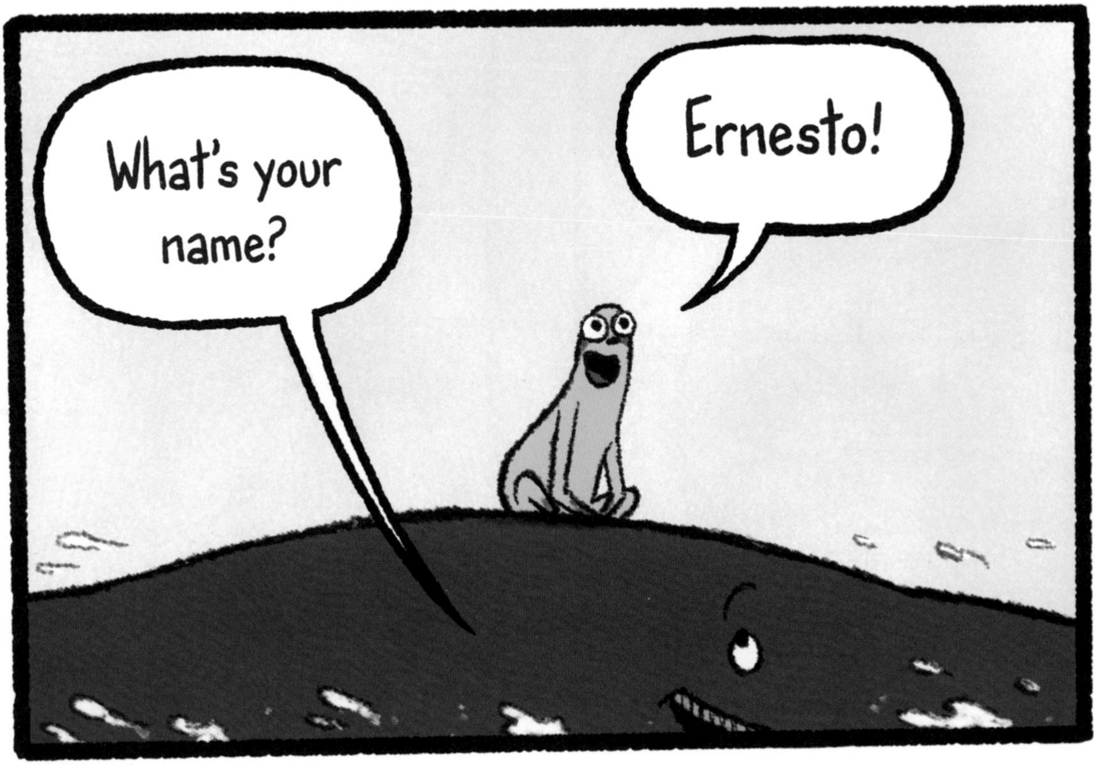
What's your name?
Ernesto!

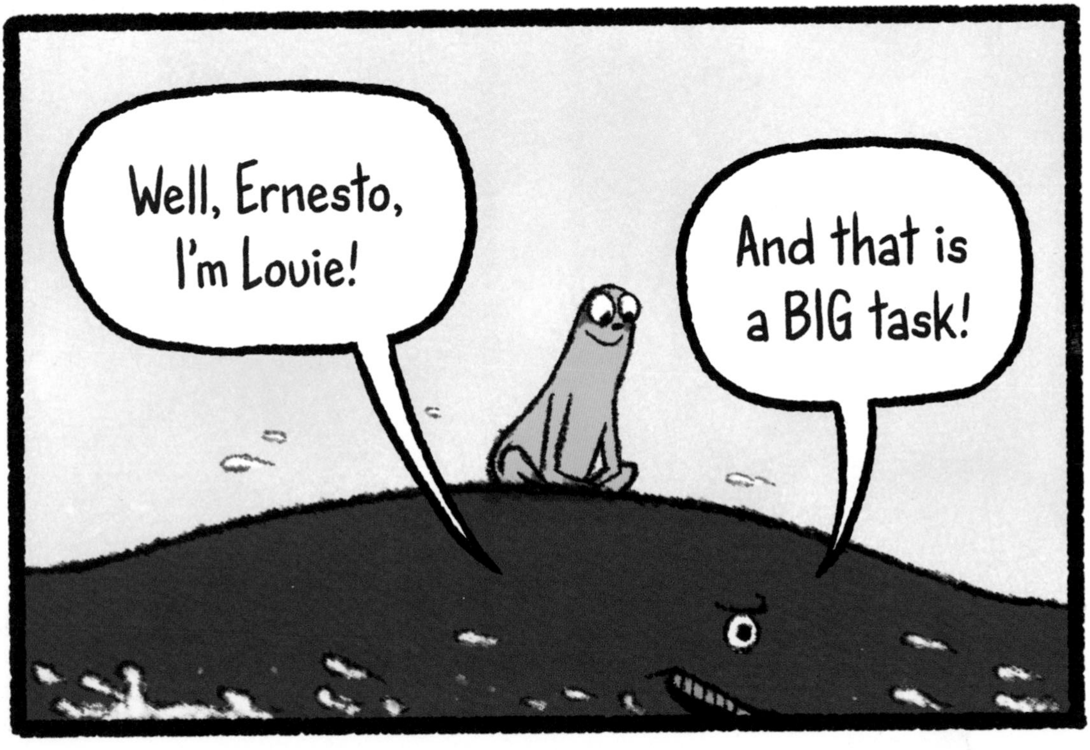
Well, Ernesto, I'm Louie!
And that is a BIG task!

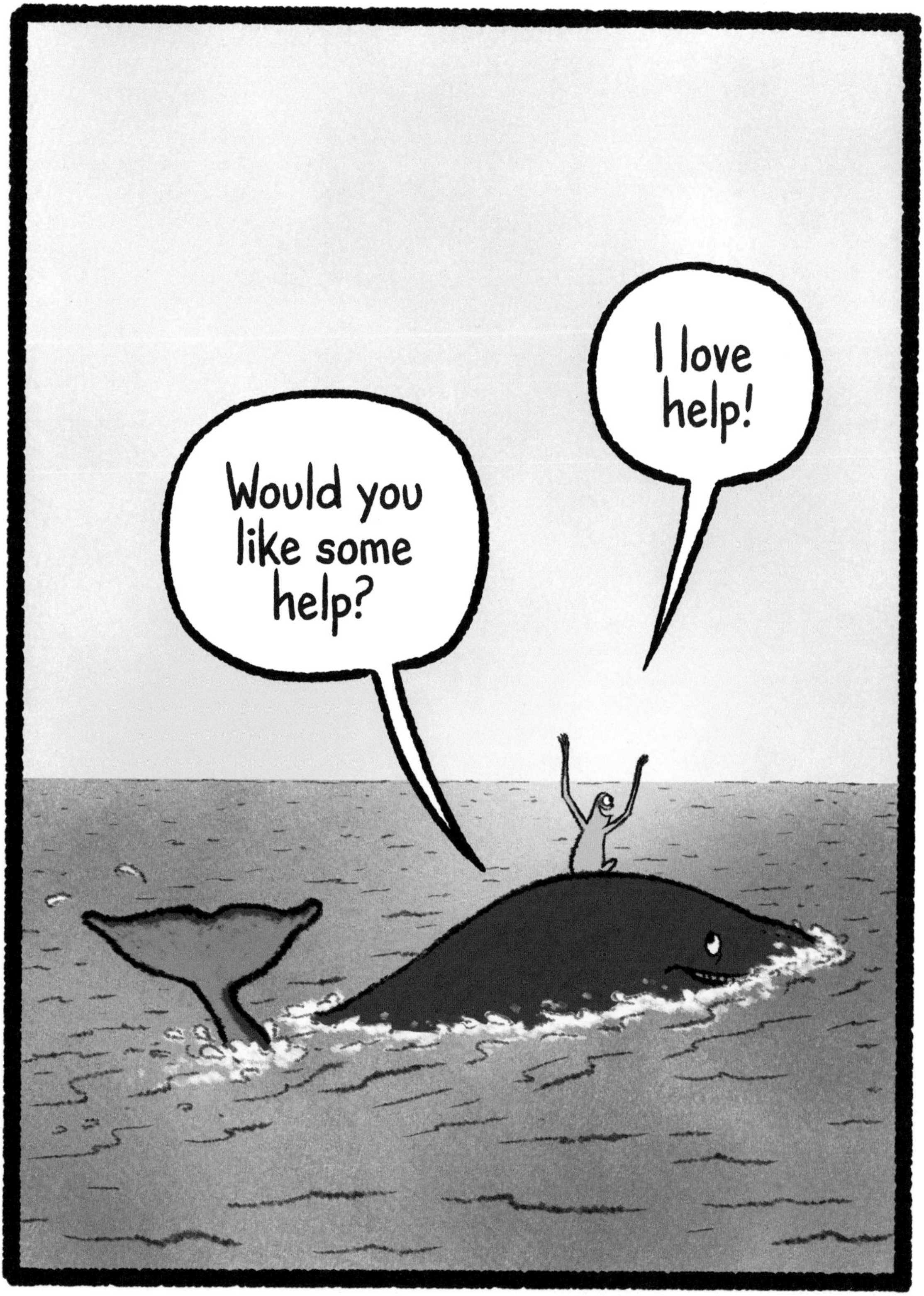
Would you like some help?
I love help!

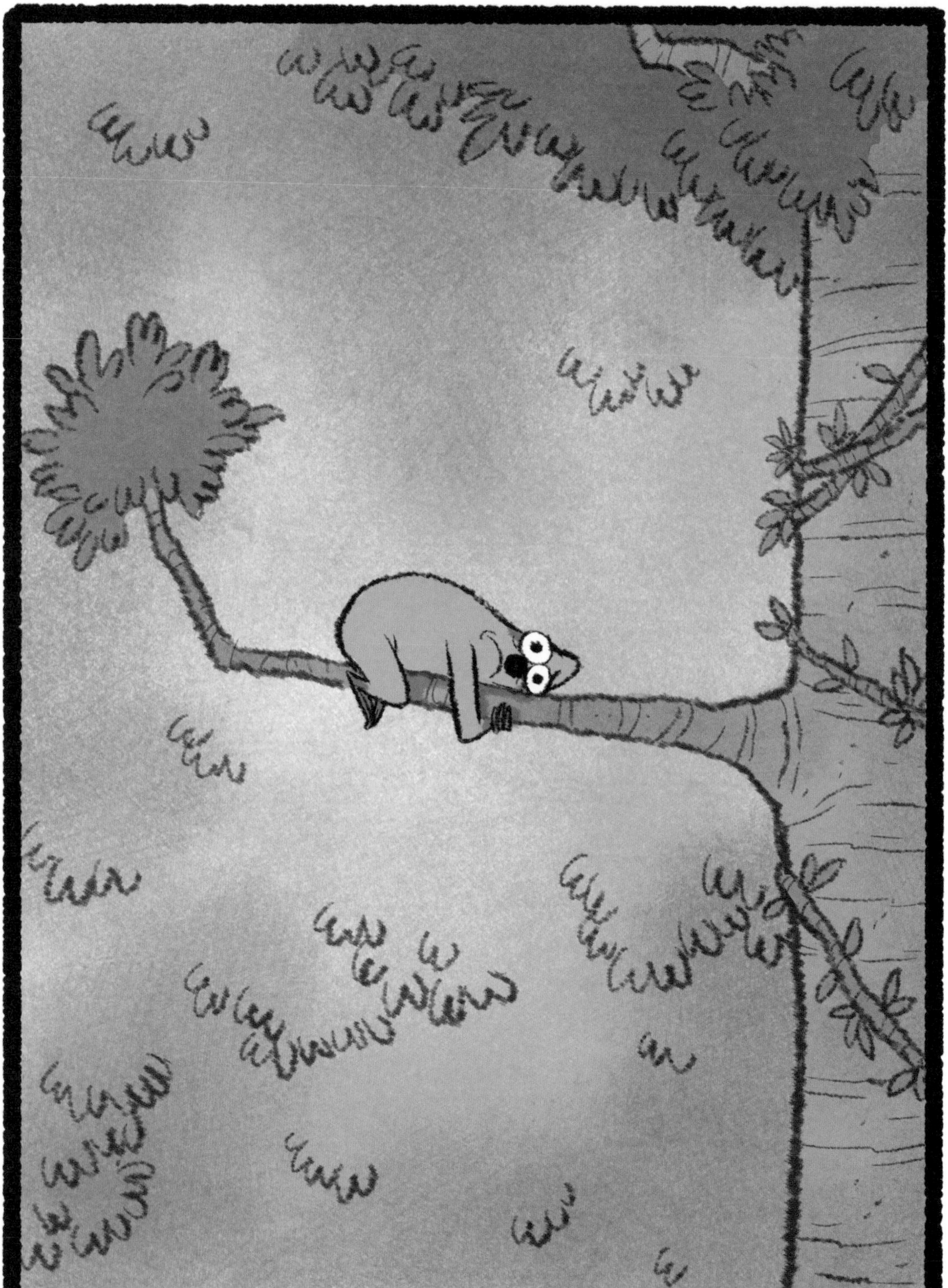

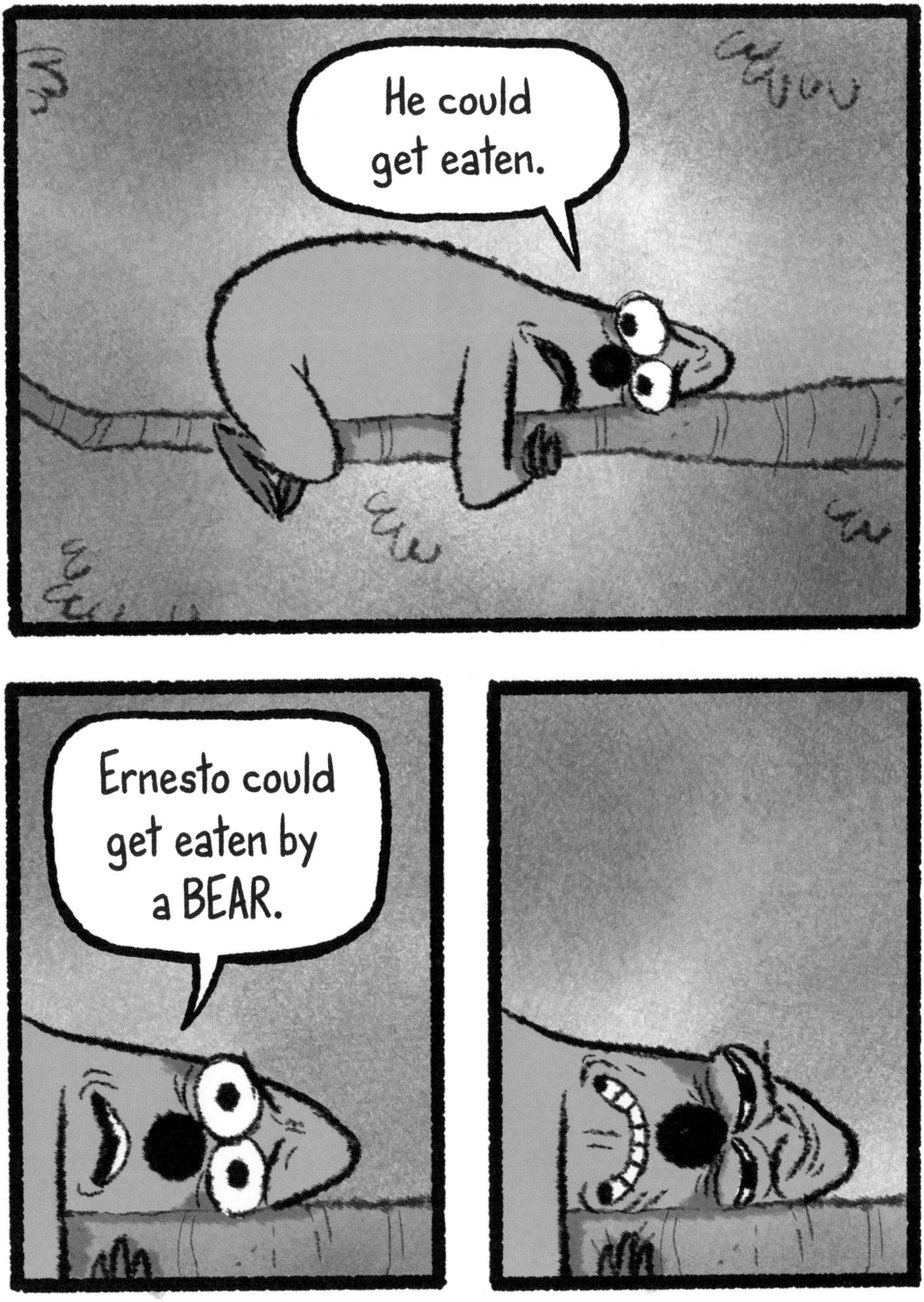
He could get eaten.
Ernesto could get eaten by a BEAR.

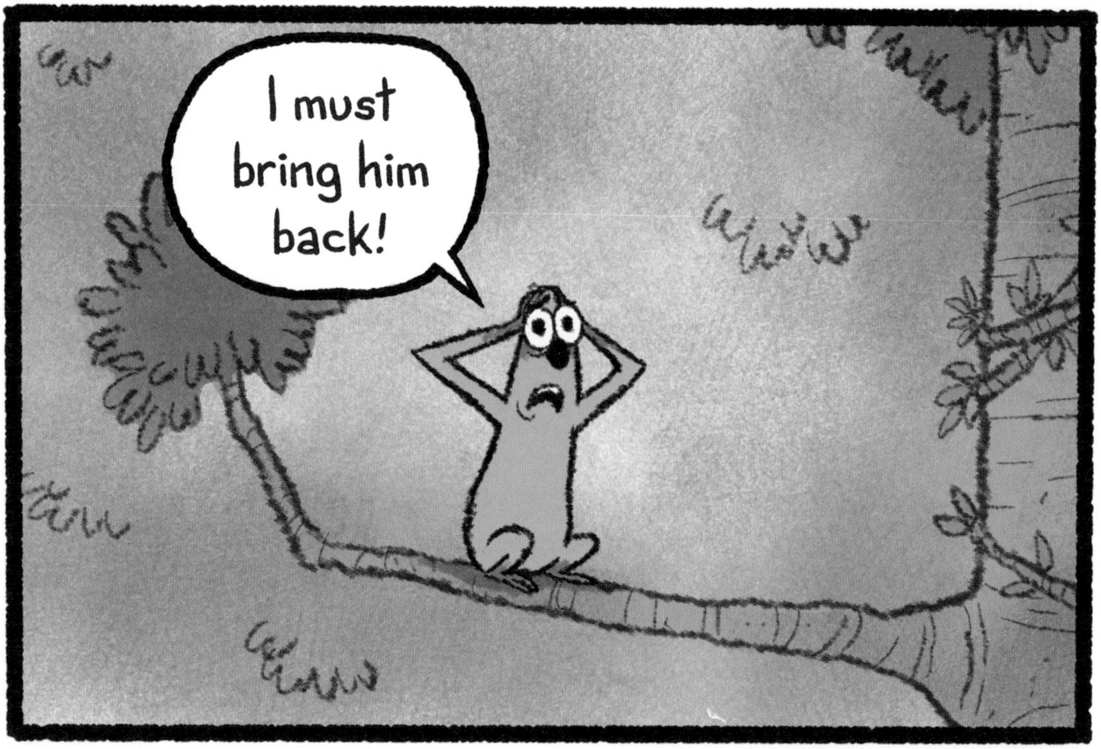
I must bring him back!

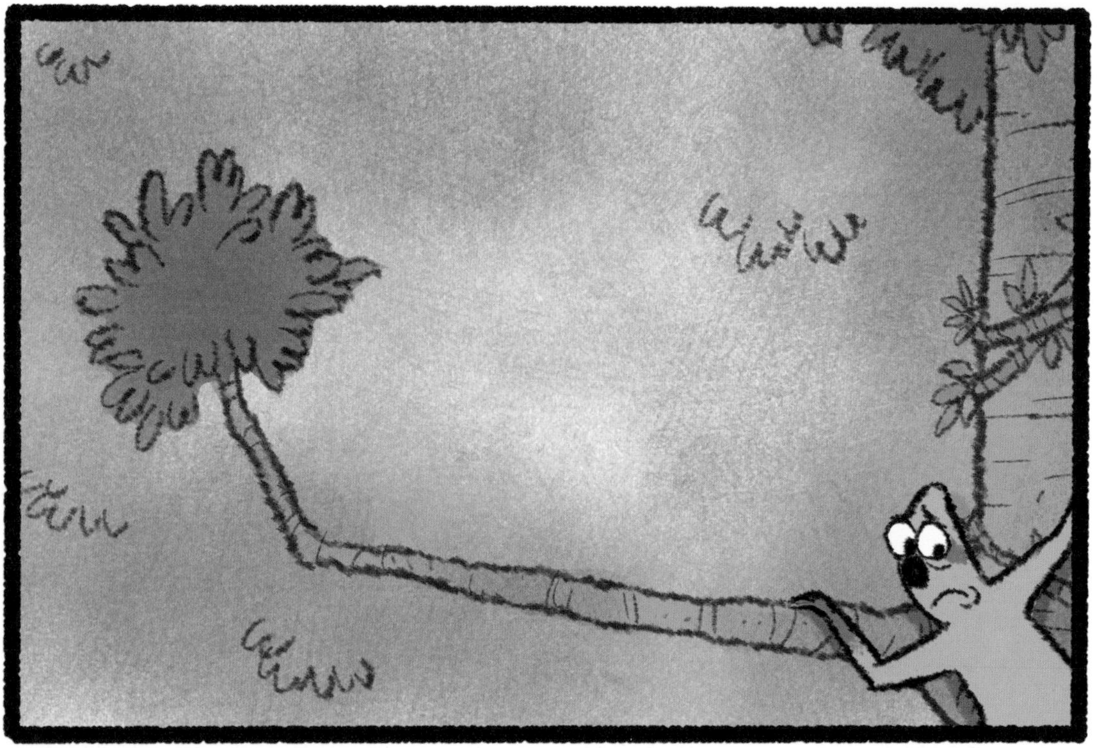

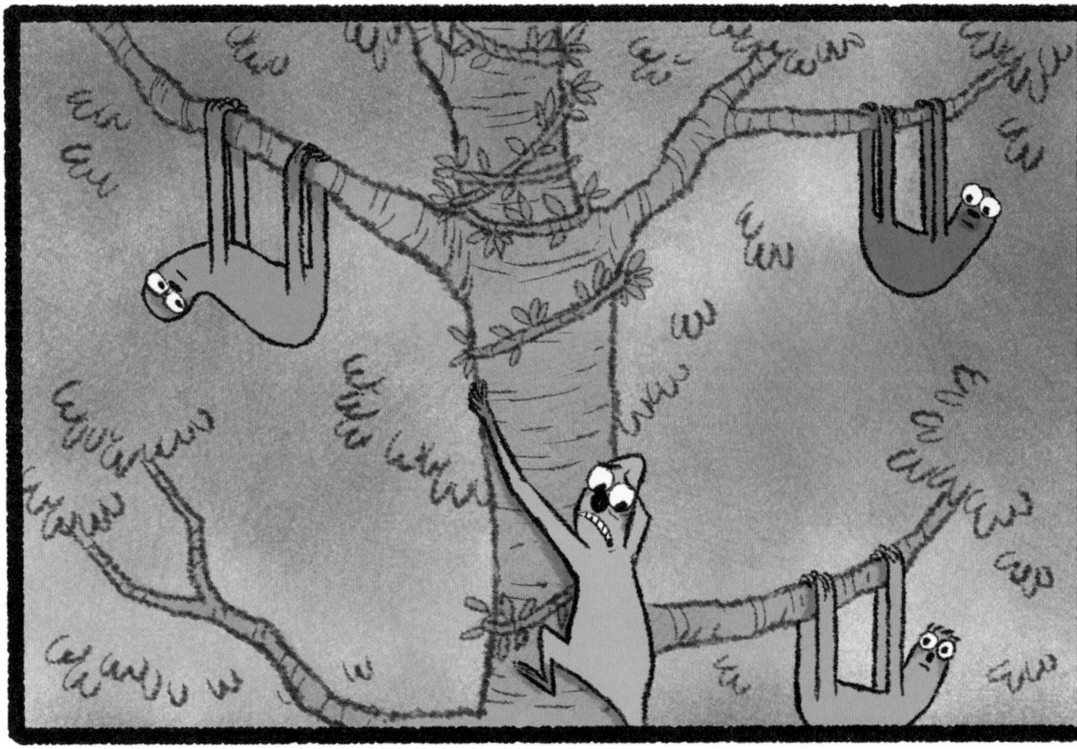

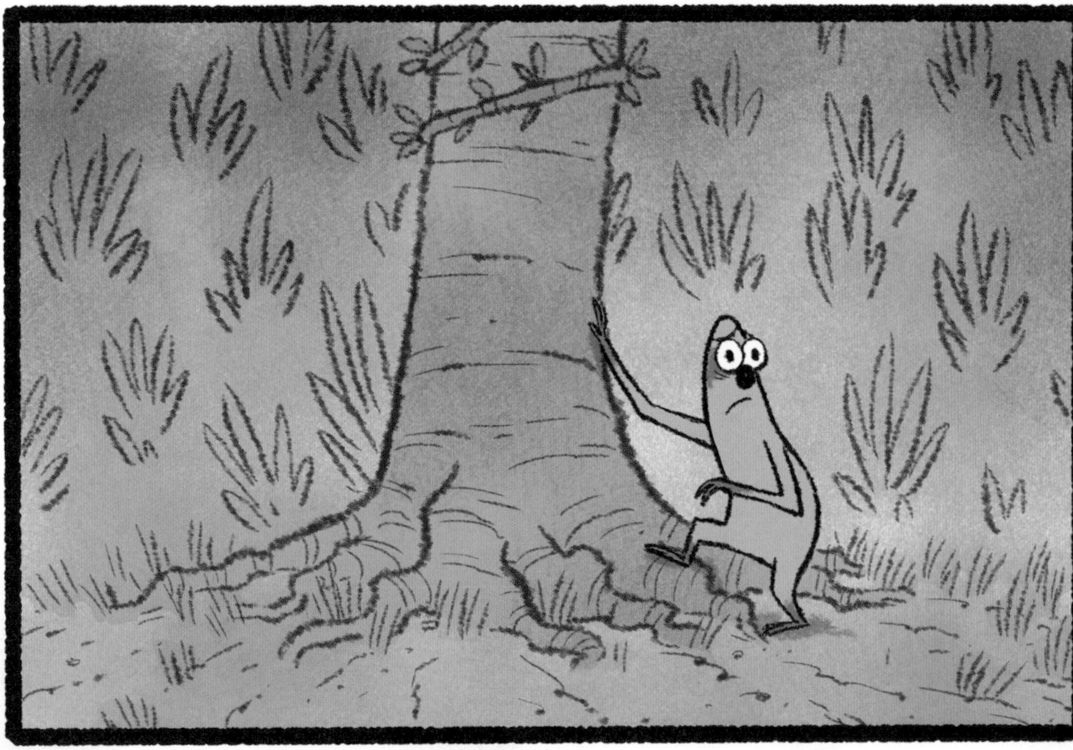

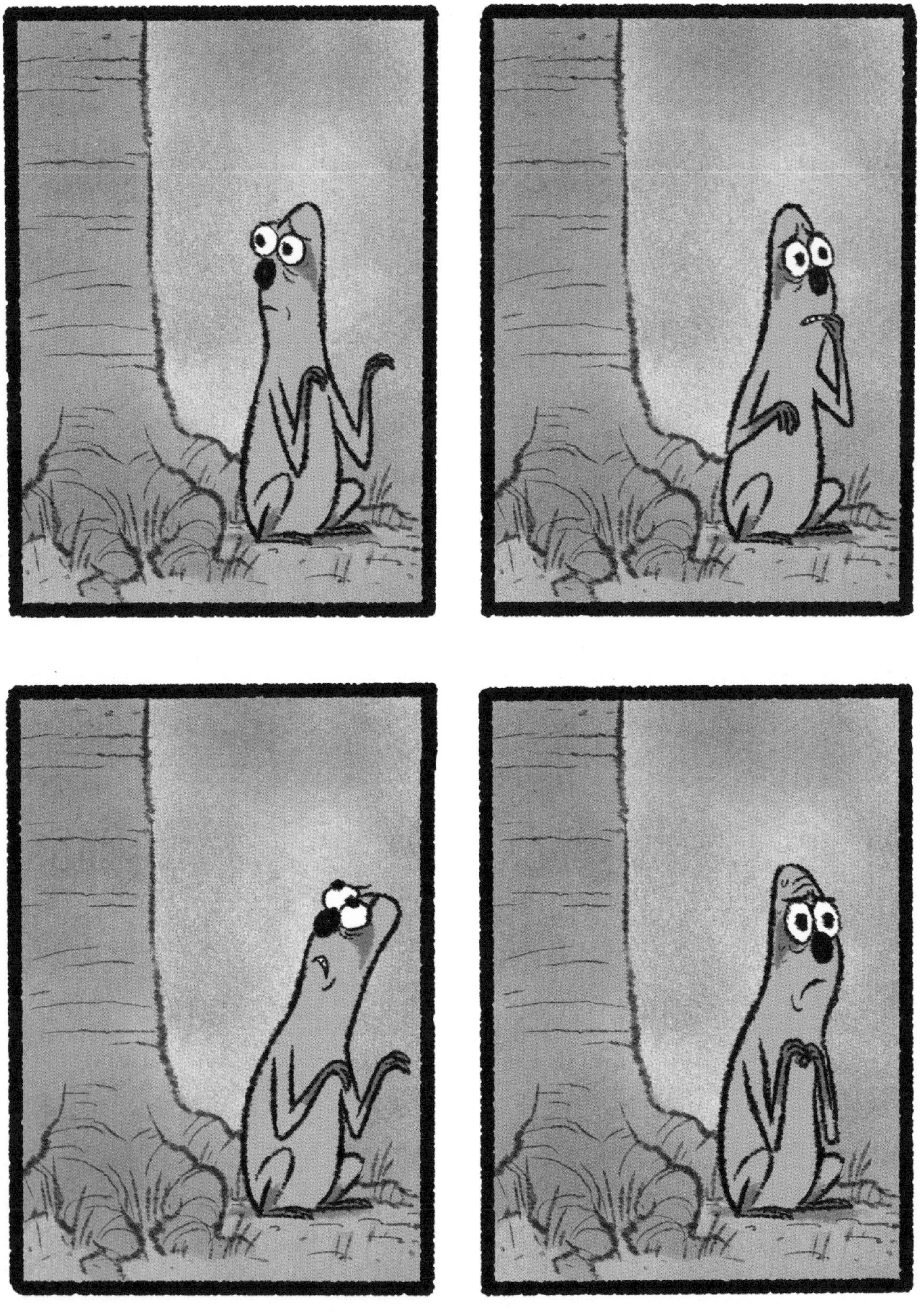

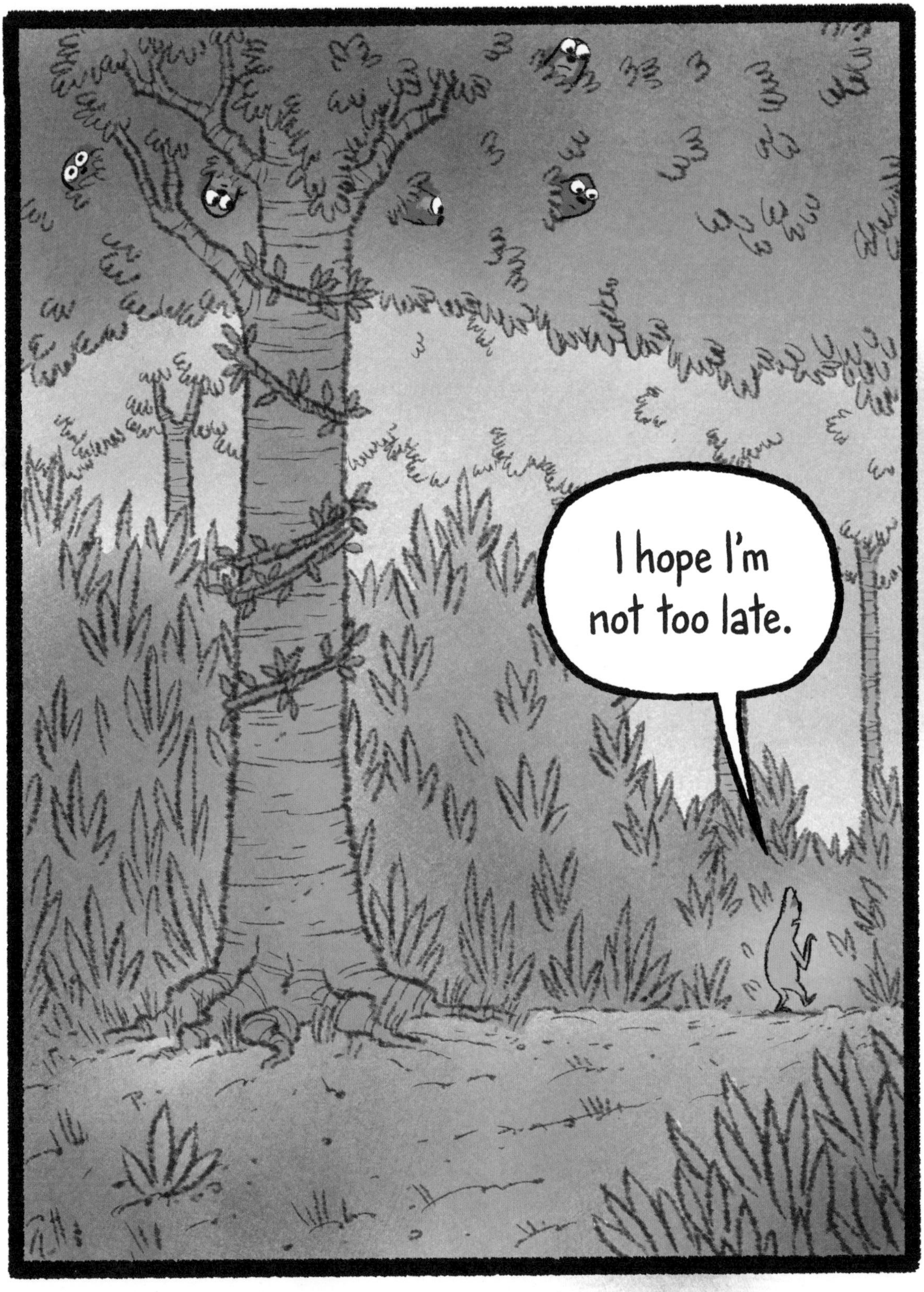
I hope I'm not too late.

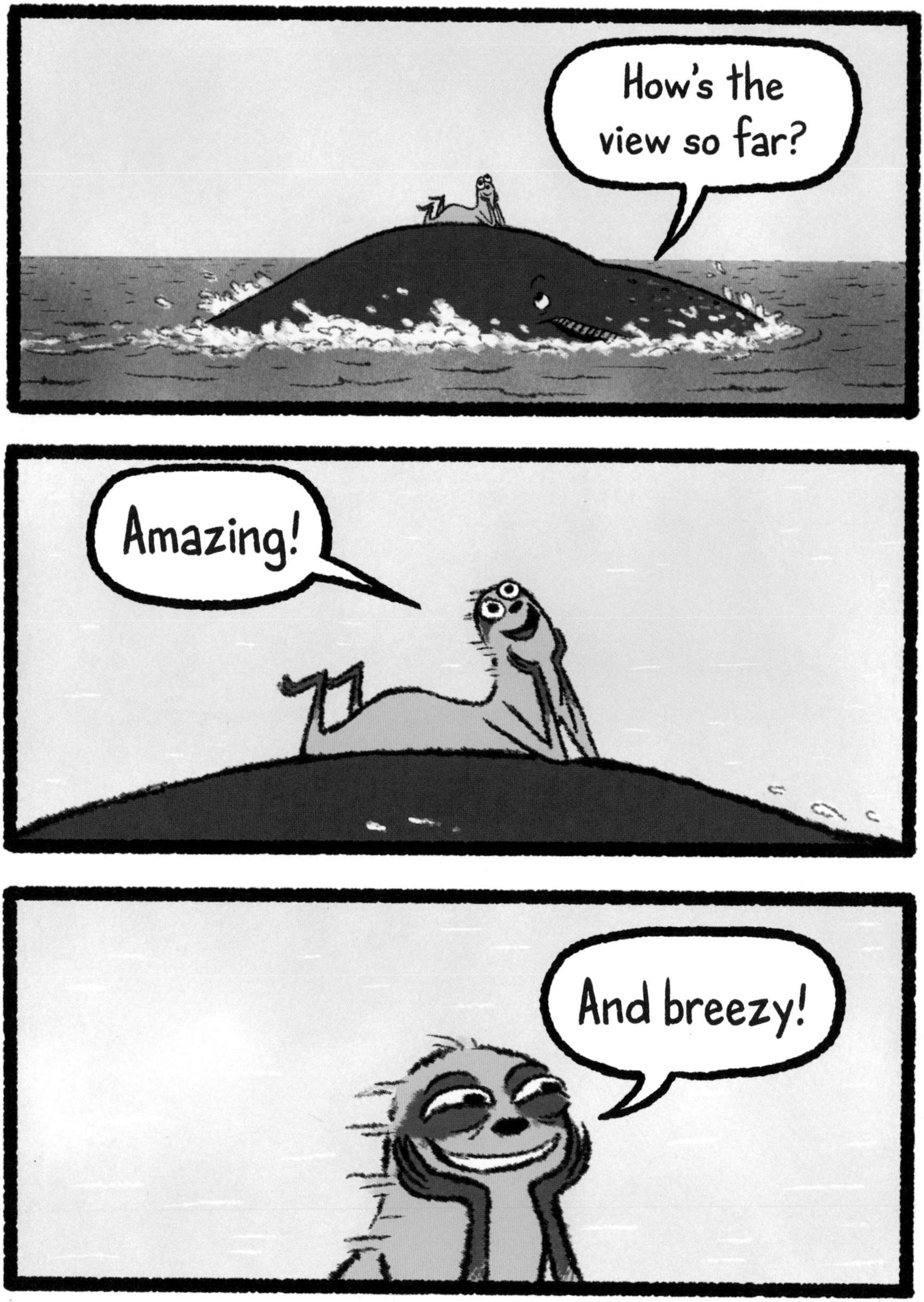
How's the view so far?
Amazing!
And breezy!

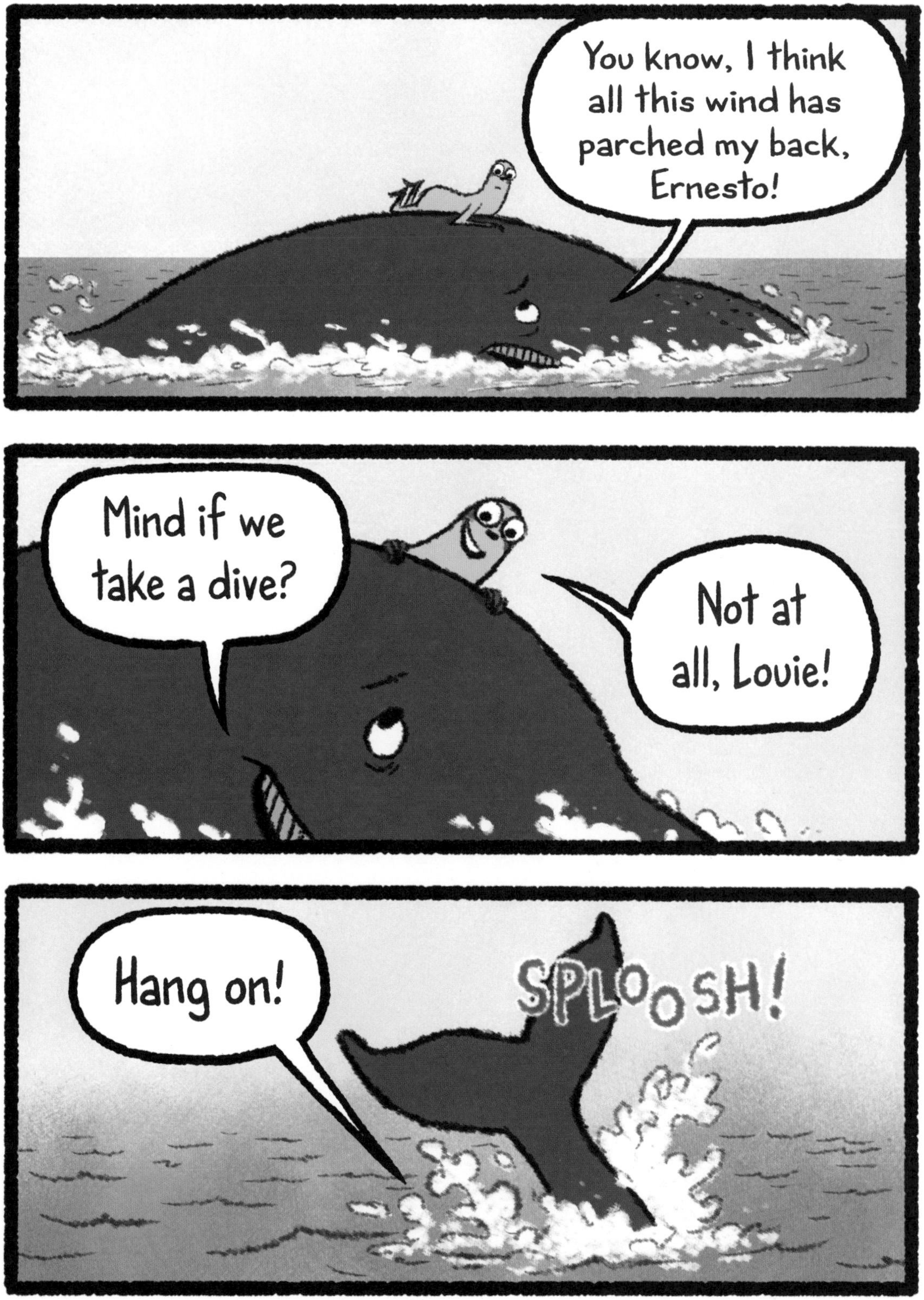
You know, I think all this wind has parched my back, Ernesto!
Mind if we take a dive?
Not at all, Louie!
Hang on!
SPLOOSH!

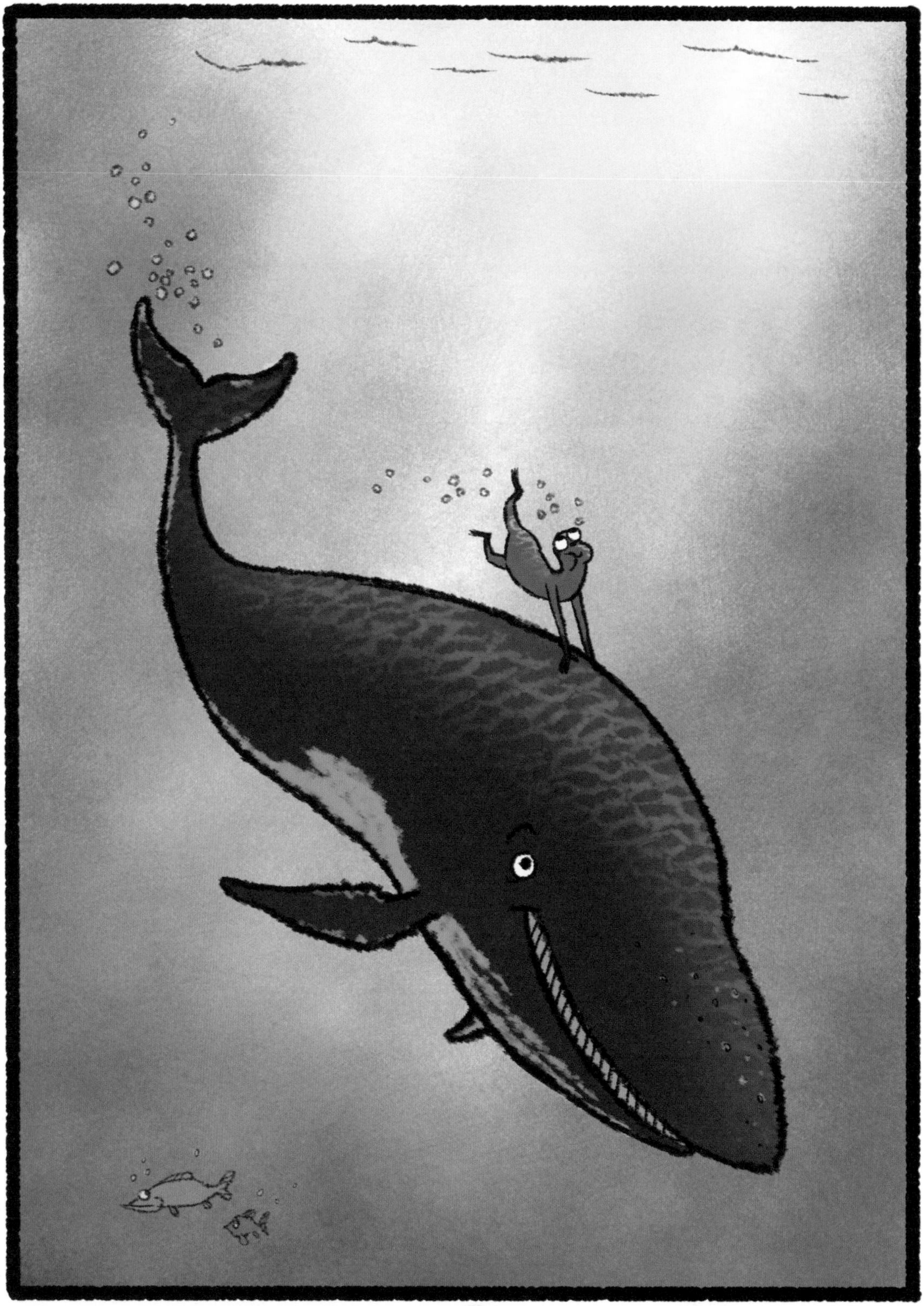

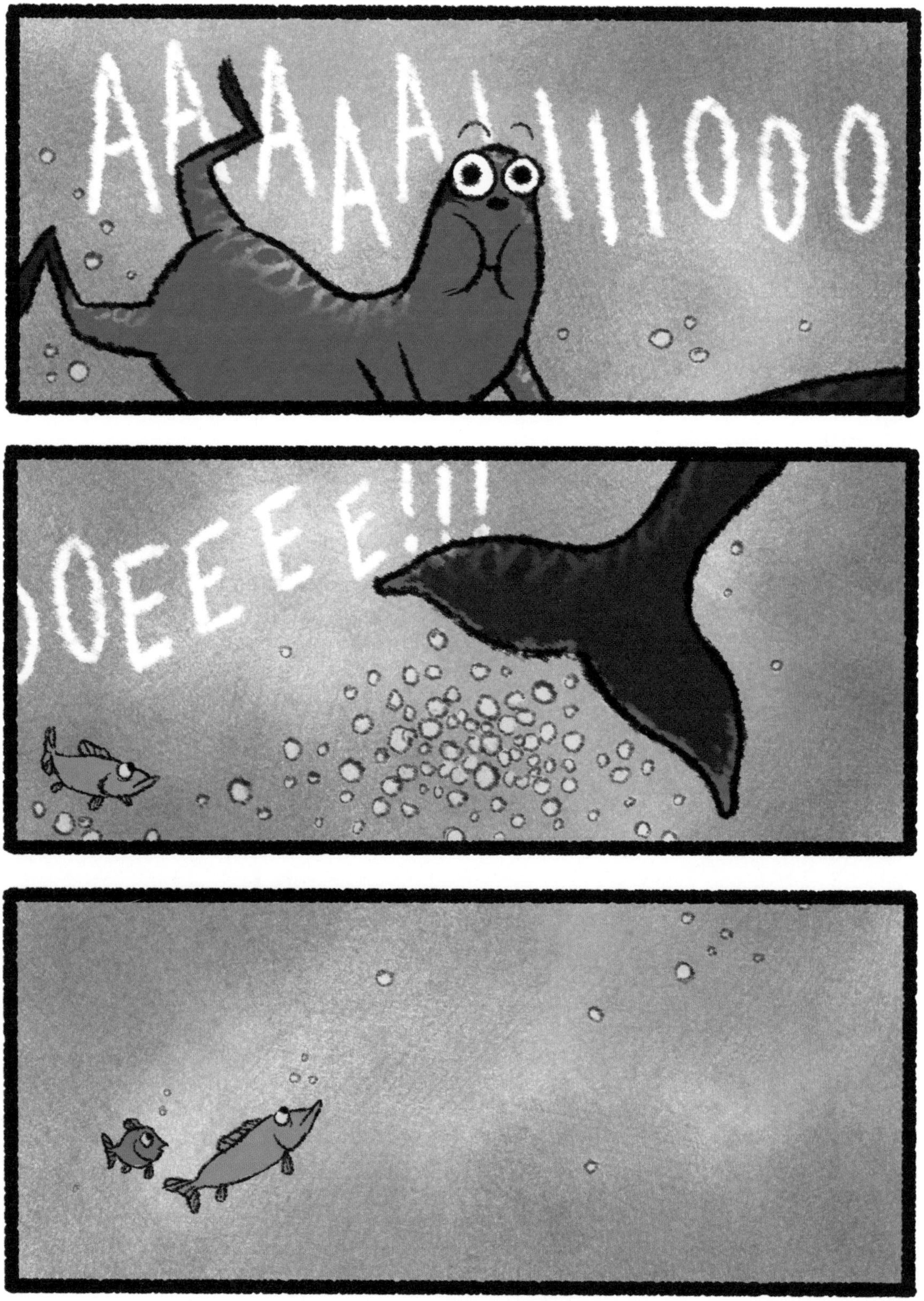
AAAAAIIIOOO
OEEEE!!!

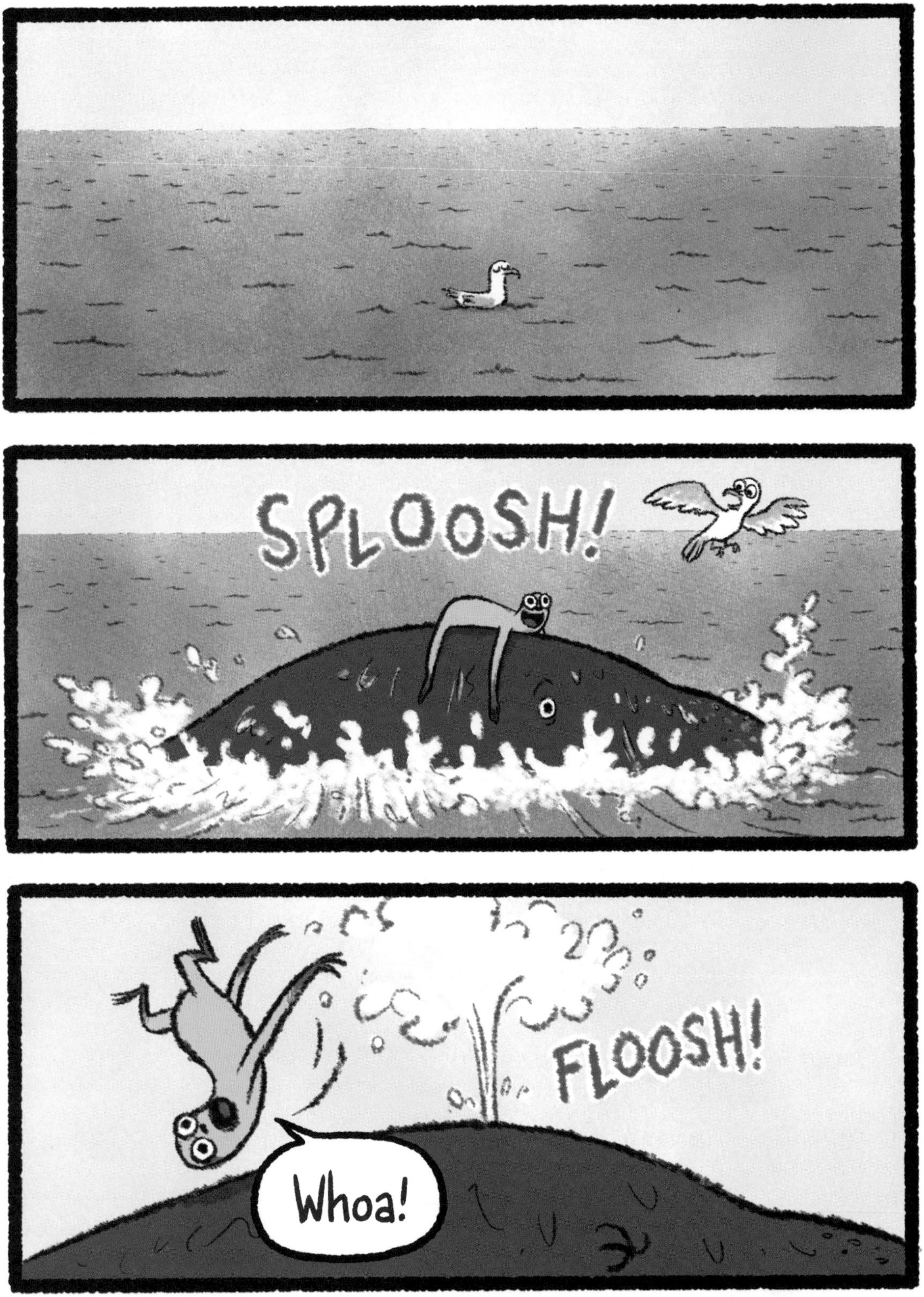
SPLOOSH!
FLOOSH!
Whoa!

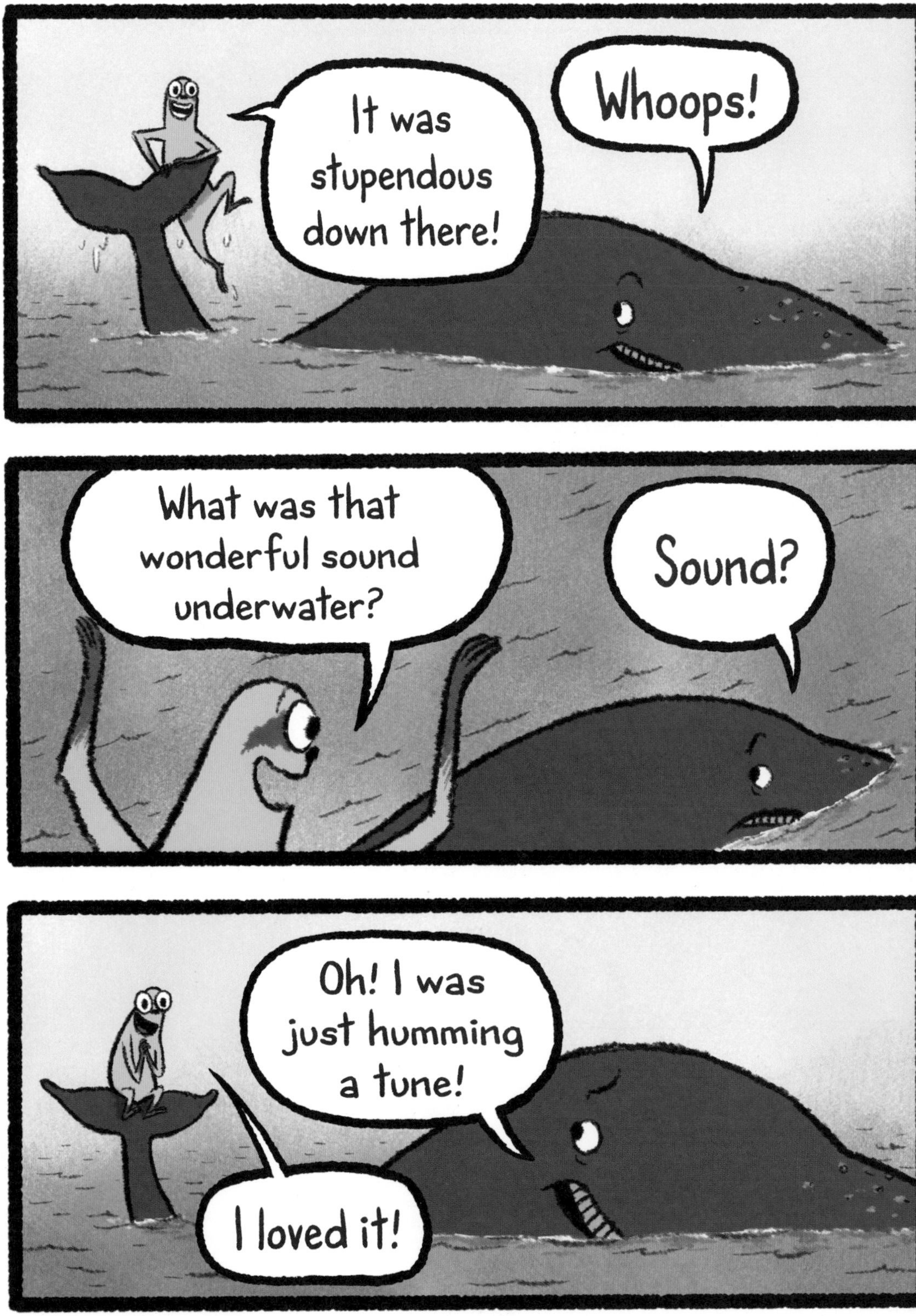
It was stupendous down there!
Whoops!
What was that wonderful sound underwater?
Sound?
Oh! I was just humming a tune!
I loved it!

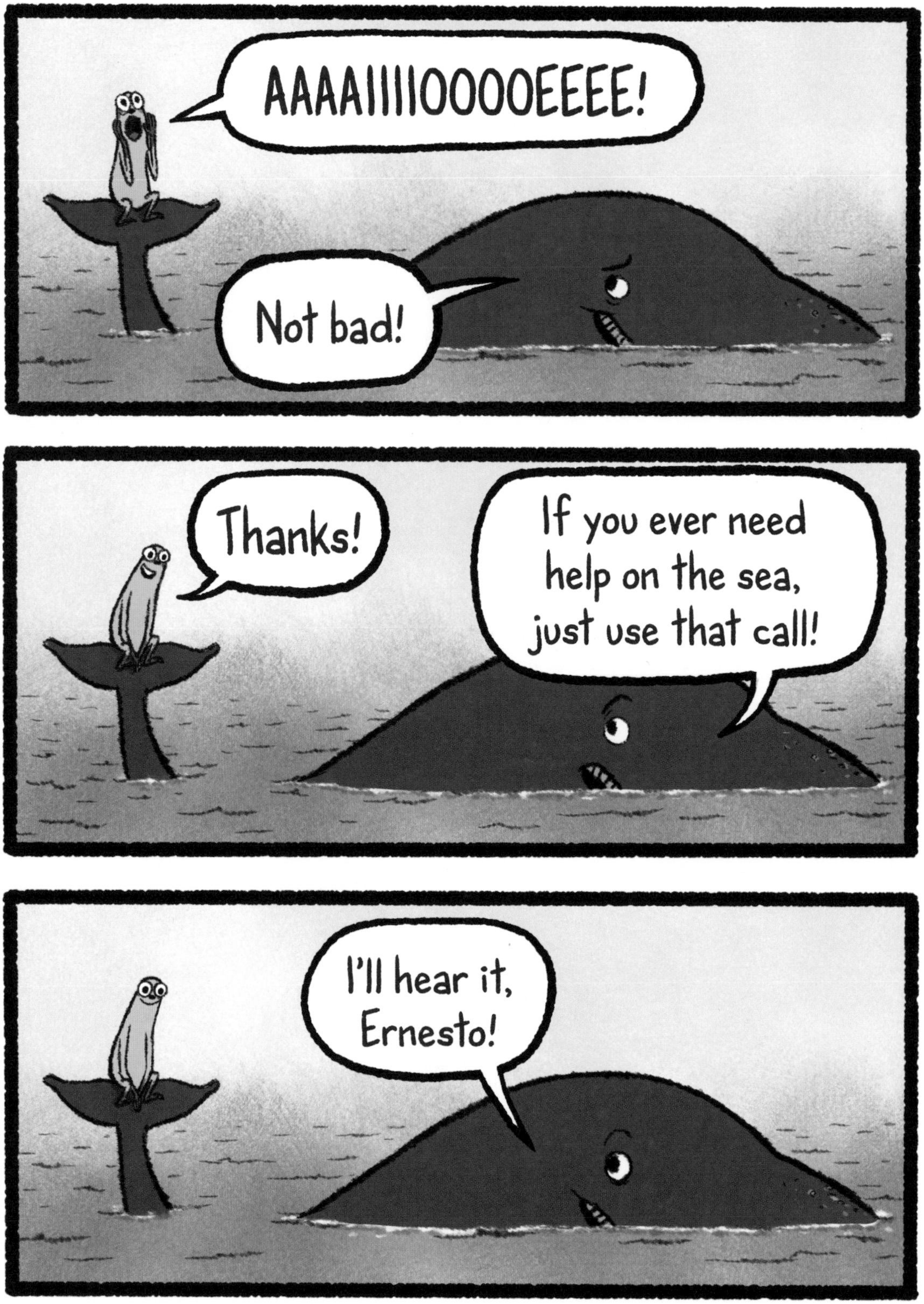
AAAAIIIIIOOOOEEEE!
Not bad!
Thanks!
If you ever need help on the sea, just use that call!
I'll hear it, Ernesto!

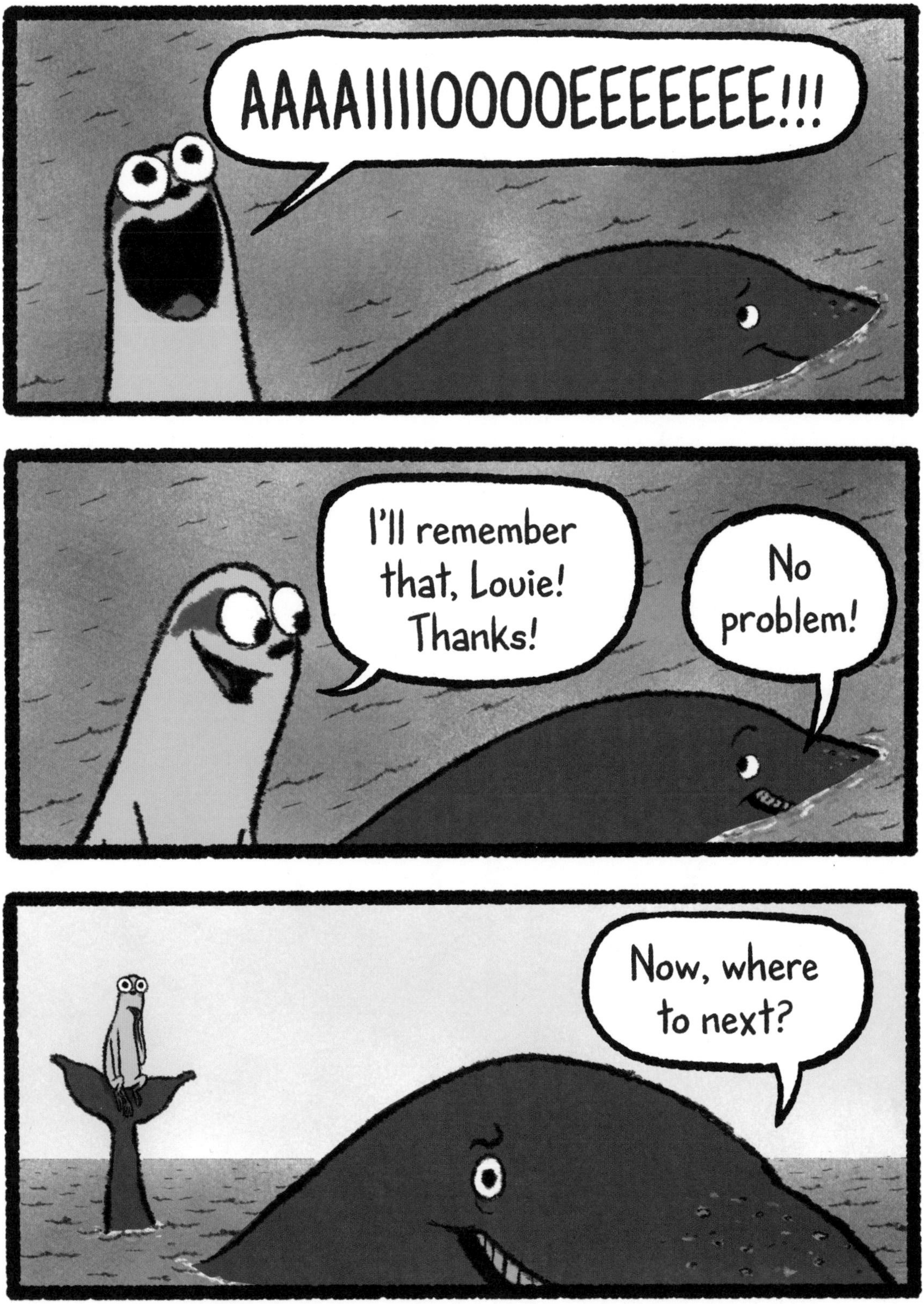
AAAAIIIIIOOOOEEEEEEE!!!
I'll remember that, Louie! Thanks!
No problem!
Now, where to next?

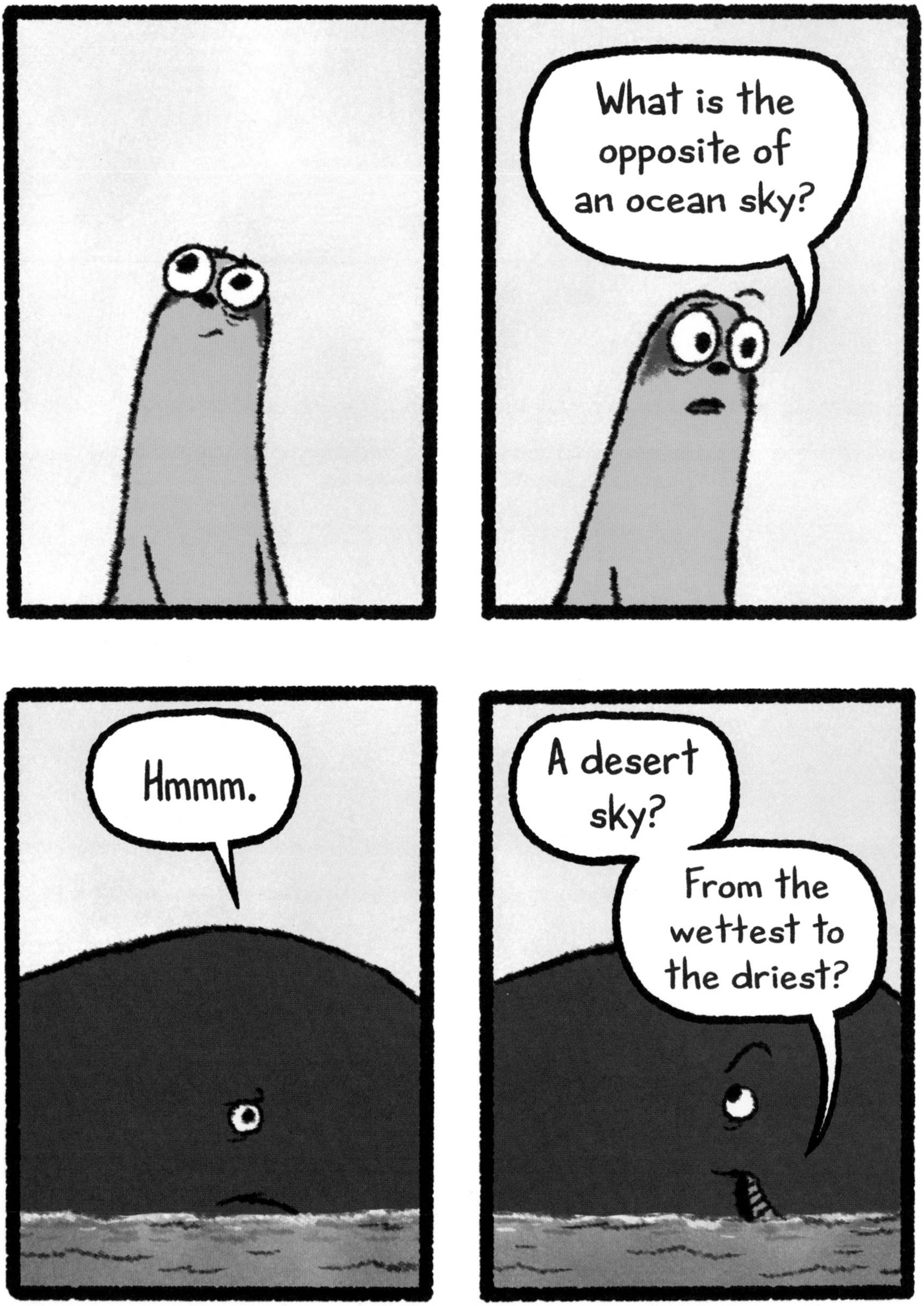
What is the opposite of an ocean sky?
Hmmm.
A desert sky?
From the wettest to the driest?

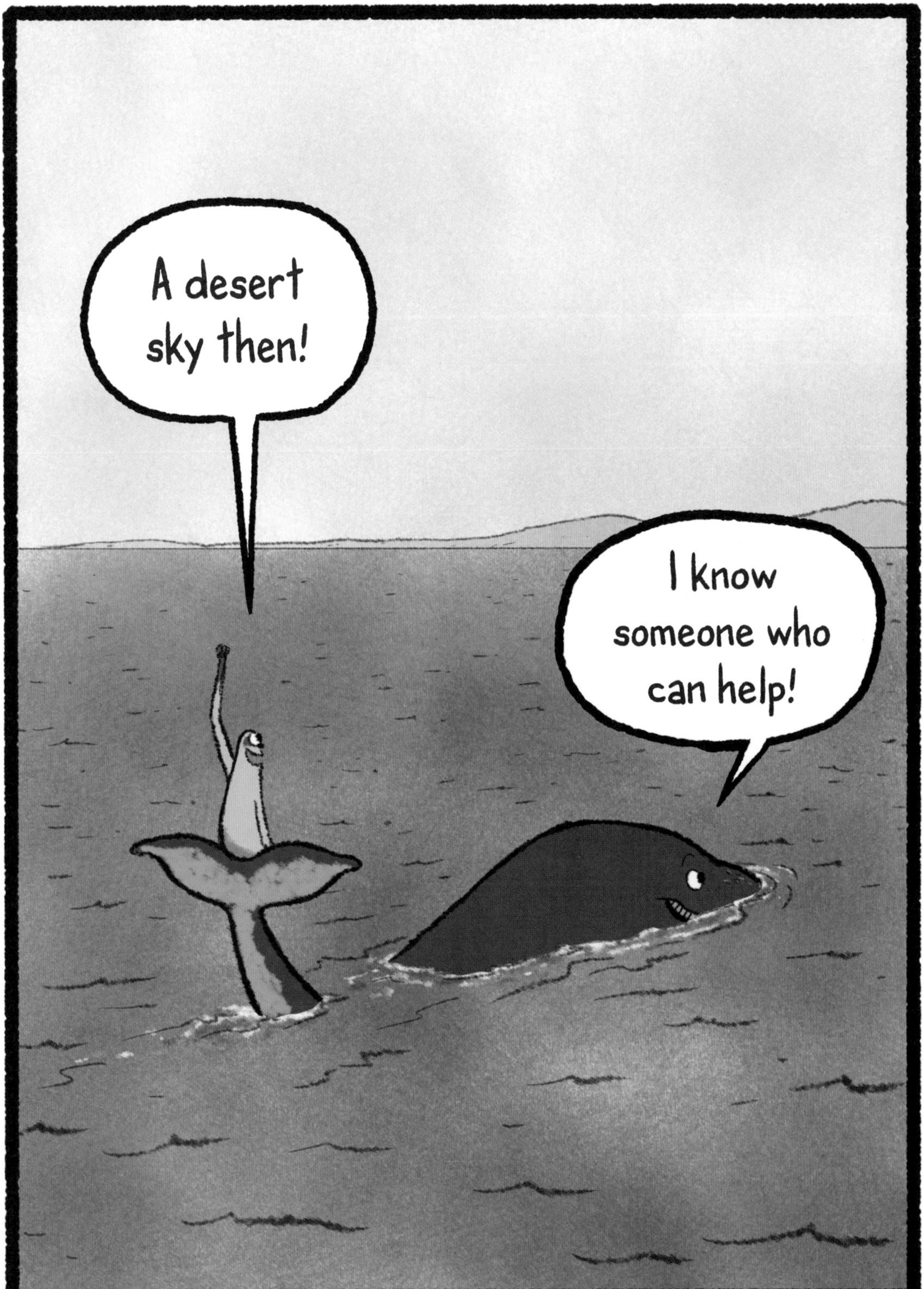
A desert sky then!
I know someone who can help!

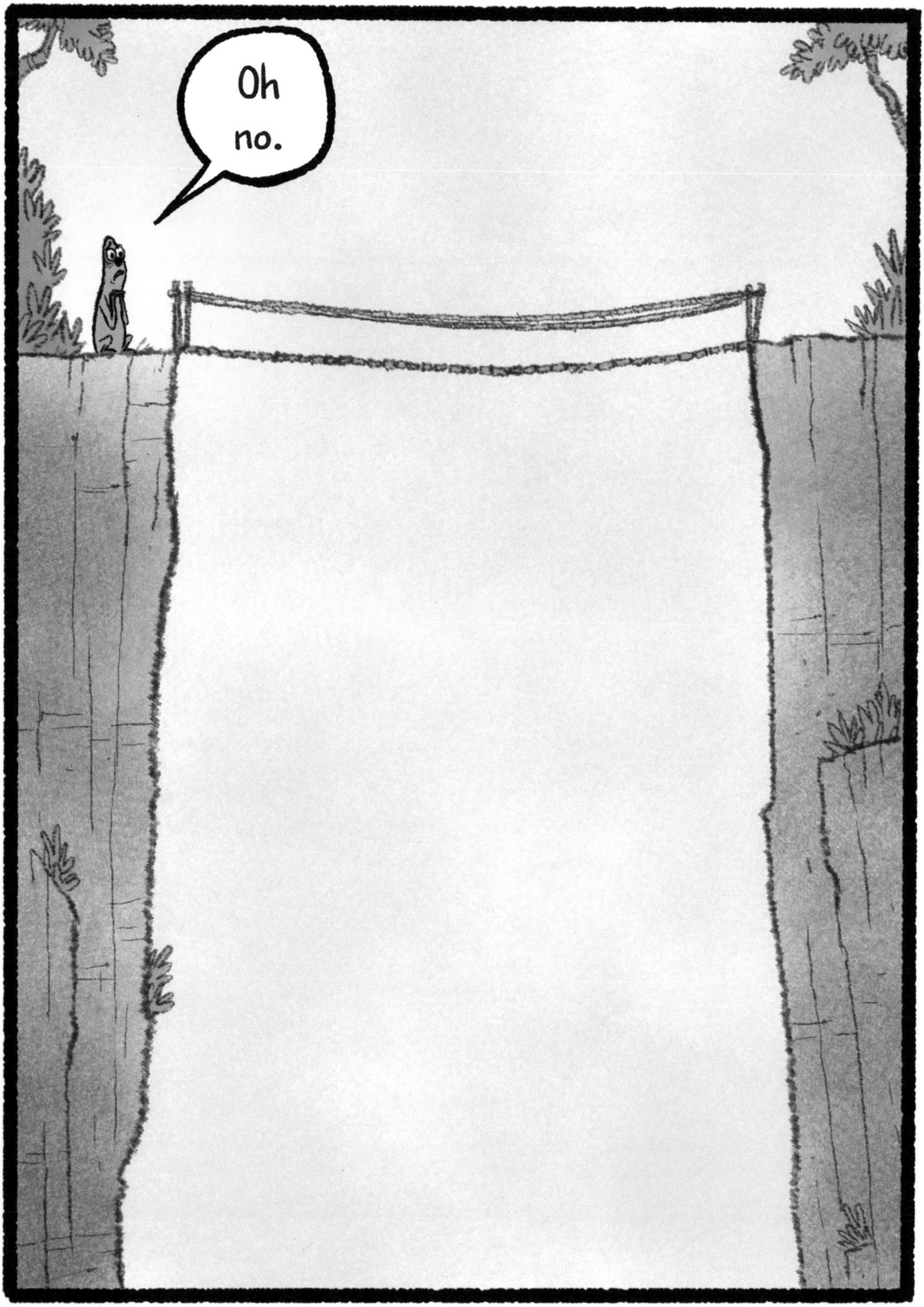
Oh no.

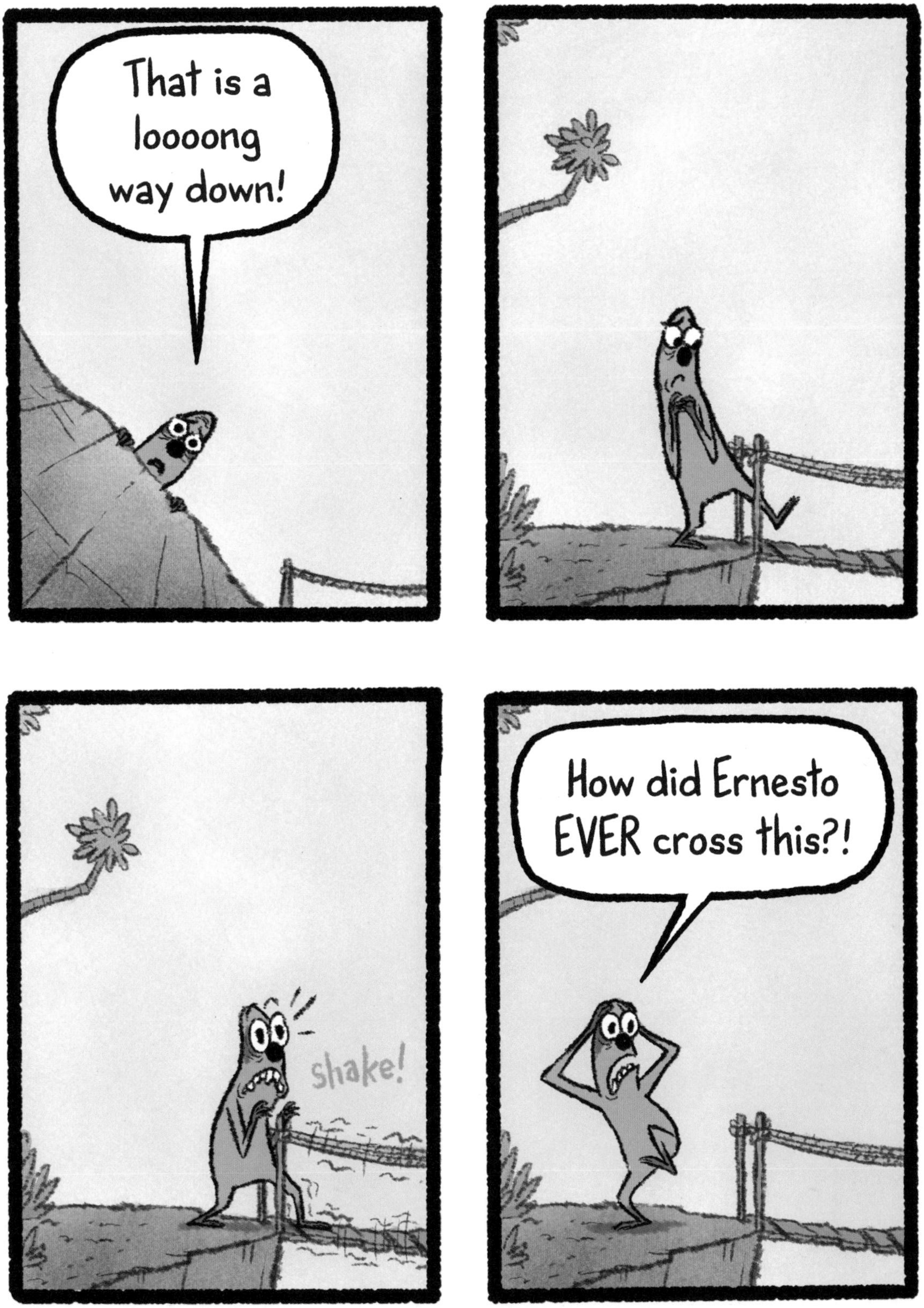
That is a loooong way down!
shake!
How did Ernesto EVER cross this?!

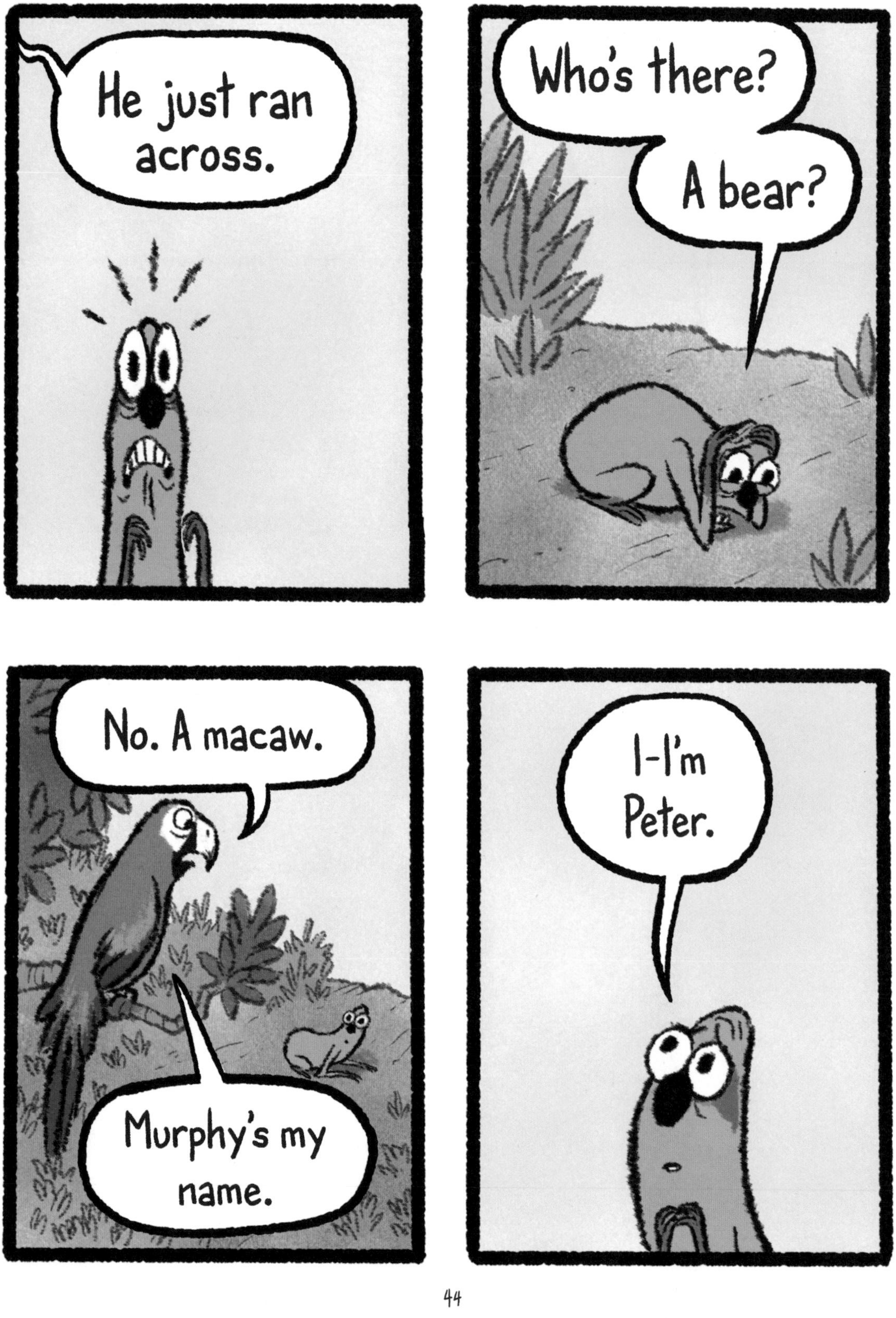
He just ran across.
Who's there?
A bear?
No. A macaw.
Murphy's my name.
I-I'm Peter.

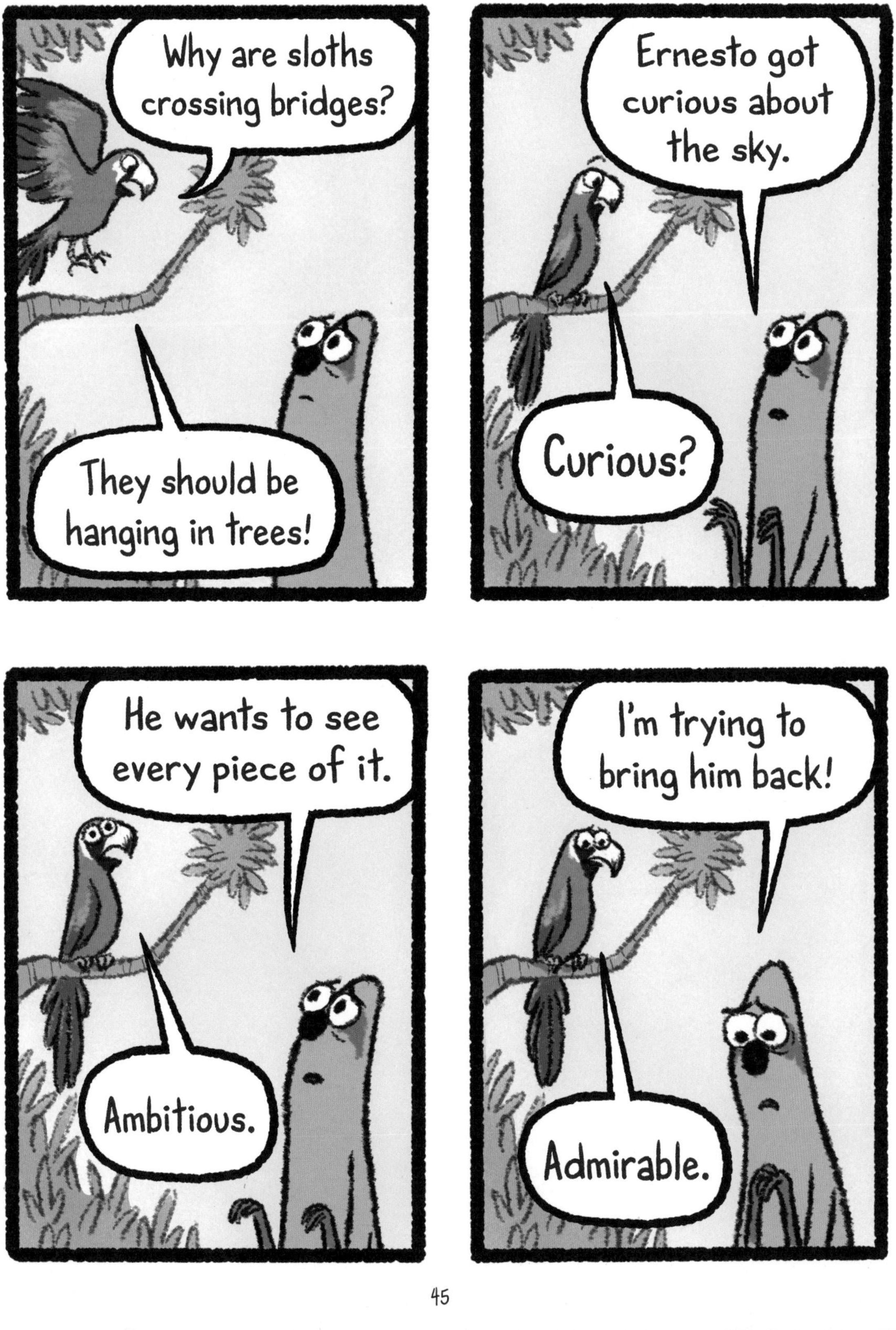
Why are sloths crossing bridges?
They should be hanging in trees!
Ernesto got curious about the sky.
Curious?
He wants to see every piece of it.
Ambitious.
I'm trying to bring him back!
Admirable.

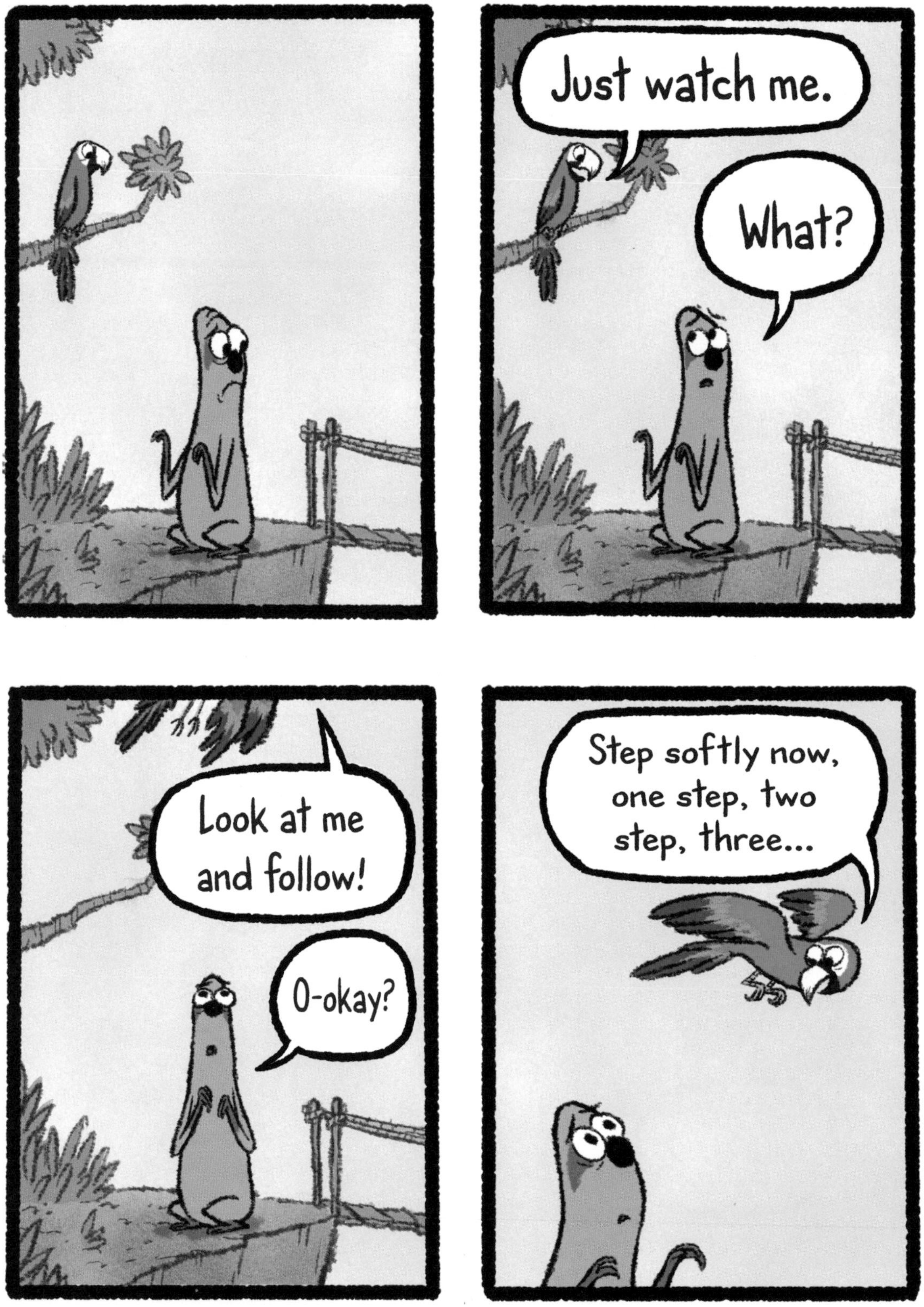
Just watch me.
What?
Look at me and follow!
O-okay?
Step softly now, one step, two step, three...

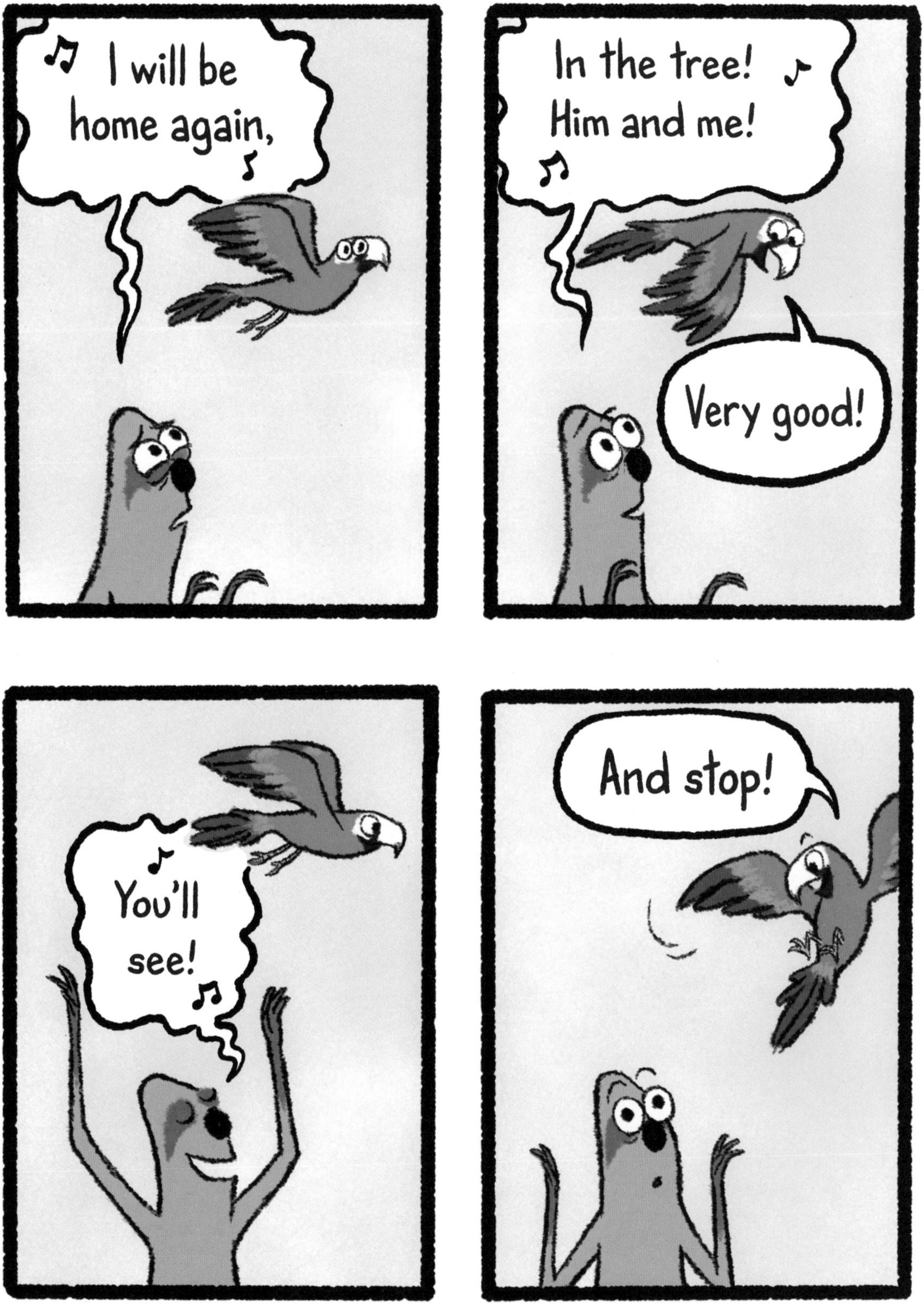
I will be home again,
In the tree! Him and me!
Very good!
You'll see!
And stop!

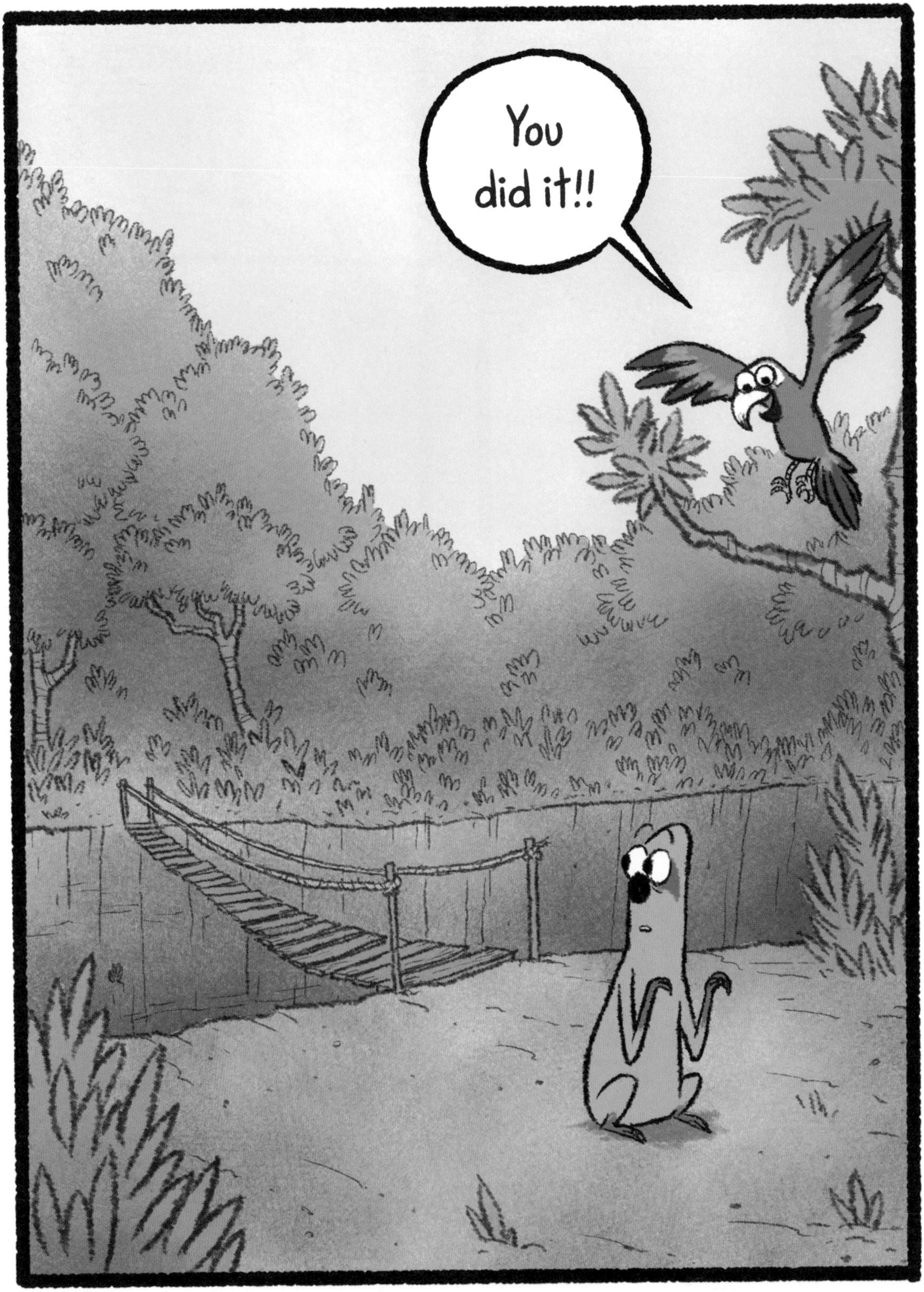
You did it!!

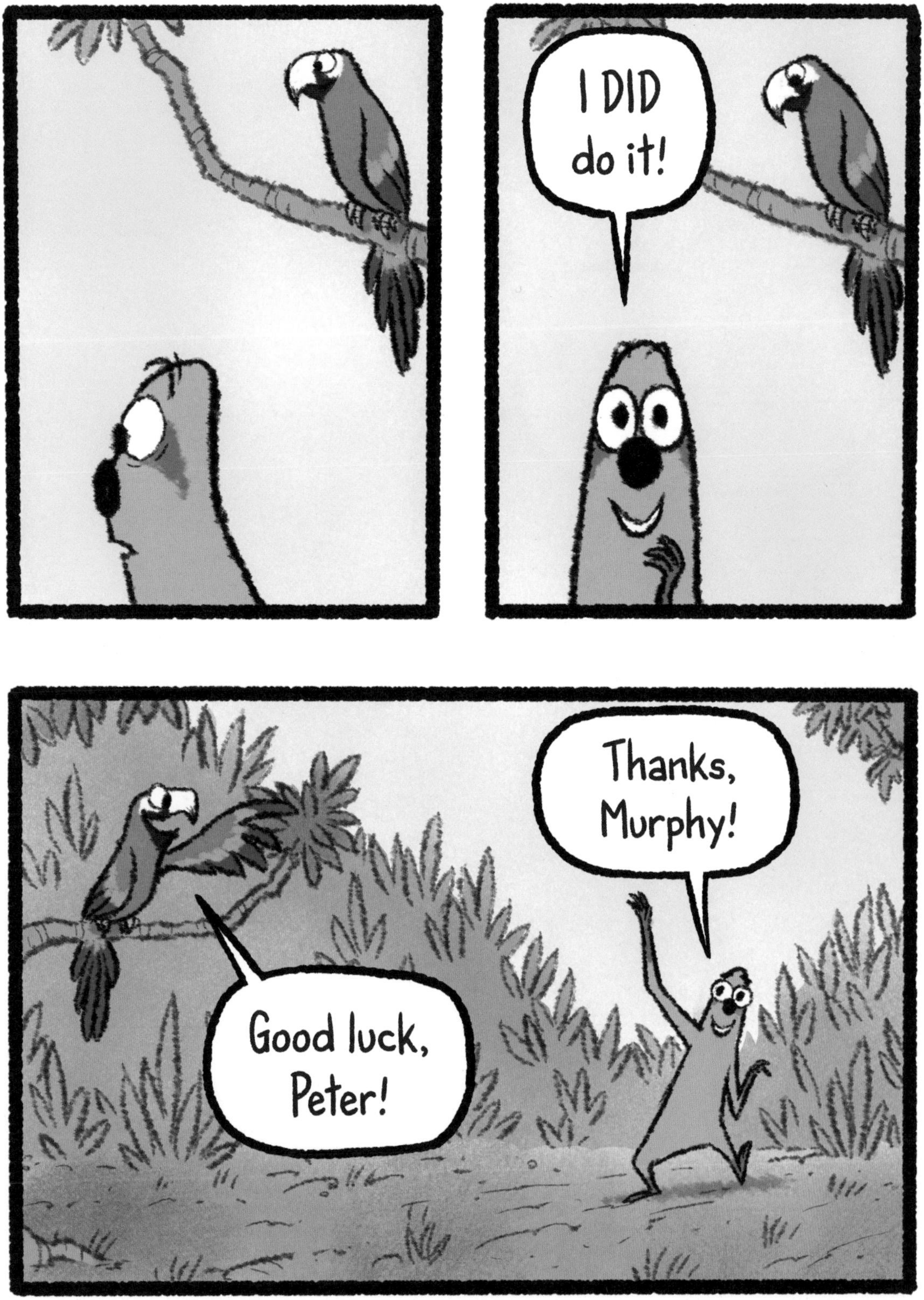
I DID do it!
Thanks, Murphy!
Good luck, Peter!

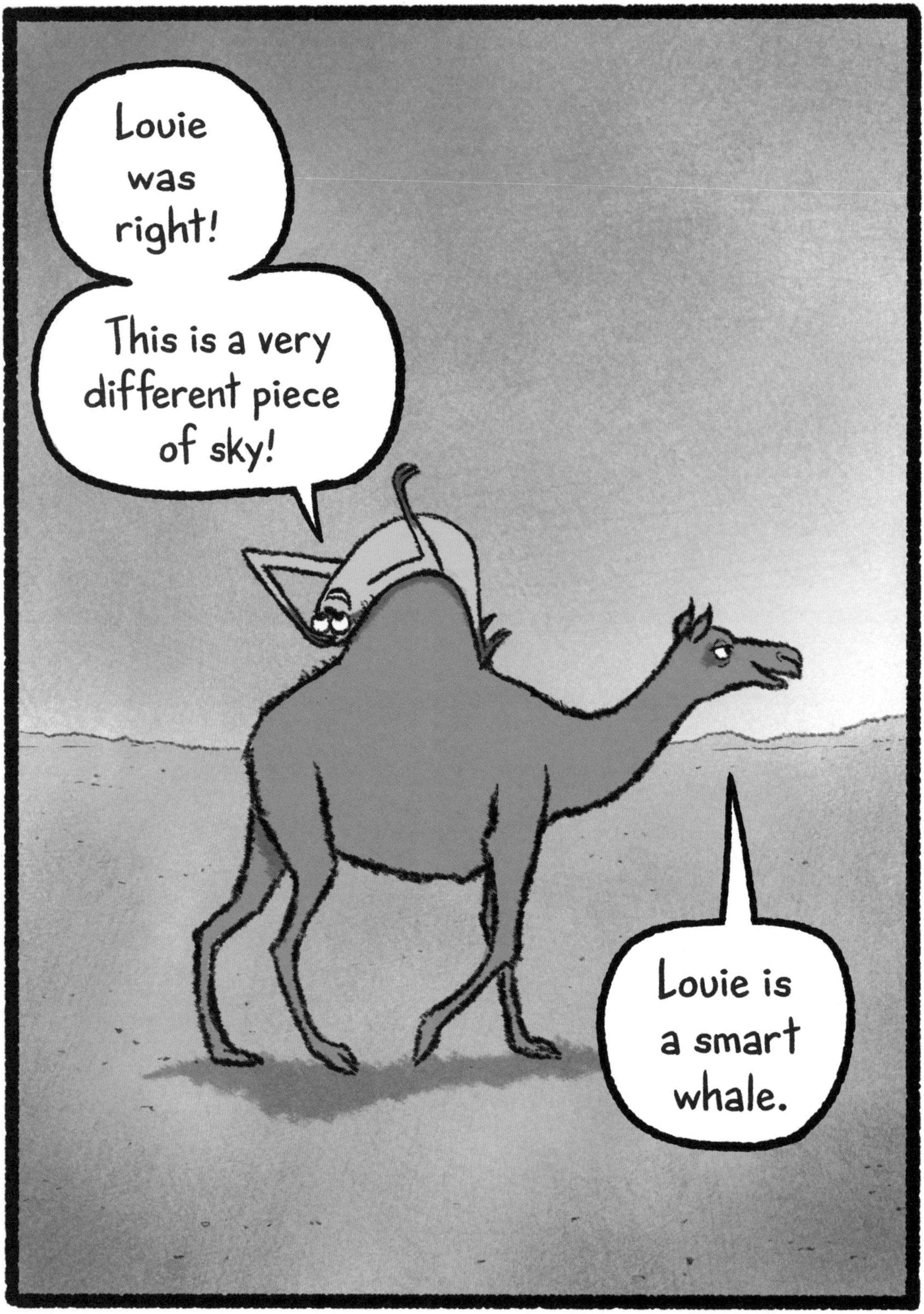
Louie was right!
This is a very different piece of sky!
Louie is a smart whale.

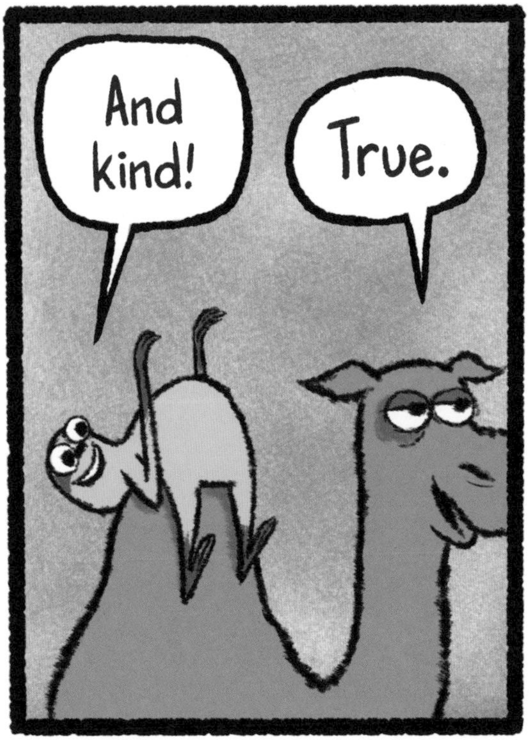
And kind!
True.

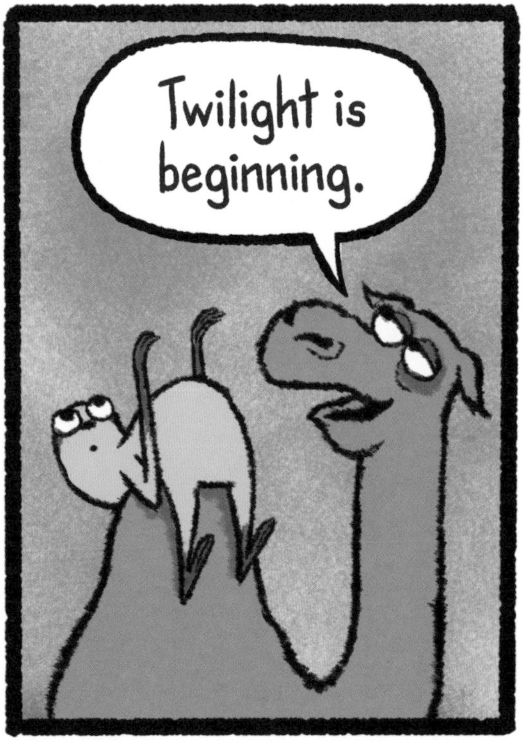
Twilight is beginning.

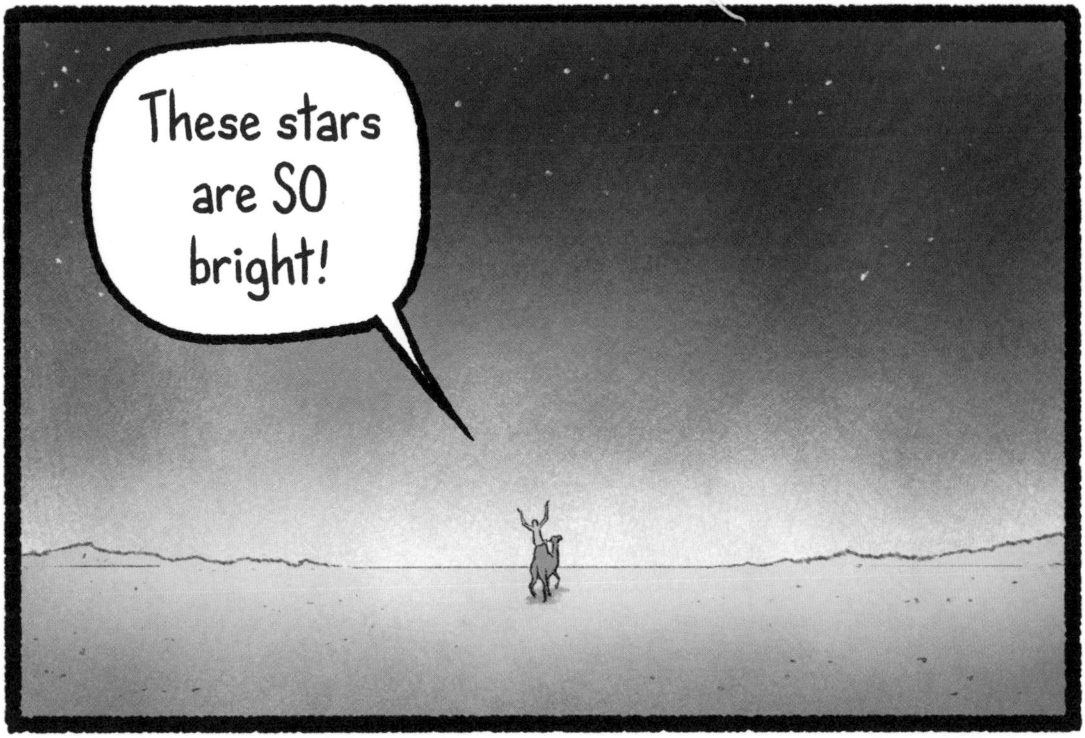
These stars are SO bright!

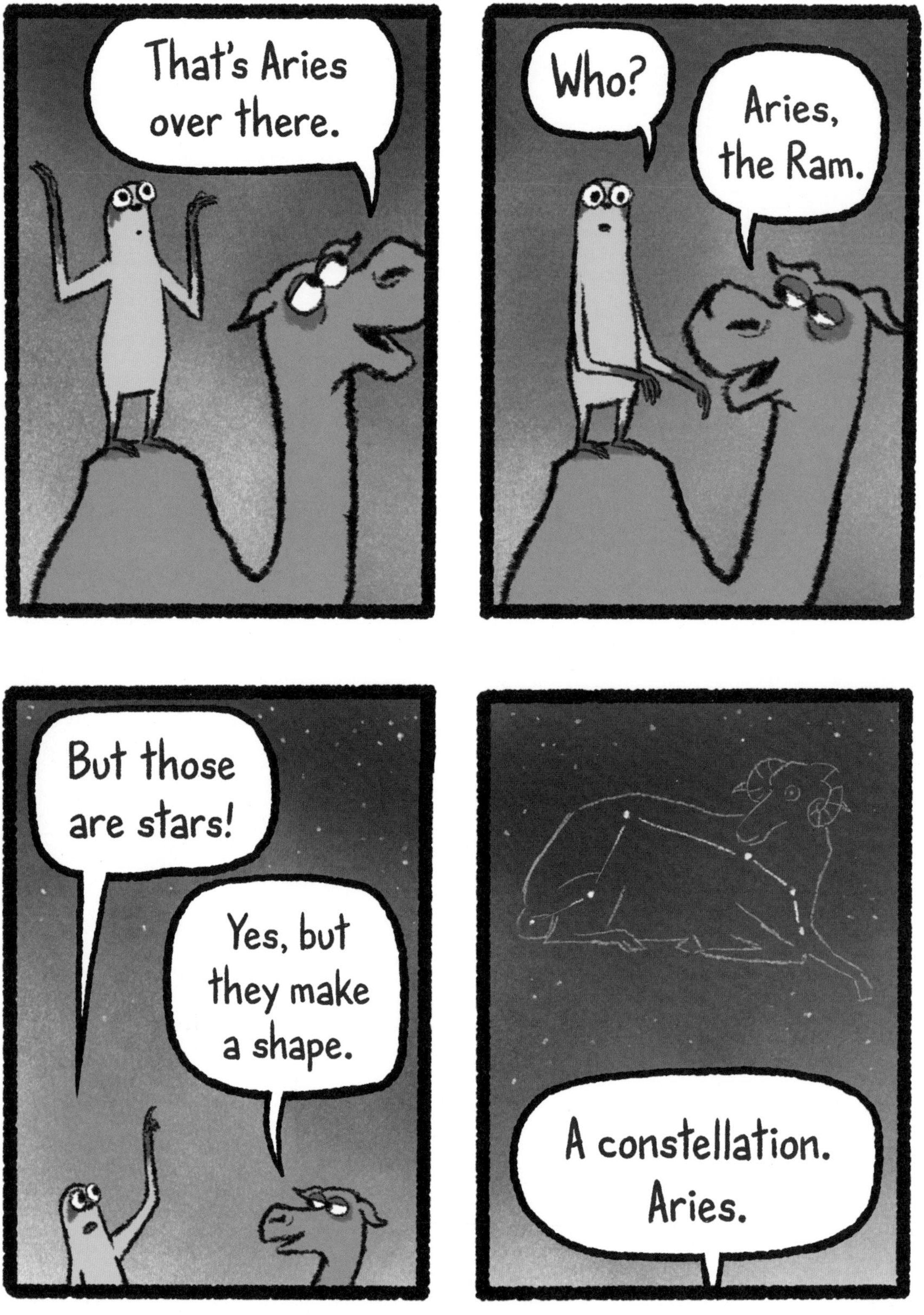
That's Aries over there.
Who?
Aries, the Ram.
But those are stars!
Yes, but they make a shape.
A constellation. Aries.

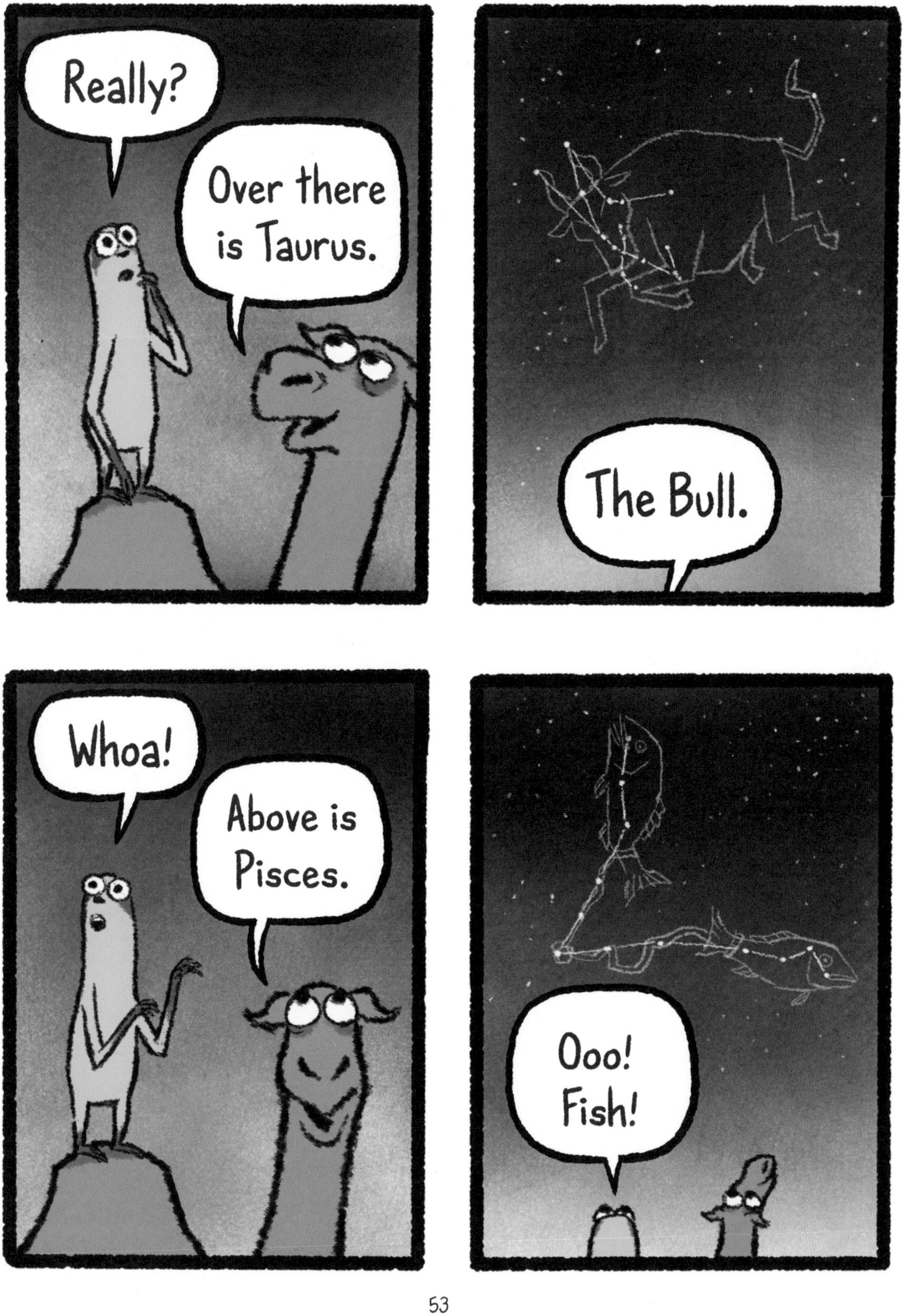
Really?
Over there is Taurus.
The Bull.
Whoa!
Above is Pisces.
Ooo! Fish!

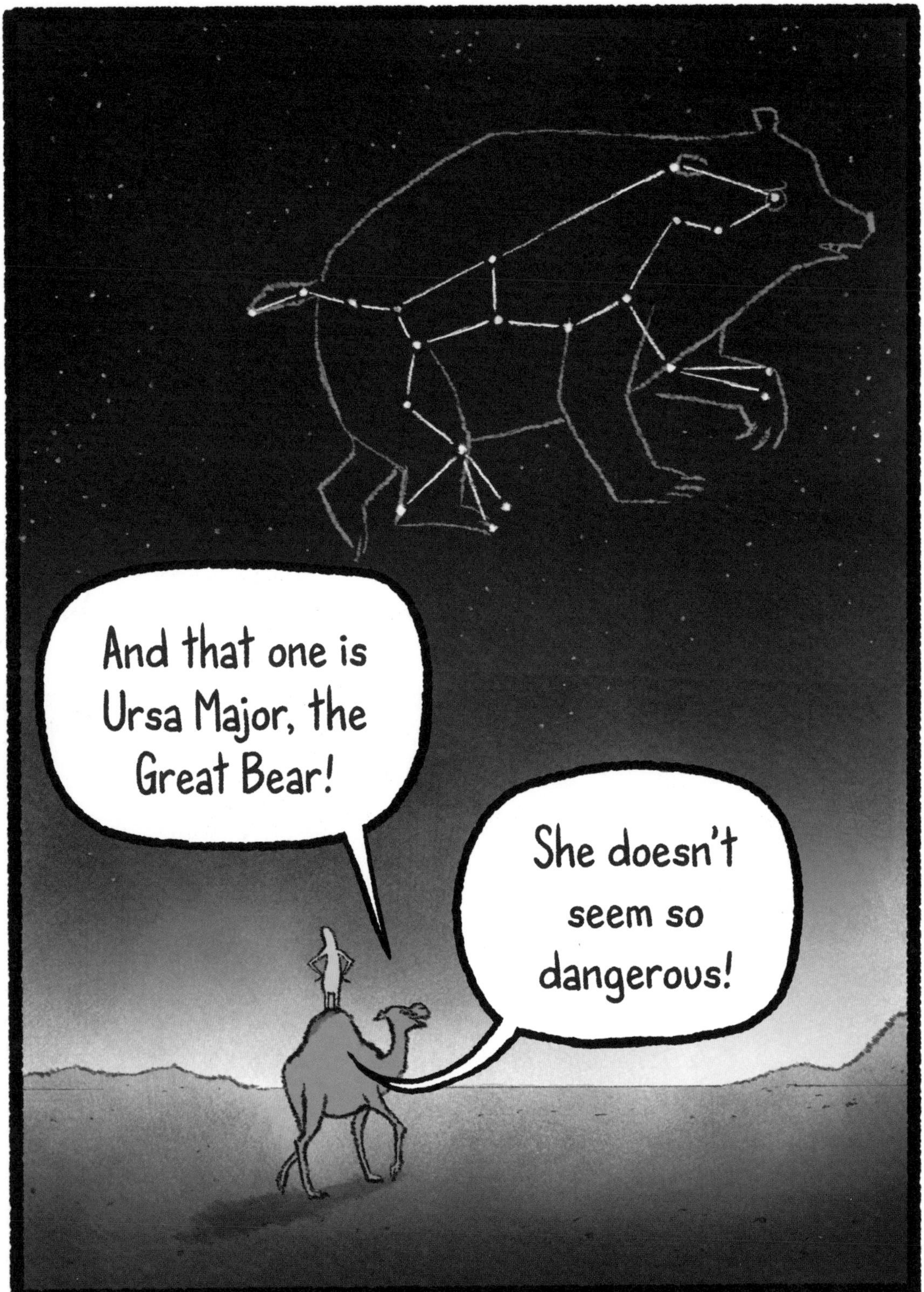
And that one is Ursa Major, the Great Bear!
She doesn't seem so dangerous!

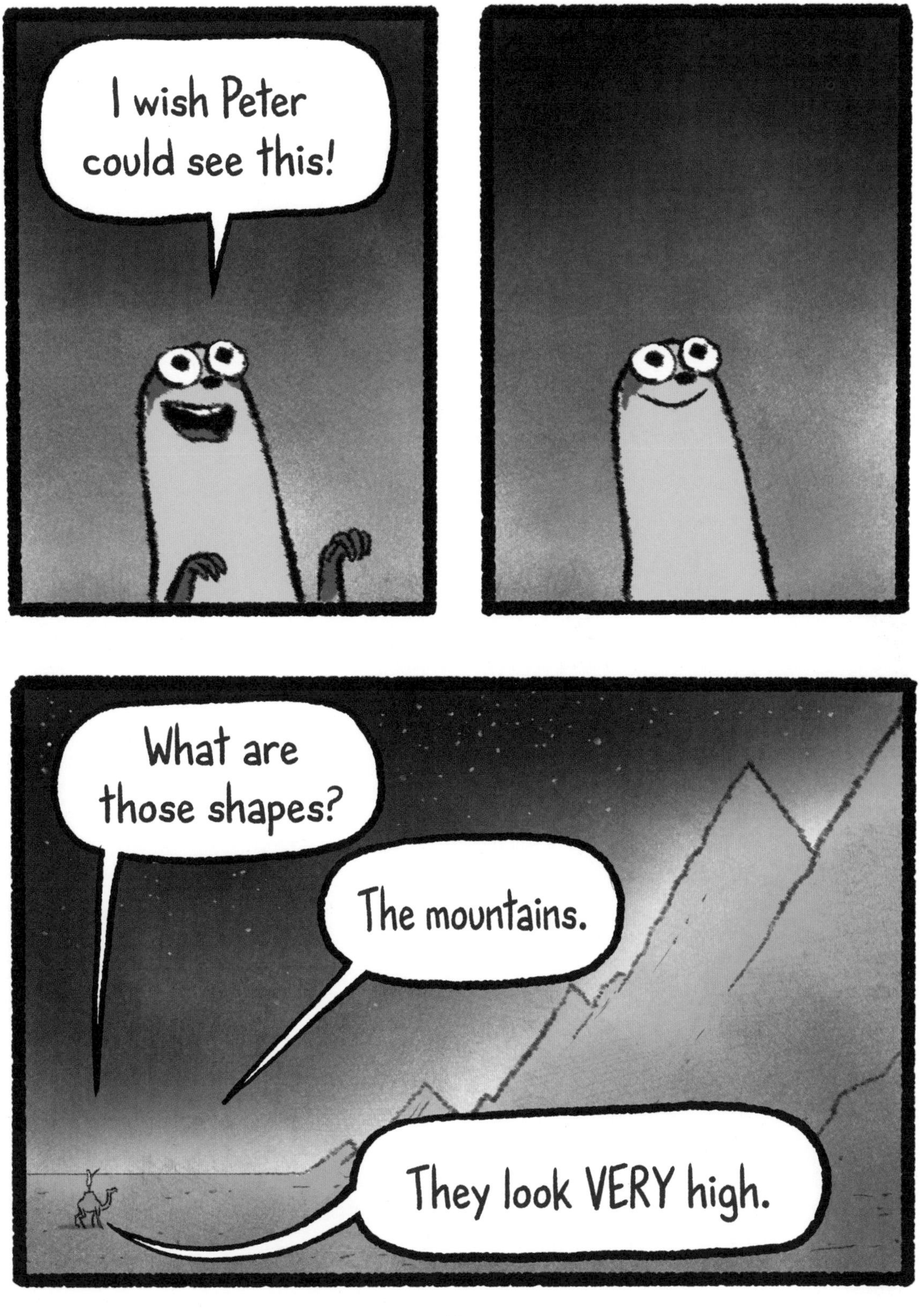
I wish Peter could see this!
What are those shapes?
The mountains.
They look VERY high.

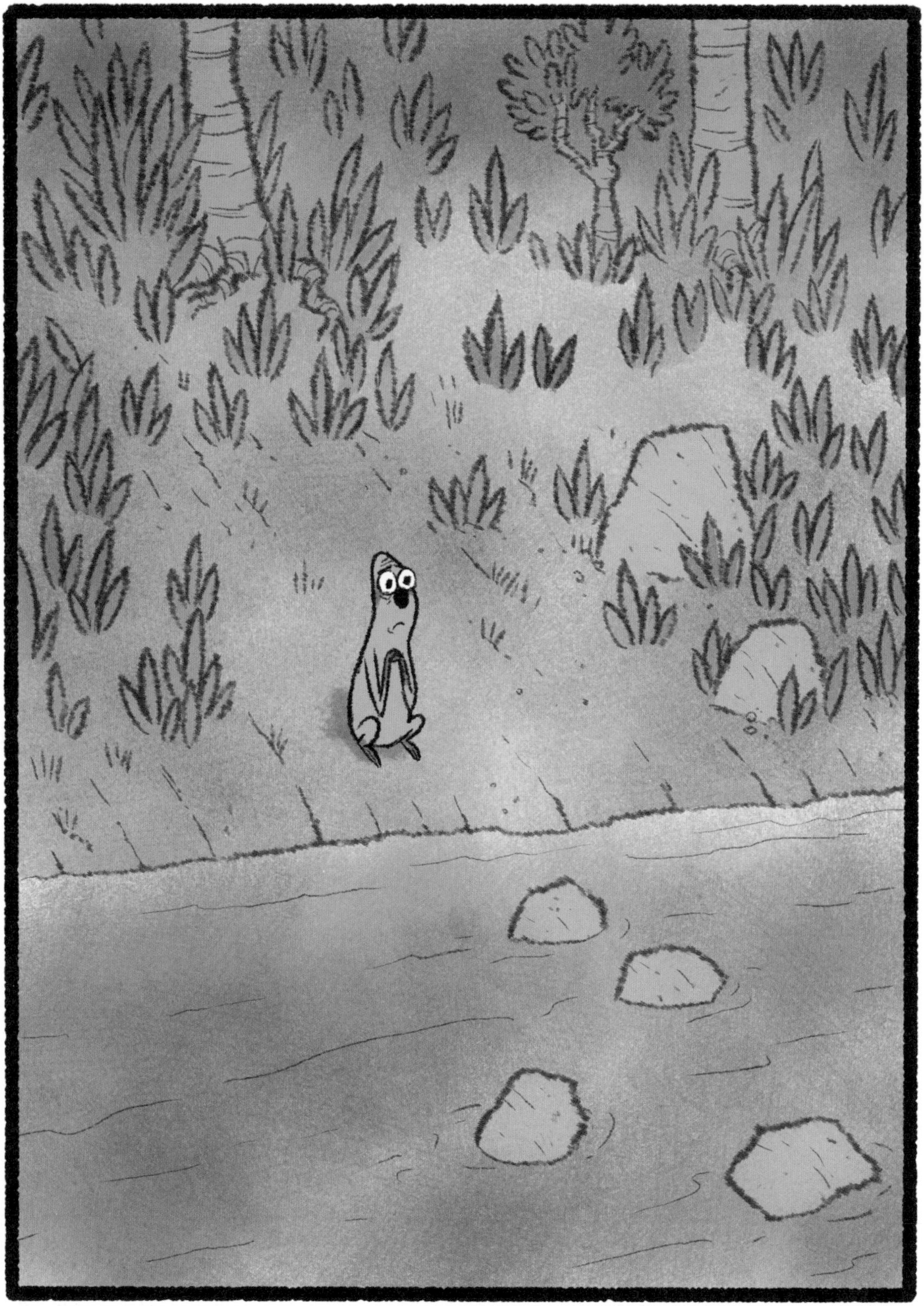

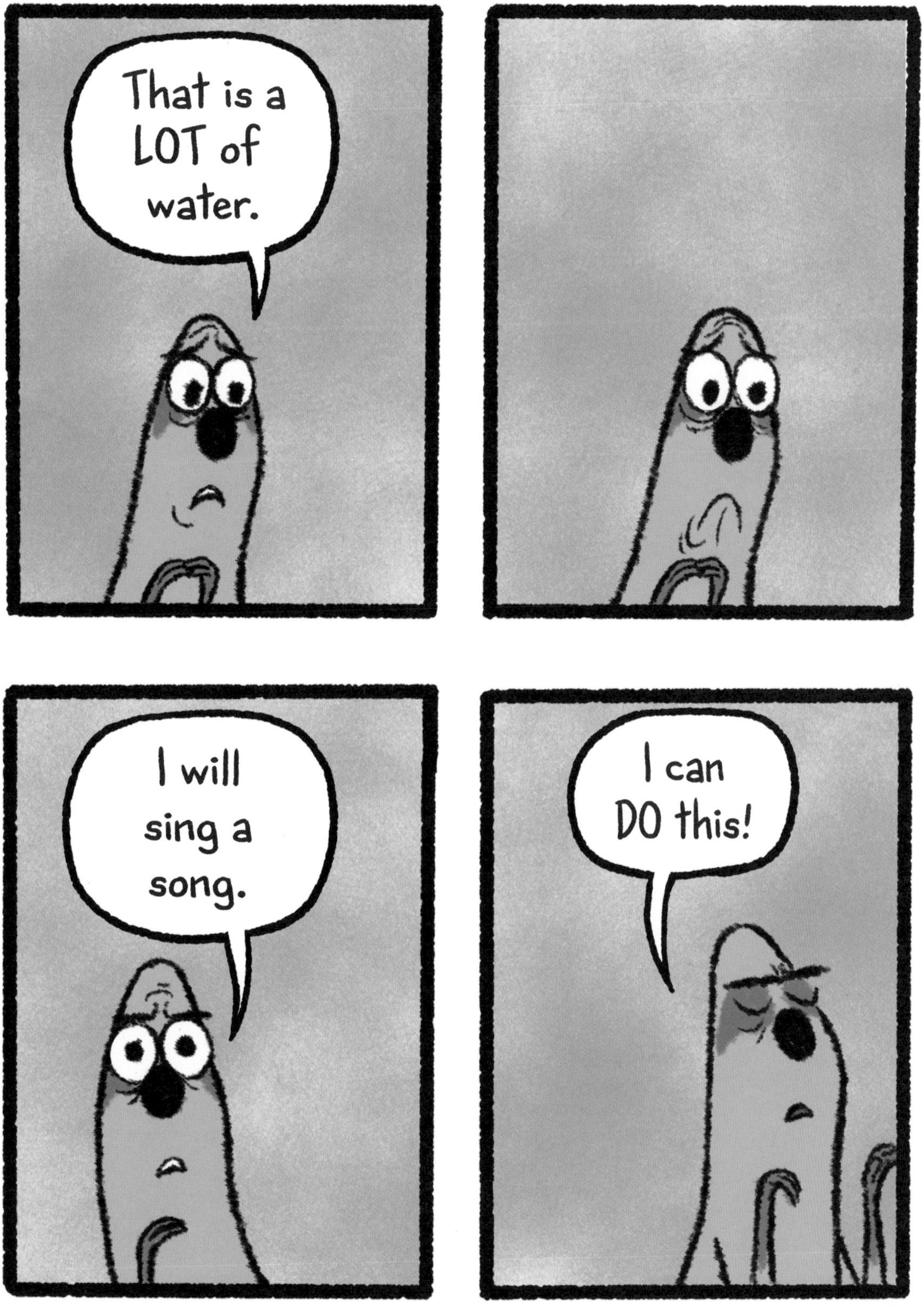
That is a LOT of water.
I will sing a song.
I can DO this!

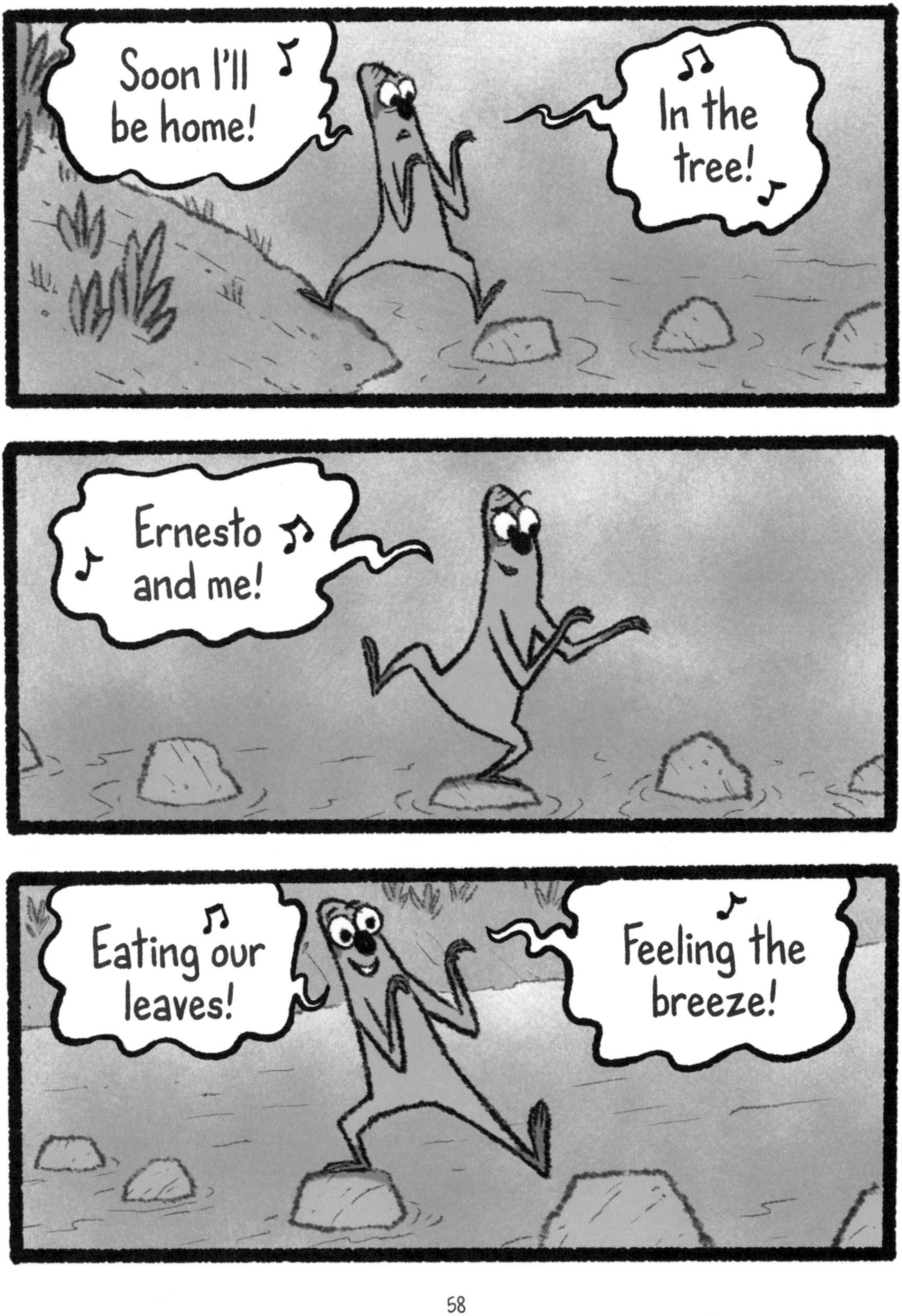
Soon I'll be home!
In the tree!
Ernesto and me!
Eating our leaves!
Feeling the breeze!

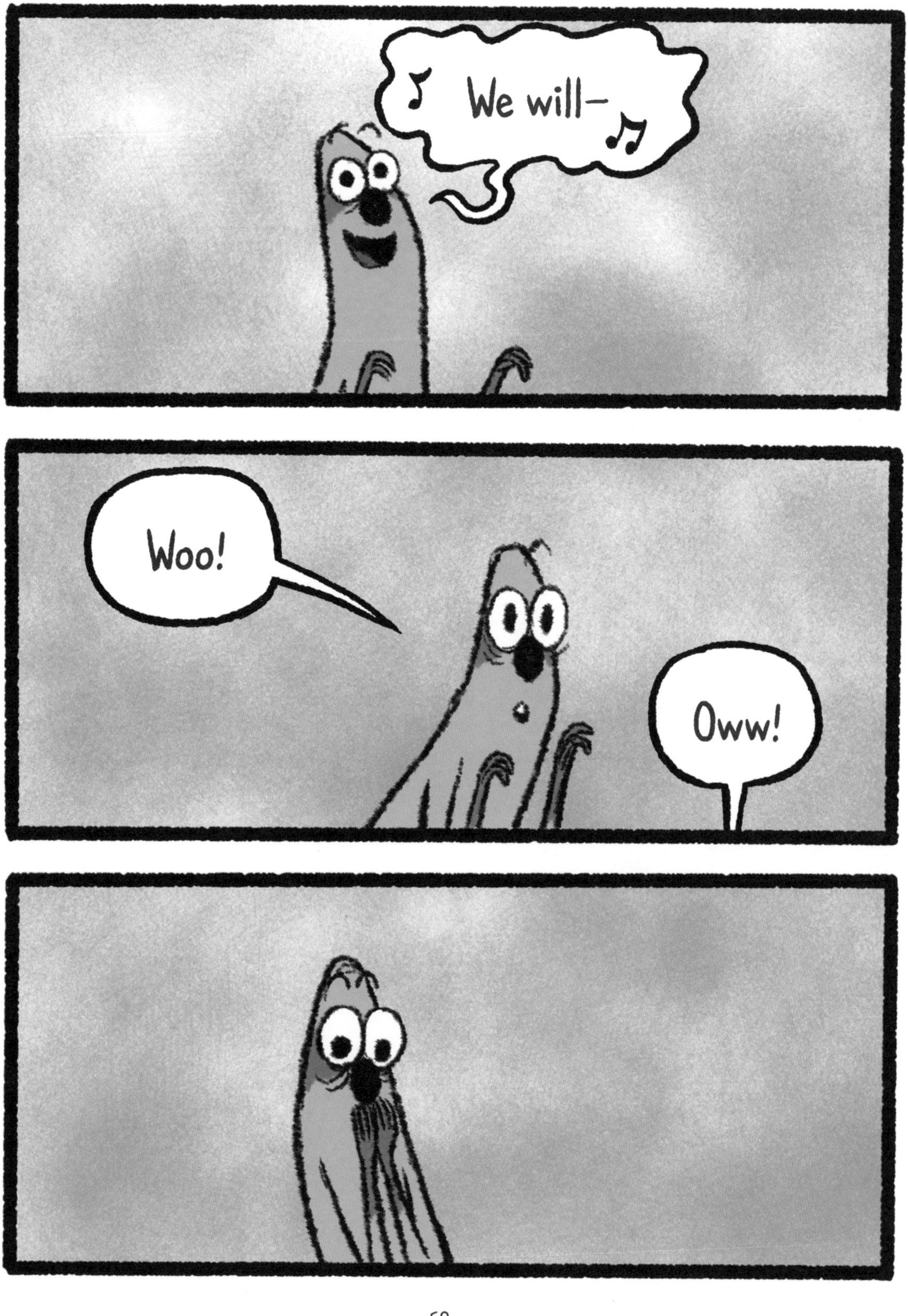
We will-
Woo!
Oww!

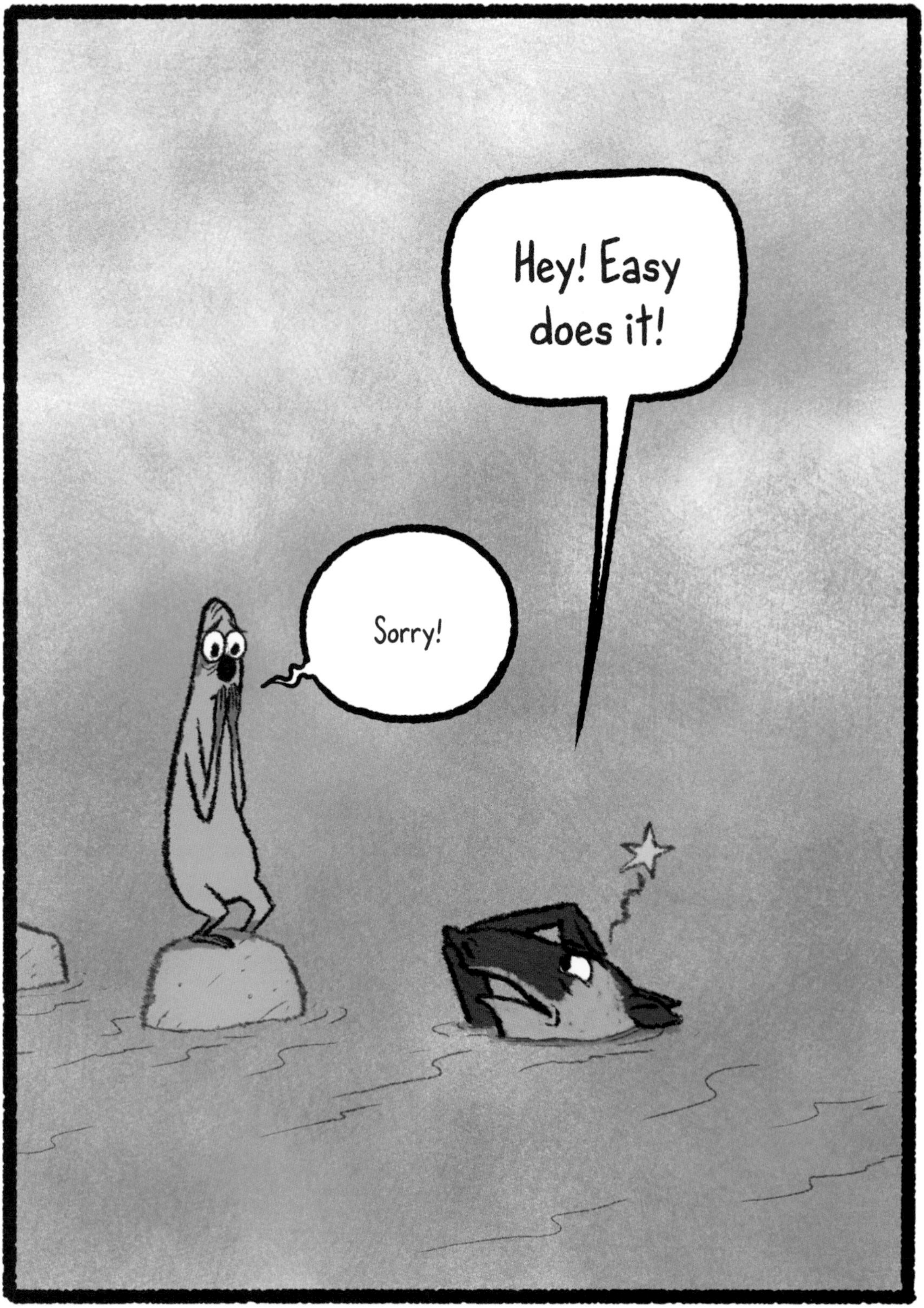
Hey! Easy does it!
Sorry!

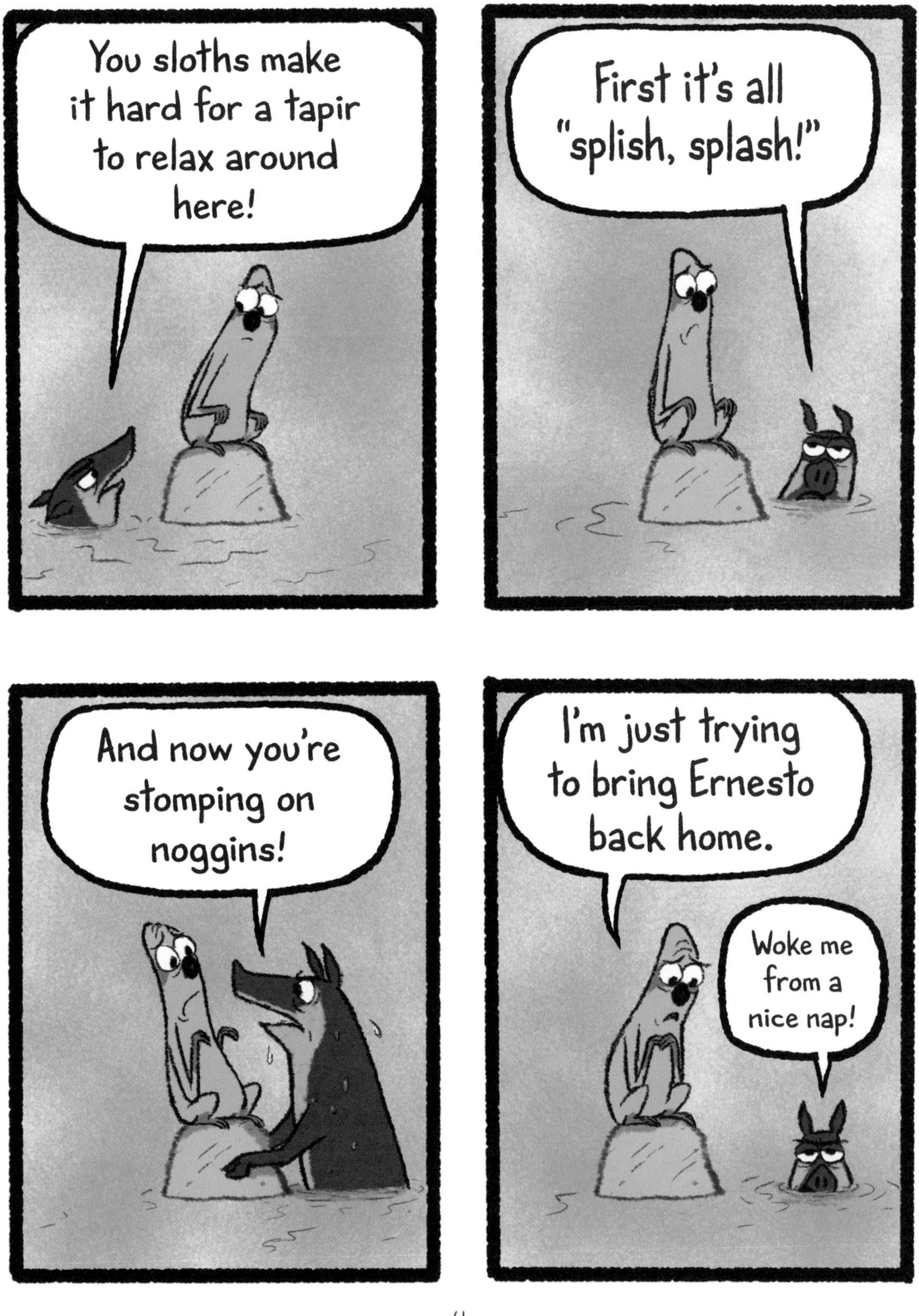
You sloths make it hard for a tapir to relax around here!
First it's all "splish, splash!"
And now you're stomping on noggins!
I'm just trying to bring Ernesto back home.
Woke me from a nice nap!

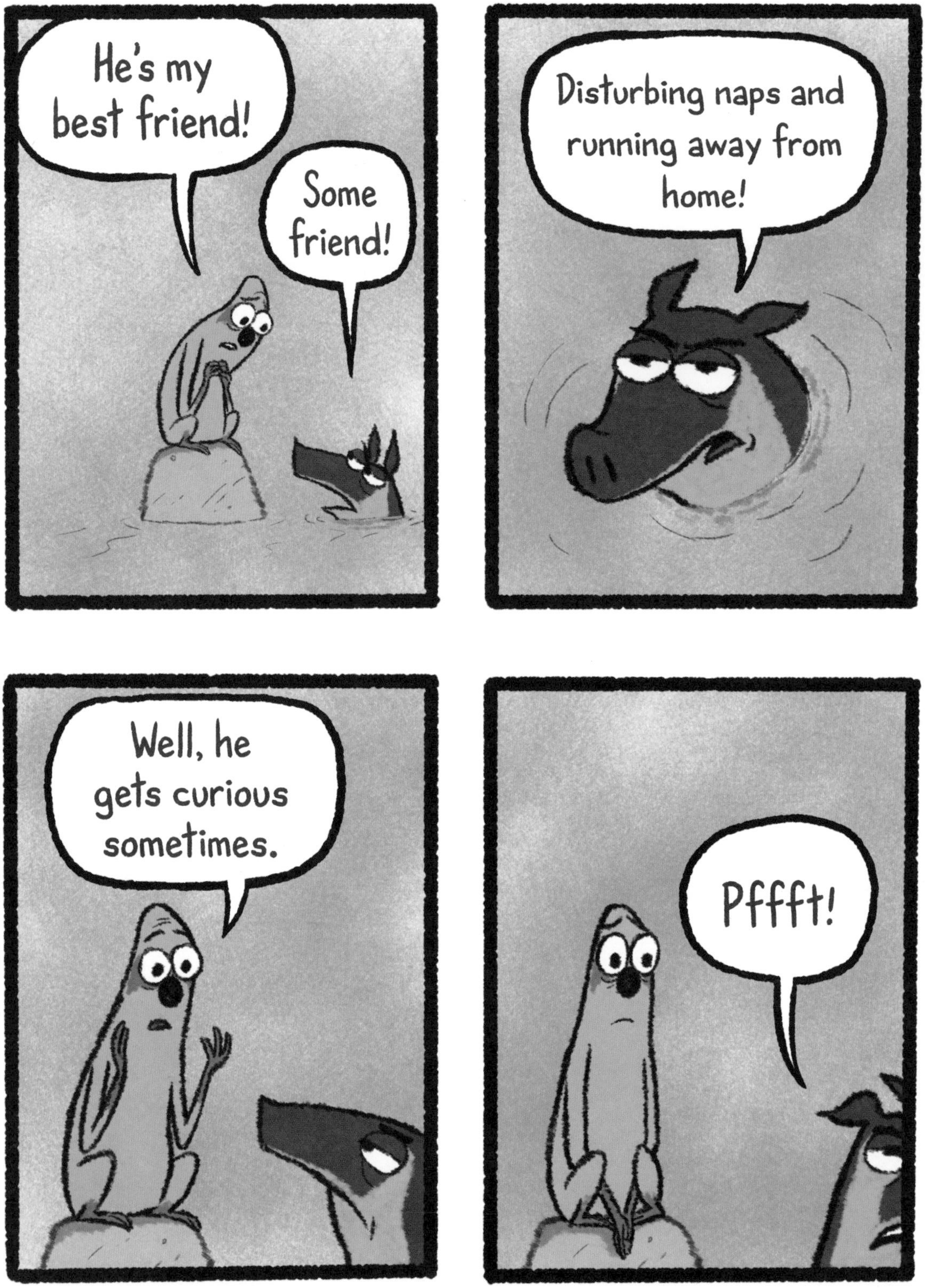
He's my best friend!
Some friend!
Disturbing naps and running away from home!
Well, he gets curious sometimes.
Pffft!

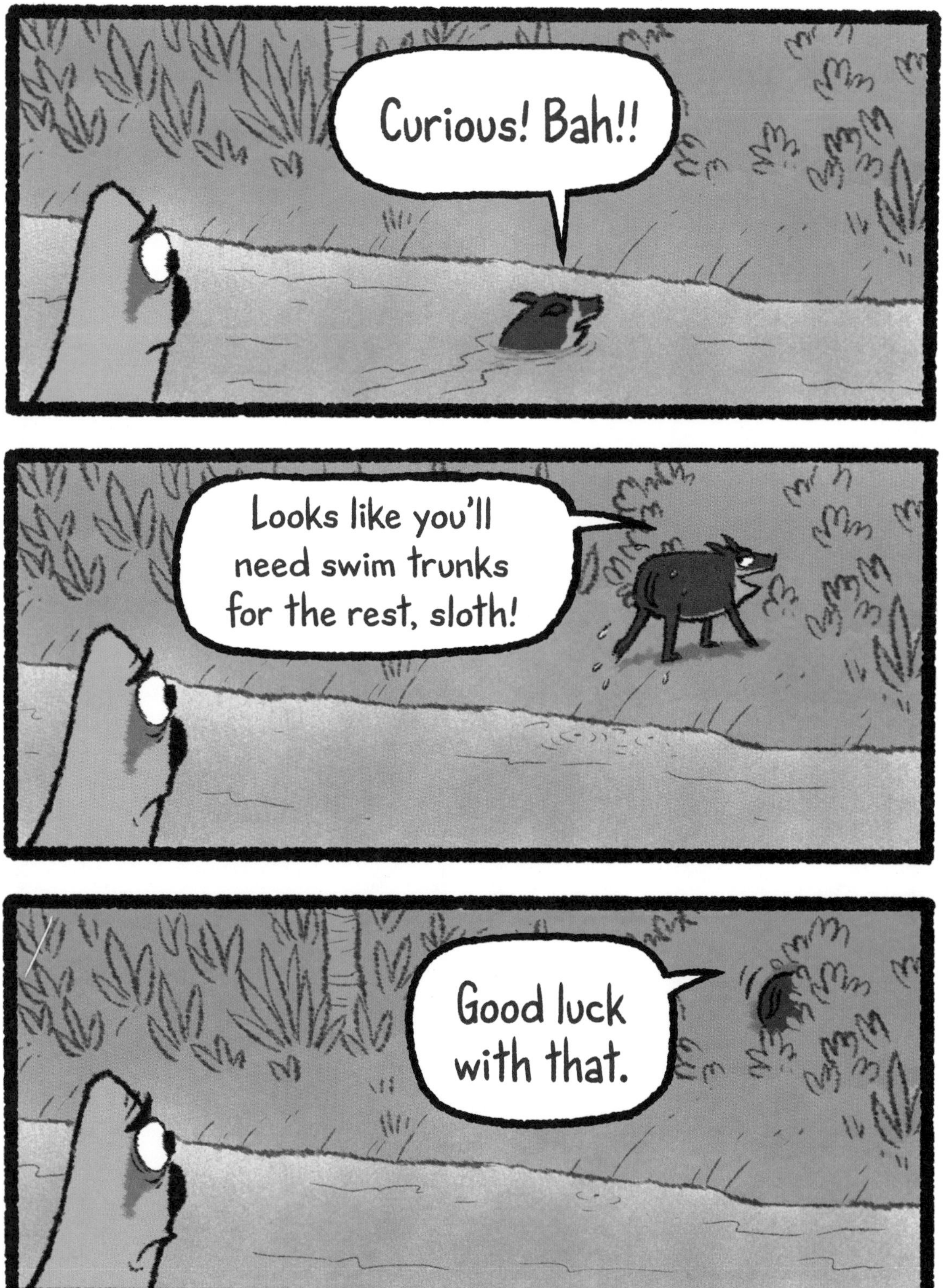
Curious! Bah!!
Looks like you'll need swim trunks for the rest, sloth!
Good luck with that.

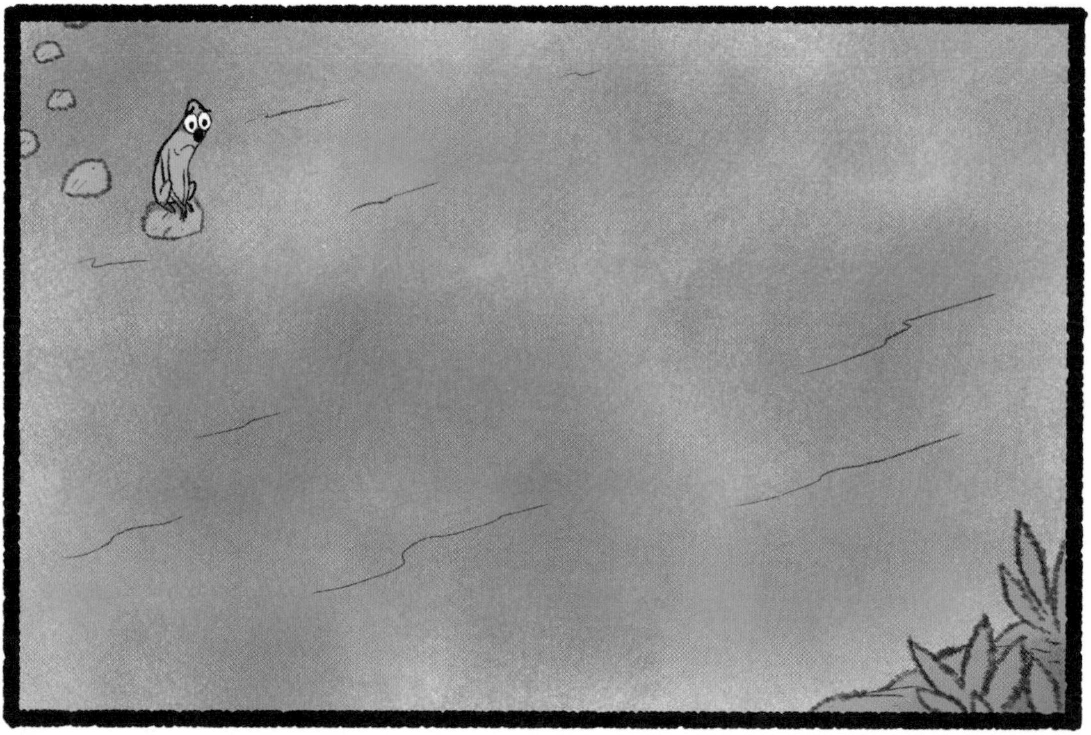

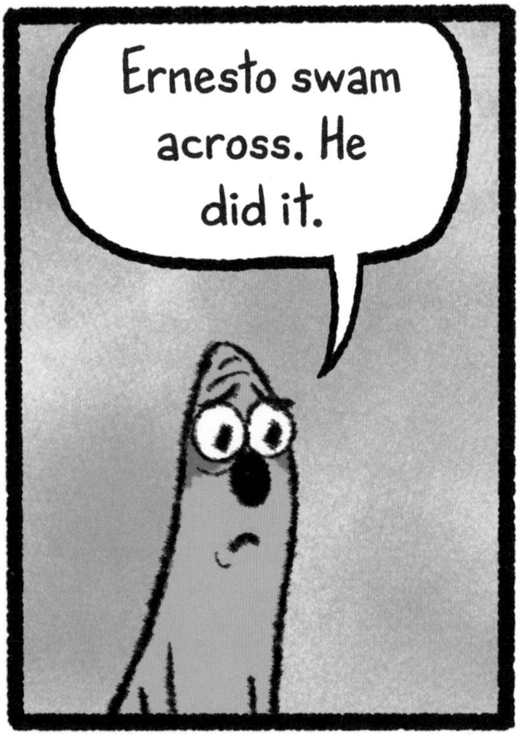
Ernesto swam across. He did it.

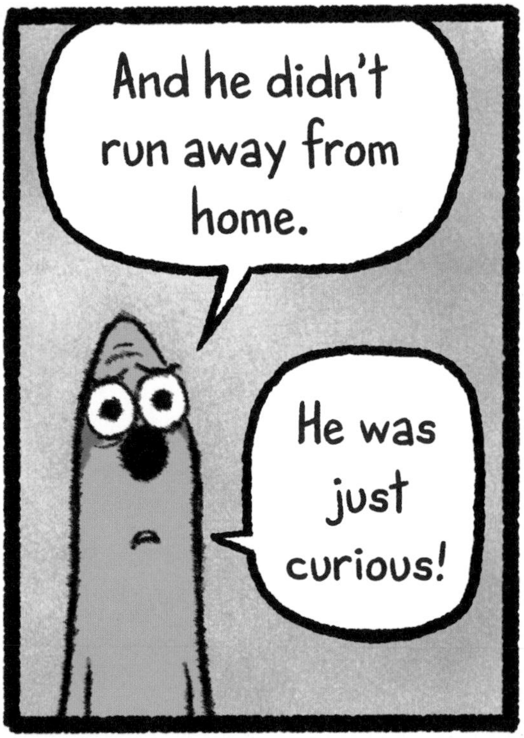
And he didn't run away from home.
He was just curious!

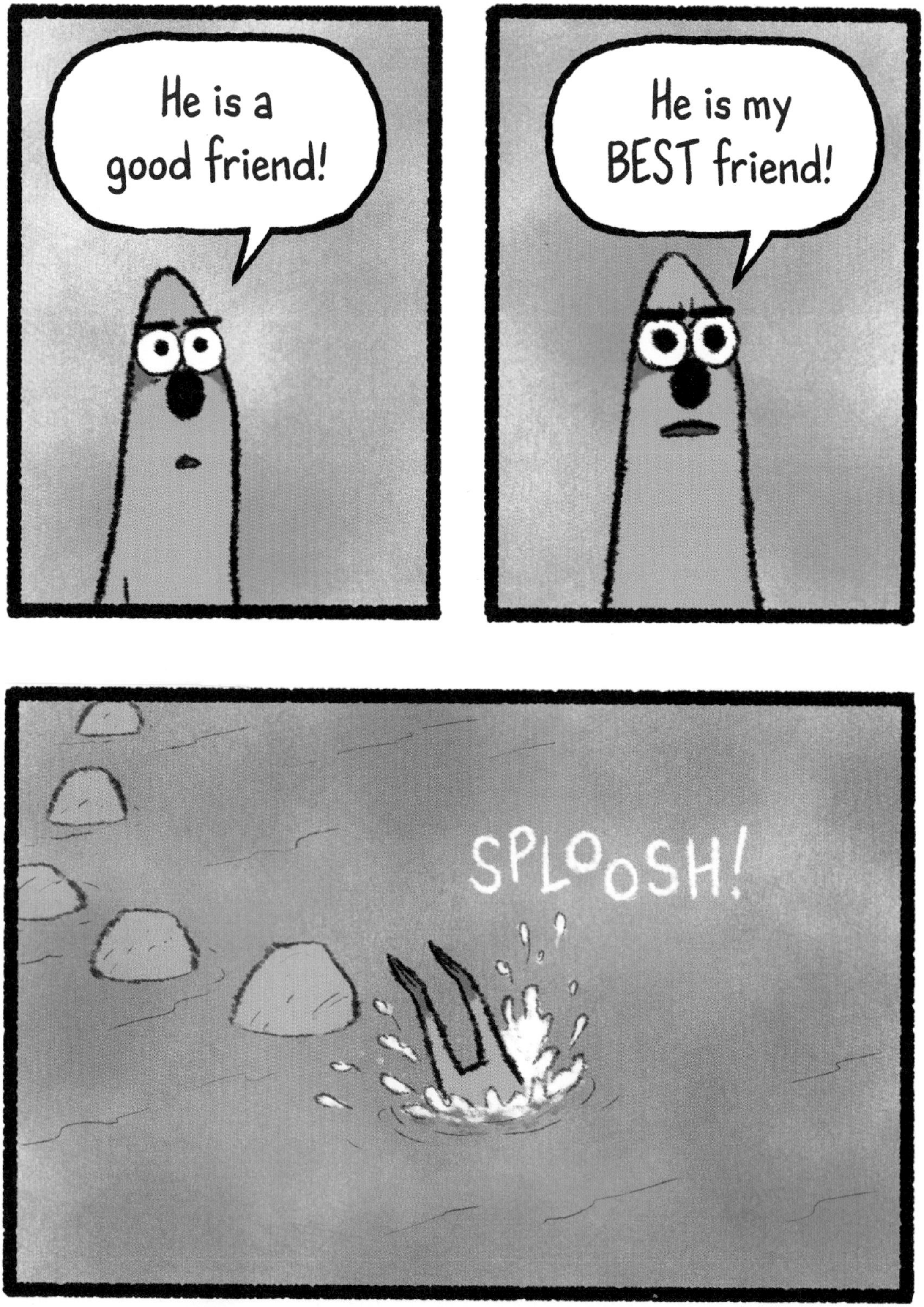
He is a good friend!
He is my BEST friend!
SPLOOSH!

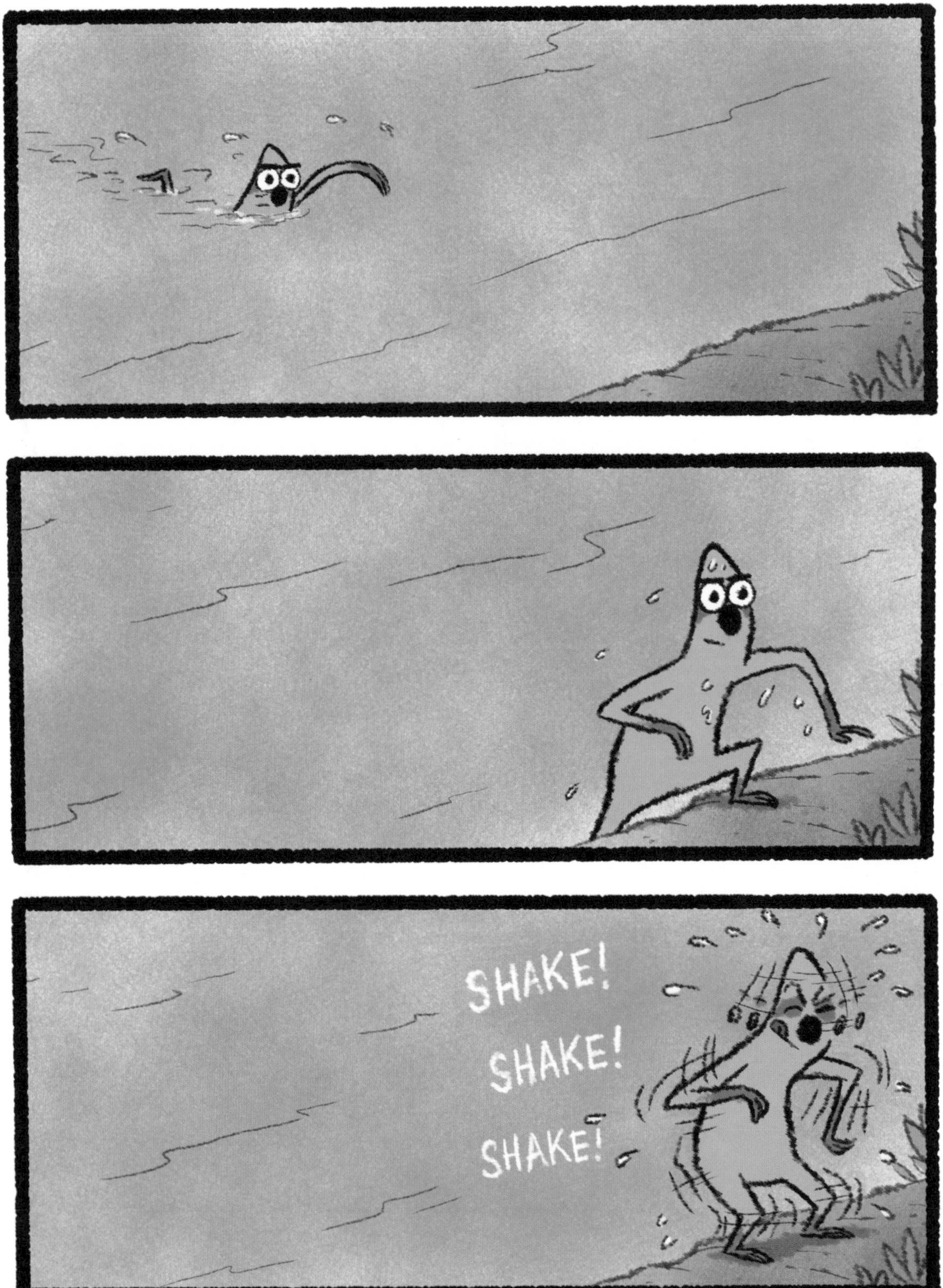
SHAKE!
SHAKE!
SHAKE!

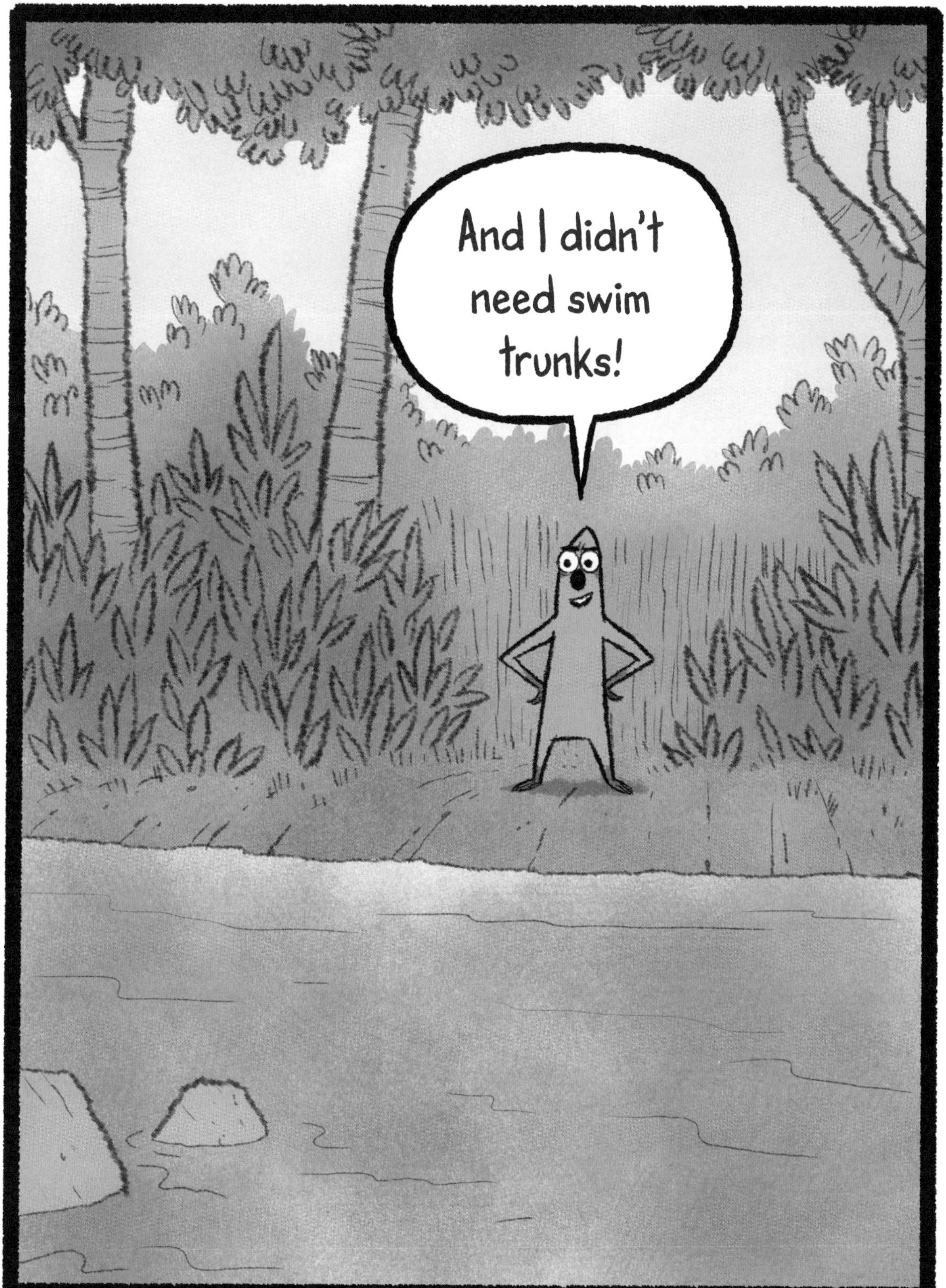
And I didn't need swim trunks!

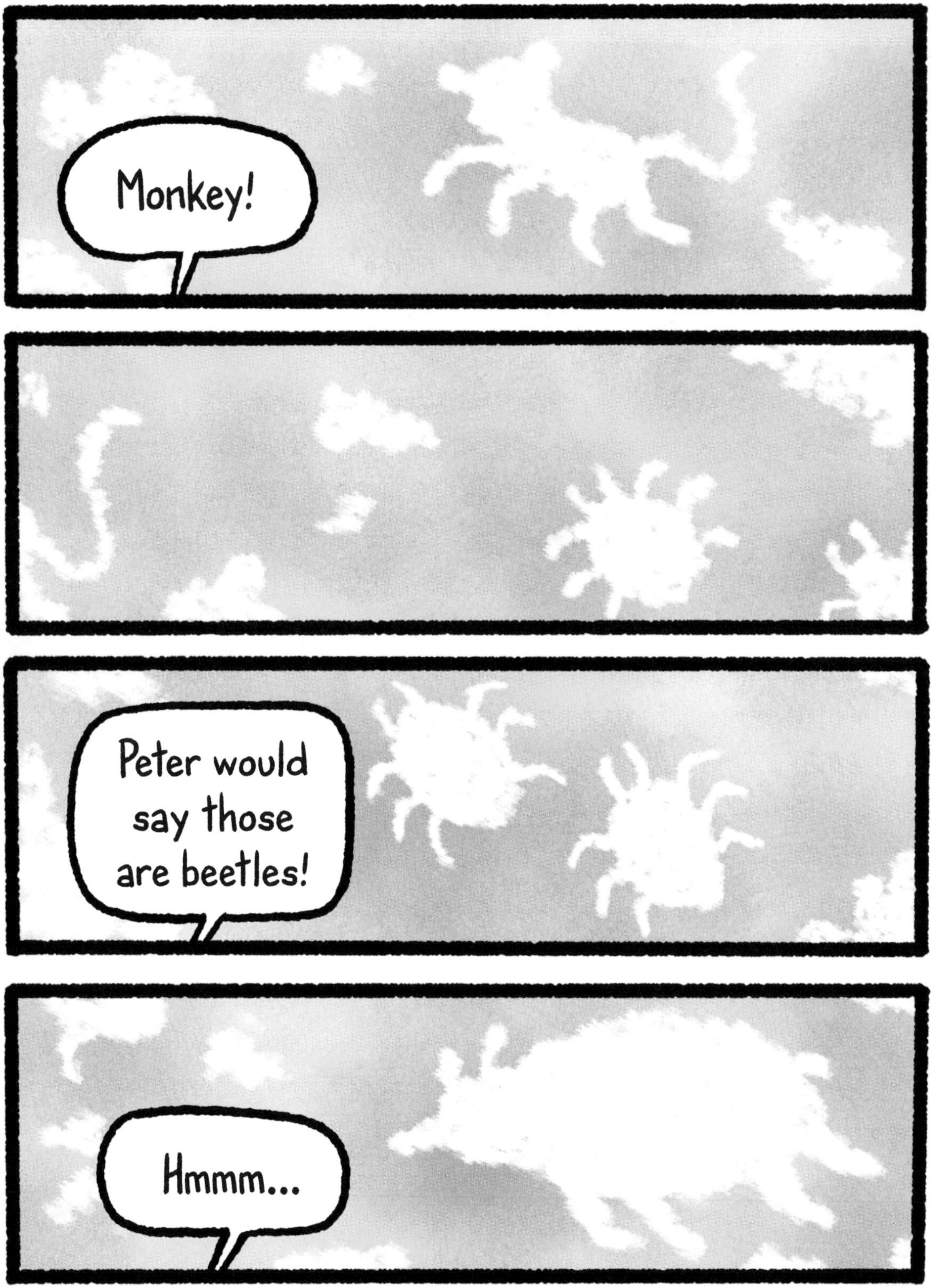
Monkey!
Peter would say those are beetles!
Hmmm...

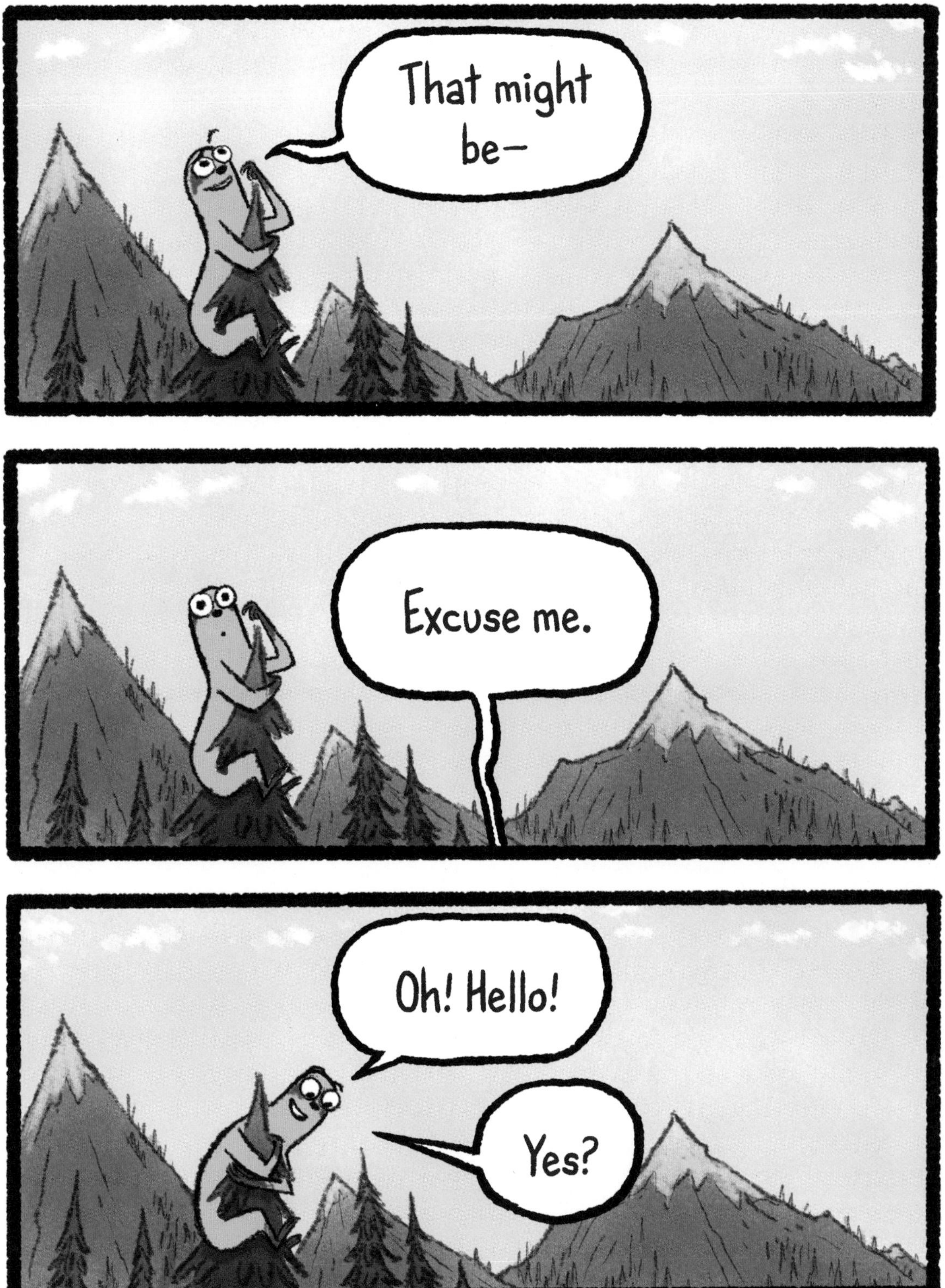
That might be–
Excuse me.
Oh! Hello!
Yes?

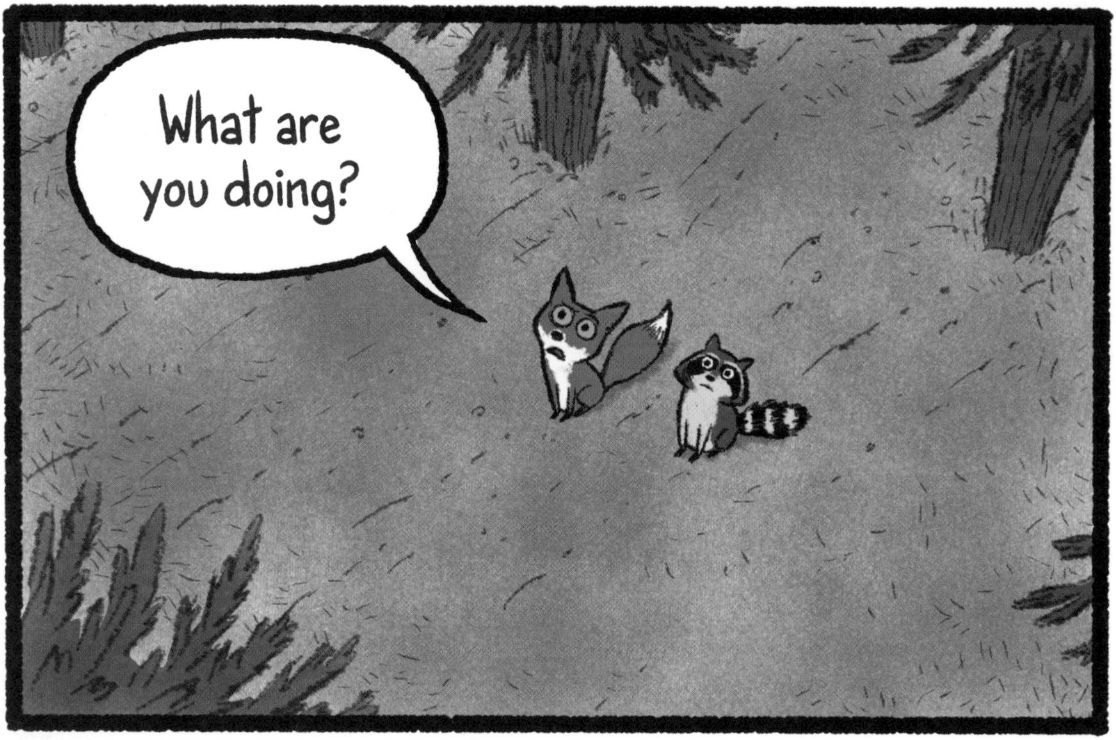
What are you doing?

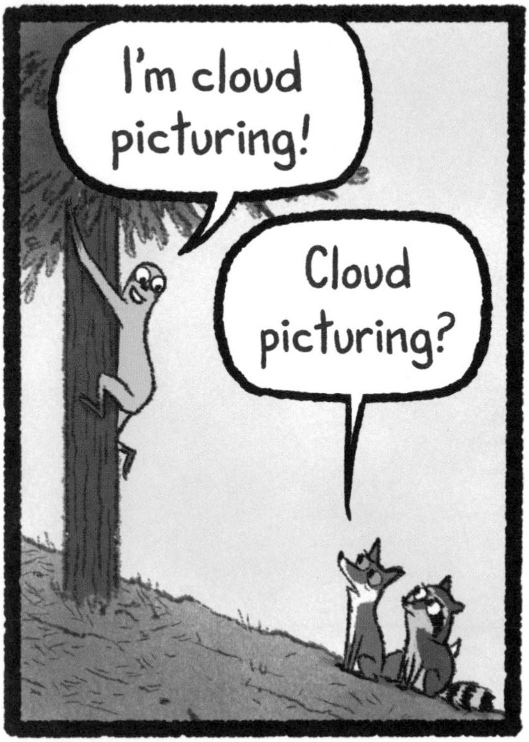
I'm cloud picturing!
Cloud picturing?

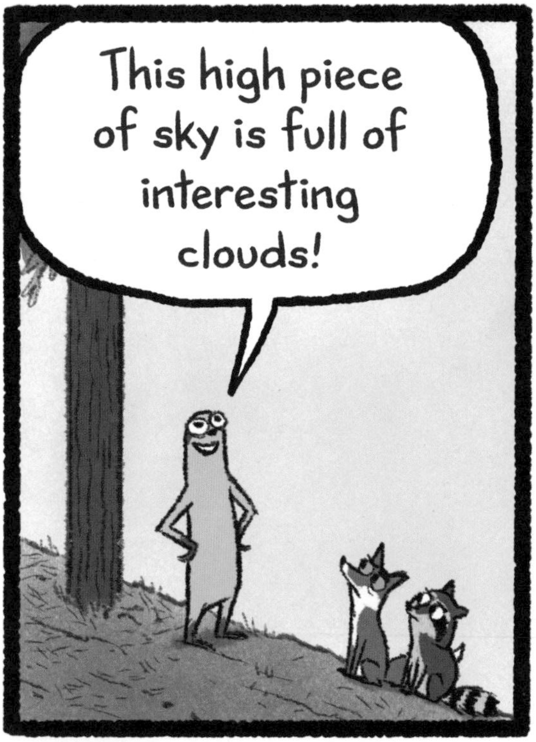
This high piece of sky is full of interesting clouds!

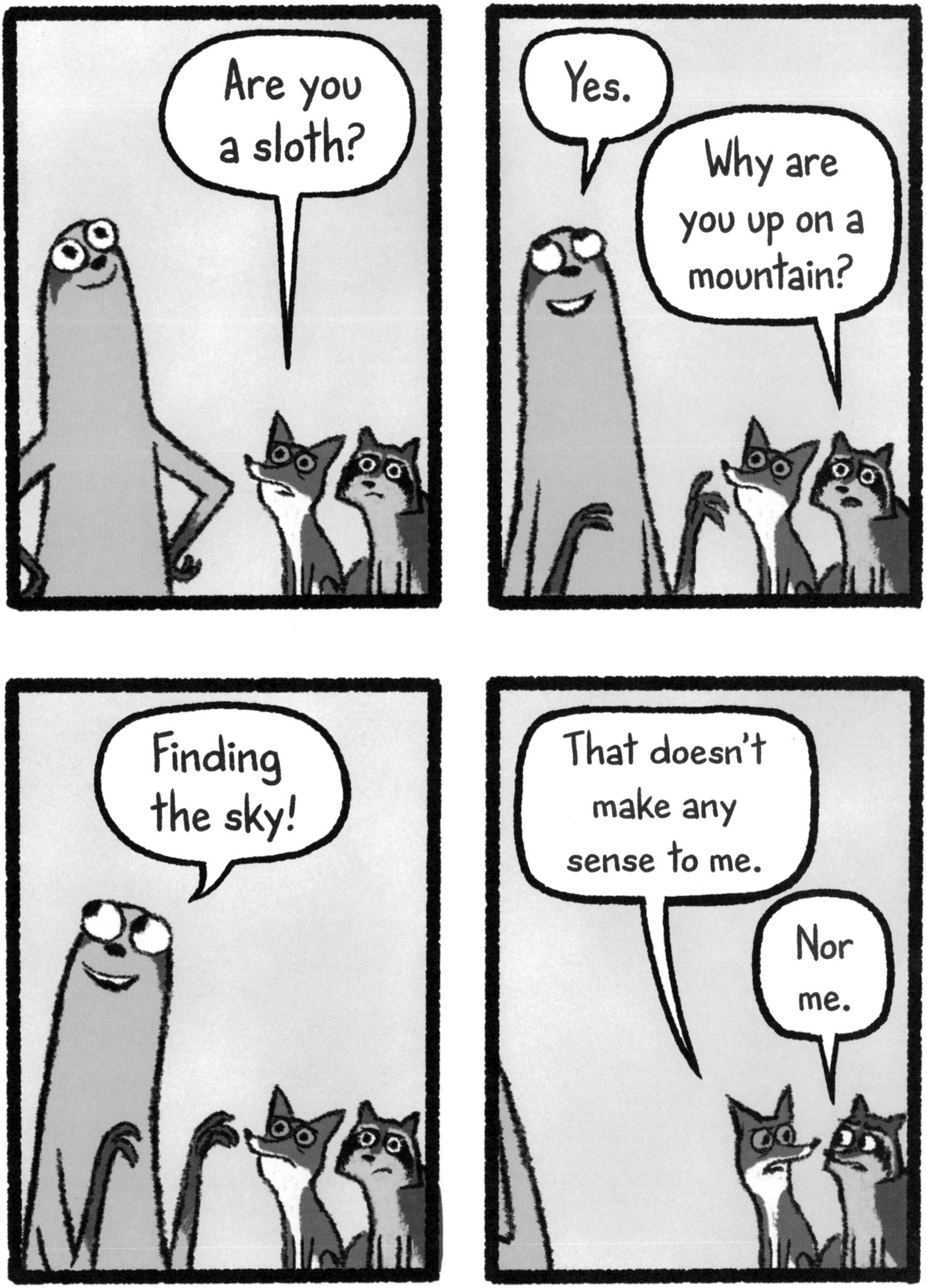
Are you a sloth?
Yes.
Why are you up on a mountain?
Finding the sky!
That doesn't make any sense to me.
Nor me.

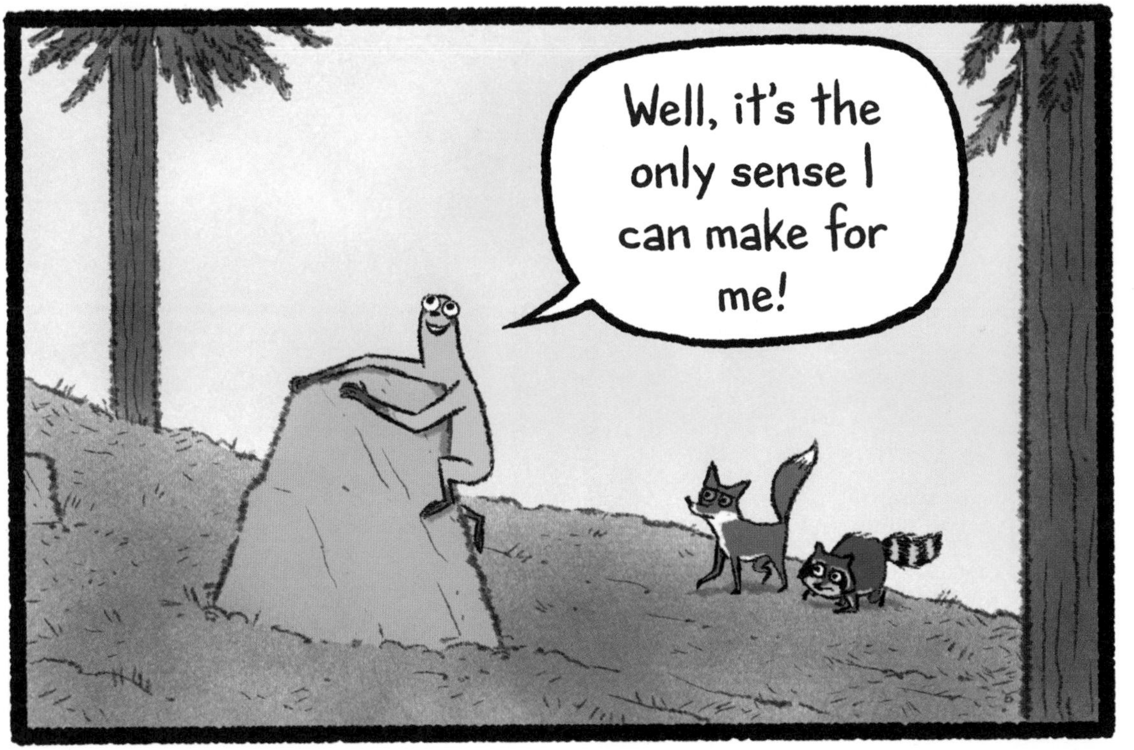
Well, it's the only sense I can make for me!

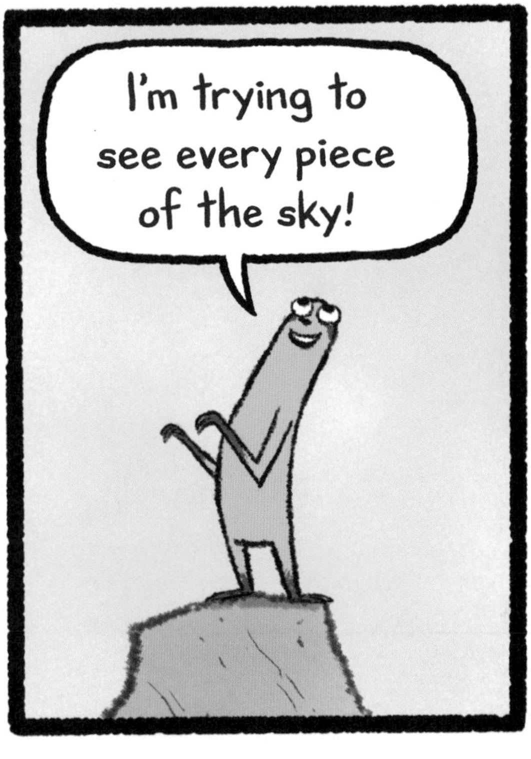
I'm trying to see every piece of the sky!

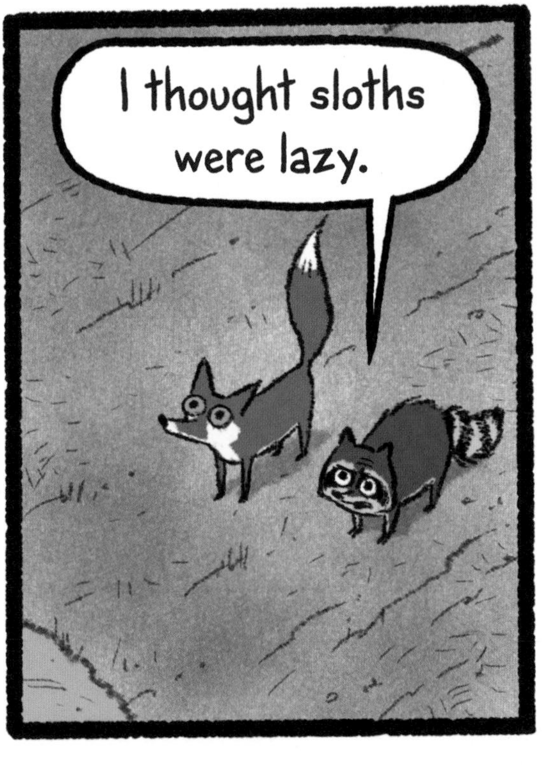
I thought sloths were lazy.

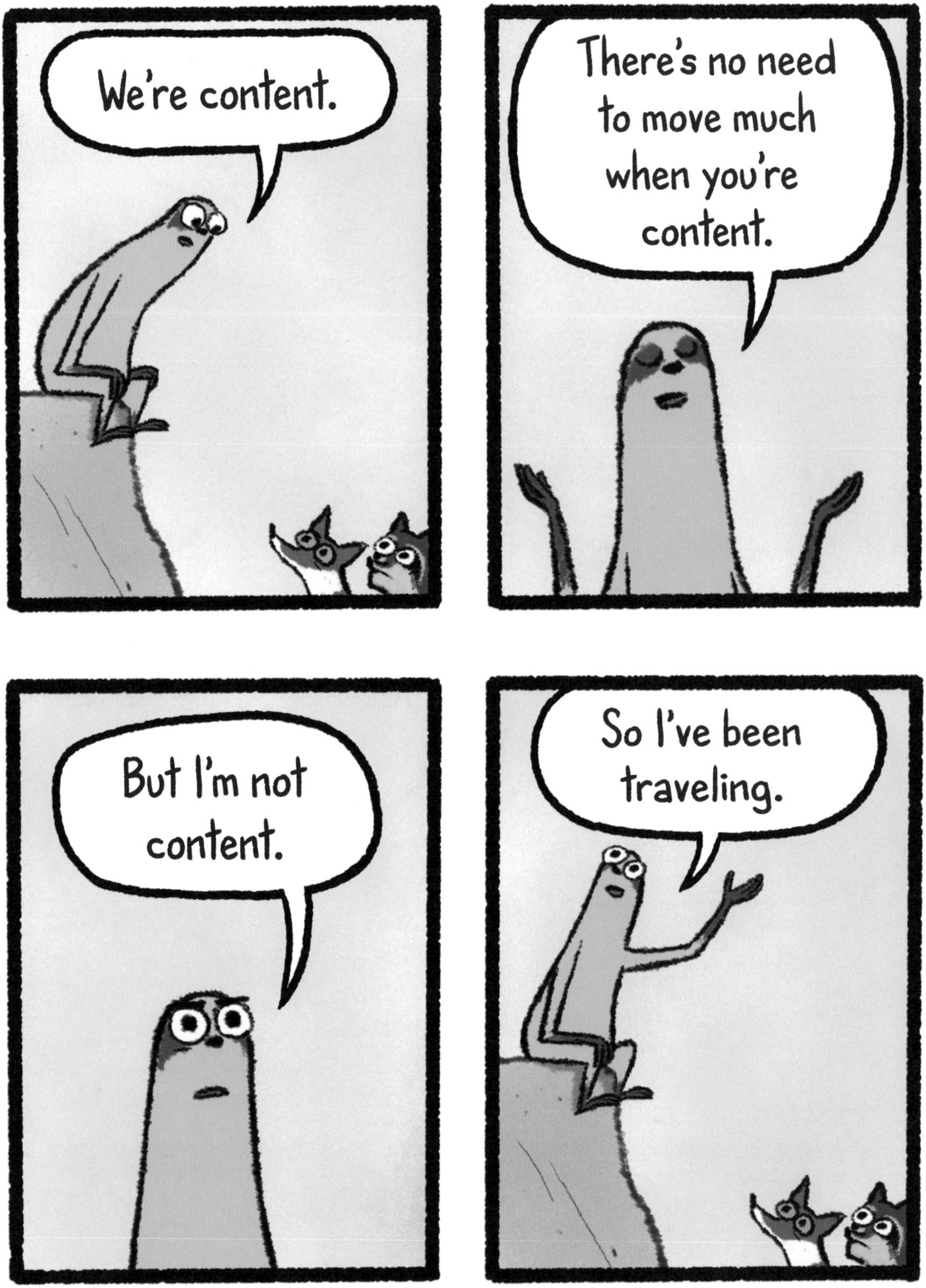
We're content.
There's no need to move much when you're content.
But I'm not content.
So I've been traveling.

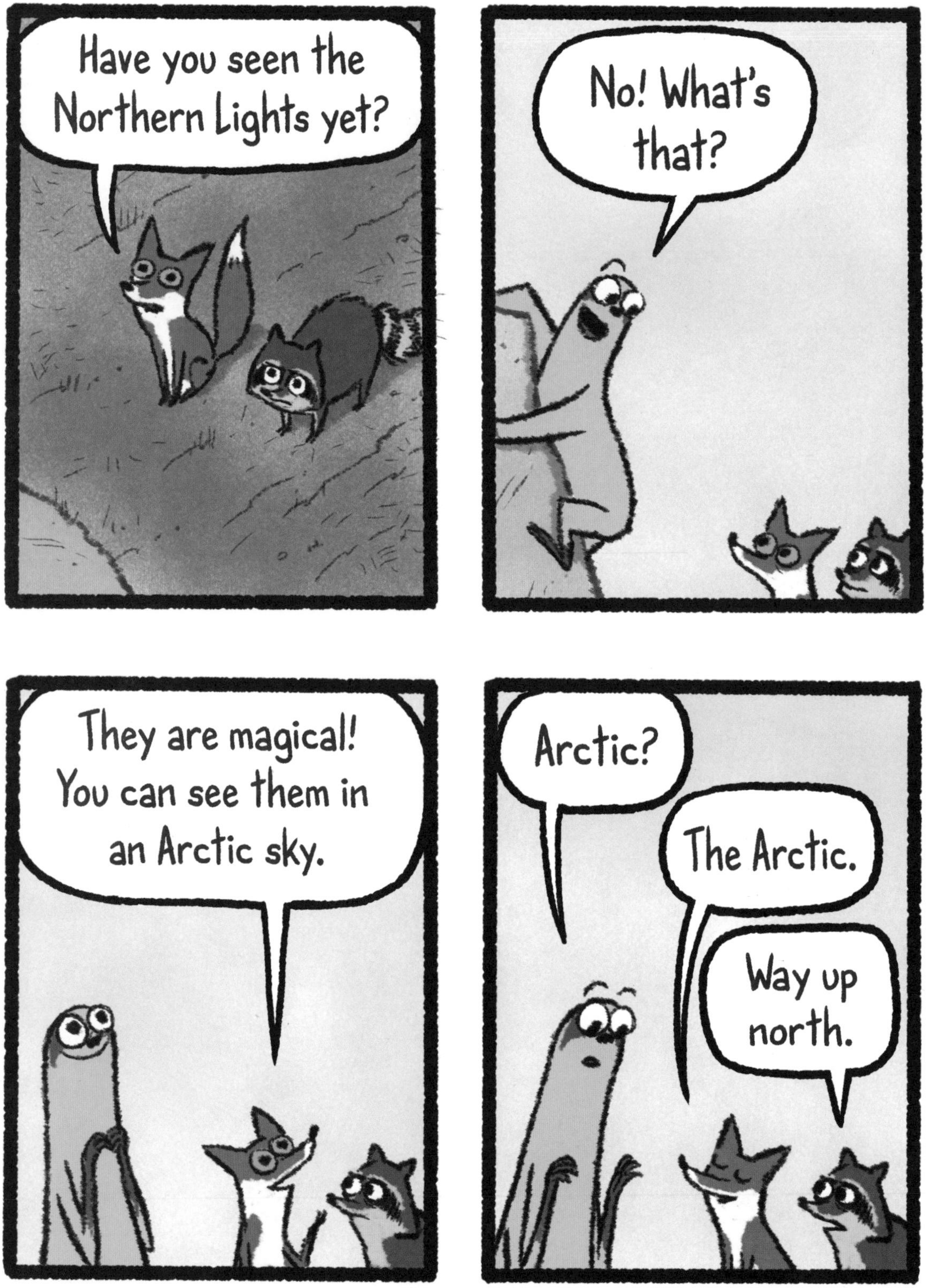
Have you seen the Northern Lights yet?
No! What's that?
They are magical! You can see them in an Arctic sky.
Arctic?
The Arctic.
Way up north.

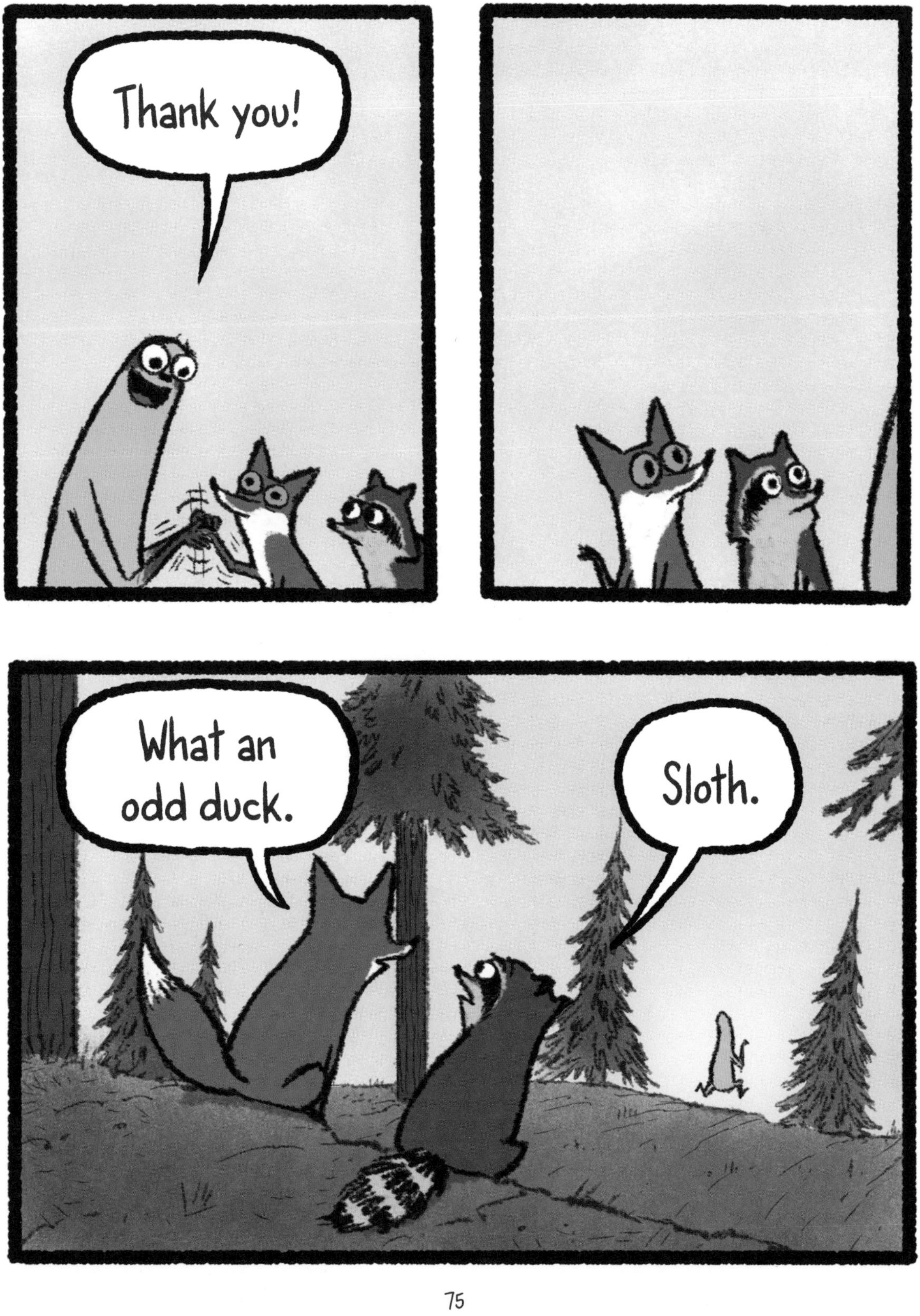
Thank you!
What an odd duck.
Sloth.

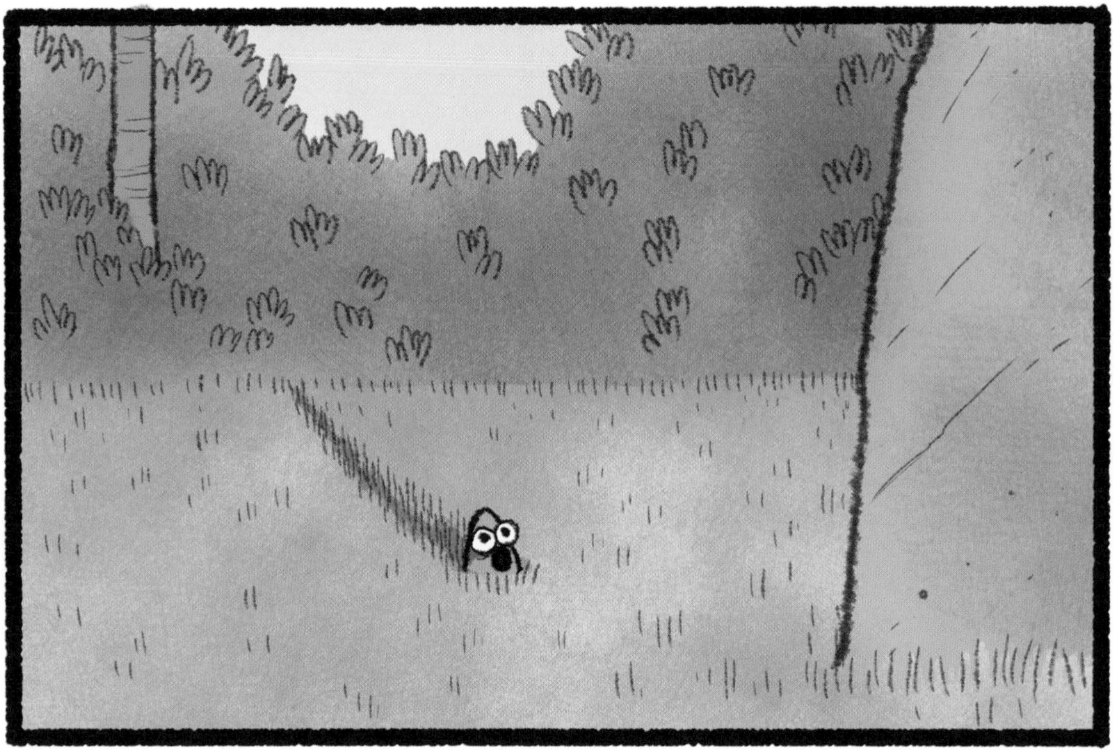

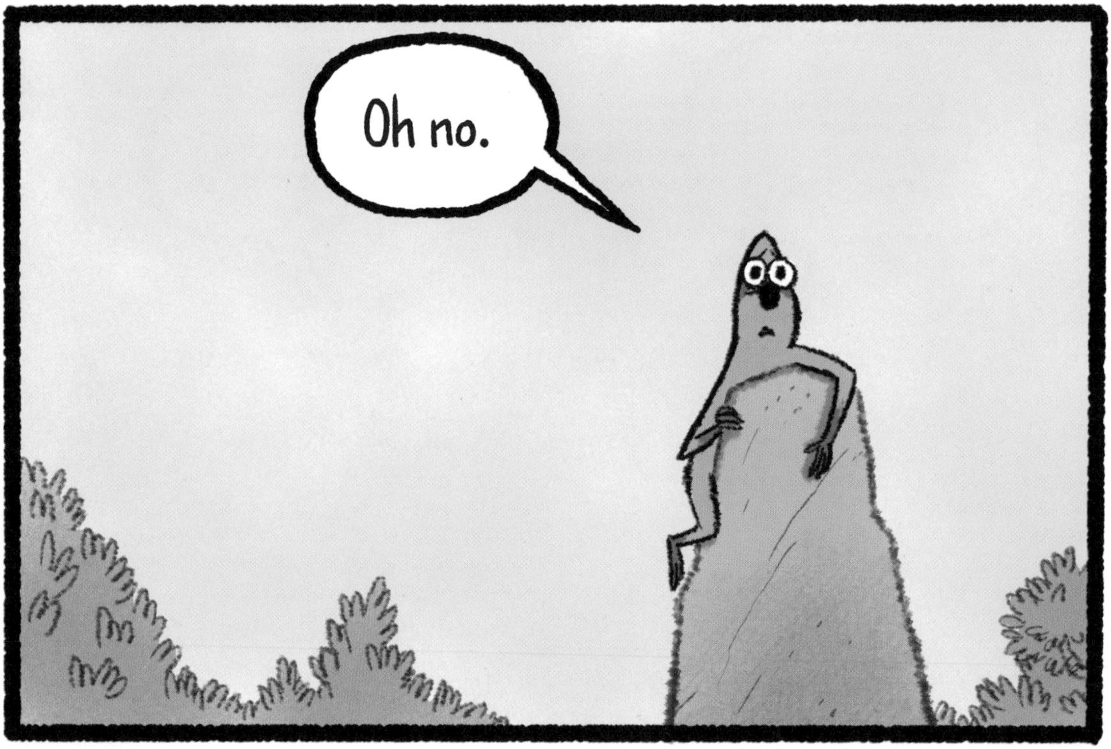
Oh no.

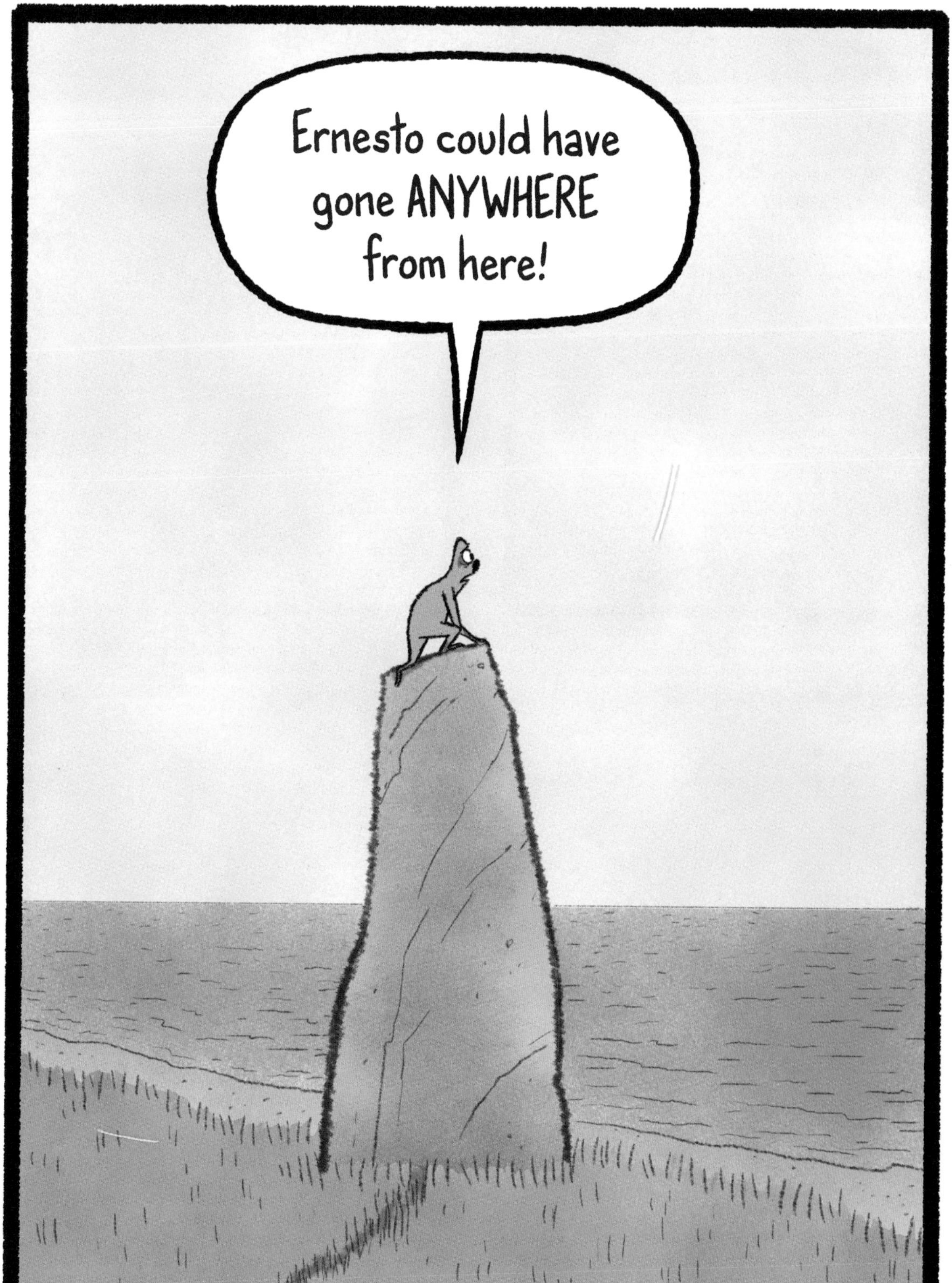
Ernesto could have gone ANYWHERE from here!

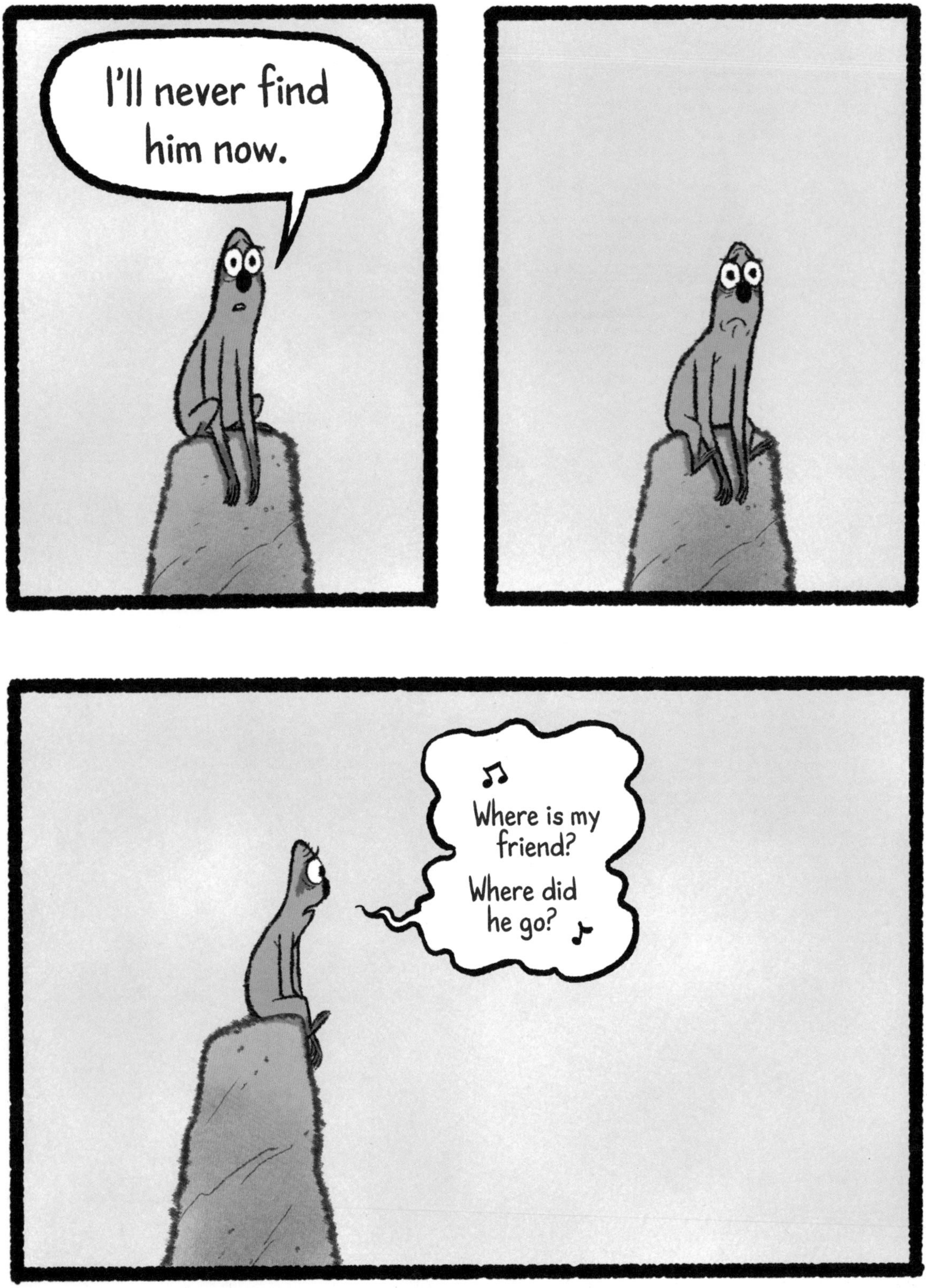
I'll never find him now.
♫ Where is my friend? Where did he go? ♪

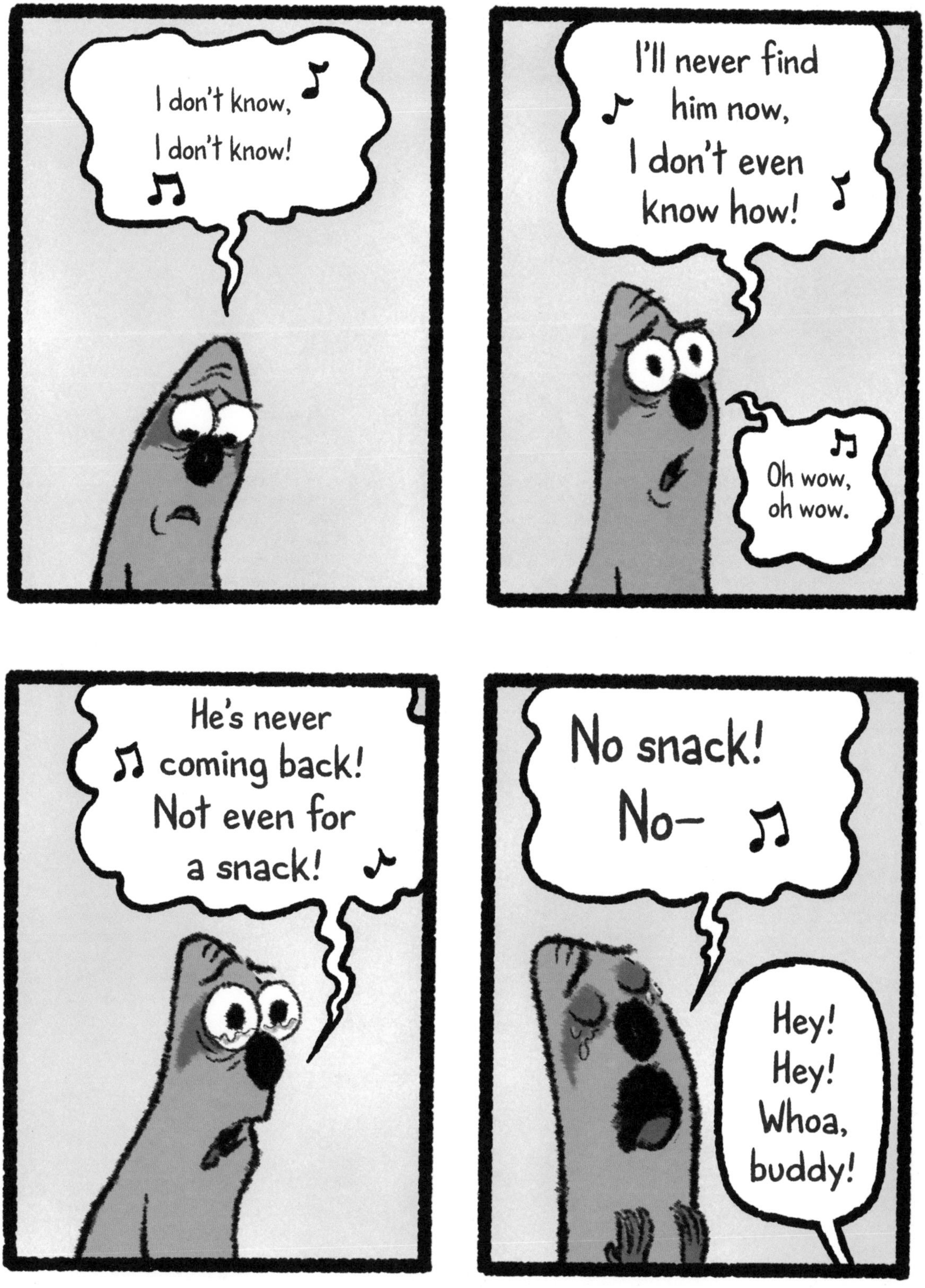
I don't know, I don't know!
I'll never find him now, I don't even know how!
Oh wow, oh wow.
He's never coming back! Not even for a snack!
No snack! No–
Hey! Hey! Whoa, buddy!

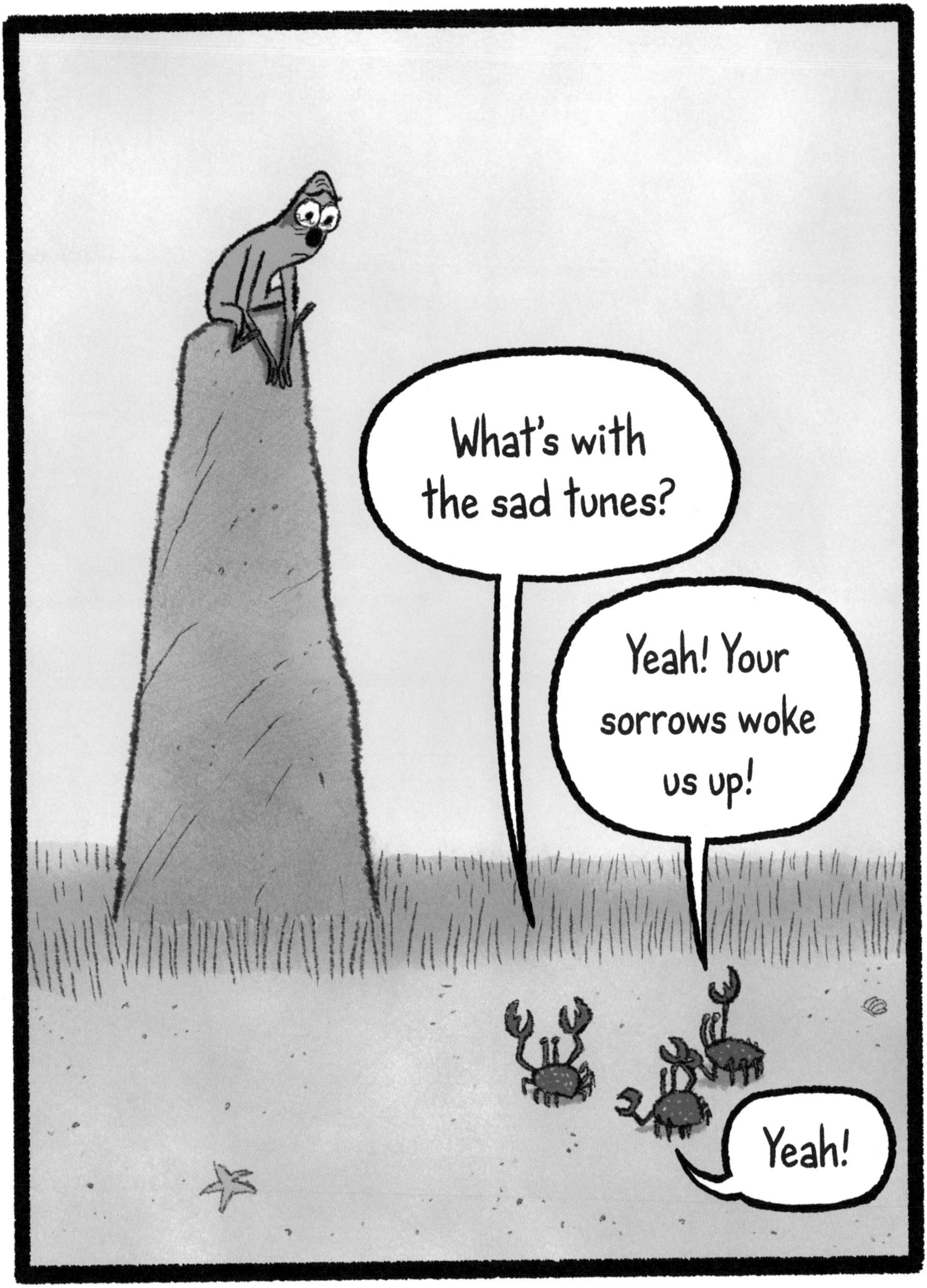
What's with the sad tunes?
Yeah! Your sorrows woke us up!
Yeah!

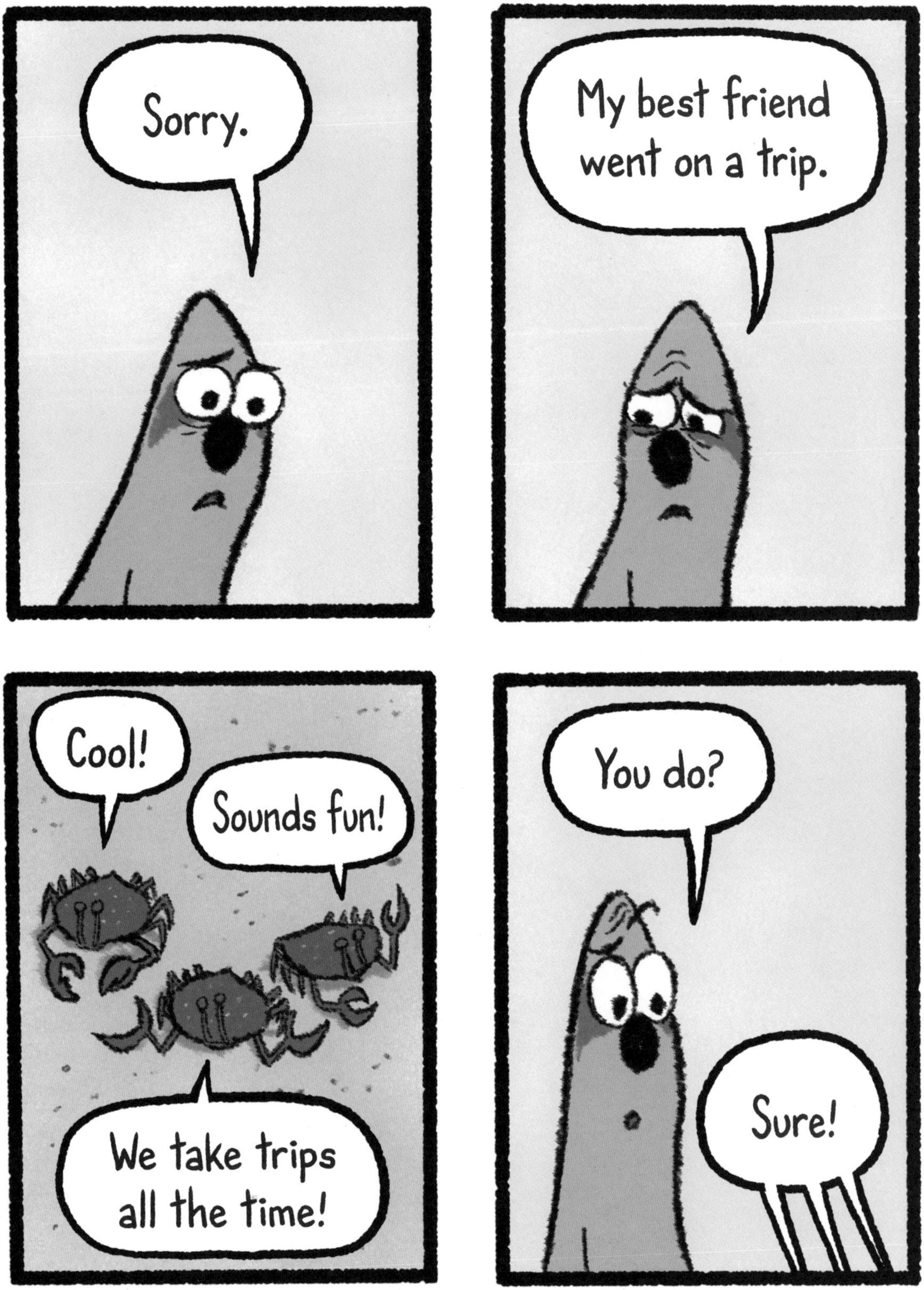
Sorry.
My best friend went on a trip.
Cool!
Sounds fun!
We take trips all the time!
You do?
Sure!

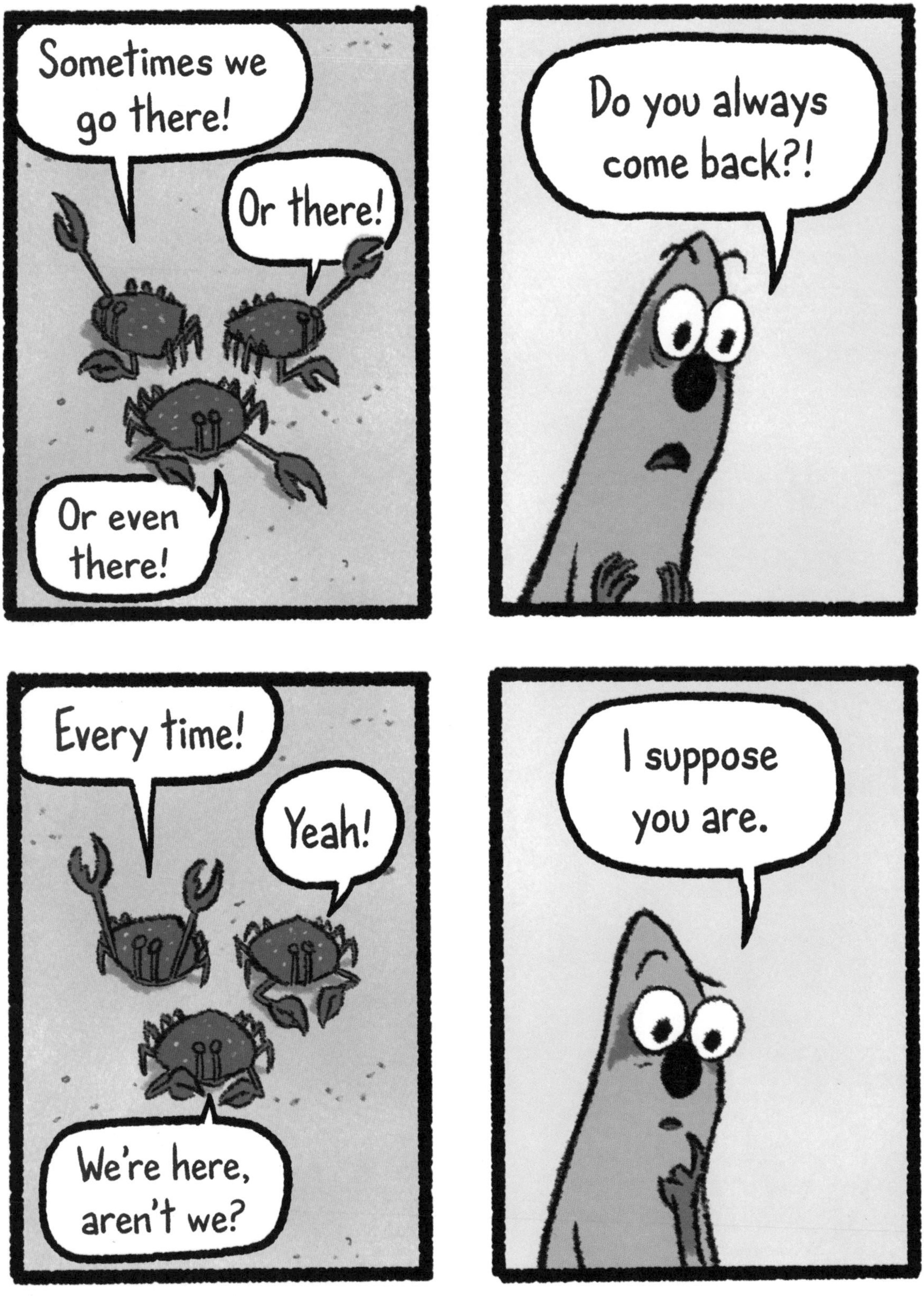
Sometimes we go there!
Or there!
Or even there!
Do you always come back?!
Every time!
Yeah!
We're here, aren't we?
I suppose you are.

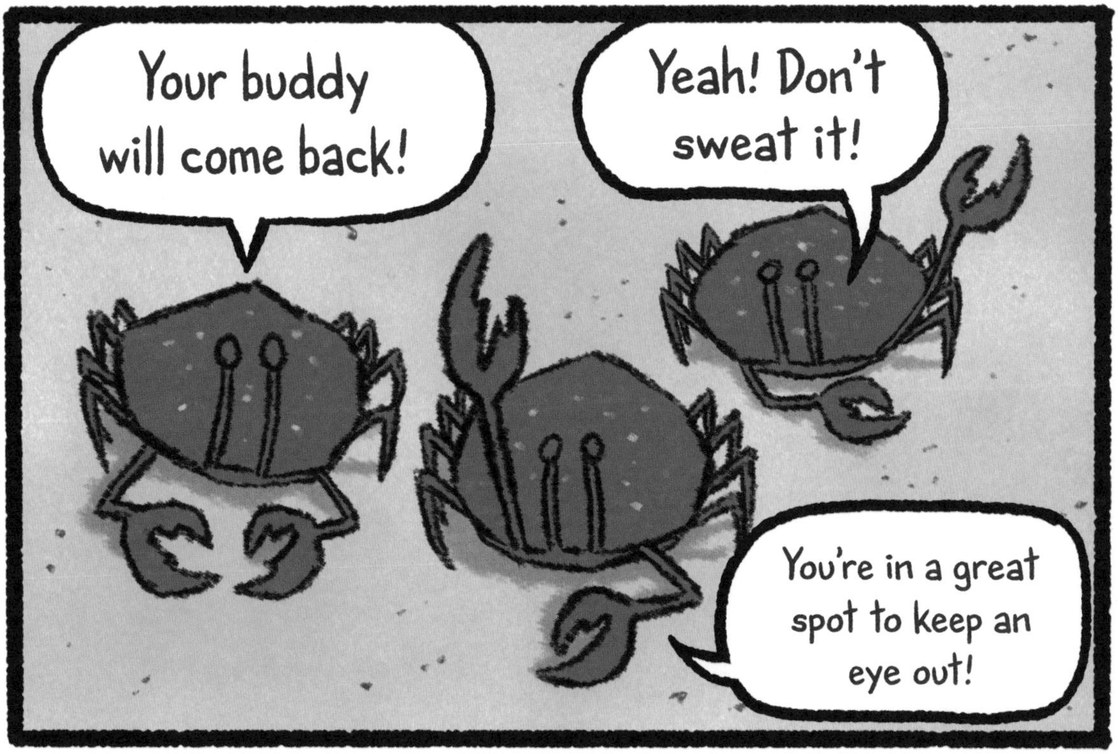
Your buddy will come back!
Yeah! Don't sweat it!
You're in a great spot to keep an eye out!

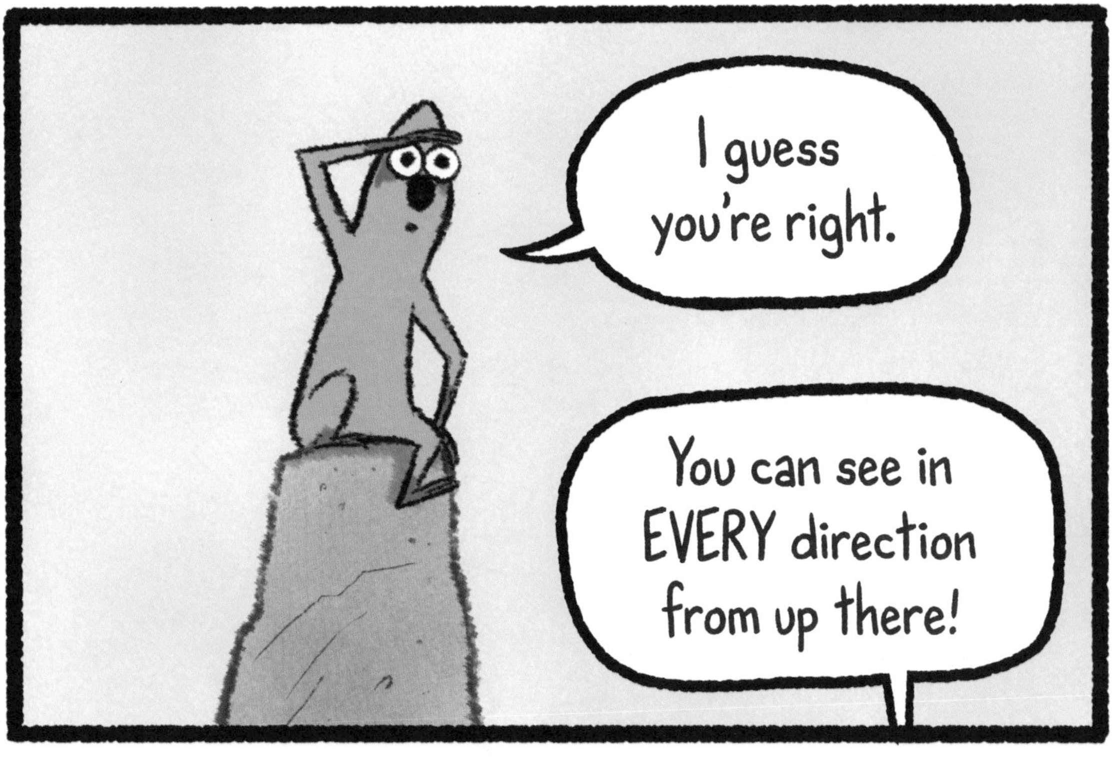
I guess you're right.
You can see in EVERY direction from up there!

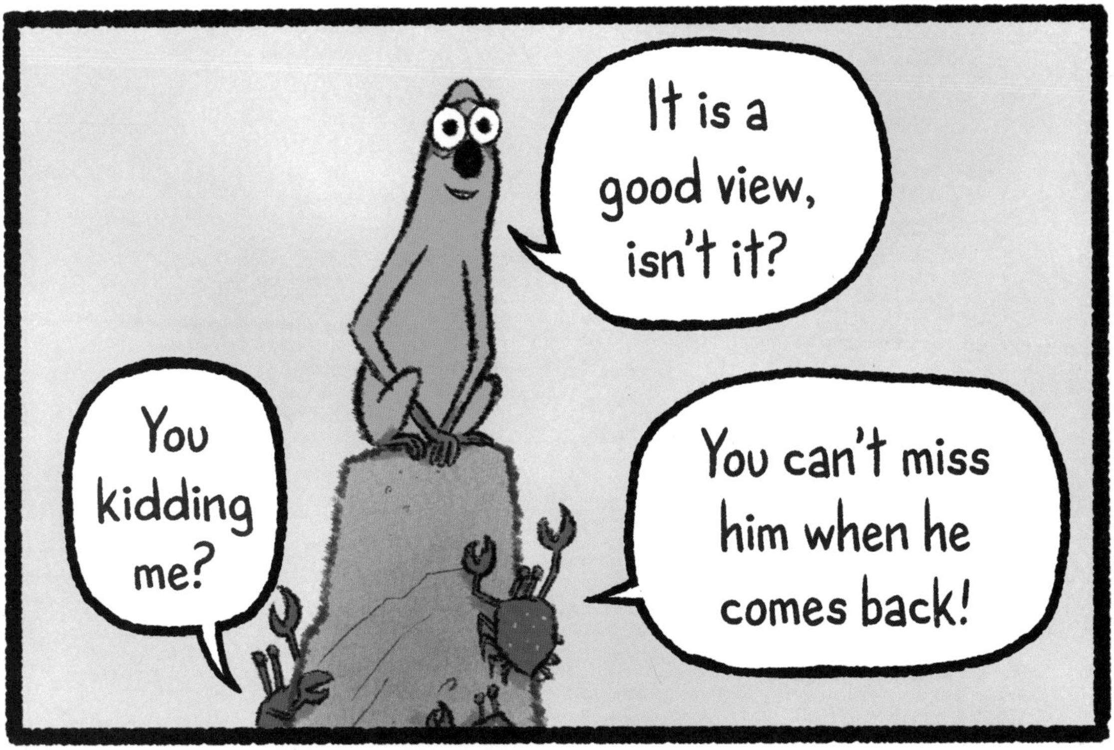
It is a good view, isn't it?
You kidding me?
You can't miss him when he comes back!

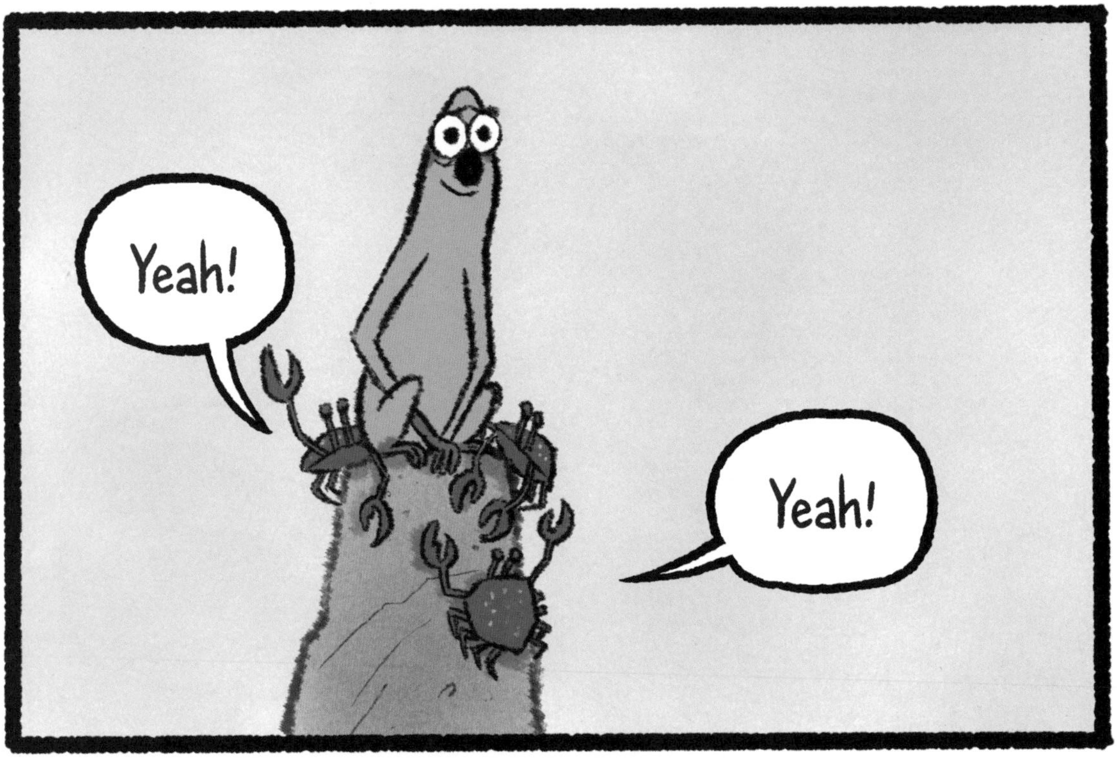
Yeah!
Yeah!

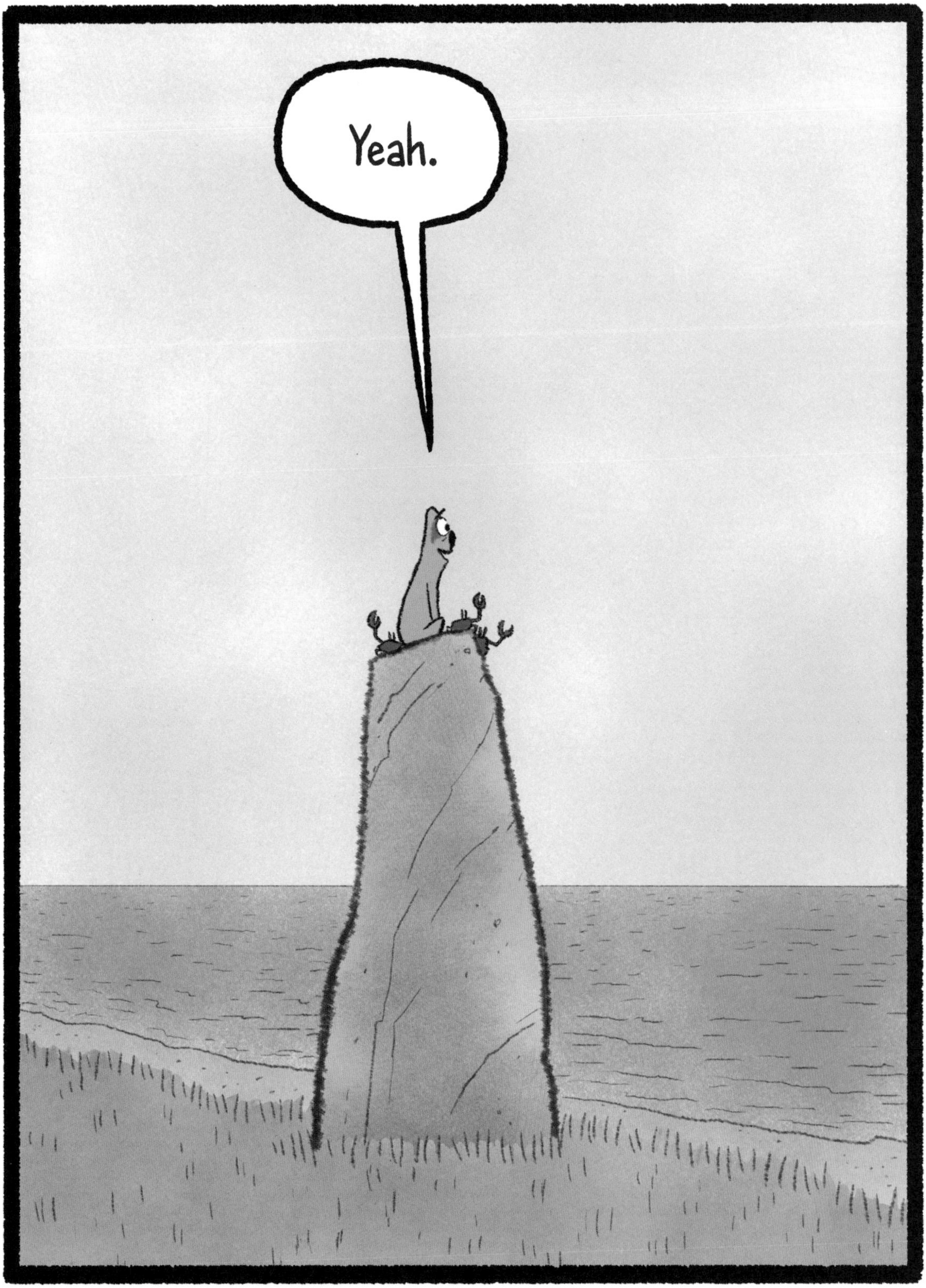
Yeah.

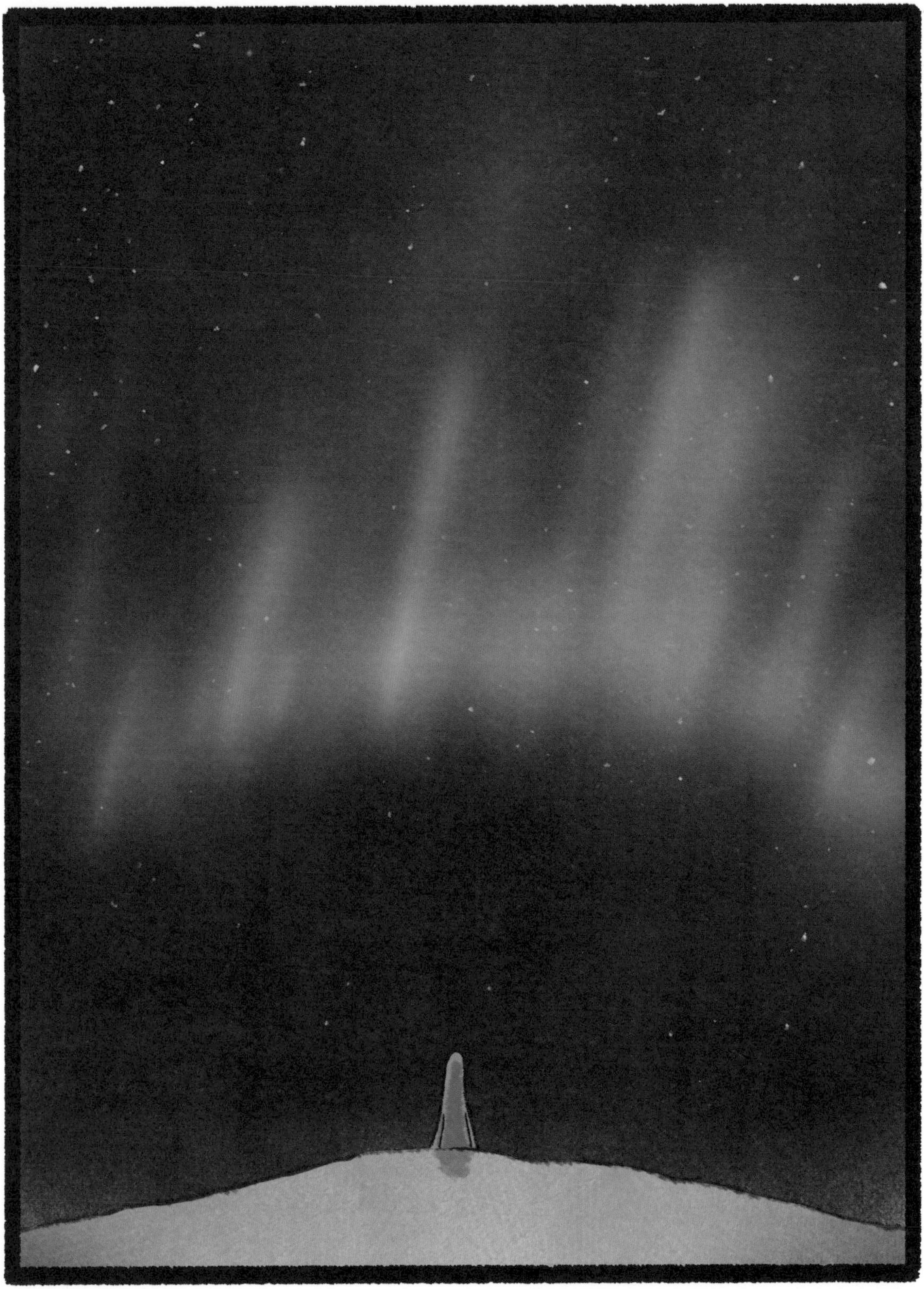

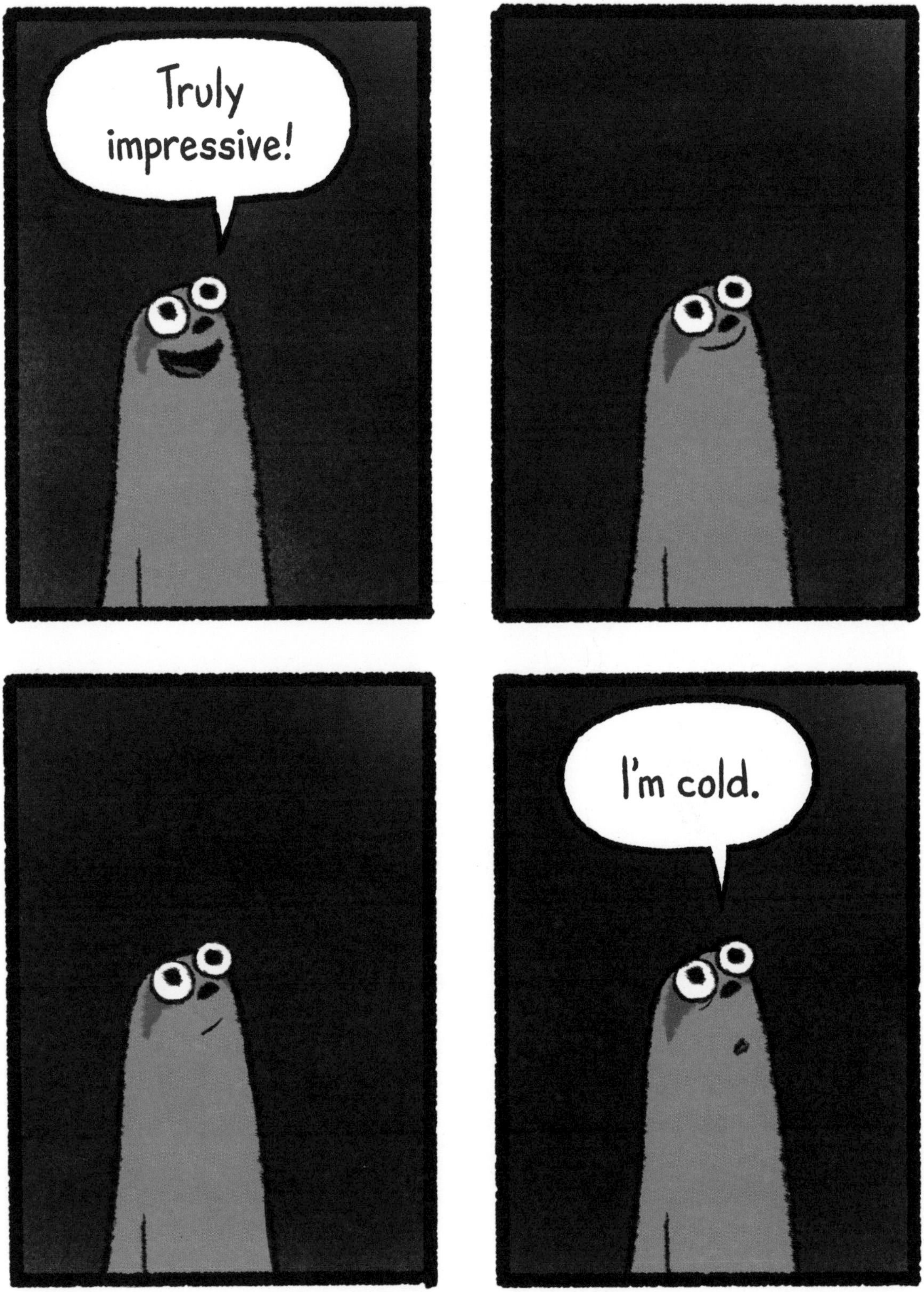
Truly impressive!
I'm cold.

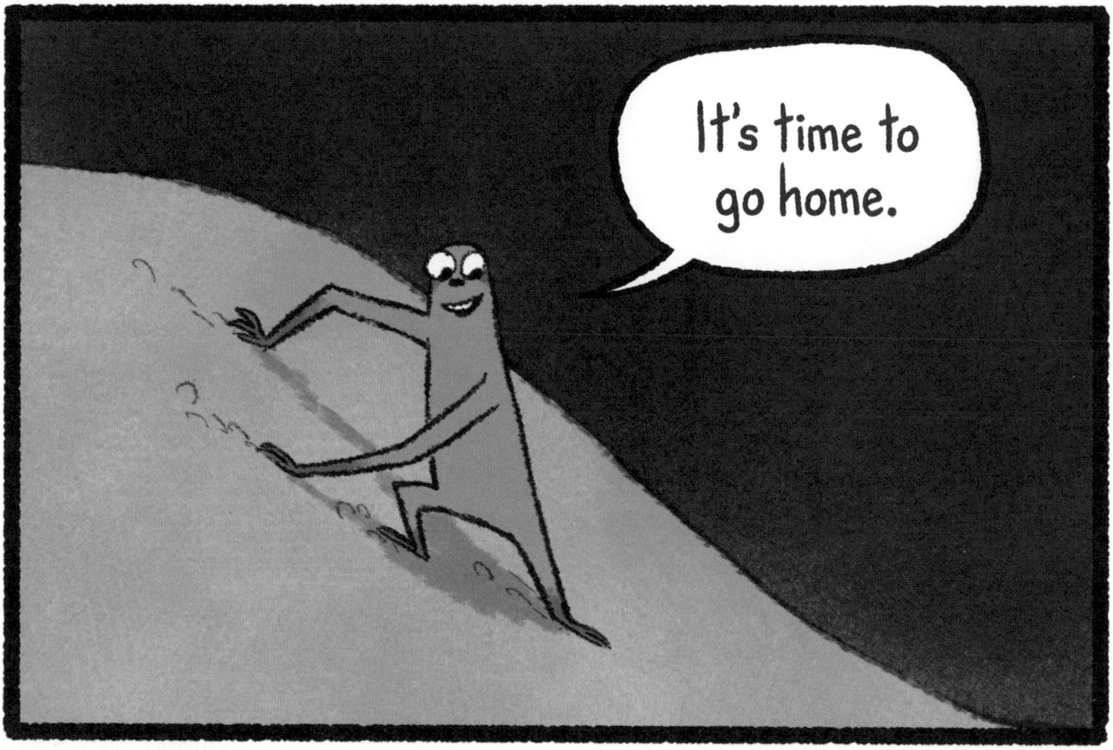
It's time to go home.

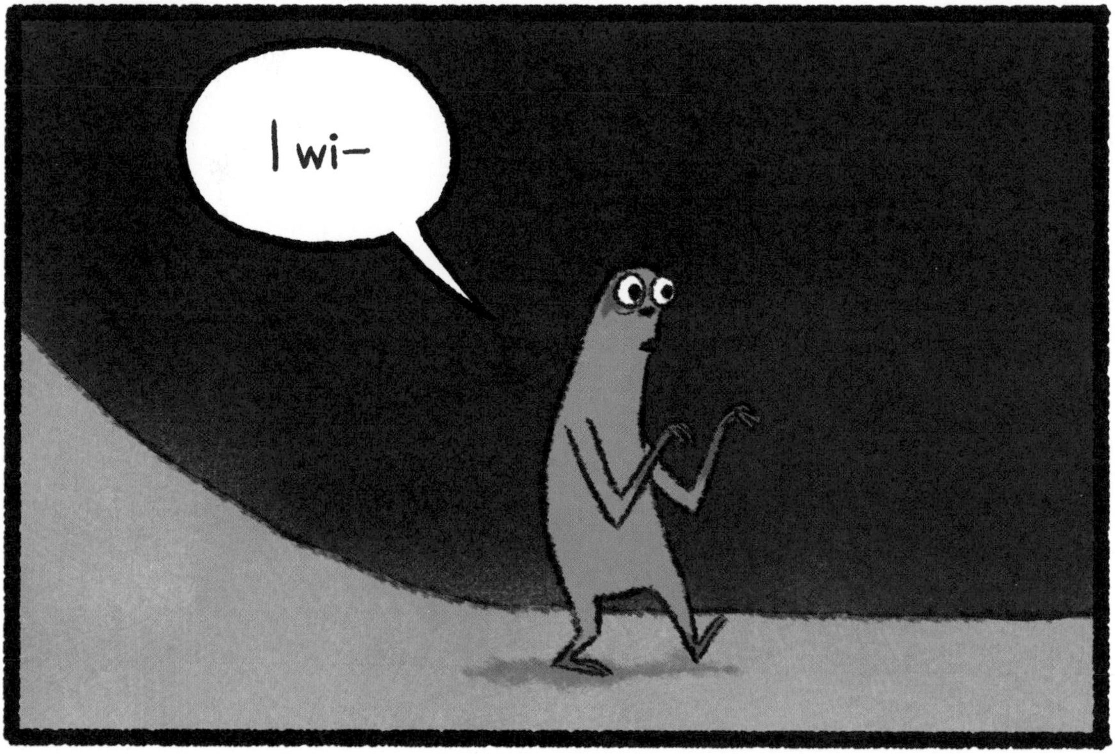
I wi–

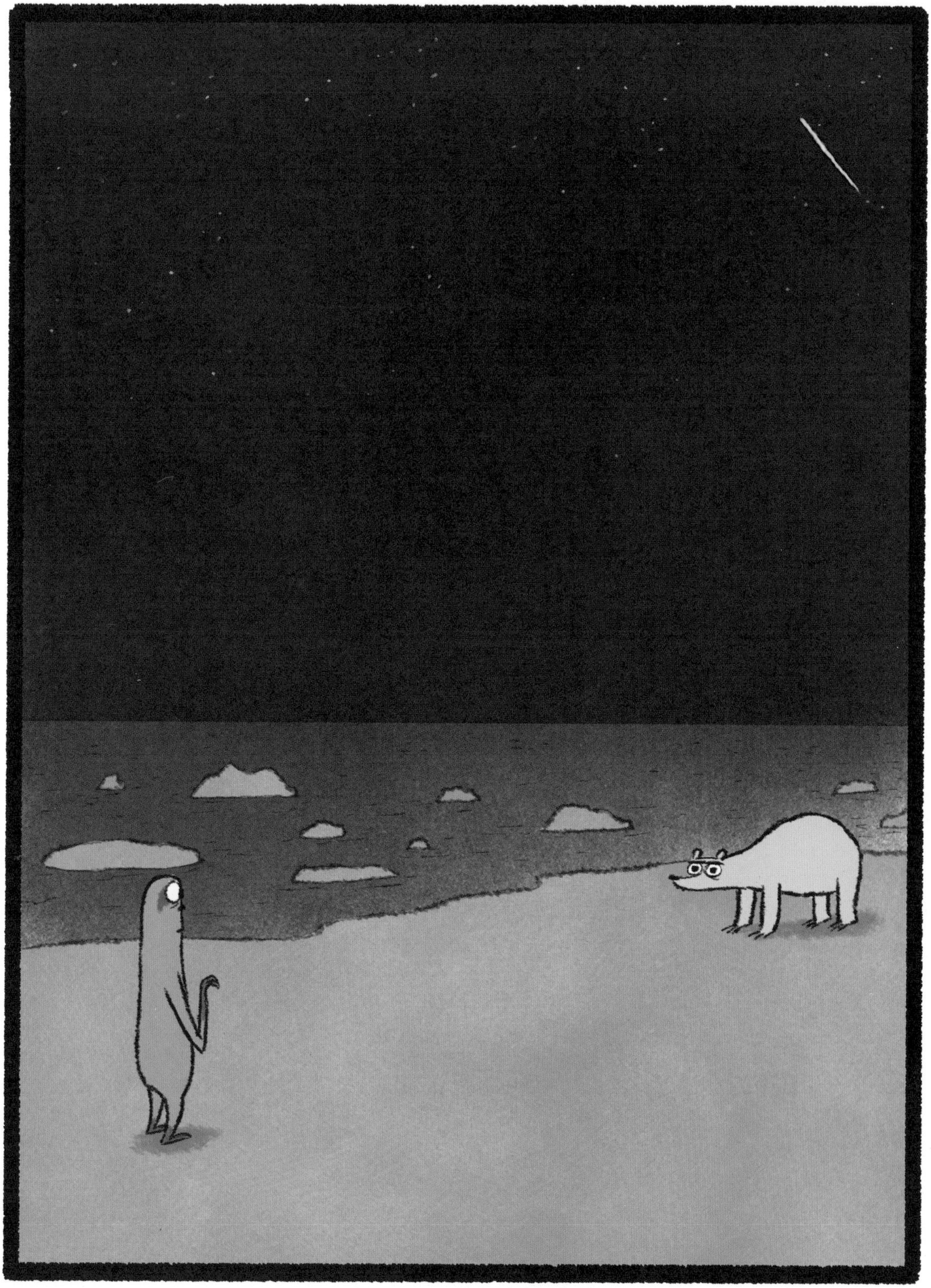

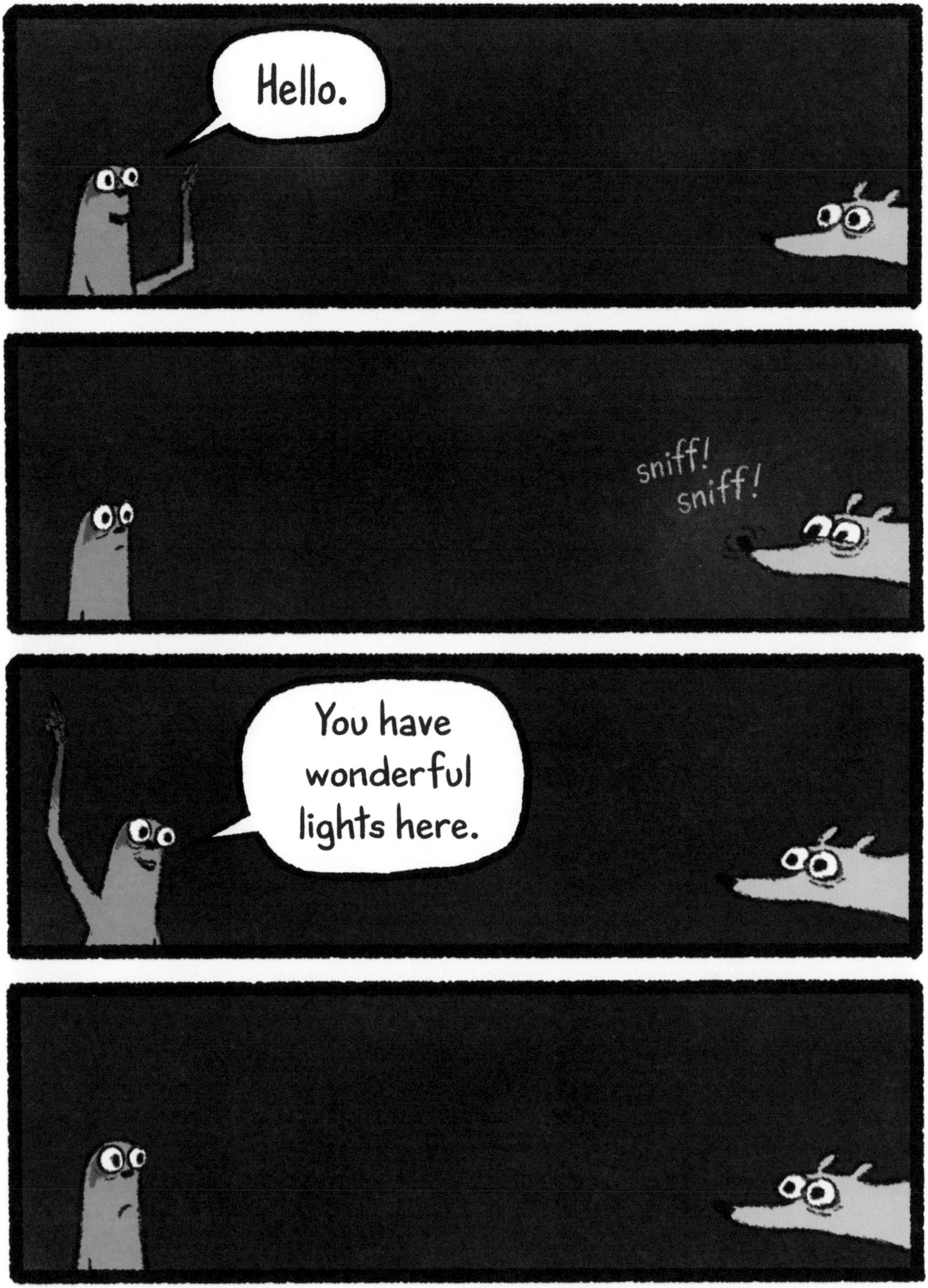
Hello.
sniff!
sniff!
You have wonderful lights here.

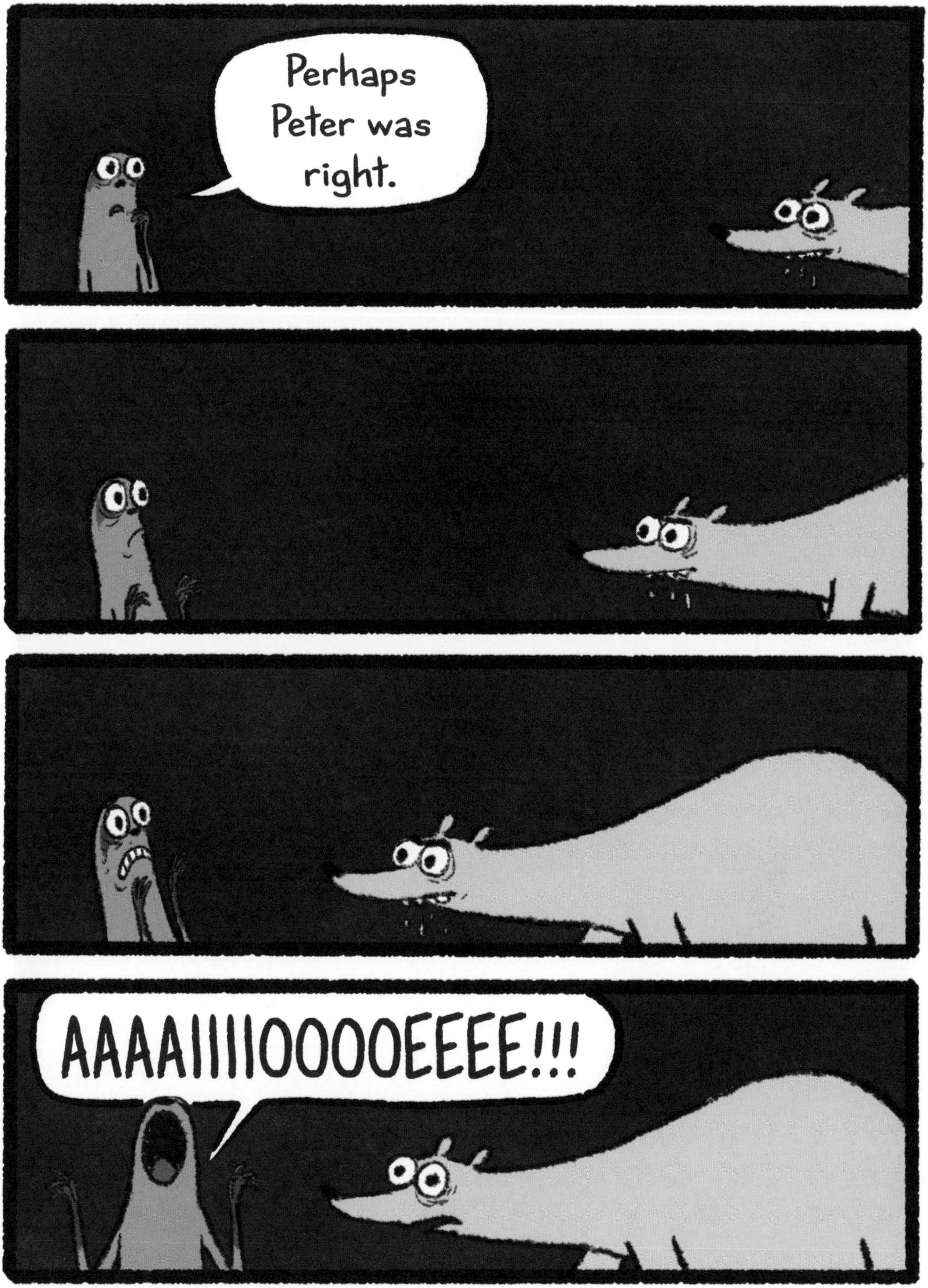
Perhaps Peter was right.
AAAAIIIIOOOOEEEE!!!

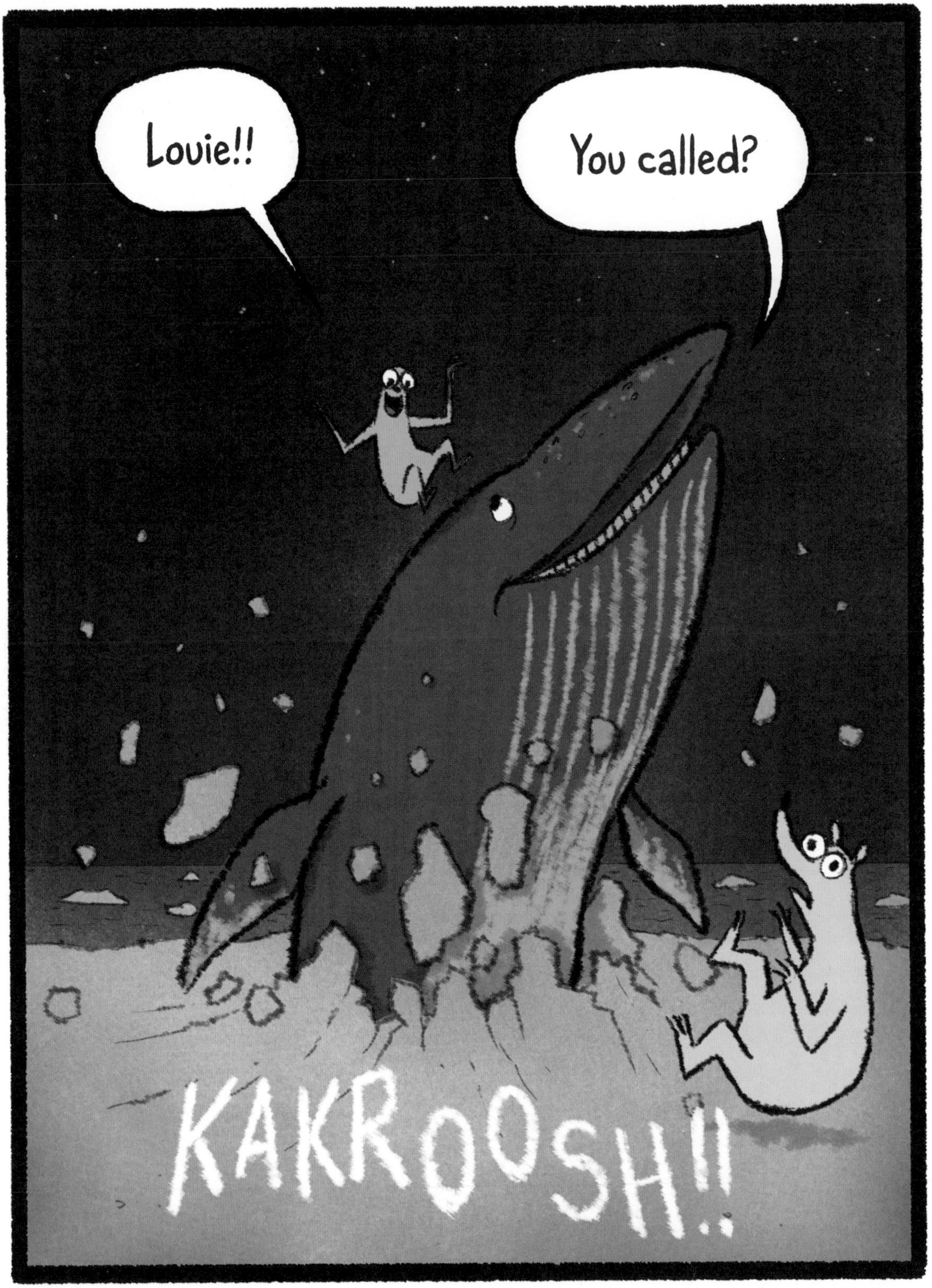
Louie!!
You called?
KAKROOSH!!

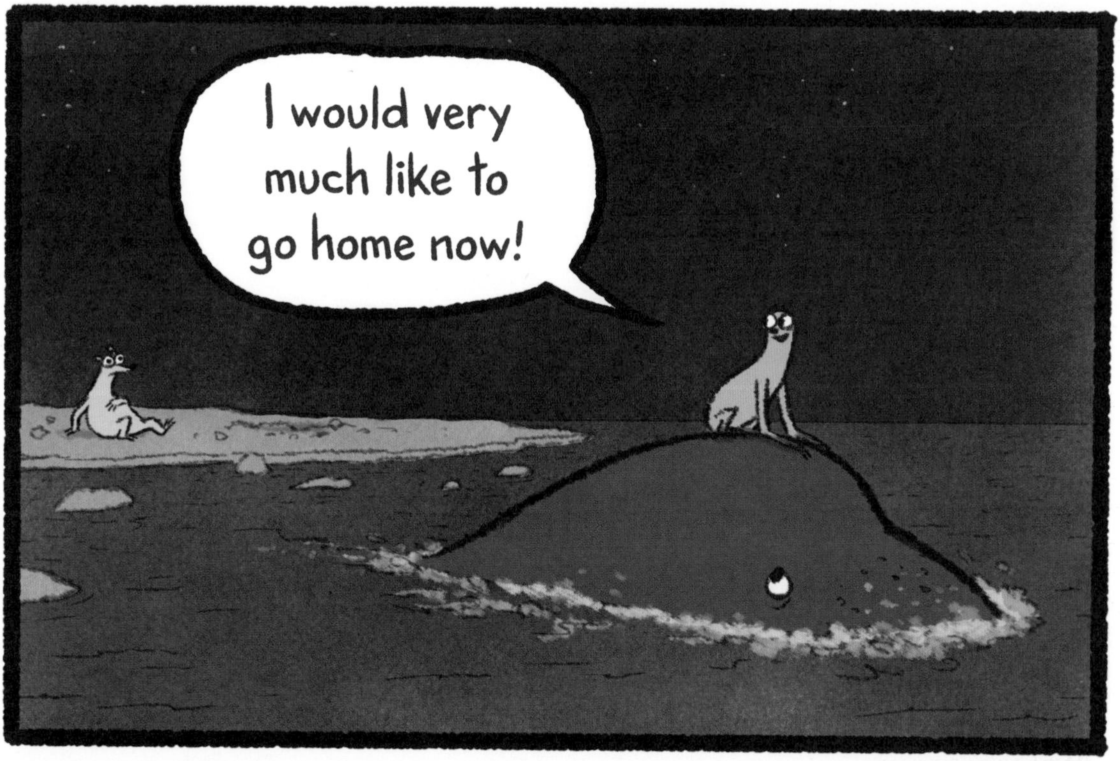
I would very much like to go home now!

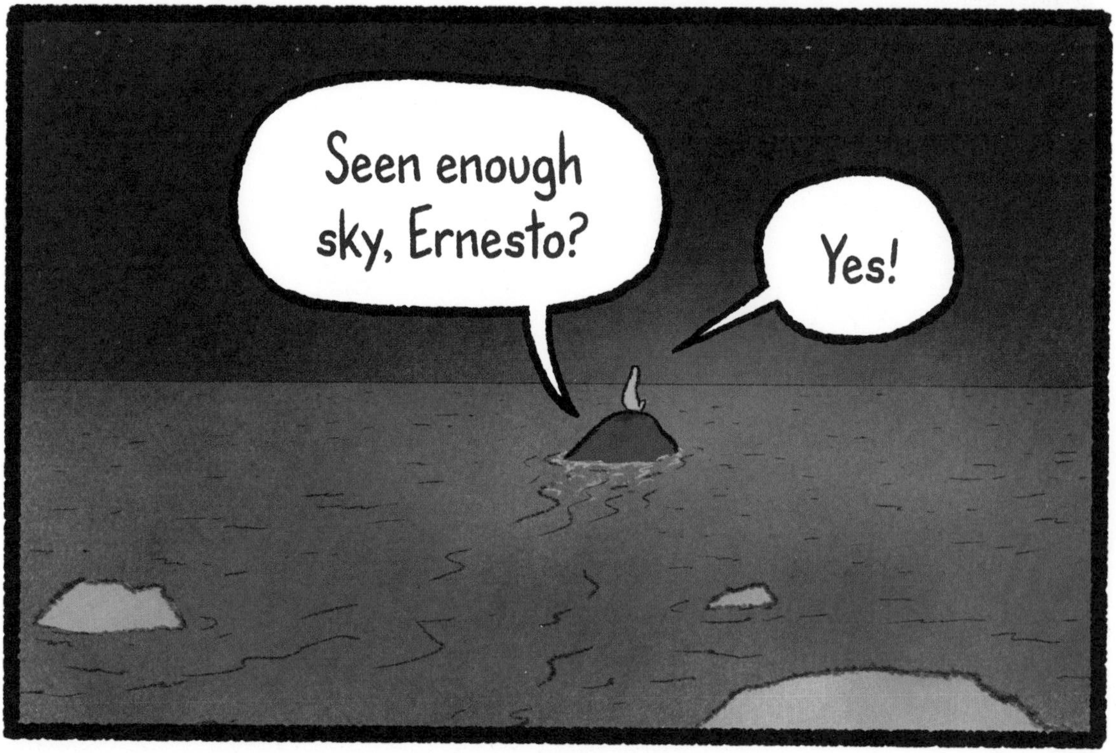
Seen enough sky, Ernesto?
Yes!

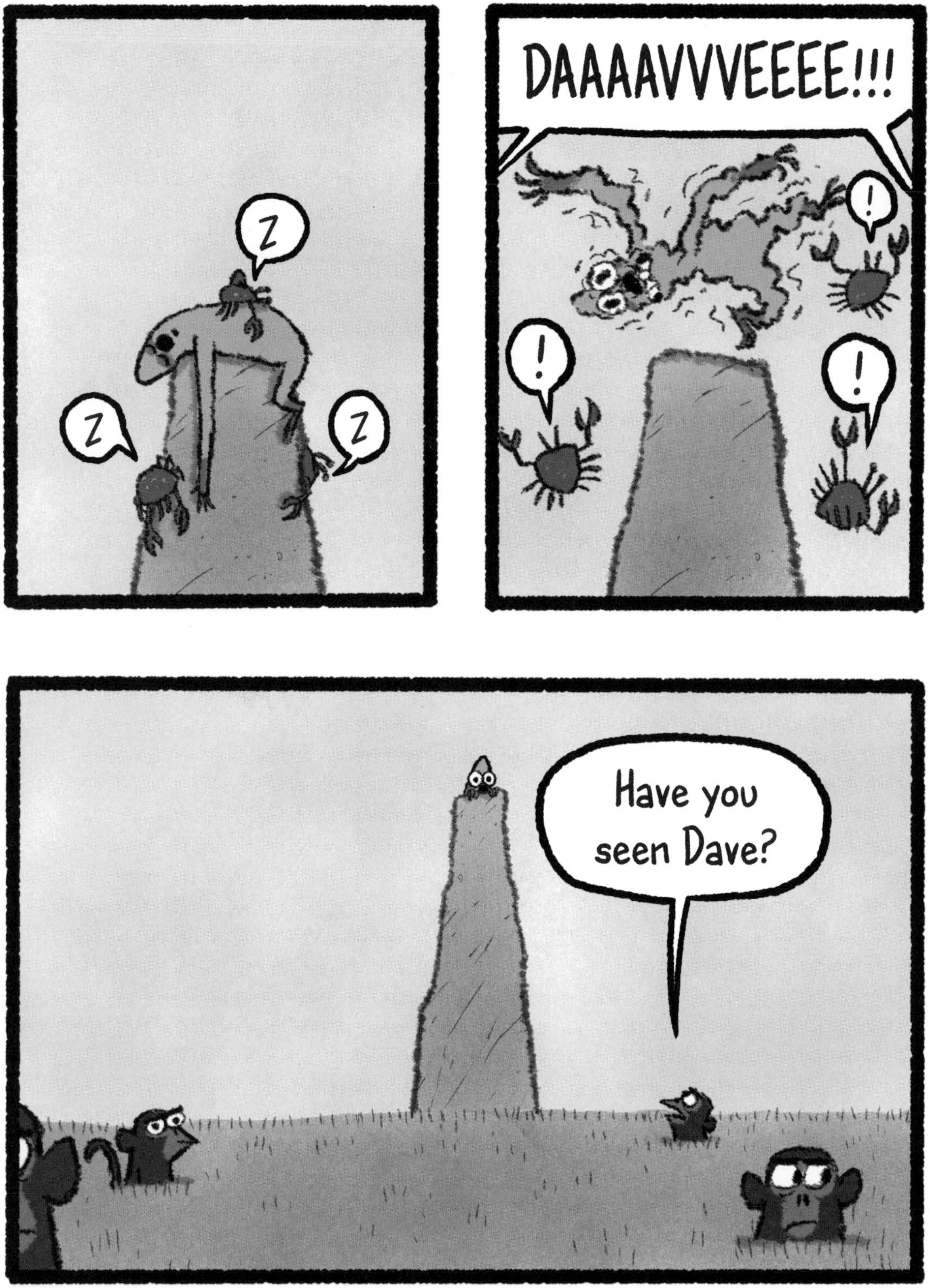
Z
Z
Z
DAAAAVVVEEEE!!!
!
!
!
Have you seen Dave?

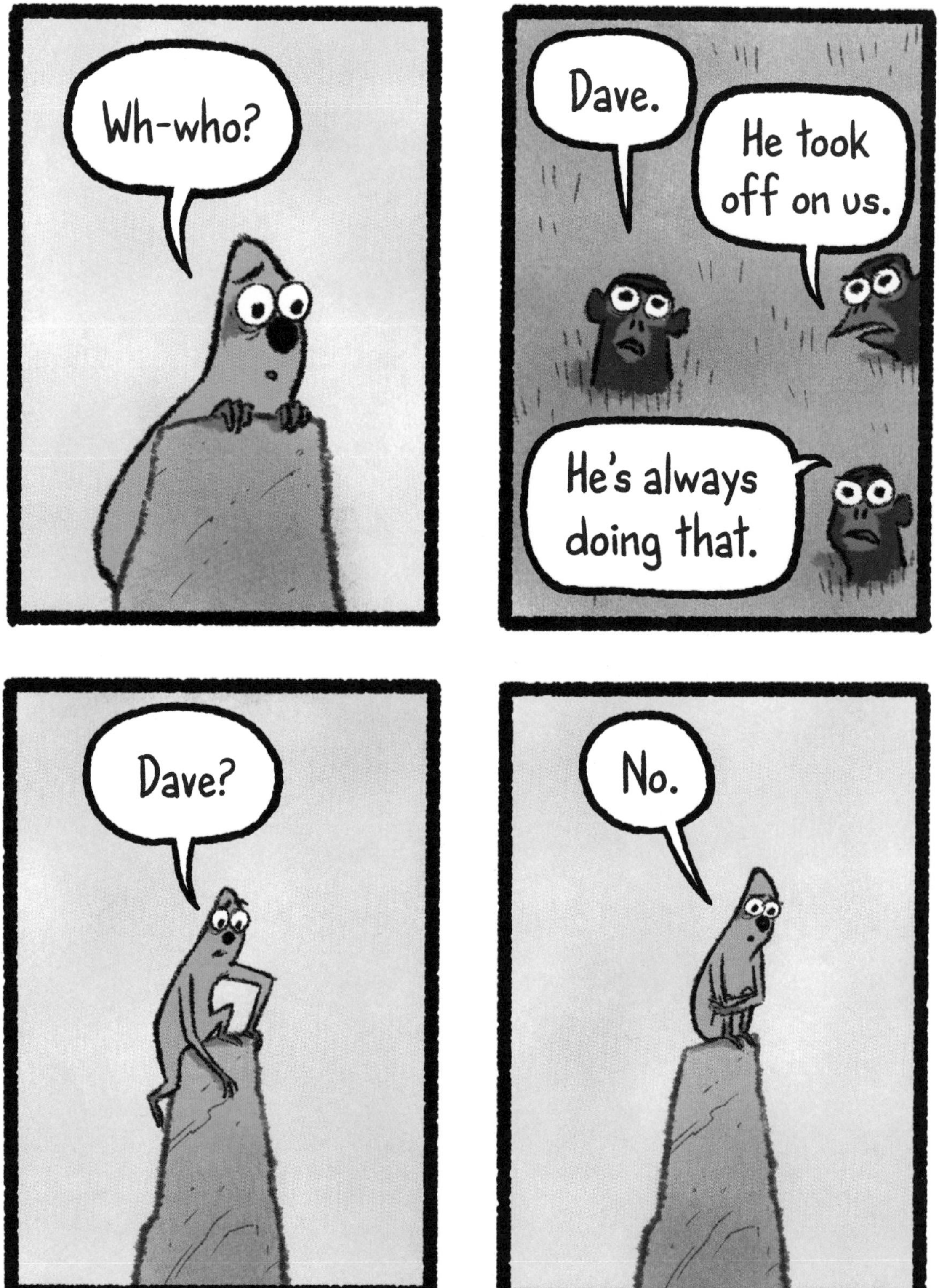
Wh-who?
Dave.
He took off on us.
He's always doing that.
Dave?
No.

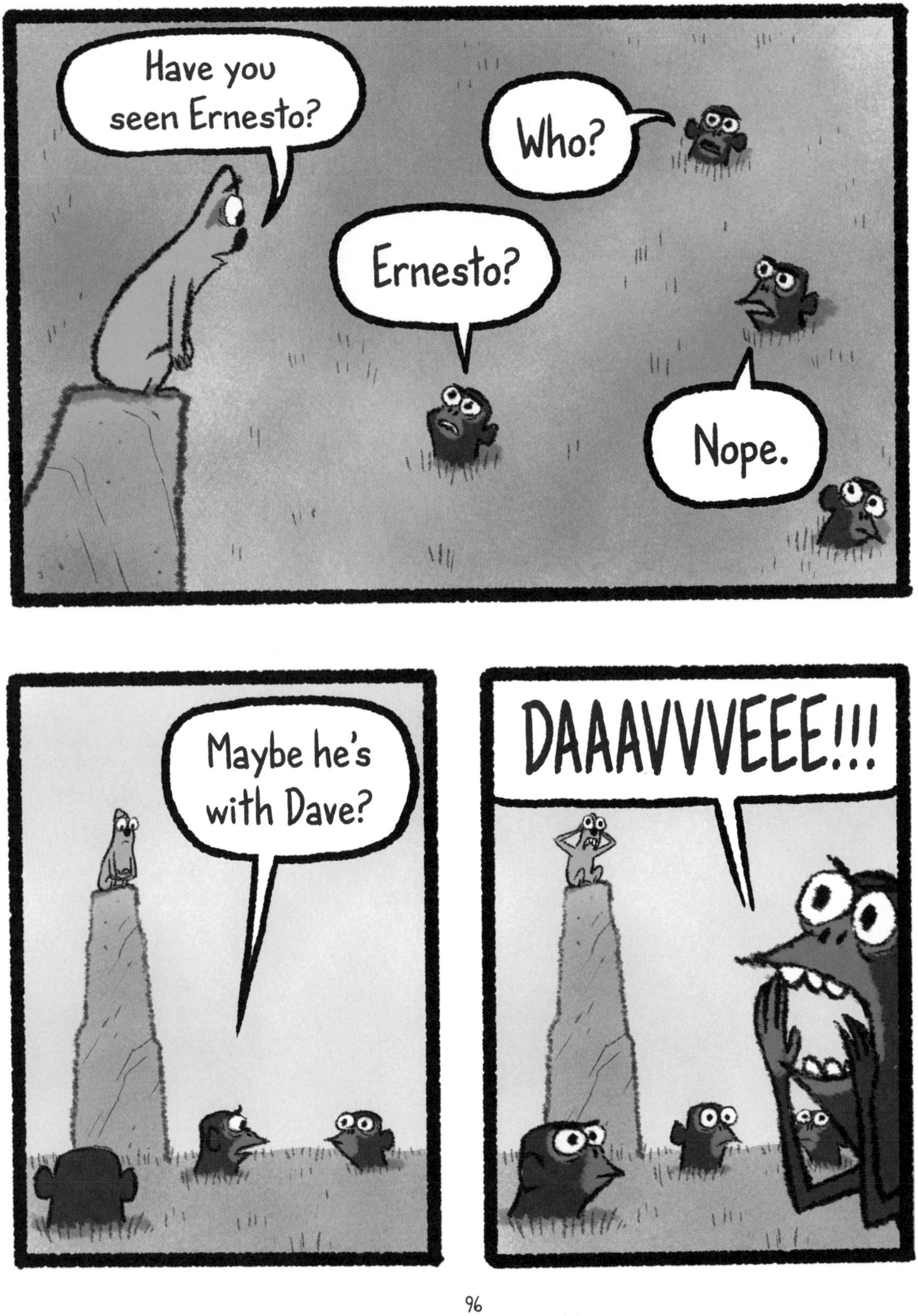
Have you seen Ernesto?
Who?
Ernesto?
Nope.
Maybe he's with Dave?
DAAAVVVEEE!!!

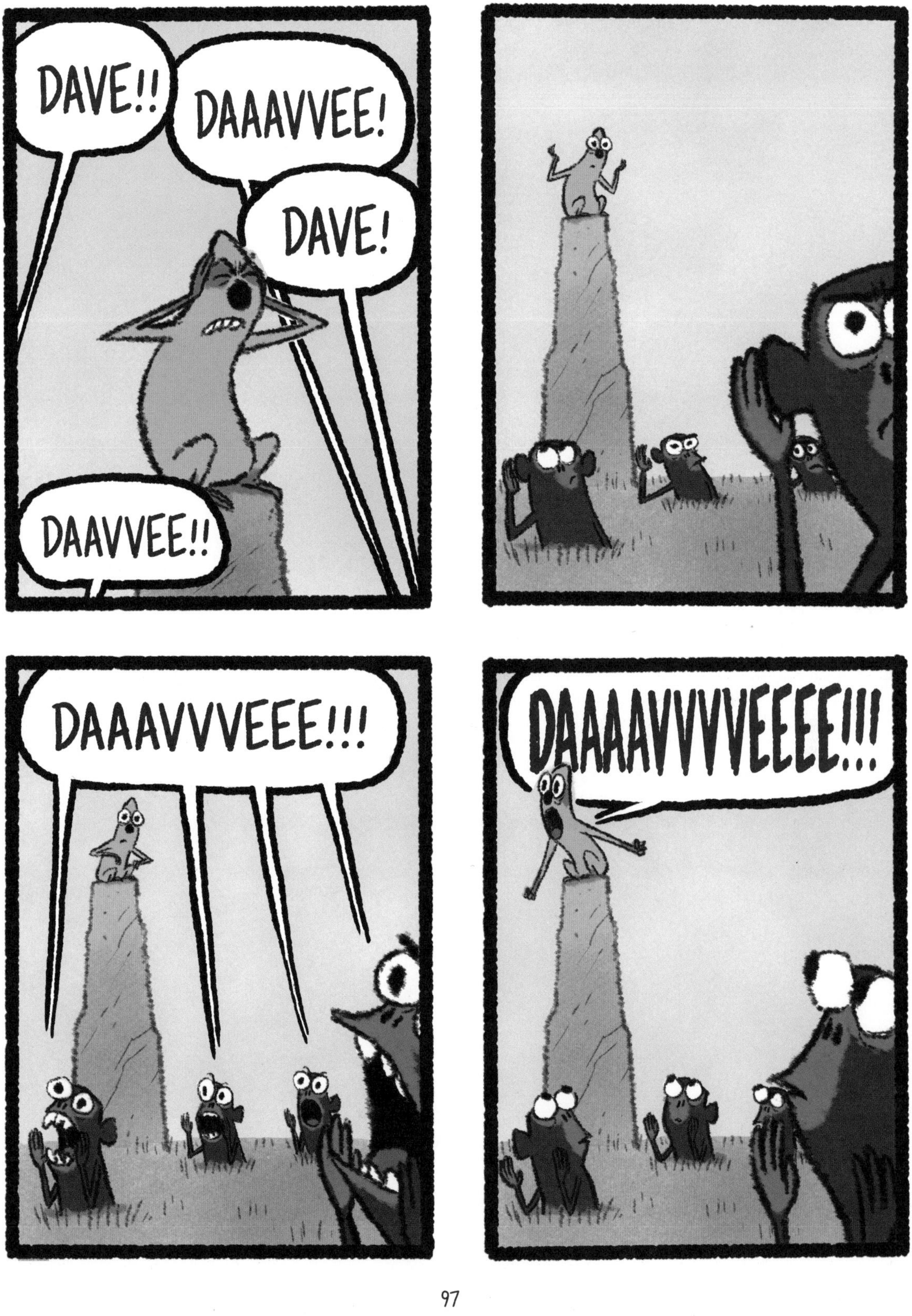
DAVE!!
DAAAVVEE!
DAVE!
DAAVVEE!!
DAAAVVVEEE!!!
DAAAAVVVVEEEE!!!

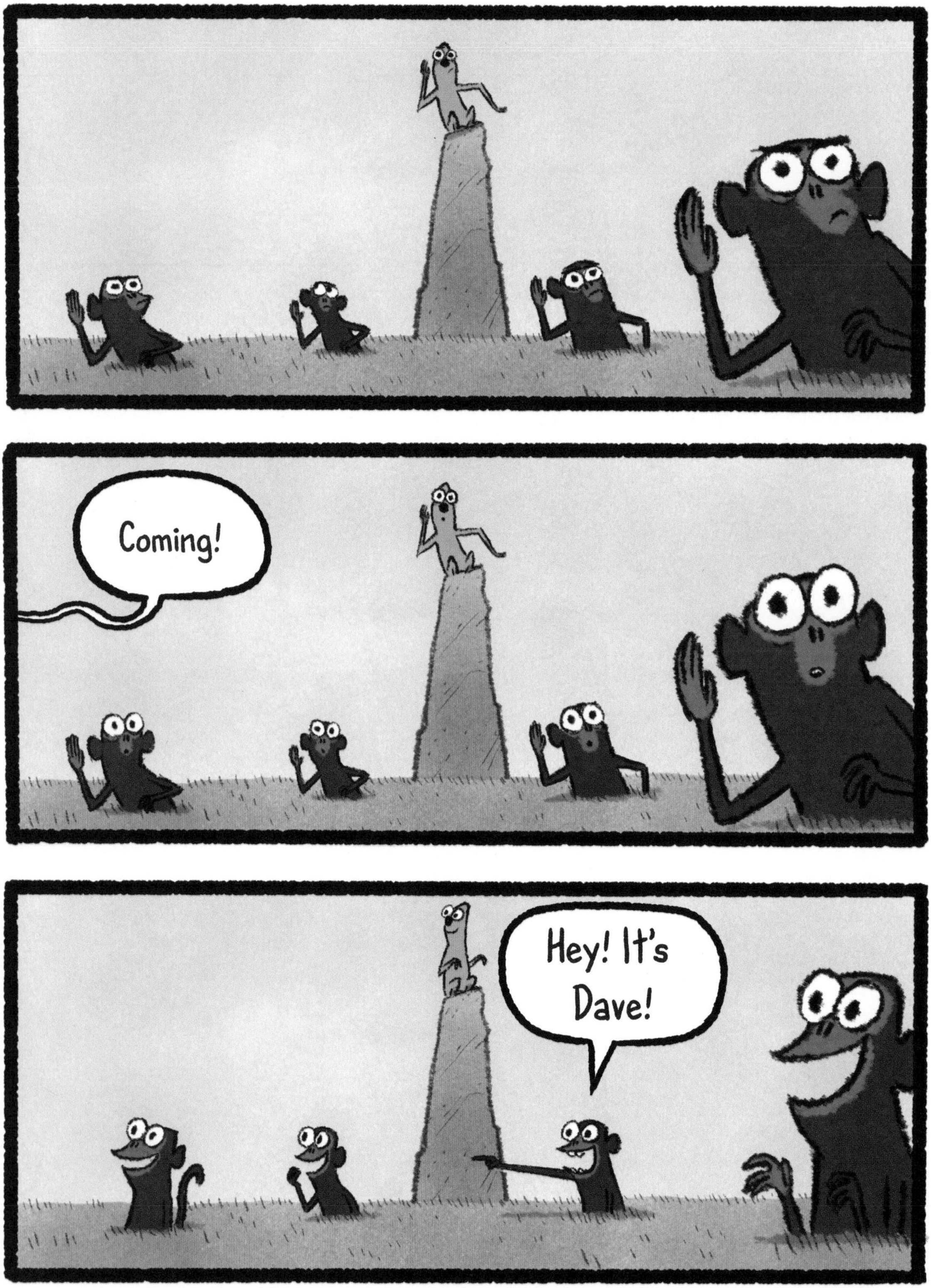
Coming!
Hey! It's Dave!

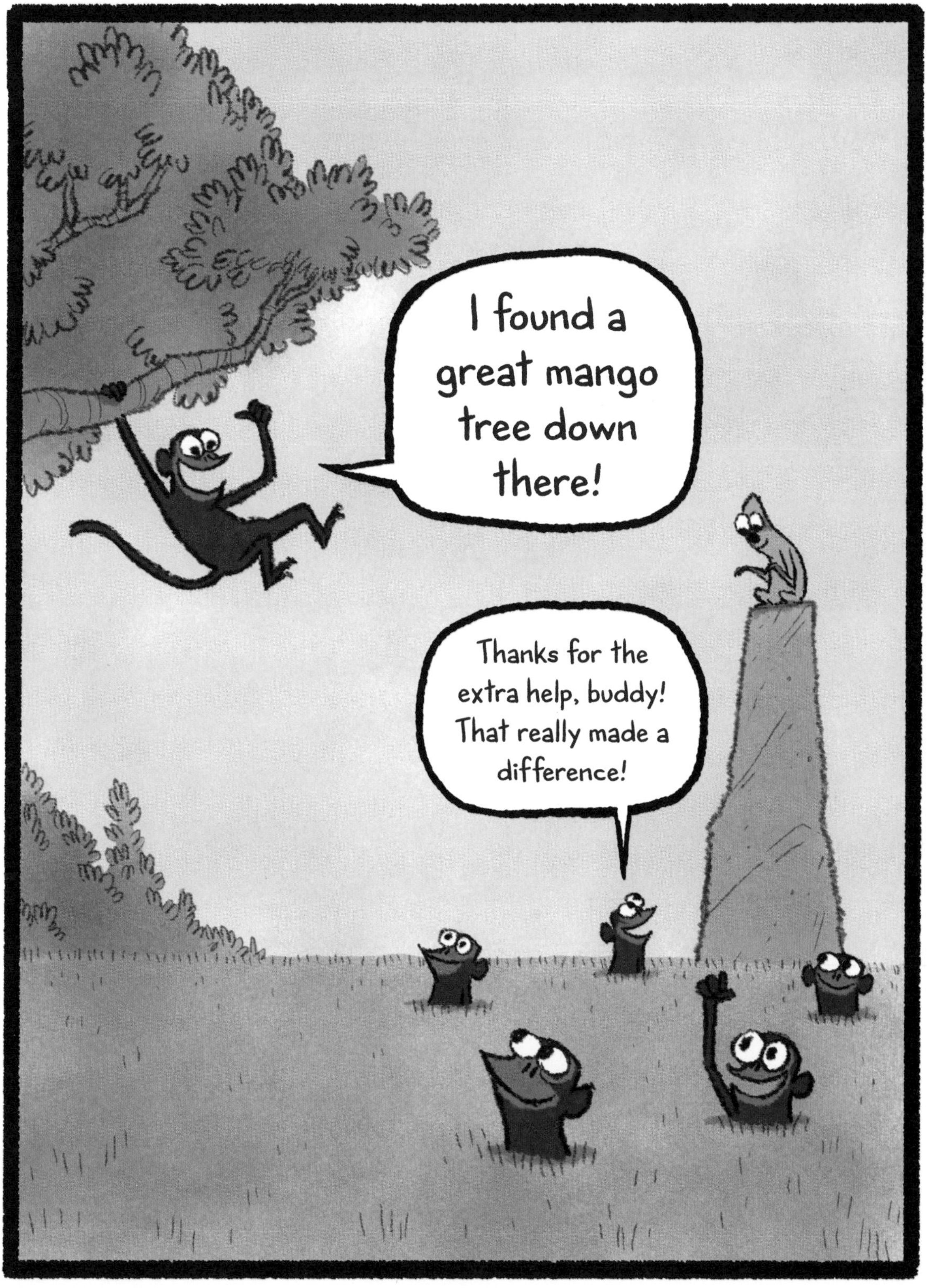
I found a great mango tree down there!
Thanks for the extra help, buddy! That really made a difference!

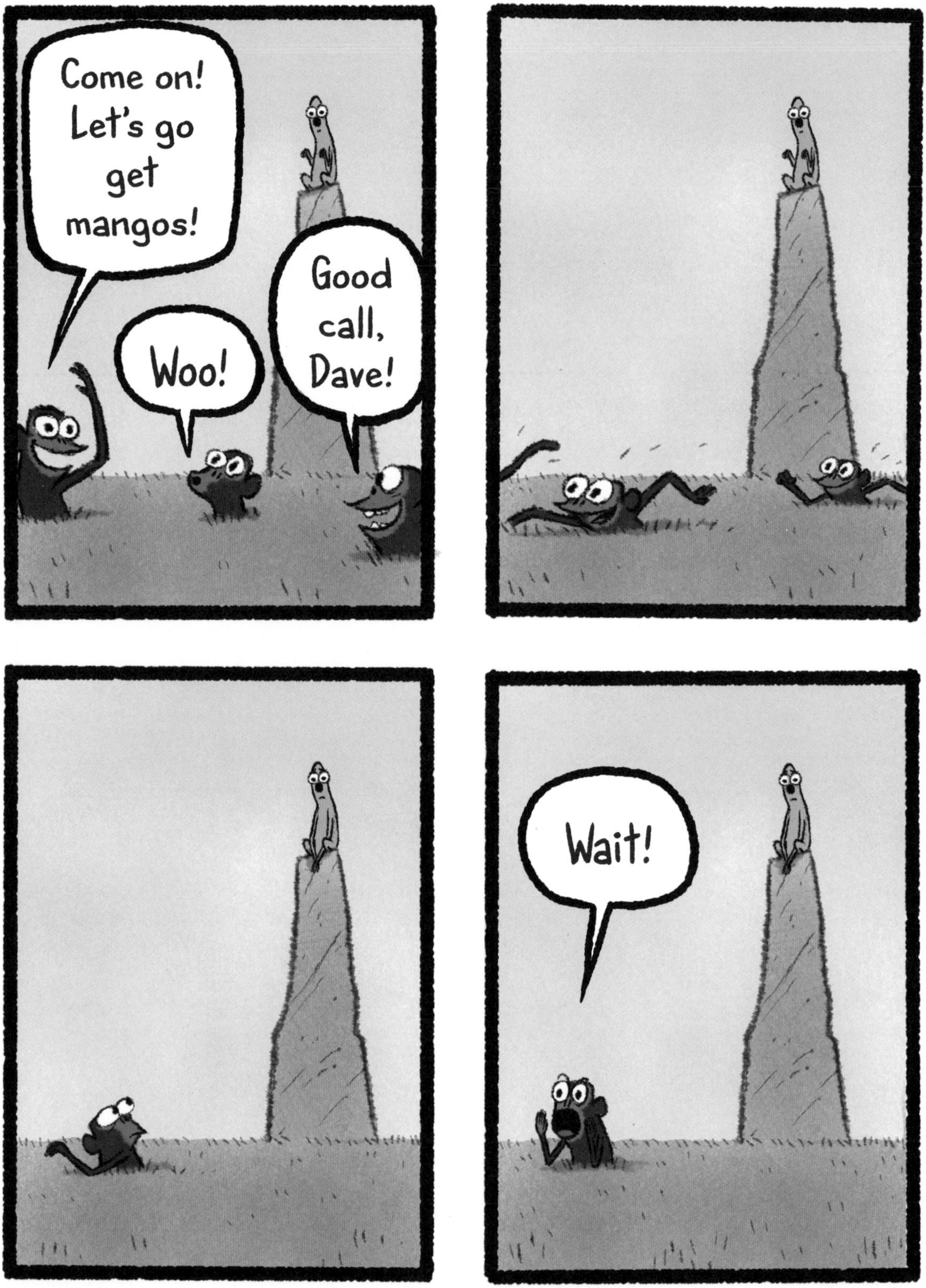
Come on! Let's go get mangos!
Woo!
Good call, Dave!
Wait!

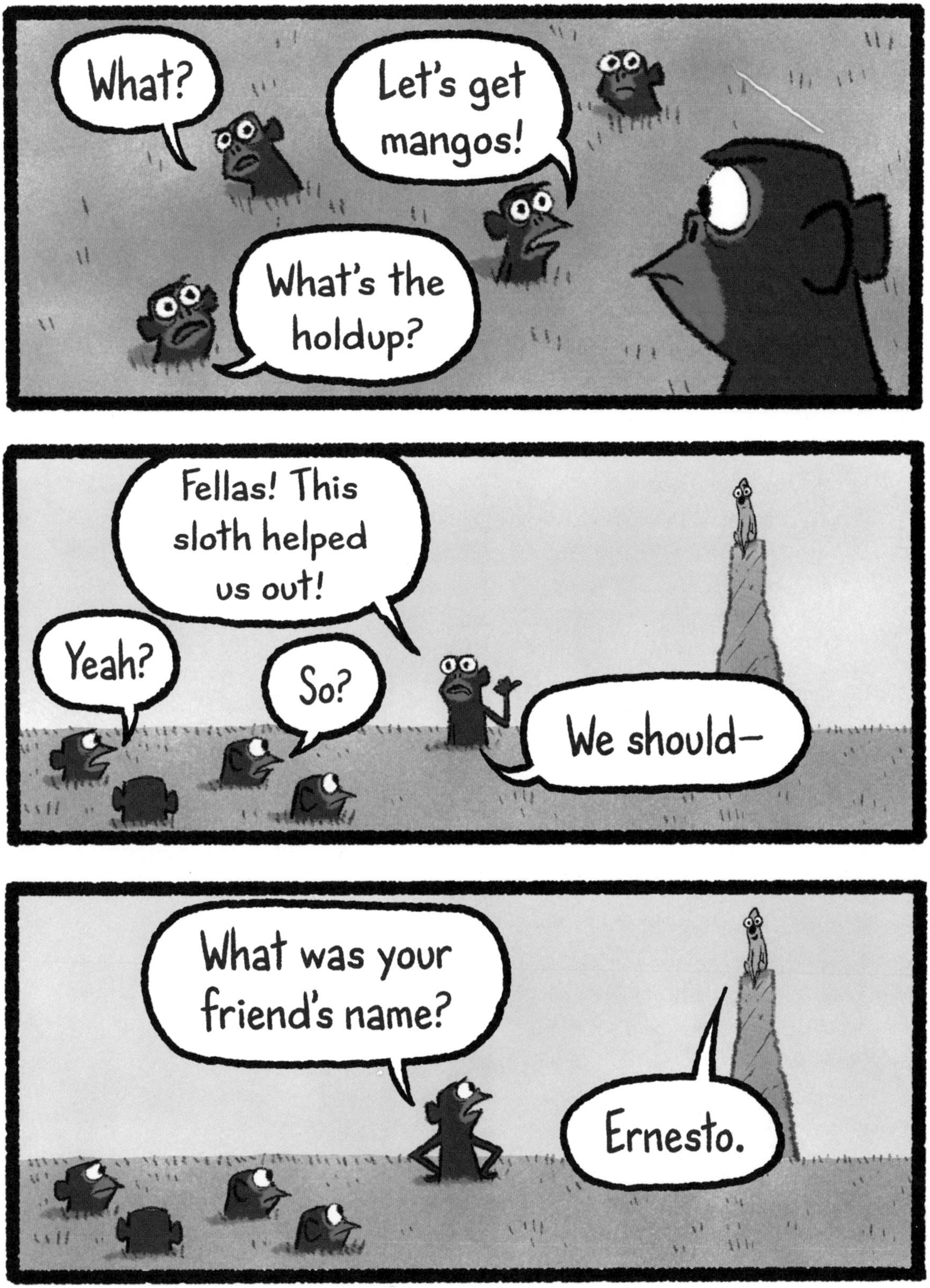
What?
Let's get mangos!
What's the holdup?
Fellas! This sloth helped us out!
Yeah?
So?
We should–
What was your friend's name?
Ernesto.

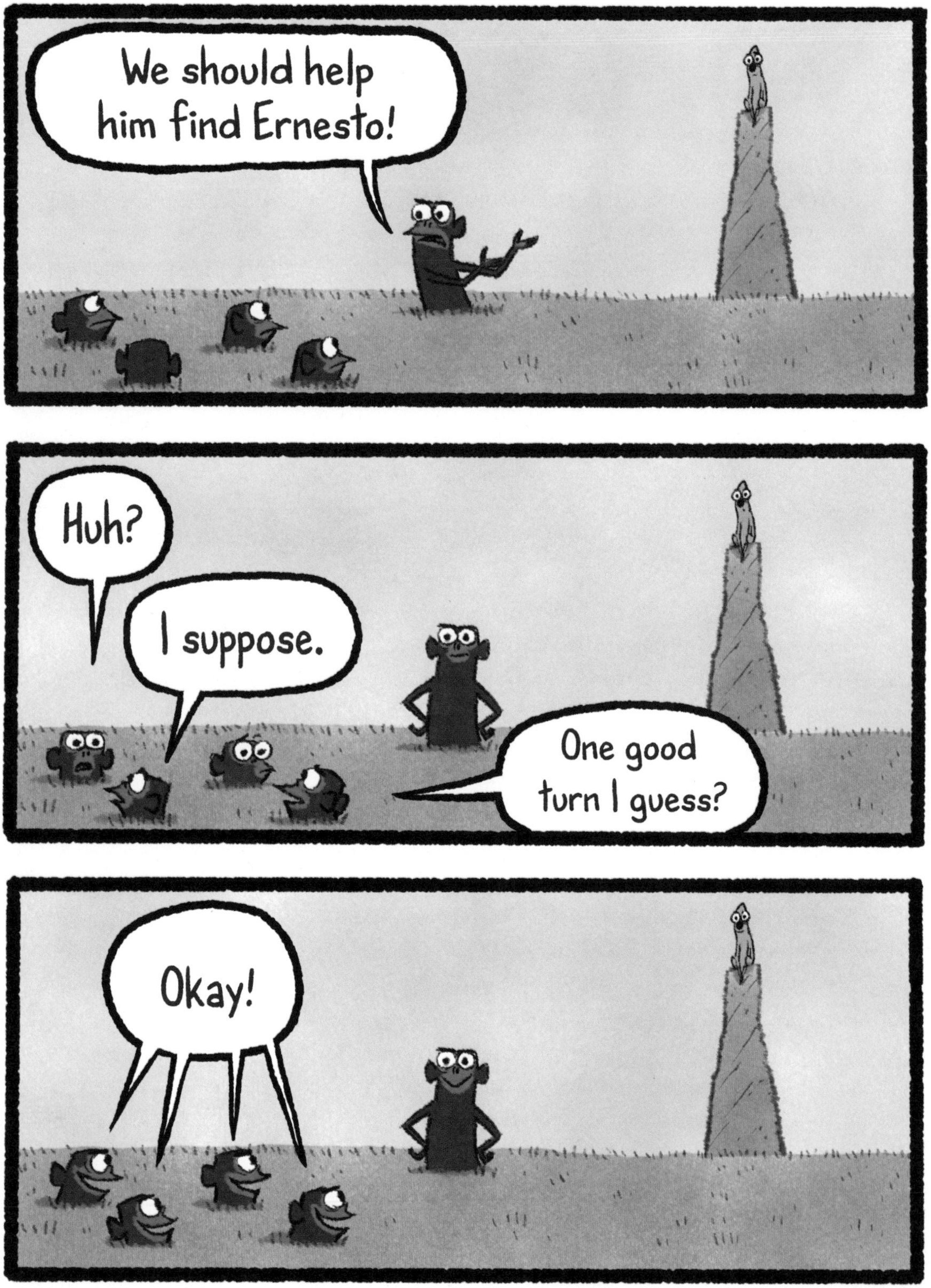
We should help him find Ernesto!
Huh?
I suppose.
One good turn I guess?
Okay!

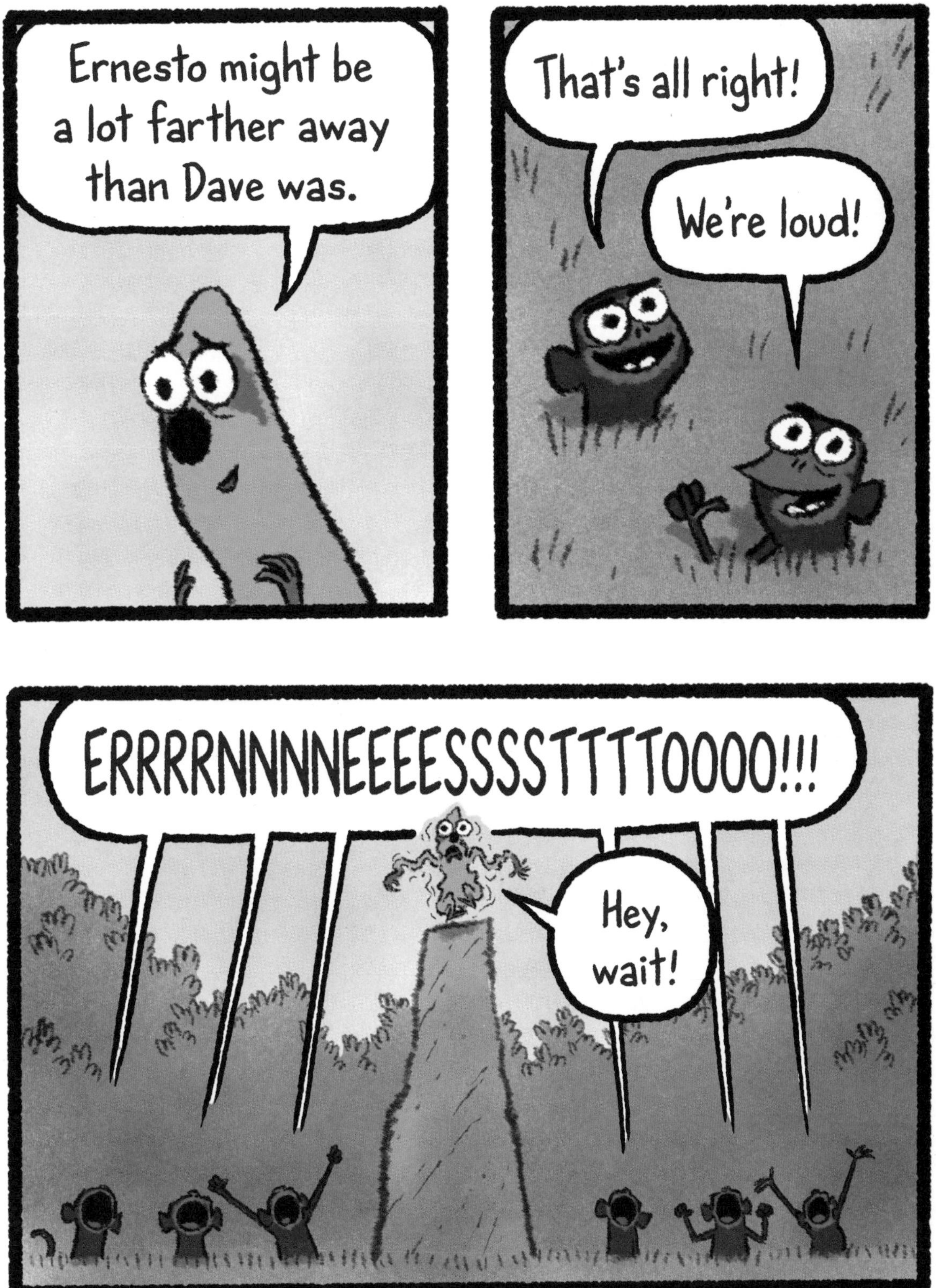
Ernesto might be a lot farther away than Dave was.
That's all right!
We're loud!
ERRRRNNNNEEEESSSSTTTTOOOO!!!
Hey, wait!

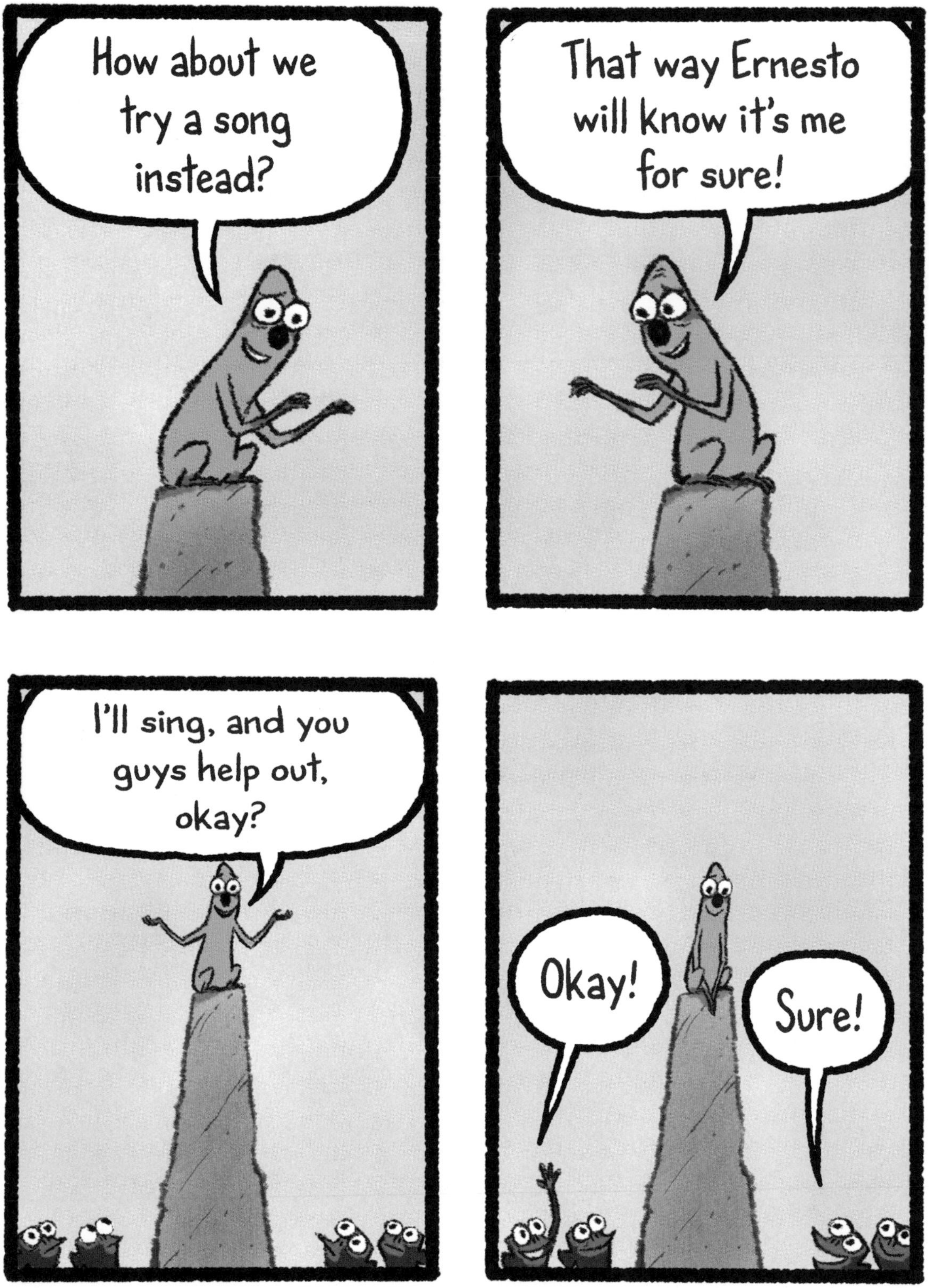
How about we try a song instead?
That way Ernesto will know it's me for sure!
I'll sing, and you guys help out, okay?
Okay!
Sure!

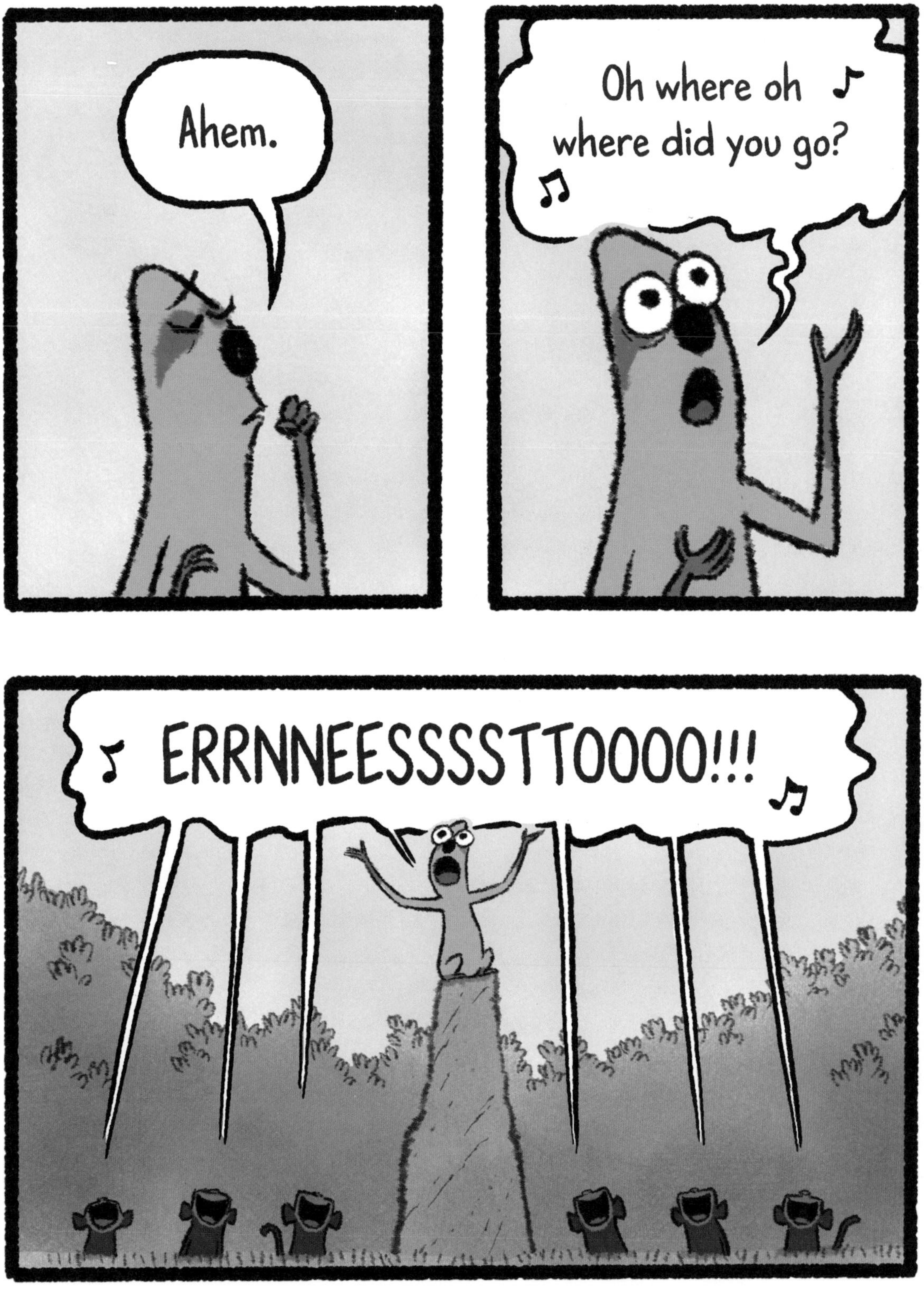
Ahem.
Oh where oh where did you go?
ERRNNEESSSSSTTOOOO!!!

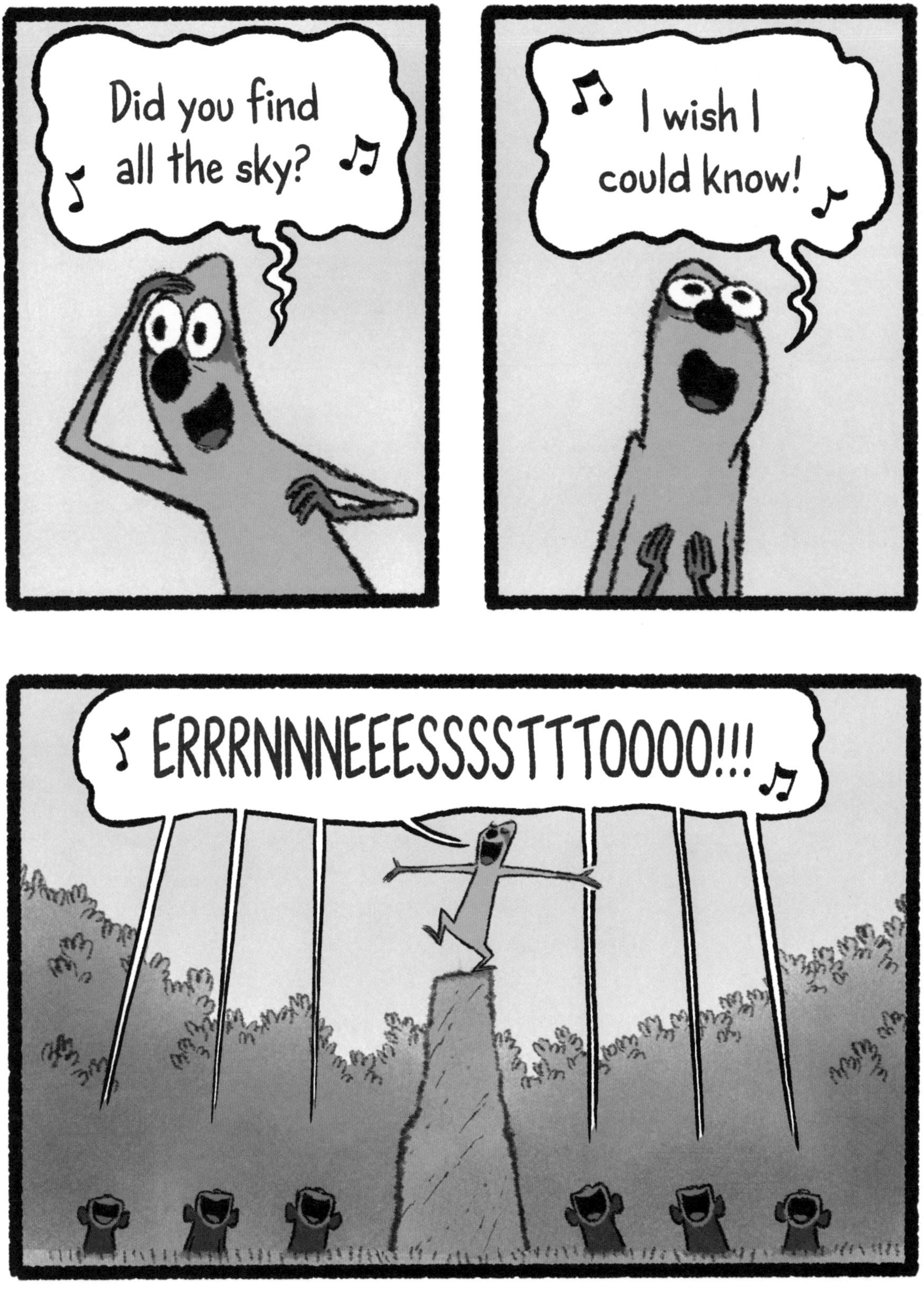
Did you find all the sky?
I wish I could know!
ERRRNNNEEESSSSTTTOOOO!!!

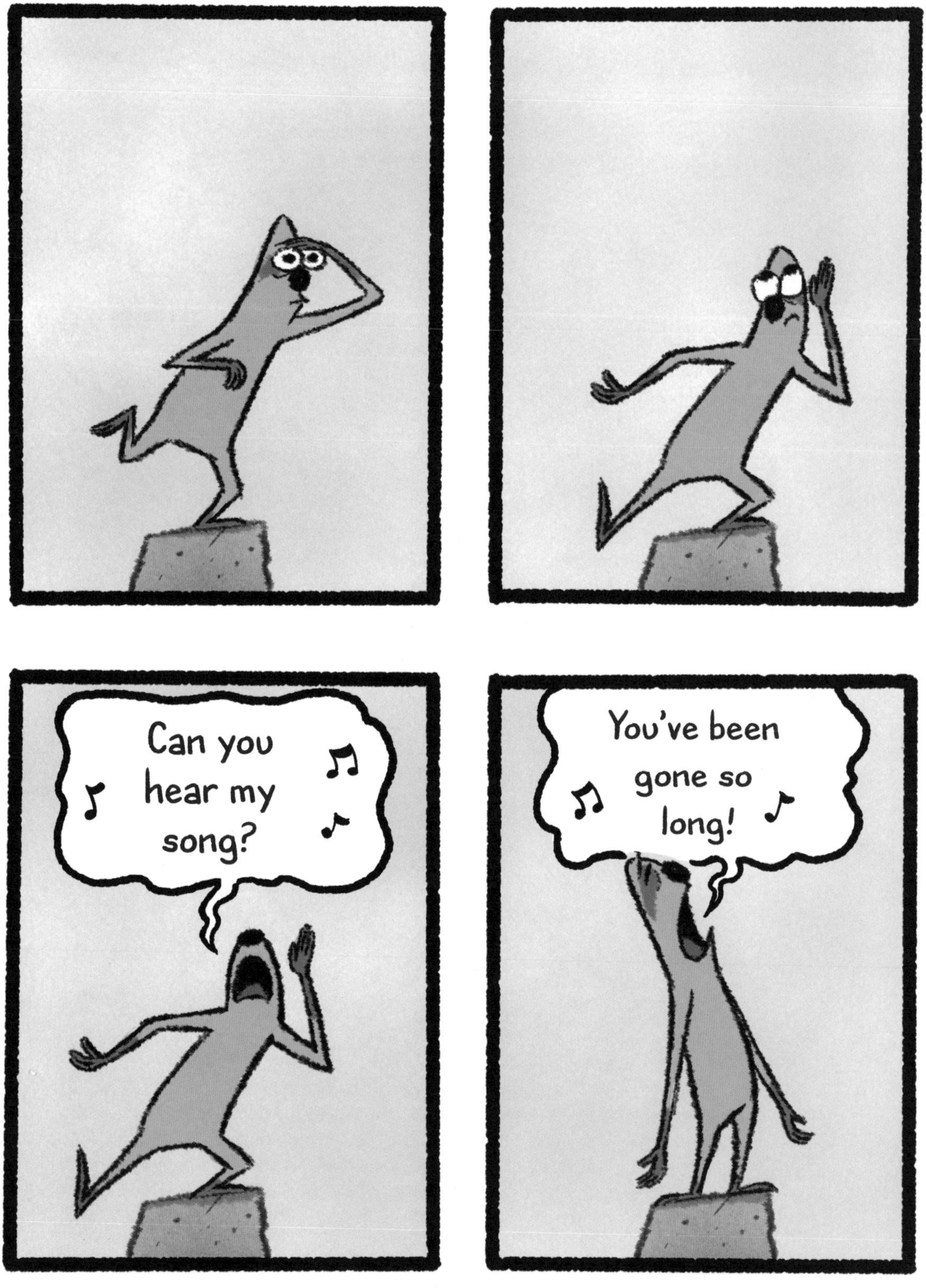
Can you hear my song?
You've been gone so long!

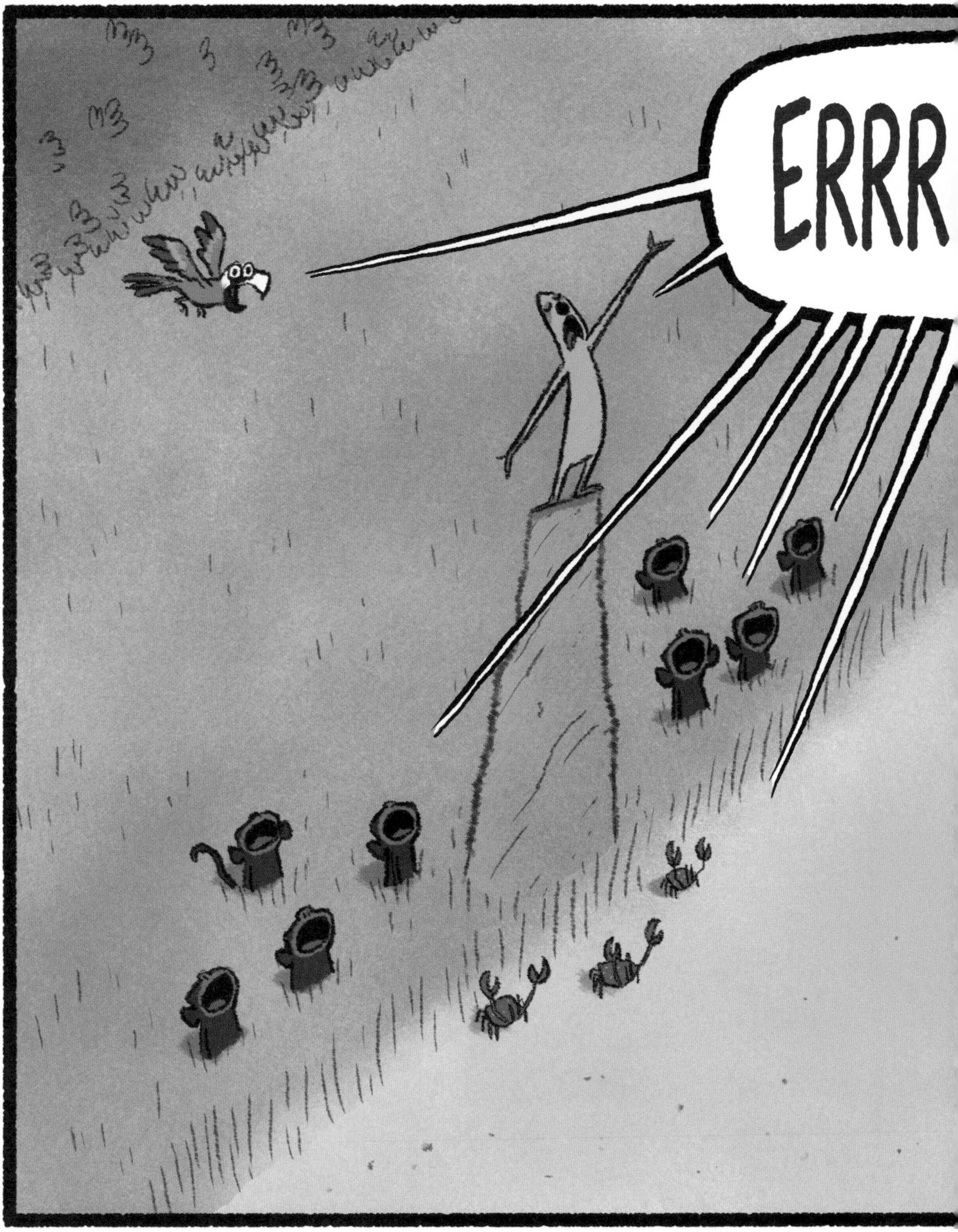
ERRR

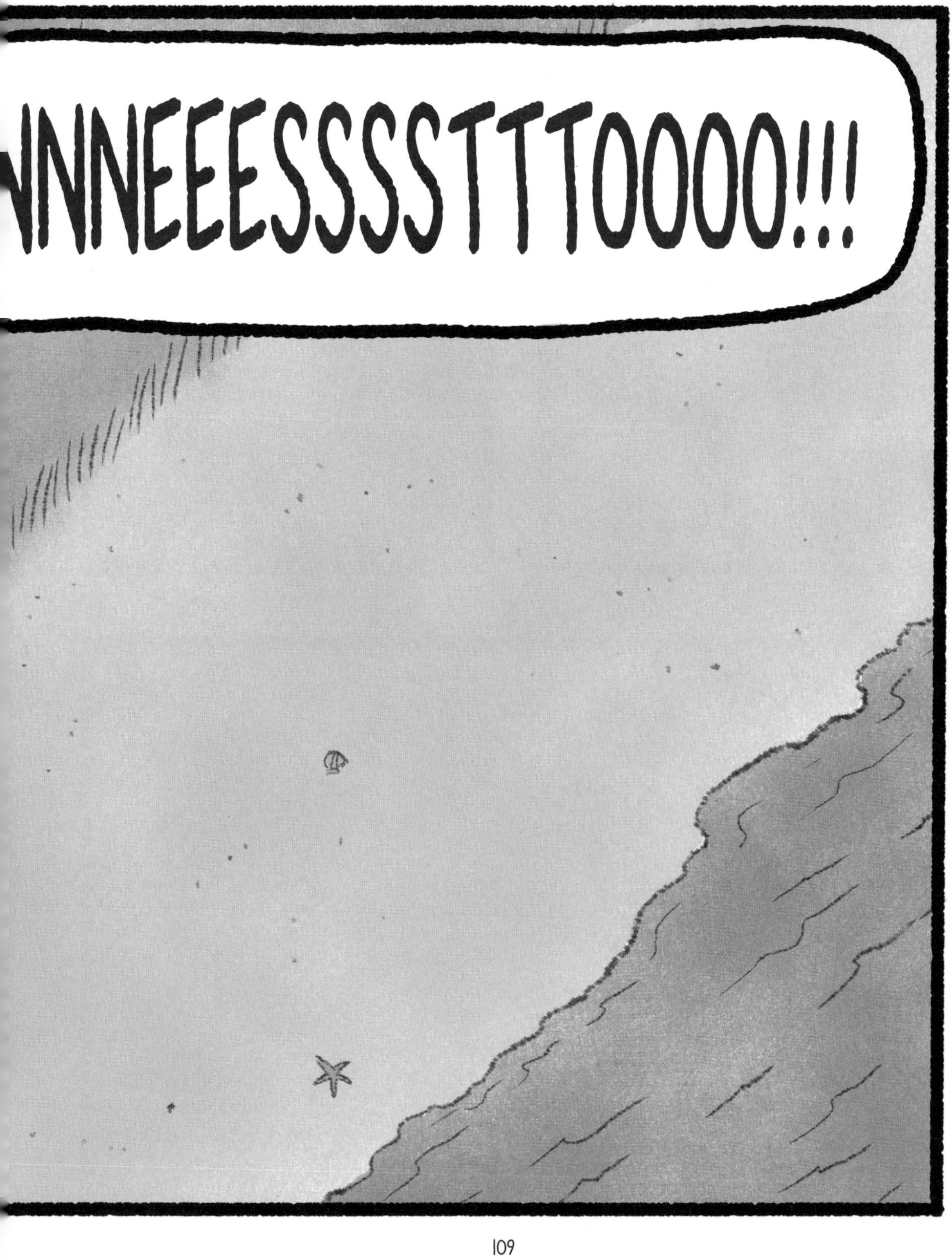
NNEEEESSSSSTTOOOO!!!

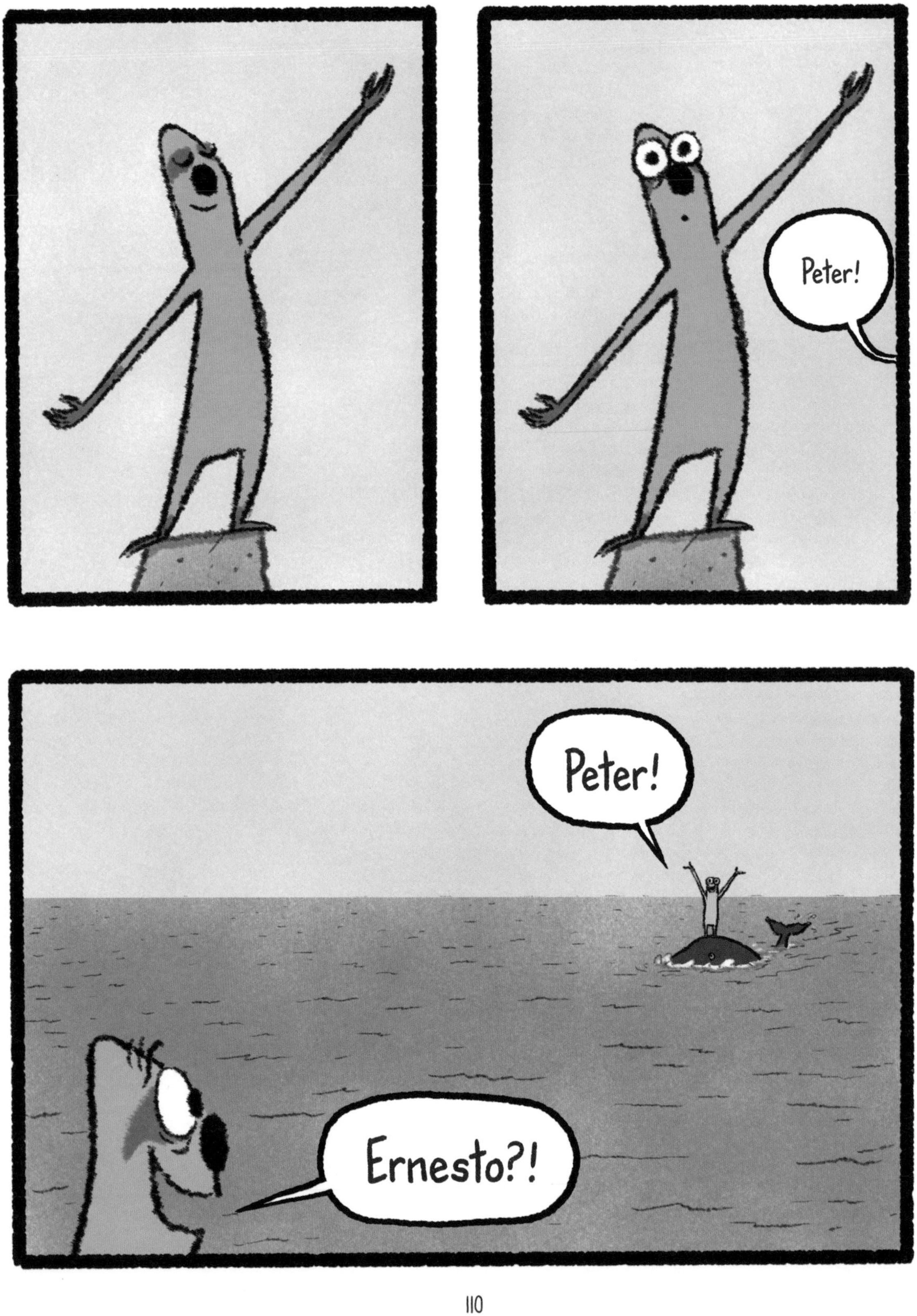
Peter!
Peter!
Ernesto?!

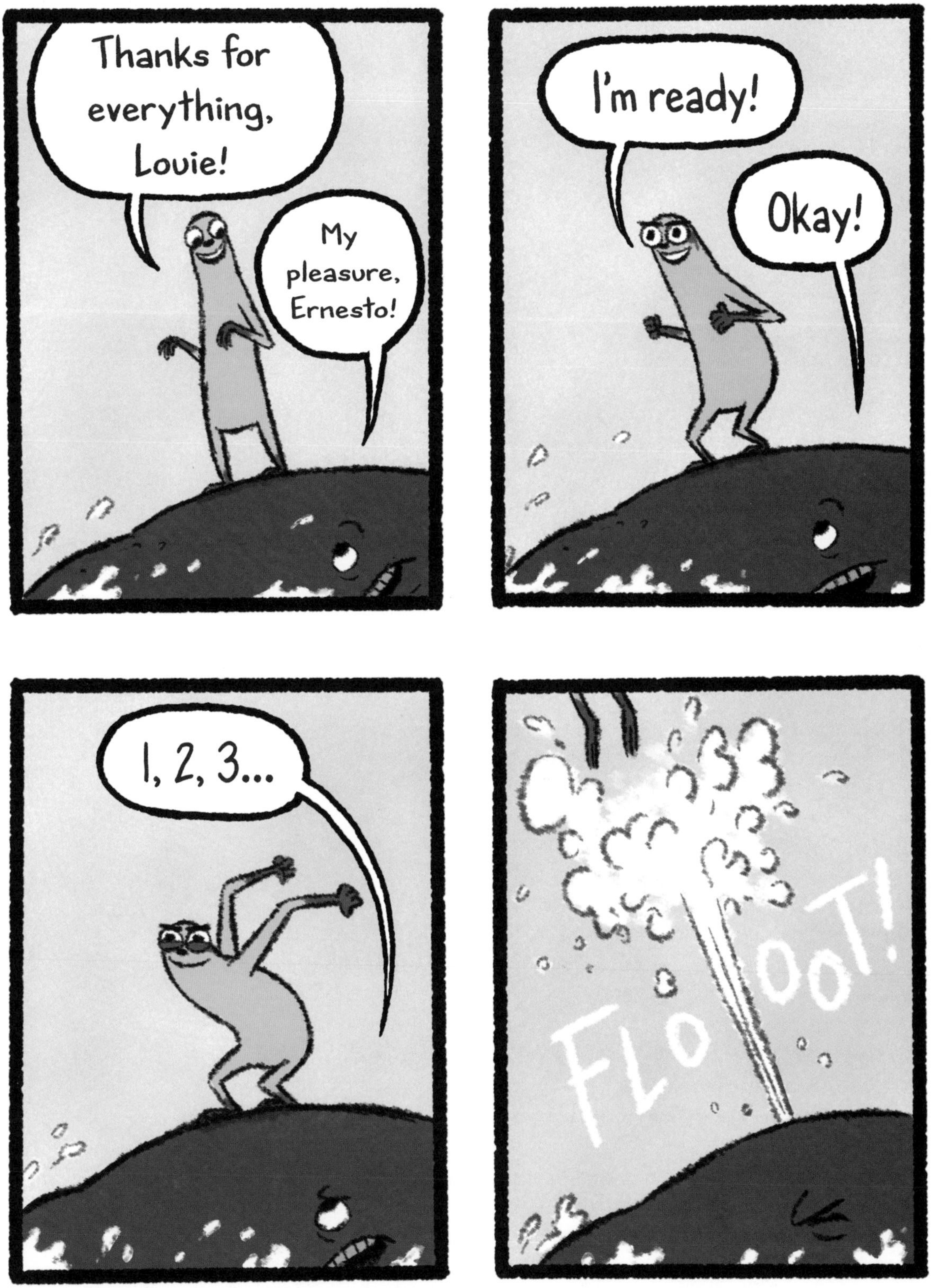
Thanks for everything, Louie!
My pleasure, Ernesto!
I'm ready!
Okay!
1, 2, 3...
FLOOOT!

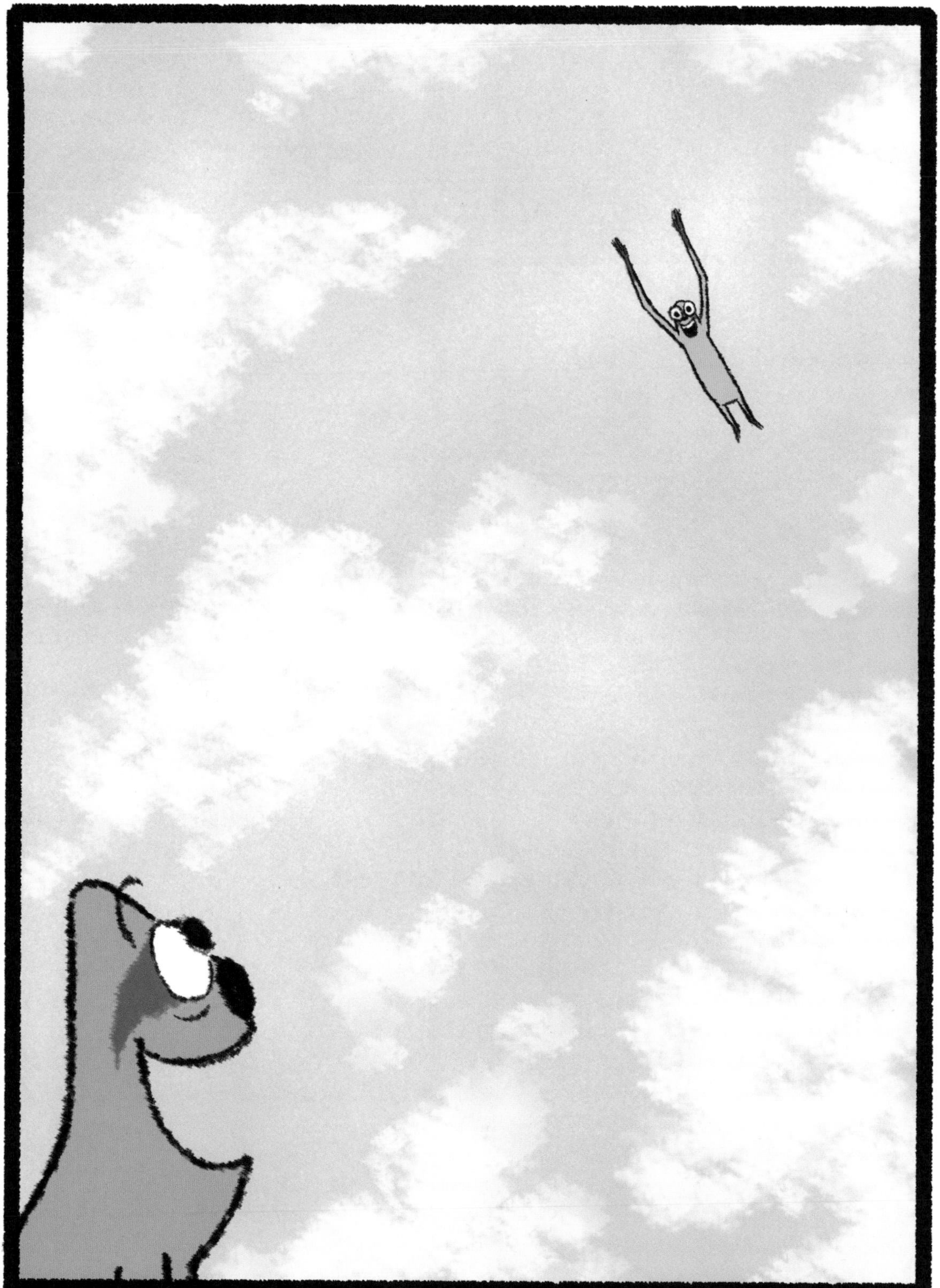

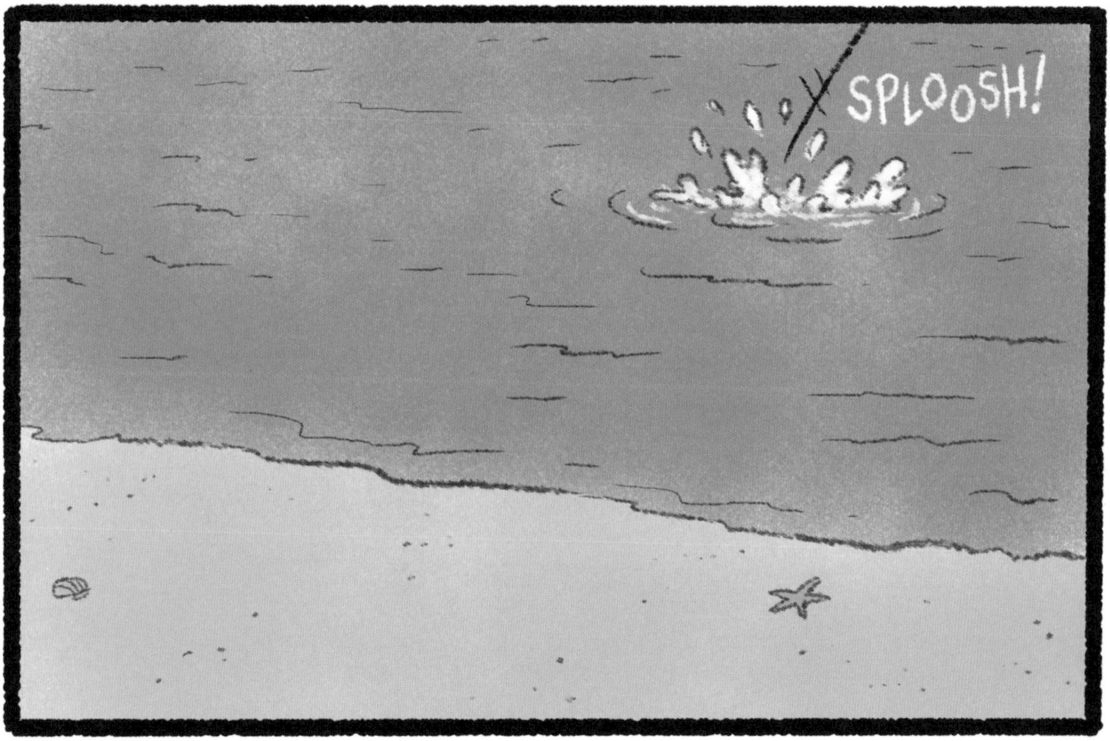
SPLOOSH!

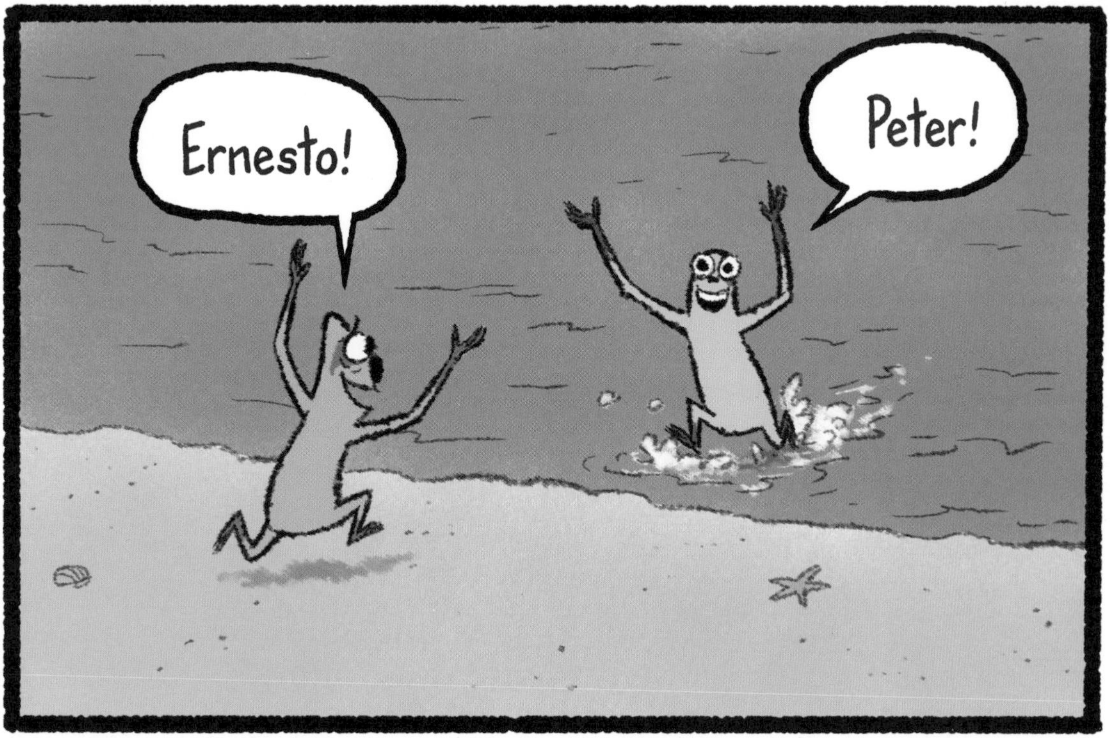
Ernesto!
Peter!

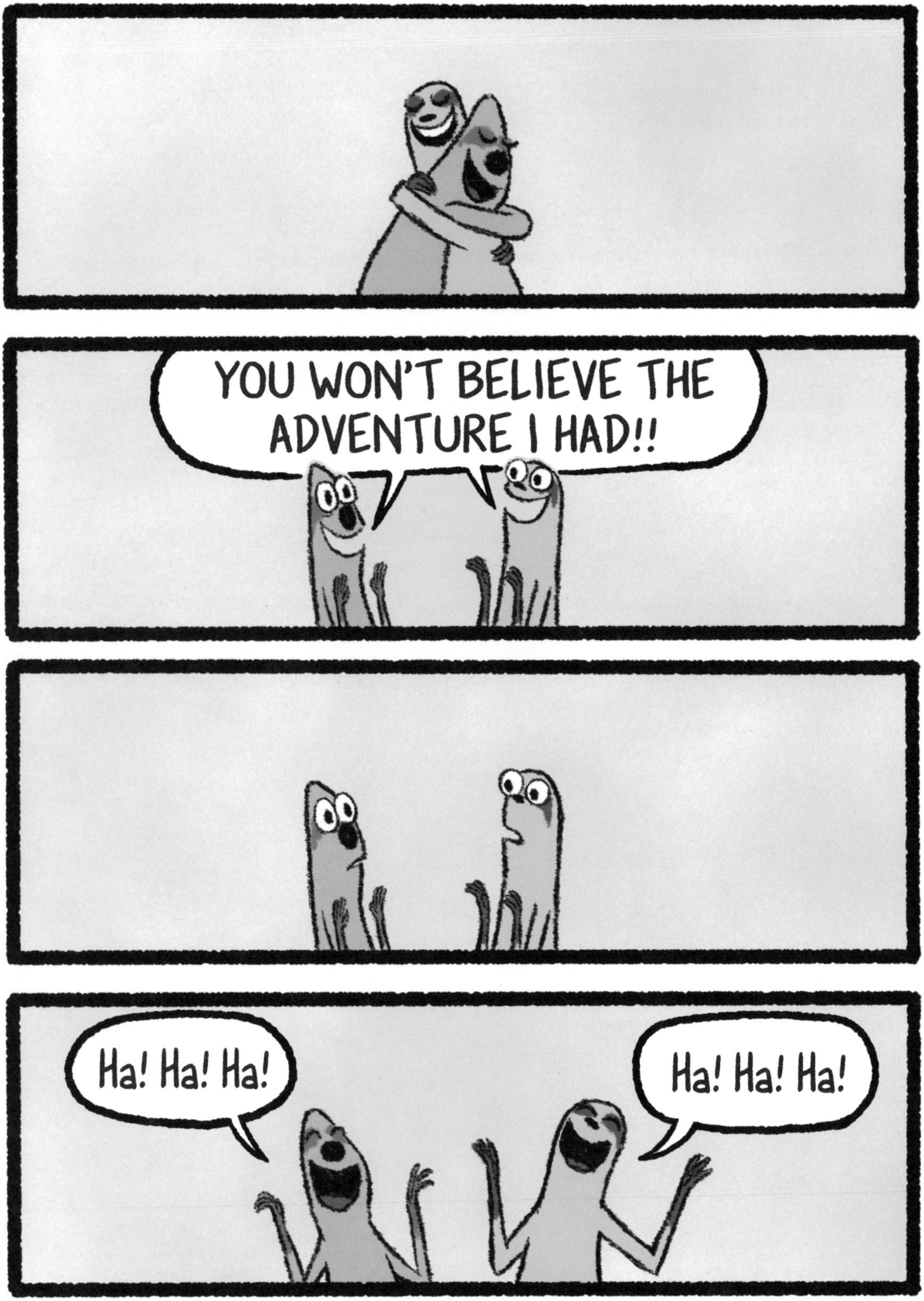
YOU WON'T BELIEVE THE ADVENTURE I HAD!!
Ha! Ha! Ha!
Ha! Ha! Ha!

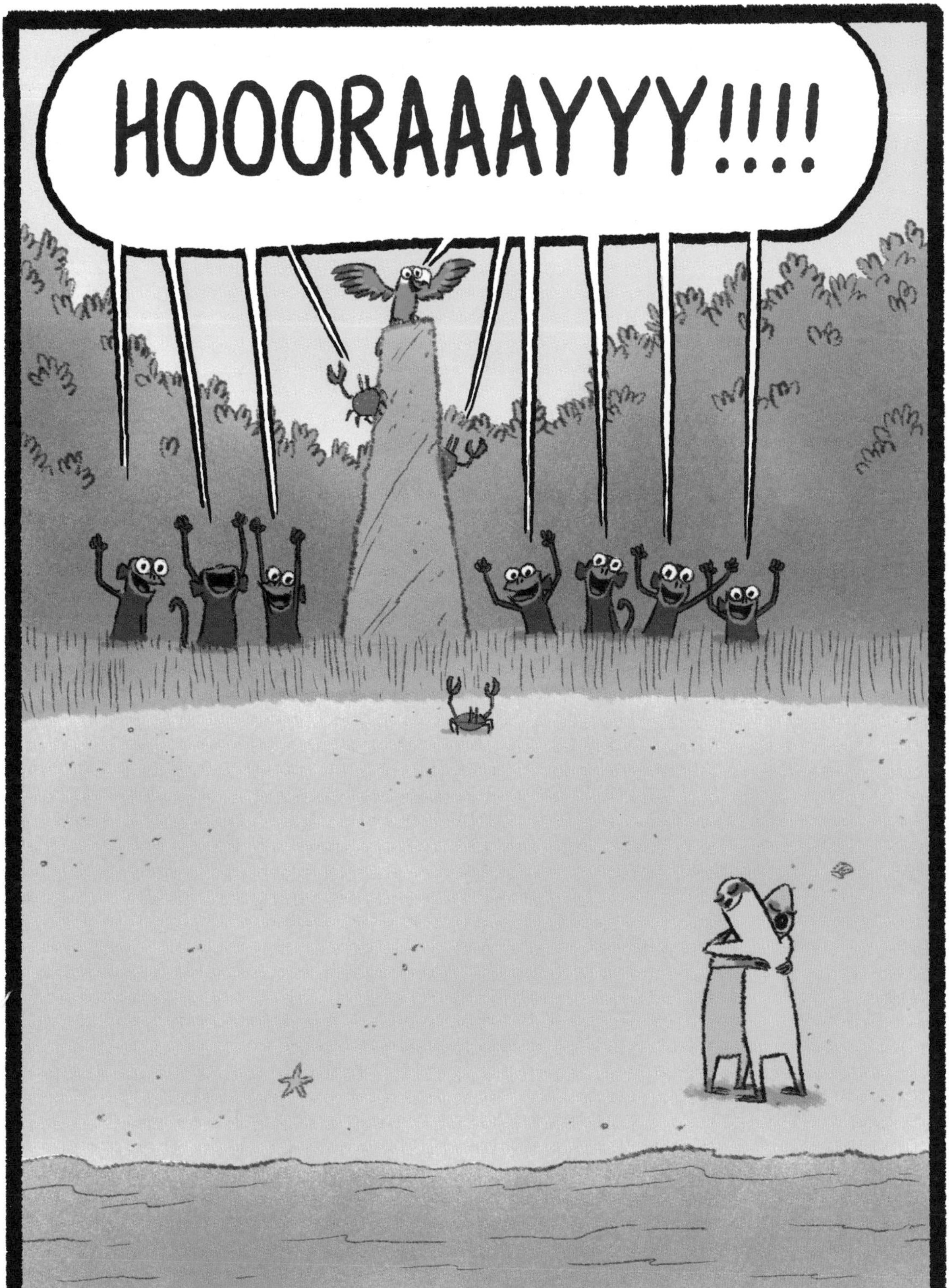
HOOORAAAYYY!!!!

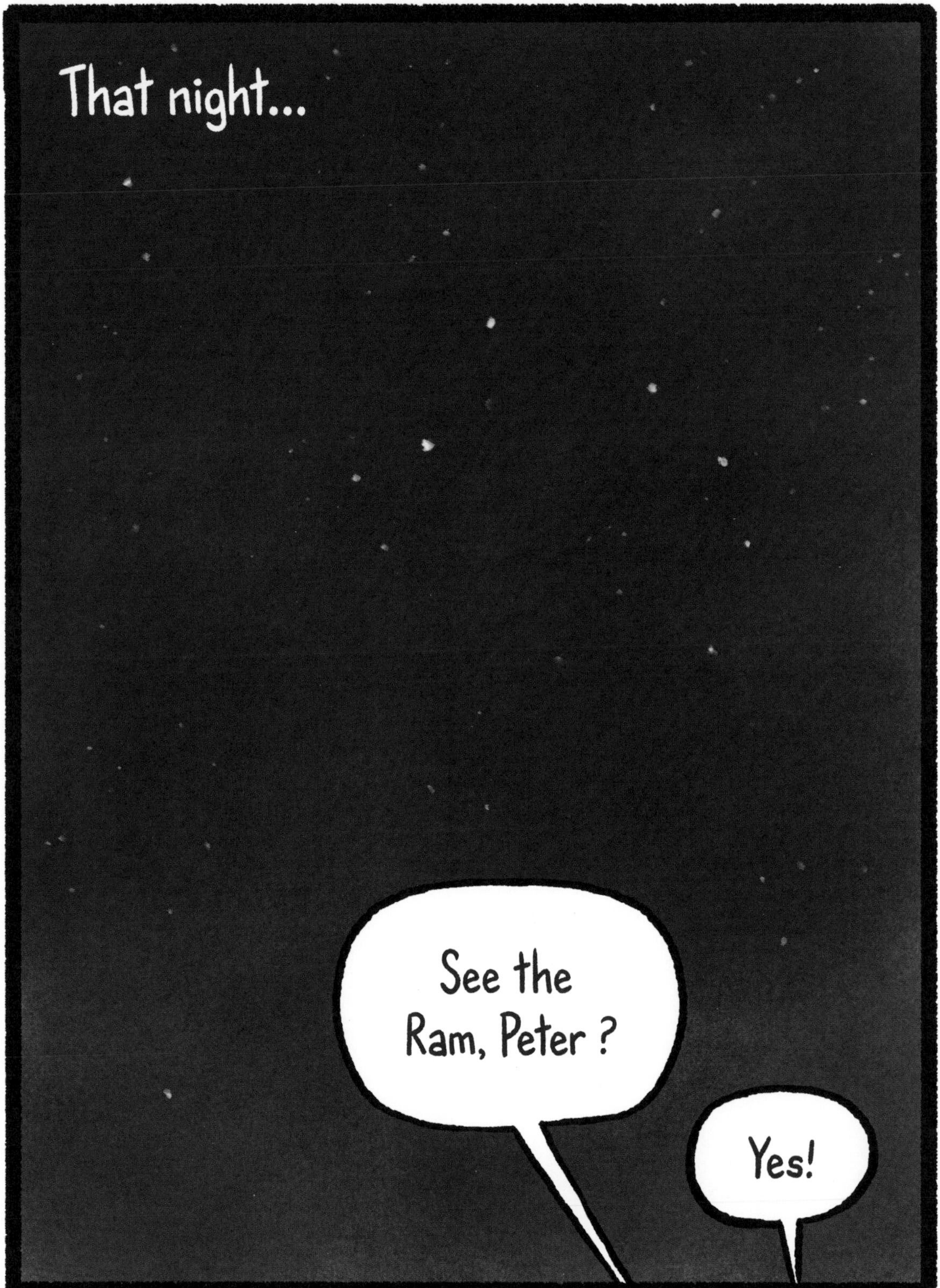
That night...
See the Ram, Peter ?
Yes!

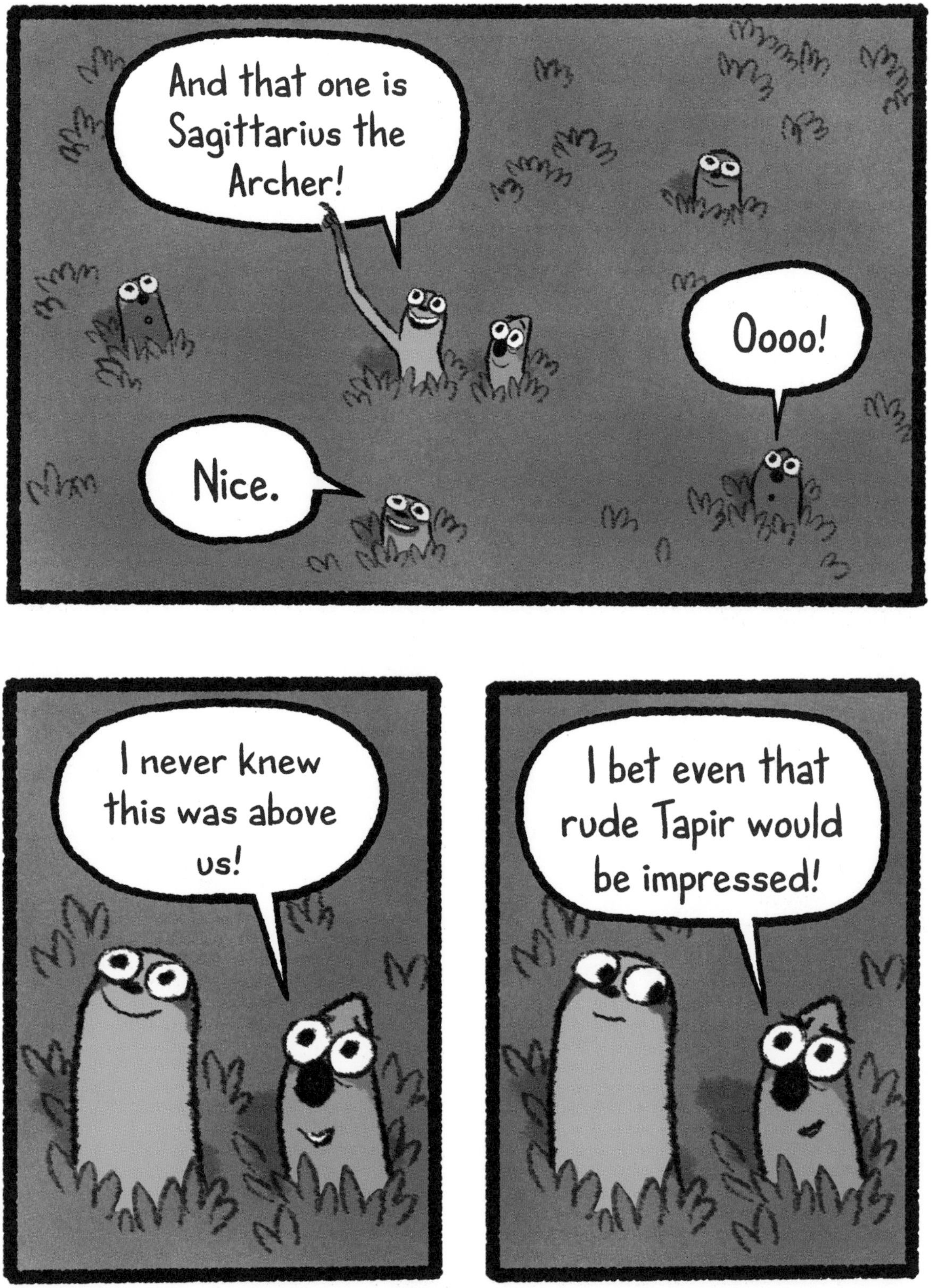
And that one is Sagittarius the Archer!
Oooo!
Nice.
I never knew this was above us!
I bet even that rude Tapir would be impressed!

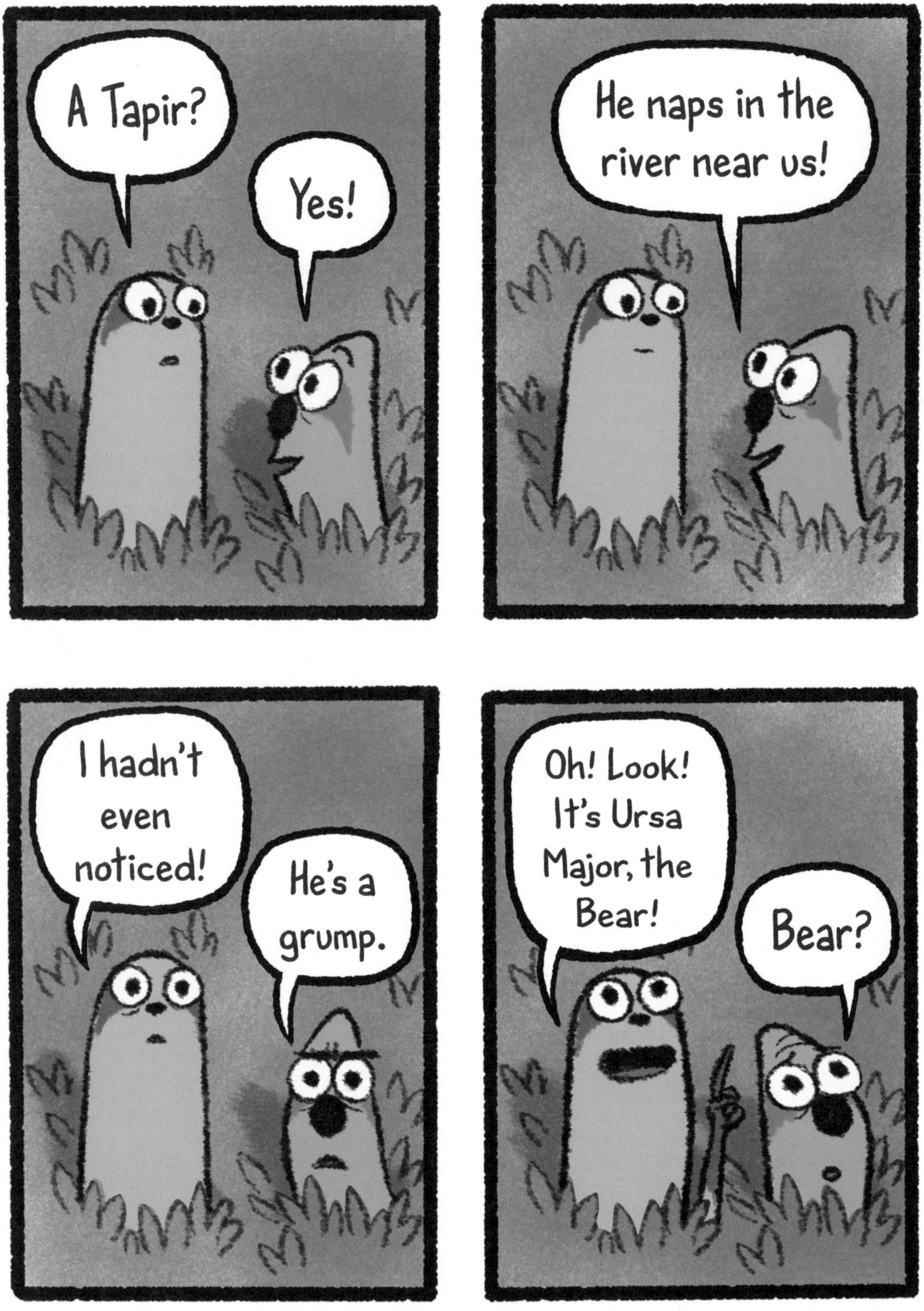
A Tapir?
Yes!
He naps in the river near us!
I hadn't even noticed!
He's a grump.
Oh! Look! It's Ursa Major, the Bear!
Bear?

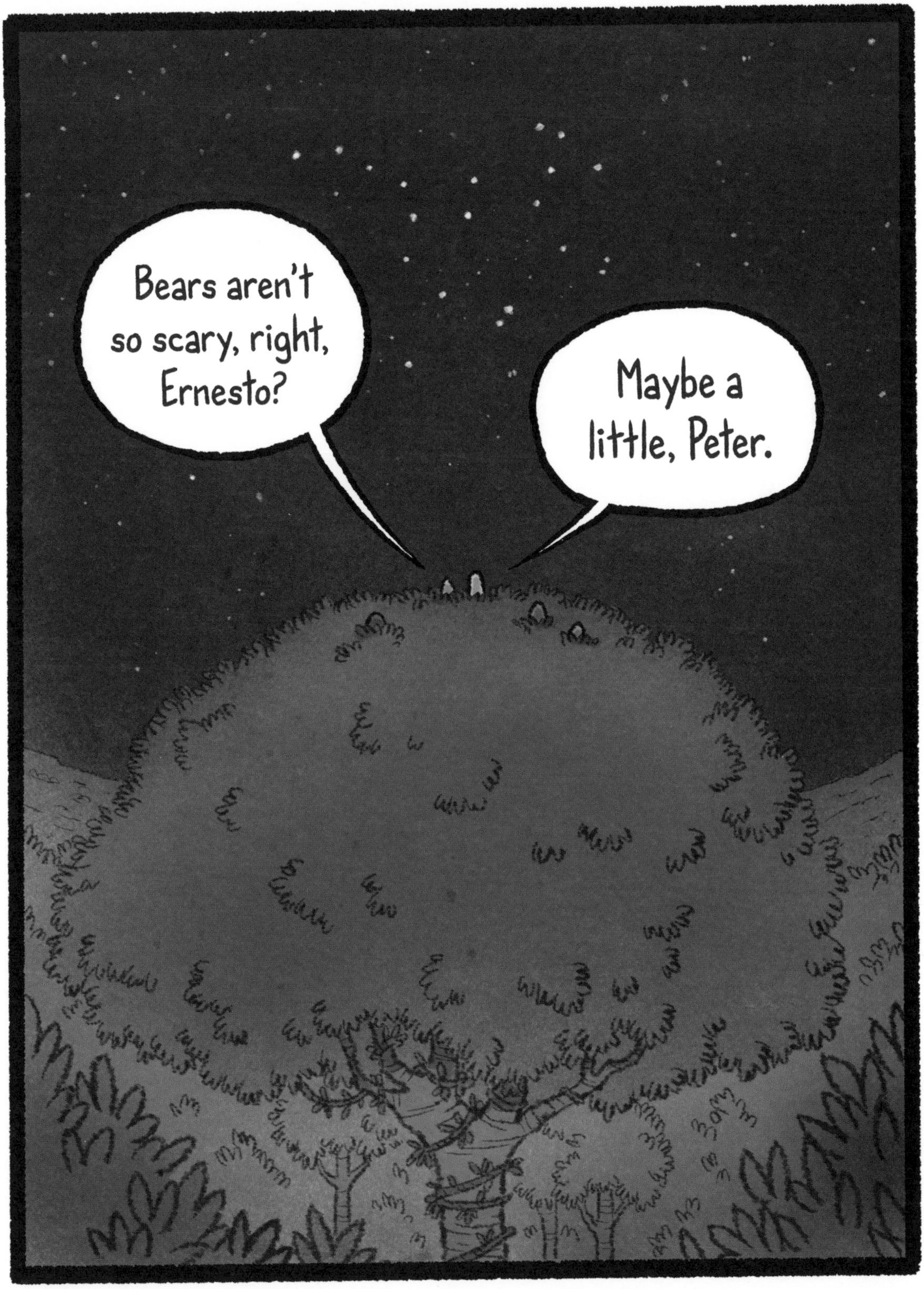
Bears aren't so scary, right, Ernesto?
Maybe a little, Peter.

Stay tuned . . .
for more adventures of

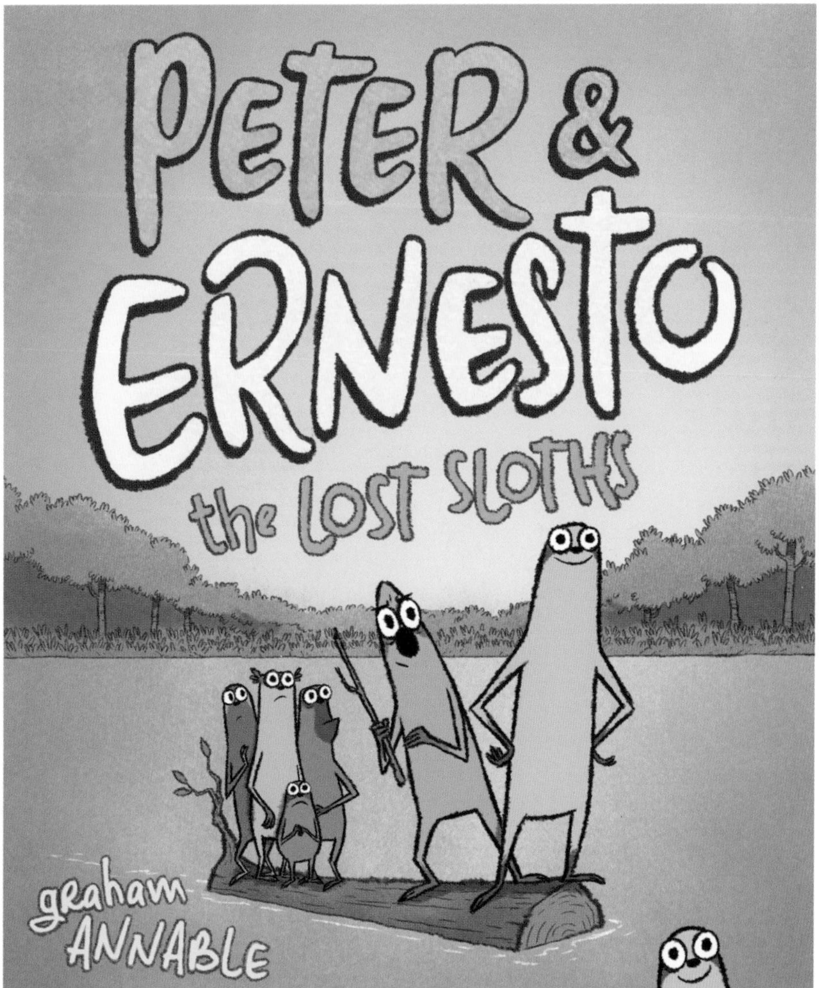
PETER & ERNESTO
the LOST SLOTHS
graham ANNABLE

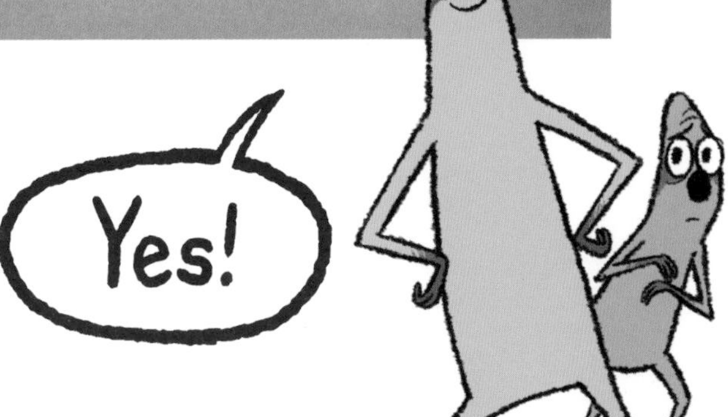
Yes!

:01
First Second

Copyright © 2018 by Graham Annable

Published by First Second
First Second is an imprint of Roaring Brook Press, a division of Holtzbrinck Publishing Holdings Limited Partnership
175 Fifth Avenue, New York, NY 10010

Library of Congress Control Number: 2017941165

ISBN: 978-1-62672-561-4

Our books may be purchased in bulk for promotional, educational, or business use. Please contact your local bookseller or the Macmillan Corporate and Premium Sales Department at (800) 221-7945 ext. 5442 or by e-mail at MacmillanSpecialMarkets@macmillan.com.

First edition, 2018
Book design by Danielle Ceccolini
Printed in China by 1010 Printing International Limited, North Point, Hong Kong

The entire story was created using customized brushes in Photoshop and hand drawn on a Cintiq monitor.

7 9 10 8 6

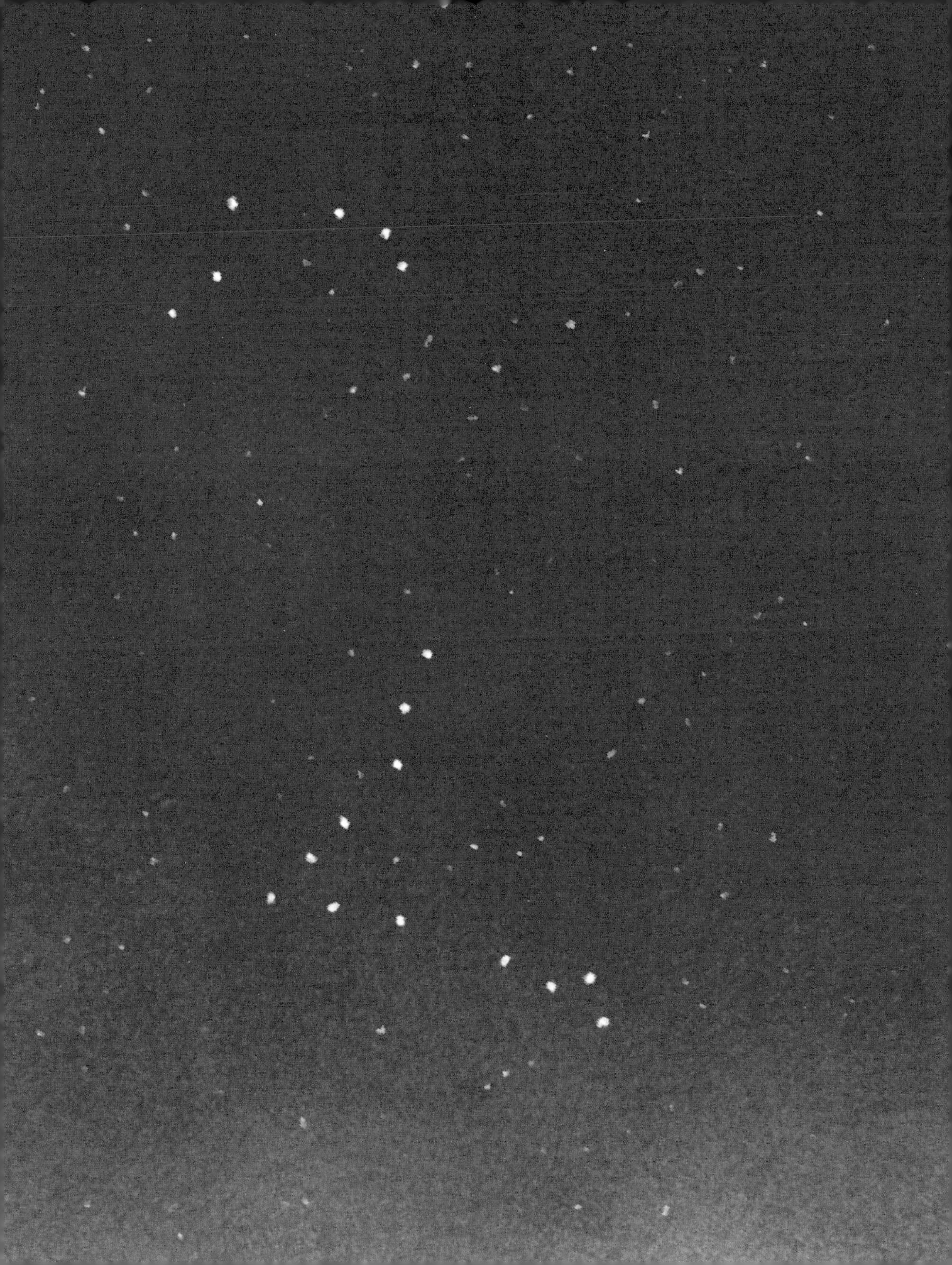